Essence bestselling and award-winning author Tananarive Due delivers a heart-stopping new novel continuing the story of descendants of an immortal line of people who are the only ones capable of saving the world.

Fana, an immortal with tremendous telepathic abilities, is locked in a battle of wills. Her fiancé is Michel. But Johnny Wright, a mortal who is in love with her, believes that if she doesn't stay away from Michel, they will become the Witnesses to the Apocalypse described in the Book of Revelation.

Fana and the Life Brothers are rushing to distribute their healing "Living Blood" throughout the world, hoping to eliminate most diseases before Fana is bound to marry Michel. Still, they cannot heal people faster than Michel can kill them. Due weaves a tangled web in this novel, including beloved characters from her bestselling *Joplin's Ghost*, in a war of good against evil, making *My Soul to Take* a chilling and thrilling experience.

PRAISE FOR TANANARIVE DUE

"Due has become a modern-day Octavia Butler, a talented storyteller who stands tall among her horror cohorts Anne Rice and Stephen King."

—*The Boston Globe*

"Tananarive Due has one of the more arresting voices in contemporary American fiction."

—*The Washington Post*

BLOOD COLONY

"Beware of spooky plot twists that will have your heart racing as you eagerly turn the page."

—*Essence*

"Due expertly mixes genres and intertwines sociopolitical issues. . . . Like the late, great Octavia Butler, she fearlessly tackles contemporary issues."

—*Baltimore Sun*

"*Blood Colony* will steal your breath on every impossible-to-put-down page. Due is masterful in crafting this thrill-ride of a tale that was truly worth the wait!"

—*New York Times* bestselling author L.A. Banks

"An elegant, scary, richly exciting tale—all that we've come to expect from Tananarive Due."

—*New York Times* bestselling author Greg Bear

"The genius of Tananarive Due is in weaving an imaginative tale so expertly that the reader is convinced she has suspended time and all reason. Her storytelling is at once intimate and wholly epic. Her characters, though otherworldly and supernatural, are profoundly relatable and eerily familiar."

—Blair Underwood, actor, director, and coauthor of *In the Night of the Heat*

THE LIVING BLOOD

Winner of the American Book Award, 2002

Publishers Weekly **Best Novel of the Year, 2001**

Los Angeles Times **and** *Essence* **bestseller**

"Stunning . . . an event of sustained power and energy. . . . This novel should set a standard for supernatural thrillers of the new millennium."

—*Publishers Weekly* (starred review)

"The pantheon of modern horror gods is a small and frighteningly talented group: Stephen King, Anne Rice, Peter Straub, Clive Barker, Dean Koontz—and Tananarive Due. If there is any justice, Due's exciting, powerful, ambitious, scary, and beautifully written supernatural thriller will be the first of a decades-long string of hits that will sell millions."

—Amazon.com

"Smart, soulful, crafty Tananarive Due deserves the attention of everyone interested in contemporary American fiction. In *The Living Blood*, this young writer opens up realms of experience that add to our storehouse of shared reality, and by doing so widens our common vision. She is one of the best and most significant novelists of her generation."

—Peter Straub

MY SOUL TO KEEP

Publishers Weekly **Best Novel of the Year, 1997**

Bram Stoker Award finalist, 1997

"I loved this novel. It's really big and really satisfying, an eerie epic that bears favorable comparison to *Interview with the Vampire*."

—Stephen King

"One of those rare gems that hook readers from start to finish."

—*USA Today*

MY SOUL TO TAKE

TANANARIVE DUE

WASHINGTON SQUARE PRESS
New York   London   Toronto   Sydney   New Delhi

WASHINGTON SQUARE PRESS
A Division of Simon & Schuster, Inc.
1230 Avenue of the Americas
New York, NY 10020

First Washington Square Press trade paperback edition September 2011

WASHINGTON SQUARE PRESS and colophon are registered trademarks of Simon & Schuster, Inc.

For information about special discounts for bulk purchases, please contact Simon & Schuster Special Sales at 1-866-506-1949 or business@simonandschuster.com.

The Simon & Schuster Speakers Bureau can bring authors to your live event. For more information or to book an event contact the Simon & Schuster Speakers Bureau at 1-866-248-3049 or visit our website at www.simonspeakers.com.

Designed by Nancy Singer

Manufactured in the United States of America

10   9   8   7   6   5   4   3

Library of Congress Cataloging-in-Publication Data

Due, Tananarive, 1966–
    My soul to take / Tananarive Due. — 1st Washington Square Press trade paperback ed.
        p. cm.
    1. Immortalism—Fiction. I. Title.
PS3554.U3143M95 2011
813'.54—dc22

                                                                                    2011013971

ISBN 978-1-4391-7614-6
ISBN 978-1-4391-7616-0 (ebook)

To my circle of voices:

Patricia Stephens Due

John Due

Johnita Due

Lydia Due Greisz

Steven Barnes

I hear you, always.

"It wants to . . . turn me into something else.
That's not too terrible, is it?
Most people would give anything to be
turned into something else."

—Seth Brundle
The Fly

. . . And so a man and woman, mates immortal born,
will create an eternal union at the advent of the New Days.
And all of mankind shall know them as the bringers of the Blood.

—Letter of the Witness

How can a disaster greater than human reckoning be a triumph?

—*Death and the King's Horseman*
Wole Soyinka

MY SOUL TO TAKE

Prologue

Puerto Rico
Ten miles south of Maricao
2016

Carlos Harris's breath rasped as he stared at the building's side entrance across the muddy courtyard. The door stood halfway open, a taunt. Or an invitation.

Carlos had scraped his arm raw sliding down from the low-hanging branches of the flowering Maricao tree where he'd camouflaged himself for the past hour, but pain was the least of his problems. Twenty-five yards from him, a stocky U.S. Army soldier patrolled the compound's gate with an M-16. A shadow hid Carlos from the guard, but for how long?

Fear stole the oxygen from Carlos's lungs.

He was miles beyond the town, past coffee plantations and bamboo forests, stranded inside the razor fencing of a two-story pale green building battered nearly white by the sun; maybe an old water-treatment plant or sewage facility. The building looked like it should have been empty, except for the mud-caked military truck and three civilian cars parked in a neat row near the main entrance's glass double doors. The soldier with the thick, sun-browned neck guarding the gate behind him might shoot him on sight.

The building's side door was midway open, stalled by its rusty hinge. All Carlos had to do was dash fifteen yards to the door and slip in. But his limbs locked as he tried to catch his breath. If he ran for the door, he might not leave here today. At best, he would be arrested. At best.

His father had warned him to let his friend with the governor's office sort through the confusion over Mami—but how could he wait? His father hadn't seen the way the coroner's eyes had shifted away in San Germán, or how the police officer in Maricao had tugged at his earlobe, itching from his own lies. His father hadn't heard their flimsy evasions at simple questions any son would ask: Where is she? What happened?

If Mami was dead, he would accept it somehow. But did they expect him to swallow the story with no proof? No body? Nothing except her purse to show that she had lived and died? Even if Carlos hadn't been a reporter for twenty-five years, he couldn't have walked away.

But Carlos had never expected to make it this far. The driver from town should have spotted him hiding in the back of his *cuchifritos* lunch truck before he'd begun his drive to the facility at dawn. The army guard should have searched the truck before waving the driver in. Someone should have seen Carlos climb out and run to the tree after the driver parked.

Truly, what kind of security was this?

Carlos was angry at the incompetence, the lies. Angry at himself. In his real life, he would never do something this crazy—this was like something Mami would do. One day, this would all be a grand joke to her.

But he was here now. The truck was long gone, and he didn't have the ATV he'd nearly killed himself riding on narrow roads the day before, when he'd first come to observe the facility. Carlos could almost hear Mami laughing at him in the rioting birds hidden in the trees. Bees circled him, humming near his ears, but Carlos was too nervous to duck or swat at them.

Carlos, I got the weirdest phone message, Dad had said when he called three days before, waking Carlos and Phoenix from dead sleep in California. Four a.m. Dad had never gotten the time zones straight, but Carlos hadn't had the chance to lay into him because Dad had repeated the cryptic phone message he'd received from an unidentified woman:

Rosa Castillo is dead. Then, the caller had hung up.

The message would have seemed absurd, except that his father couldn't reach Mami, and none of her neighbors had seen her in days. Dad was still recovering from hip surgery, so Carlos had flown to Puerto Rico to find her, chasing her ghost like a detective.

Her girlfriends from the gallery in Old San Juan had told him about their hiking trip to El Yunque, and how Mami had stayed behind to take photographs. A park ranger at El Yunque remembered the woman Carlos described: she'd joined a family from Hong Kong on an impromptu trip to Maricao. *Sólo se vive una vez*, she'd told the park ranger when she changed her plans: "you only live once." Because that was Mami. No planning. No consideration.

In Maricao, Carlos had finally gotten lucky. Or so he'd thought.

The wild-eyed tourist from Chile had drawn Carlos a map to the facility, afraid to lead him there. The tourist had sworn he'd seen six bodies loaded into a truck from the hacienda, the little hotel, in the middle of the night. The authorities had been dressed in plastic suits from head to toe, as if there had been a radiation leak or a terrorist attack. The man's worry for the spirited *Negrita* with silver braids had made him follow the truck into the rain forest.

The stranger had met Mami only twice in the plaza, but he said he'd liked her and urged her to see a doctor when she complained of a stomachache. Then she was gone. And those radiation suits! It was all so suspicious, he'd said, the way the police wouldn't answer questions, just like Chile under Pinochet. Then the hacienda where the bodies had been found was closed right away, the manager among the missing.

What were they hiding? Fury welled up in Carlos, silencing his fear.

Carlos's legs were churning before he realized he was running for the propped door, his breathing so loud in his ears that he was sure the guard could hear him. His legs were rubbery, ready to fold, but he bounded up the two concrete steps and peeked inside the open doorway first: he saw a short, narrow hallway, part of an L intersection from the main hall. Three doors on each side, two open, four closed. No soldiers. No one in sight.

Carlos slipped through the building's open door, barely nudging it, in case touching would set off an alarm. He was glad it didn't close behind him, because God knew he might need it again. One of the open rooms was six strides from him, the lights off, so he ran to the doorway just as he heard voices from the wider hall.

He didn't have time to see if he was alone before he closed the room's door behind him; the click rang in his ear like a gunshot. He pushed in the lock, another terrifying click. Only then did he whip his head around to see if he'd stumbled into the lion's den.

But he was alone.

The room was a small office, three drab metal desks without cubicles. The walls were rimmed with wire bookshelves that were mostly empty except for a few piles of papers and paperback manuals. Something white near the window caught Carlos's eye, and his heart rejoiced: a lab coat was hanging on the desk chair!

Shivering with gratitude, Carlos grabbed the coat and flung it on. It was short at the sleeves, too tight—maybe it was a small woman's—but it felt like his armor and shield. His lungs opened, allowing him to breathe.

The room smelled dusty, as if it hadn't been aired out in years. The desks were old and scuffed, but the wire shelving was new. So was the slender tablet computer sitting open at the desk where he'd found the coat. Carlos hadn't thought to bring gloves—one in a long list in his plan's oversights—but he tapped the computer screen and prayed for a miracle.

The opening screen flared, bright blue. A username was saved in the top field behind a row of dots, but the password field was blank. He cursed. Had he thought he could type in his mother's name and find a complete report?

Carlos peeked through the window's vertical blinds, saw the side of the guard's checkpoint. The bulky soldier was pacing with his gun slung across his shoulder, bored.

What now? As Carlos panicked, his mind went white, skipping like an old LP.

The desk drawers were bare, emptied long ago. Carlos rifled through the papers and manuals on the wire shelves, but the pages were crammed with unfamiliar symbols. Chinese? No . . . Korean. A thick manual looked like a medical journal, judging from the photographs of deformities inside, but he couldn't read a word. Carlos cursed again.

As his adrenaline wore off, he felt wearied by the futility of his plan. What would Phoenix say if she saw him now? His father? His capture would make international headlines. He was transforming into a crazed stranger, and over what? A tourist's delusion?

Still, Carlos left the sanctuary of the office with the manual under his arm to complete his costume, keeping his face down as he scanned the hallway. It was still empty, but he wouldn't have time to search every room.

He saw a handwritten sign in bright red at the end of the hall, near the fork. The sign had an arrow pointing to the right, like a trail of bread crumbs. OBSERVATION, the sign read in English. A matching sign was posted on a nearby stairwell door; this time, the arrow pointed up.

Carlos opened the door to the stairwell and found it empty, too, lighted by fluorescent bulbs that flickered and buzzed.

Another sign waited at the door on the second floor, and Carlos opened it without giving himself time to change his mind. Bright lighting assaulted him, and he shielded his eyes with the manual. His reflection stared back at him from a glass panel five yards in front of him that stretched nearly the length of a long, narrow room.

Several voices nearby spoke in a gentle babble. A dozen men and women were huddled to the right of him, at the far end of the room. They stood with their noses close to the glass like students on a class field trip to the aquarium. About half of them wore lab coats like his, but none was dressed like a soldier. None had a gun. One of the men was speaking English with a heavy Asian accent, his voice too low to hear. They were so absorbed, they did not notice him.

Carlos suddenly didn't care who they were—he cared only what they were looking at.

He took three confident strides to the glass, and his reflection melted from sight as he stared down. Thirty feet below, he saw what looked like a makeshift autopsy room, six rolling metal tables arranged in two uneven rows of three. The space was a giant stage, and he stood in its balcony.

On every table lay a body. Nude. Uncovered. The bodies lay in tight fetal balls, as if they fought the cold even in death. Clenched fists were raised to their faces. Two of the bodies were very small. Children.

"... If it was airborne ..." a woman's voice said, soft as cotton.

"... Within such an isolated infection area ..." murmured the man with the Asian accent.

Carlos's chest quaked. His heart was a boulder ramming his ribs. The room below swayed, and he leaned on the glass to keep his balance. The cryptic call to his father had not been a joke or a lie. The Maricao tourist's story had not been a paranoid fantasy. His terrible new knowledge guided his eyes ... and he saw her.

Her bright white hair, prematurely gray since she'd been in her forties, was braided in ordered cornrows that curled around her ears like a schoolgirl's.

But everything else was wrong.

Her brown skin had been leached of pigment like the walls outside, chalky and pale. And she had aged twenty years since he'd seen her at Christmas, leathery skin hanging from brittle bones. She looked like a ... husk. She might have been a hundred years old. The child in him mouthed her name, his lips pressed to the cold glass.

Carlos Harris knew his mother's corpse on sight.

PLAGUE

And the blood shall be to you for a token
upon the houses were ye *are:*
and when I see the blood, I will pass over you,
and the plague shall not be upon you to destroy *you,*
when I smite the land of Egypt.
—Exodus 12:13

Where's my keys and ride?
Lemme give my map a shout.
This party's gettin' tired.
This dream is all played out.
—Phoenix,
"Time 2 Go"

One

Paso Robles, California
One Week Later

Phoenix was recovering from her steep morning run as the black Mercedes SUV approached on her path, bouncing along the dusty, unpaved road from her house half a mile up the hill. The SUV had been spotless ten minutes before, when she'd told the driver to turn left at the vineyard on the corner and follow the road. Now it was coated with the white dust swirling behind its massive tires.

The Mercedes was a hydro, at least, but it was still a portrait of privilege. When so many children in Los Angeles didn't have food or medicine, the L.A. County plates told Phoenix that the driver lived in an oblivious world. She knew that world: hell, she had *owned* that world, once. Some people just hadn't figured out how bad it was yet.

Phoenix smiled when the SUV stopped beside her and a tinted window slid down. The young man driving shut off the music playing loudly from the speakers—"Gotta Fly," she noticed. Old-school. As she'd suspected, the driver was a fan. Or a reporter.

"Phoenix Smalls?" the driver said. He had a sheepish, youthful grin. "I didn't recognize you with your hair like that."

While her mother was undergoing chemo, Phoenix had shaved off most of her own hair in solidarity, and they'd both played dress-up with wigs. After Mom died, she'd kept her head shaved to hold on to her memory, and because she liked her altered appearance. Dark peach fuzz. Rebirth, as her name had always promised her.

"Harris," Phoenix corrected the man. She'd been married to

Carlos Harris for a decade, but most people still knew her by the stage name she had kept to honor her father.

"I apologize, Mrs. Harris," the young man said. He was black, with a stylishly thin mustache, his scalp shaved nearly as close as hers. He wore a small earring with a dangling gold cross. She might have thought he was handsome, back when she noticed a stranger's looks. "When I asked you where your house was, why didn't you tell me who . . . ?"

He had asked for directions when his vehicle was still shiny. He hadn't recognized her because he'd barely looked at her, his grim eyes somewhere faraway.

"That wasn't what you asked. But yes, I'm Phoenix Harris. And that was my house."

She had known he wouldn't get past the gate. She had relented and put up the fence when Carlos pointed out how many people came looking for her house each year. Most sojourners left flowers or gifts like crafts or poems without knocking, but a few were clearly unhinged. The day Carlos persuaded her to put up the fence, he'd found something in a shoe box on their front porch that he'd never described—and she didn't want to know about. The horrified look on his face had been enough.

A white pickup truck rumbled past them in the opposite lane. Phoenix didn't recognize the driver, who waved when he passed. His radio blared with the farm report and news of more drought. Phoenix hoped he was headed higher into the hills, or to see the Kinseys.

"If you're a reporter, call my manager," Phoenix said.

"All due respect, Mrs. Harris, but your manager doesn't return her calls."

Phoenix's cousin sent her new emails about phone messages each day, but Phoenix ignored most of them. When Carlos was in town, she barely bothered to check her email once a week. Now, she was on a constant lookout for news from him. Her wristphone buzzed when new messages arrived, but this morning, so far, only silence.

"Not her fault," Phoenix said. "I don't do interviews. It's all in my book, *Joplin's Ghost*. The rest is just for me, my head, and my family. Sorry."

The SUV's engine purred, docile as the expression on John Wright's face. "I'm not a journalist," the man said. "More like a producer."

He was about twenty, but looked closer to twelve despite his mustache. No surprise there: youth was the engine that powered music. She'd dropped her first album at his age. Younger.

Phoenix frowned, shoving her hands into the pockets of her light jacket. Now that she had stopped running and her skin was cooling, she noticed the bite in the fall air. Meteorologists were predicting another cold, dry winter to lay waste to her neighbors' vineyards.

Phoenix resumed her walk up the hill, toward home. "Wrong answer," she said. "I'm not performing anymore. You might have heard."

"What about Port-au-Prince?"

"That was different," she said, still walking. She had come out of retirement six years earlier, almost as soon as she quit, for a free concert in Port-au-Prince to help rebuild Haiti after the earthquake. "That was to save lives."

"This is to save lives too, Mrs. Harris," he called. "Hear me out for ten minutes?"

Phoenix stopped walking. Only the empty house sat ahead, full of waiting. Her son, Marcus, was at his friend Ronny's for the weekend, riding horses and playing his GamePort.

Phoenix turned back to the idling SUV. "The answer is definitely no," she said. "But what's your name?"

"I'm John Wright. I work for—"

"Doesn't matter," Phoenix said gently. Her voice was firmest when it was soft. "But I'm honored for the invitation, Mr. Wright. I'm sorry you wasted your drive from L.A. Come on up to the house. I'll get us some tea, maybe fix you a bite. At least you'll have a story."

"Want a ride?" he said, his grin suddenly hopeful.

Phoenix shook her head, waving behind her.

She would make it home the way she did every morning, walking on her own.

• • •

Ten minutes later, John Wright climbed out of the waiting SUV to greet her with the polite pat on her upper arm that had replaced the handshake, especially in the cities. Swine flu and its descendants had spawned distaste for hand-to-hand contact, and talk of the deadly new infections sealed the custom. Phoenix patted his arm in return, adding a tender squeeze for emphasis. *Sorry I'm such a hermit.*

Phoenix hadn't understood hermits until she'd become one; now she was addicted to quiet. For her, the noise had begun when her father was shot dead backstage at her first major concert, and it had never relented until she stopped performing. Prince had warned her years ago: *When you get to the top of the mountain, you'll see. There's nothing up there.* Sarge's death had dimmed the bright lights of her ride early on. Sometimes what waited on the mountaintop was far worse than nothing.

"I can't thank you enough, ma'am," the young man said, reaching for his briefcase on his passenger seat before he climbed out and closed the vehicle's door. She noticed the embossed gold CWH insignia stamped across the case's leather, and a globe logo she recognized.

Suddenly nervous, Phoenix hugged her arms across her chest. She planted herself in Wright's path. "Does this have something to do with my husband?" she said.

Wright looked confused. "Your husband? No, ma'am."

If he was lying, it was too late to undo it now. She had literally led him to their doorstep. She forced herself to relax, uncrossing her arms. " 'Ma'am' makes me sound too damn old," she said. "I'm just Phoenix. Follow me."

"Can't thank you enough, Phoenix. My employer is a big fan."

Like most visitors, John surveyed her ranch house's exterior with surprise. The front yard was dry, the grass brown and thirsty. Phoenix suspected that many of her neighbors watered their lawns, but Phoenix wouldn't waste water on grass even if it were legal. She used her water ration for the garden, where she needed it. She and Carlos had talked about laying down concrete or arranging stones, but so far their yard was only dying.

John Wright followed Phoenix as she climbed the wooden front porch steps, past the porch swing for two and its cushion that needed washing. The house was three thousand square feet but looked much smaller from the outside; sun-faded and modest. The porch and roof were visibly in need of repairs that neither she nor Carlos had interest in. The cracking antique wooden wagon wheel leaning beside the living room picture window was a holdover from the original owners, making her house look like a cheesy western motel. She and Carlos had laughed about it.

Phoenix opened her door, which was unlocked. The door could use paint, she noticed.

John Wright froze in the doorway, looking alarmed.

"Not what you were expecting?" Phoenix said.

"It's not that," John Wright said, and his voice had changed, deepening. "I was just thinking: are you alone? And you're inviting a stranger into your house?"

Now he sounded like Carlos. She couldn't dare tell Carlos that she'd invited a stranger to the house while he was gone. Carlos had enough to worry about without thinking she was crazy.

Phoenix's mind flashed an imaginary headline: MUSIC STAR MURDERED IN HER HOME BY STALKER. She became aware of how close John Wright stood to her, how he was six feet of wiry, lean muscle. Maybe she'd been lulled by his boyish face, or the cross dangling from his ear. Maybe she'd thought she was protected from bad news because Carlos was already in so deep. Maybe she should have peeked inside the unspeakable box Carlos had found on their porch the day he insisted they fence off the world.

"I'm also a security consultant for my employer," Wright said. "I'll only come in if you promise me you'll never invite someone like me into your house again."

"Someone like you?" Phoenix said.

He handed her a business card and a photo ID. Both identified him as the Public Relations Director of Clarion World Health Corporation, headquartered in London, New York, and Johannesburg. In his photograph, he wore his hair in short dreads the way Carlos did.

"Damn, you're in PR?" Phoenix said. "That's worse than a producer."

John Wright didn't smile. "I'm someone you don't know," he lectured her while she glanced at his identification. "No background check. No staff. You don't even have a dog?"

"We did. She died." She handed back his ID and business card, convinced. "Are you coming in or not? You're letting out all my heat."

John Wright shook his head ruefully, but he walked inside. "I don't mean to sound like your father, but—" He bit off his words, mortified. He knew about Sarge, of course. Sarge's murder had been a question on *Jeopardy!*, back in the day.

"Shame you're not trying. You sound just like him," Phoenix said. She closed the door behind him. Talking about Sarge didn't cut as deeply as it had when she still heard the gunshots in her sleep, but the pain was always there. "And you're right. I shouldn't trust you, but I do. People say I'm psychic, so maybe I'm believing my own hype. But trust me at my word: I will slap myself before this ever happens again. Satisfied?"

"I can work with that," John Wright said. "Just want to be sure you understand the value of what you're protecting, Phoenix. That you know who and what you are."

His eyes went to her house, her walls, her floors, sponging up everything in sight.

He was eager to tell the story.

TWO

When she returned from the kitchen, Phoenix found John Wright in her dining room, mesmerized by the walls.

Phoenix's family rarely ate at the stately Tuscan cypress dining room table, so Carlos and Marcus had surprised her for her thirty-fifth birthday by transforming the space into her trophy room. The walls were a museum of gold and platinum records, concert photos, and framed newspaper and magazine headlines. Phoenix no longer knew that cocky girl in the photos. She hadn't wanted to wilt the proud grins on the faces of her two favorite guys, but those memories made her lose her appetite.

John Wright was standing so close to the framed CD jewel case from her Joplin album that a puff of his breath might have knocked it from the wall.

"Let's stay in the living room," Phoenix said. She raised the serving tray she had brought. "Tea's from Madagascar, but the bread is homemade. Multigrain honey cranberry."

"Wow," Wright said, his eyes still traveling the biography on her walls.

Phoenix cut his pilgrimage short, tugging the back of his suit jacket, pulling him away. "Don't want the bread to get cold," she said.

In the living room, Wright squirted his hands with the sanitizing-lotion dispenser on her coffee table without being asked, caution or good manners. She gave him his mug of tea and a plate of lightly toasted bread, still warm from the oven. Sitting across from him on the sofa, she relaxed with her first sip of Madagascar red.

John Wright crossed his legs in his crisp, dark corporate slacks.

His shoes shone like black glass. PR flack or not, she congratulated herself on her instinct to invite Wright inside. For five whole minutes, she hadn't worried about Carlos. She would give Wright thirty minutes, ask him to leave, and begin worrying again. A thirty-minute break from worry was a gift.

Her living room was more tasteful than the exterior, overly crammed with African and Asian tables and masks that had decorated her pop star's mansion in Beverly Hills. Phoenix and Carlos didn't own a television set, so the living room looked like a library, with shelves stubbornly filled with books even though she and Carlos both read more e-books than paper books nowadays. But e-books didn't *smell* like books, or add dignity to a room.

"You said a ghost helped you write that music?" Wright said. "Scott Joplin's?"

After a decade of reverence and ridicule, Phoenix couldn't answer that question again in this lifetime. She'd written her book, which had exhausted her, and now she didn't like to talk about Scott Joplin, even to Carlos. She felt like a widow, although her encounters seemed to fade into fantasy as years passed. Some days, it was easy to believe that there had never been a ghost, just like her critics had always said.

"Next subject, please," Phoenix said, barely hanging on to her smile.

Wright looked embarrassed. "I only ask because it shows the profound power of your music. Your appeal defies easy understanding." He reached into his inside jacket pocket and pulled out a small vial filled with a translucent red liquid that looked like strawberry Kool-Aid. "Have you heard about Glow?" John Wright said.

Phoenix scooted away from Wright, although her eyes were bewitched by the vial. The Department of Homeland Security had warned about terrorist ties to Glow in national press conferences, before the droughts stole the newscasts. Before the new flu deaths.

"Glow is illegal," Phoenix said.

Wright stood the vial upright on her table. Sunlight from the window speared the liquid, making the tabletop shimmer in violet red beneath it. "In the United States and Europe, yes," Wright said. "Only because it defies easy understanding. It's legal in thirty African nations, throughout the Middle East and Israel, and in China. Soon? Here, too. We're working on the FDA. But we can't wait. Glow cures diseases, including one much worse than the flu. You can help Clarion get a step ahead of the pandemic."

The word *pandemic* made her wonder about Carlos. Phoenix suddenly realized that Wright looked familiar despite his haircut. *John Jamal Wright.* His photo should have told her sooner. Carlos would kill her when he got home, if he made it back.

"We've seen you on the news," Phoenix said carefully. "And not in the good way."

"To the FBI, Martin Luther King was a communist," Wright said, shrugging. "Change is a tough business. Health corps thrive on the sick, not the healed. They don't want us to succeed." He sounded twice his age.

"I'm not a doctor," Phoenix said. "Or a revolutionary. I'm not even a singer anymore, except in the shower. I'm a mom who's homeschooling her seven-year-old son. And who bakes damn good bread, which you haven't even tasted, by the way."

Wright nodded, taking his first bite. "Good," he agreed. "But you forgot one thing: you're a powerful force. Your music reaches people and makes them believe in something bigger than themselves." He lowered his voice to a hush. "No touring, no press junket. A one-night concert. We're ready to heal the world—we're already doing it—but we need you."

Heal the world. Phoenix almost chuckled. She had been full of herself, too, at his age.

"Some free advice?" she said. "Too much hype makes you sound crazy. I know."

"I'm just telling the truth, Phoenix." His unblinking eyes believed every word he said.

"Me too, John. How old are you?"

"Twenty-one."

"And you already know the truth?" Gentle skepticism in her voice. "Lucky you."

"Yes. Lucky me," Wright said. "Truth came to me one day. Got me in some trouble. Yeah, it got me on the news. Then, the truth exonerated me. That same truth will heal the world. But even truth needs a messenger. Ask Mark, Luke, and John."

Phoenix had expected him to start flinging biblical references, but she had to fight not to roll her eyes. Her wrist vibrated with a text message from an unfamiliar number:

JUST LEFT SAN JUAN. IN NY TONIGHT. CA TOMORROW.
Phoenix shot to her feet, as if the words carried an electrical charge. Carlos was on his way home!

When he'd called last night from his throwaway phone, Carlos had bemoaned the long lines at the airport and the Health Department's dictates. A TSA official had told him he had to stay in Puerto Rico for thirty days' quarantine. He'd ducked out of his exit interview and was sure he'd narrowly escaped being arrested. But something had changed. *Thank you, God.*

"Do you believe in miracles, Phoenix?" Wright said.

Phoenix exhaled a sigh of relief so powerful that her body shuddered. Until that moment, she had been preparing for the idea that she might not see Carlos for a long time. Or, just possibly, ever again.

"I believe in miracles today," she said. "My husband's on his way home after a long hassle. His mother got sick and died suddenly. He thinks . . ."

She was bursting to tell someone, but thought better of it. Carlos had made the mistake of blogging his theories about his mother's sudden illness. He'd taken the internet page down right away, but the damage had been done. He'd been banned from flying, threatened with arrest. He said he'd never seen Puerto Rican officials in such fear and hysteria.

"I'm profoundly sorry for his loss," Wright said. "But your husband's mother would still be alive if she'd had this vial of Glow."

Phoenix didn't believe in miracles in a vial. Mom had agreed to try Glow toward the end, and Gloria had pulled every string in search of the fabled Underground Railroad. The doctor who had analyzed the vial Gloria brought back said it was saline with red food coloring, and it might have done harm if she'd injected it.

"The hard sell doesn't work for you, John," Phoenix said. She picked up the waiting vial and held it out to Wright, noting the warmth of the glass against her palm. Rumors said that real Glow was warm to the touch, but that thought only made her angry. It didn't help her now. "Take it. I wish you hadn't brought an illegal substance into my home without my permission."

"Please, Phoenix—keep it," Wright said. His eyes pleaded with her.

"I don't shoot up drugs," she said. "*Any* drugs. Don't make me ask again."

Wright pursed his lips, so disappointed that his eyes narrowed. He returned the vial to his hidden pocket. "I'm sorry. I meant it as a gift, but . . . it's only a gift if you're ready. My employer wants to keep you around a long time."

"Tell your employer I'm doing fine," Phoenix said.

But that wasn't true. *What about the lump?*

Phoenix could lie to John Wright, but not to herself. She felt a tiny lance of pain in her right breast as she remembered. Sometimes she thought she could feel her breast squirming, changing shape. Vivid, ugly imagination. But moving or not, she knew the lump was there. Her hand brushed it in the shower each day. After losing her mother to breast cancer five years earlier, Phoenix would have thought she'd rush to her doctor's office at the first sign of trouble. She'd promised Mom she would guard her health. Instead, much to her amazement, she wasn't picking up the phone to call her doctor. She expected to each day, and never did.

As soon as I know Carlos is all right, I'll call, she thought, a new variation of the vow she'd been making for nearly a month. Maybe the psychic part of her was steering clear of doctors because a doctor would make it real.

Wright studied her face. "You can lock the vial in a drawer and never touch it," he said. "It doesn't need refrigeration. Take your time. Have it studied by someone you trust. Keep it for when you need it. Authentic Glow is very hard to find in the States. Some of the trash products are only poison."

"I have to ask you to leave now."

"I'm sorry, Phoenix," he said, stepping away, hands slightly raised. "If you knew what I knew, you'd understand why I'm trying so hard. I really only came with a simple request. . . ."

Phoenix was already leading him to the door.

"One night only," he went on, following her. "Johannesburg. A concert for worldwide health care. Lifesaving treatments for adults and children. I know you don't need money, but we'll donate five million in any currency to your favorite charity." He spoke faster as they neared the door, fumbling with his briefcase to bring out a glossy black folder.

"Five million for one night? Must be expensive damn tickets."

"Tickets are free. We're not raising money—we're raising awareness."

Nice touch, Phoenix thought. But she donated plenty of money through her foundation. She and Carlos had been living on a fraction of her earnings since she'd retired, designating the rest to charity and Marcus's college fund. She had long ago run out of things to buy.

"I don't do airplanes," she said. "And I don't sleep away from home. Not anymore."

"Name your venue," Wright said, holding the folder out to her with the same pleading expression. "What about L.A.? Four hours' drive, and you're back in your own bed."

Phoenix opened the front door, inviting in the dry, cool air. "I'm sure you can find a whole lot of other folks who'd be happy to help. I'll tell my cousin to send you some names."

"My employer wants *you*, Phoenix," Wright said, nearly breathless. "She's a lifelong fan. It's not a stadium or arena concert—it's intimate. With two or three songs, you can help spread the word about Clarion."

"You mean Glow," Phoenix said. She wouldn't let him PR his way out of illegal drugs.

"Do your research, Phoenix," Wright said. "In this folder, you'll find a link to a website set up by independent medical scholars, one at Harvard Medical School, one at Cambridge. A Lasker Award winner is on our board of directors. Glow *heals*. The only side effect is a mild euphoria. We're running out of time to fight the propaganda. This new infection in Asia . . ."

Despite herself, Phoenix's heart jumped with thoughts of Carlos. "How bad is it?"

"Bad," he said. "We have doctors on the ground in North Korea, so we've penetrated the news blackout. We're ninety-five percent sure it's airborne. It's a tragedy."

Airborne was a scary word. Carlos had overheard that word and tested it in his blog. "How tragic?"

Wright blinked, lowering his face to hide the mania dancing in his eyes. "The question may not be how many will die—the question is, how many will survive?"

Phoenix felt icy panic, until she remembered Wright's gift for overstatement. Why was she asking his opinion anyway? But even if John Wright was a quack or a nutball, she and Carlos both needed to research the infection. Ignorance was no longer an option.

Phoenix took the black folder. "Is your card in here?"

Wright brightened. "Yes. And—"

"Fine. I'll keep this. I'm sorry to kick you out."

"Yes, ma'am," he said. "I mean thank you, Phoenix. For trusting me this far. Your music has been a gift to all of us." He wanted to gush more, but held himself back.

Phoenix watched Wright retreat to his soiled SUV. He waved before climbing back in to fire up its oversized engine. Below her elevated property, the dusty road wove down to sprawling acres of dry farmland and ghostly vineyards. More than her lawn was dying.

"You said your boss is a fan," Phoenix called. "Who is she?"

Phoenix saw the beatific transformation on Wright's face as he grinned. Wright worshipped the woman he worked for. She hoped John Wright hadn't fallen victim to a religious cult the way so many restless souls she'd known in Hollywood had.

"You don't know her. Not yet," Wright said, his grin shining. "You'll meet her soon."

John Wright said it as if he knew her future.

Three

A broad-shouldered man stands at Jessica Jacobs-Wolde's kitchen counter, stirring a bowl with slow, careful strokes while he watches her out of the corner of his eye. He slumps across the counter on one elbow, his face hidden by a shadow escaping the light from the bright rows of jalousie windows.

Not her husband, David. She left David sleeping in their bed upstairs. Besides, this man has the wrong shoes. Wrong posture. Wrong smell . . . shoe polish. And Old Spice, a smell older than David's. The man's face turns slightly, and light cleaves to his dark skin. Jessica blinks three times, more weak-kneed with each blink.

The man is her father.

Jessica's father died when she was eight, in 1978. But now he's in the kitchen as if he belongs with her in 1997, stooped over as he stirs the cobalt-blue bowl she and David bought in Key West. Nineteen years have passed, but she knows his wide shoulders, salt-and-pepper hair, the small gap between his front teeth.

Time and death haven't changed her father a bit.

But his clothes aren't right. At first, he was wearing his dusty work boots, and in the next breath he's in his gray Sunday suit with shiny black shoes reeking of Kiwi shoe polish—his only church suit, the one he was wearing when they closed the gleaming rose-colored casket and lowered him into a maw in the earth.

I'm dreaming, she thinks, a late realization. She has to be.

"Thought I'd make us some breakfast," Daddy says.

How *dare* he just show up now, out of the air! What has taken him so long?

Before she speaks, she talks herself down from her anger. Isn't he always near them when she and her daughter, Kira, climb down into the tiny burial cave at the foot of their front yard, near the mailbox? Don't the neighbors talk about ghosts in the mossy live oak trees? Maybe it has taken him twenty years to find her.

"Daddy?" Her voice reverts to childhood, almost too soft to hear. Her father stirs with his wooden spoon. Pancakes and fried eggs were all her father knew how to cook. It's Daddy, all right.

"'Mornin', baby girl," Daddy says.

"What are you doing here?" She can't say Daddy a second time.

His clothes change again, melting. Now he's wearing his brilliantly aqua blue Miami Dolphins jersey, number 72. Bob Greise. Daddy has gone to the Orange Bowl to see the Dolphins play all season long, sparking a fuss with her mother. The tiles on the kitchen counter turn powder blue, like the ones in their childhood home. When Jessica blinks, the tiles pale back to white.

Is Daddy trying to trick her? Daddy's face isn't quite in focus. She blinks again. Now he looks like David.

"You've been gone a long time, Jess," he says. Her father had never called her by David's nickname for her. When he was alive, he told her and her sister, Alexis, to stop letting neighborhood boys call them Jess and Alex because it sounded too tomboyish. "Come on back with me, before you can't anymore. We miss you, Jessica."

"Who's 'we'?" Jessica is surprised at how angry she sounds.

"You know who I mean, mi vida," Daddy says patiently. He heats a skillet on the stove, and butter sizzles sweet in the air. She has never heard her father speak Spanish, but his accent is flawless. He sounds like he grew up in Spain. Daddy's voice drops to a whisper. "Fana. Me. Alex. All of us."

What's he talking about? Her sister, Alex, isn't dead!

"Alex isn't with you, Daddy," she says. "She's still here. And who's . . . ?"

She already can't remember the other name.

As if the stranger's name broke the spell, Daddy is suddenly gone. The skillet sizzles without him, the butter turning brown. No

Daddy. An echo of his bright jersey still plays behind her eyes, but his absence hangs in the room.

Jessica holds her breath, waiting for him to reappear, her mind raging with questions and regrets. She is exhausted from grief. She wants to go back to bed, but her nightmares would come if she tried to sleep now.

"Daddy?" she whispers to the empty room, trying the word on her tongue again.

"Lord, girl, you're burning up the butter!" Bea says from the kitchen doorway. Her loose, multicolored batik tunic fans across her arm like a choir robe.

Her mother was in last night's nightmare, Jessica suddenly remembers. Something about an airplane. Her heart. The memory fragments are sharp as glass, like physical pain.

Still here.

Jessica clasps her mother's warm hand, running her fingers across the soft, fleshy ridges of her knuckles, moistened with the Giorgio lotion Jessica gives her for Christmas every year. And the scent of Zest soap from her neck.

"Something just scared the *crap* out of me," Jessica says. Already, holding her mother's hand, she feels better. "Not you. It was . . ."

"Ommmmmm!" Kira hums, chiding her from behind Bea's skirt. "You said a bad word, Mommy! *Crap* is a bad word."

Jessica is surprised to see Kira up and already dressed for school—in her pink Flower Power T-shirt and slightly too-short blue jeans she wore because she loved the pink belt. Her sneakers clash in bright orange.

Jessica feels sick to her stomach. A sour taste prods the back of her throat.

"Well, let's see what Gramma can whip together," Bea says, opening the kitchen cabinet.

"Kira has school, Mom. I'll fix her cereal."

"Hush," Bea says. "We have all the time in the world."

Kira gives Jessica her prettiest bright-eyed stare. "I love you, Mommy!" Kira says, and crushes herself against Jessica for a tight hug. "Forever."

Jessica kneels to the kitchen linoleum on one knee to hug Kira and savor every part of her. The sure, steady fluttering of her heartbeat. Her tiny rib cage. The sweet Crest toothpaste on her breath. The honey scent of her uncombed hair.

Honey? Bees. Her nightmare tries to surface, but Jessica fights it back.

"You need to let her go and give her to me, Jessica," Bea says. "She's my best helper."

Kira cheers, flying to Bea's side by the stove. Smoke rises from the skillet, Bea and Kira are hard to see.

"Jessica, go fetch me some flour from the cellar," Bea's voice says in the smoke.

The smoke is pluming, filling the kitchen, but Jessica sees the cellar door wide open in her path. Two steps, maybe three, and she'll be inside the doorway. *We don't have a cellar,* Jessica thinks, but there it is. A bright light shines, and a shadow moves against the wall.

Maybe it's her father. Maybe this is where he wanted her to follow him.

Kira gaves a small cough, and Jessica's head whips around. All she sees are smoky profiles, one taller, one tiny. The kitchen smells like sweet-spicy incense.

"Mom . . ." Jessica begins. She has a thousand things to say. A thousand questions.

"Don't worry about Kira," Mom says. "I've got her, baby. You go on, now."

"Bye, Mommy!" Kira calls, and Jessica's throat burns with pain.

The shadow in the cellar moves again. A disembodied arm beckons, or seems to.

"Daddy?" Jessica says, and goes toward the open cellar door. The incense smell is stronger from downstairs. Bea and Kira giggle behind her.

Jessica takes her first step down the cellar stairs.

But it isn't a cellar, just as she'd thought. It's the burial cave at the end of their driveway with smooth dirt walls, built by the Tequestas to store arrowroot: Kira's outdoor playhouse. The most charming fixture of her yard. Jessica's favorite place.

Jessica doesn't remember a doorway from the house to the burial cave. But here she is.

In 1997, she reminds herself. *Still here.*

Jessica hunches over to walk down into the cave.

A man sits cross-legged against the packed dirt of the cave's far wall. The cave is bigger than Jessica remembers it—as big as their bedroom. This time, the man isn't her father. He is nude. His face is hidden in a bright light, but she knows his body.

"Why are you in here?" Jessica says.

"You know why," her husband says. "For you, Jessica. To find you." His voice sets her soul afire.

"You haven't lost me," she says. "You're right here."

Slowly, he shakes his head. The light plays across the burnished skin of his face, unbridling his beauty. His face brings tears to her eyes.

"The man in the bed upstairs isn't me," he says. "He's a memory, Jessica. A lie."

When he says the word *lie,* the ground shakes beneath her, a rumble. Her stomach aches.

"It's not a lie," she says. "I taste it, touch it, and feel it every day. I'm still here."

"It's a dream you made for yourself."

Suddenly, she can't remember her husband's name. The cave is dimming around her. She feels sleepy, her eyes coaxed open by the light on her husband's face.

"We live at 296 Tequesta Road," she says. "I work for the *Miami Sun-News.* I'm a reporter. We have a five-year-old daughter named Kira. She's right here. And so is Mom. My mother is cooking break-fast with Kira right now."

Her husband's jaw clenches with what looks like anger, but in the light she sees it's pain. "We lost Kira, Jessica," he says. "We lost your mother."

"That's not true!" Jessica screams.

Tears water her husband's cheeks. "I wish it weren't, Jess. If I could make your dream real and step back into time, I would find a way to spare you all of it." He swallows a sob. "I would change everything. But I cannot. We cannot. I dream of your memory, too. I wish we could travel back together."

For the first time, Jessica remembers her husband's true name: Dawit.

"You lied to me," she says.

"Yes."

"You stole everything."

"Yes." A whisper.

And yet, she loves him. Her love for him is deeper, somehow, than her love when she had known him only as David. But their love was brighter then. Innocent.

"Then why shouldn't I stay here?" she says. "Why shouldn't we be happy?"

"We will be happy again, Jess," he says. "We can."

"How?"

She can't remember everything about her nightmares yet, but she is waking from her dream. Not the cave—somewhere else. An underground temple. Another child.

Not Kira. Her first daughter is dead.

Fana. Her second child's name.

Fana is where Jessica's nightmares begin.

Four

Carlos Harris's forehead beaded with sweat as he made the long walk from the North American Airways terminal, his heavy backpack slung across his shoulder as he passed encamped crowds, bland food courts, wailing toddlers. Blinding white floors. He needed to piss, but a K-9 officer and German shepherd posted near the bathroom changed his mind.

Tranquilo, he told himself. *Don't draw attention. Slow and easy.*

A flock of Asian flight attendants walked in the opposite direction, dragging flight bags, nearly identical in their purposeful strides, jet-black hair and blue paper face masks stamped with the Korean Air logo. Carlos was sure he saw their eyes study his face, one after the other.

Come mierda. What now?

Quickly, Carlos wiped his chin and neck, checking his palm for blood. He found a bright red smudge and wiped it on the seat of his pants. He'd nicked his face during his quick shave in the plane's bathroom, but he'd rid himself of the patchy facial hair that had drawn stares in San Juan. He didn't want stares. He didn't want anyone to notice him, to remember him. Just another guy strolling through LAX. God help him if he caught the eye of lurking paparazzi.

The letter was in his shoe. After his father had finally gotten through to his old Yale roommate, Ramon Garcia in the governor's office had promised Carlos he could leave San Juan without delay. That was nearly a week ago, but Carlos had a copy of the letter folded in the sole of his shoe, on Garcia's official stationery from La Fortaleza. Reasonable deniability. Since then, Carlos had been told by six local officials that he was forbidden to leave—one had even given him admission papers to El Presby Hospital to begin a "voluntary" quarantine—and he had ducked behind a parked taxi to elude his escort. But if anyone challenged him, he would produce Garcia's letter and claim ignorance. *A fugitive? Me?*

Carlos had expected to find police and God knew who else waiting for him in Miami, at Kennedy, and again at LAX. His muscles ached from tensing for capture.

Carlos melted into the stream of travelers heading downstairs to baggage claim, although he'd left his suitcase behind so he could travel with only his backpack. His computer had been seized by police in San Juan.

A sign posted in bright red letters warned him that once he crossed the yellow stripe on the floor, he could not return to the terminal. He kept a pleasant look on his face as he approached, although three TSA officials observing the line were staring straight at him.

Someone tugged on Carlos's arm from behind.

"Excuse me, sir?" a woman's officious voice said. "Where are you flying from?"

Adrenaline drenched Carlos's body, a bucket of ice water. He stopped in midstride, frozen while he held his breath. The folded paper in his shoe seemed to pulse.

A woman's blond head bobbed into Carlos's view. She was middle-aged and full-faced, with tired eyes. Sunglasses on top of her head pinned her hair in place. No uniform. No badge. No handcuffs. Just another passenger.

"Where you flying from?" the woman said again. She looked harried.

Maricao, Carlos wanted to say. "JFK."

"I thought so! Where'd they say our bags are?"

"I . . . don't know." He hadn't checked a bag, and he'd run out of things he could say.

She waded ahead without a smile or a thank-you.

No alarms went off, no shouts were raised, as Carlos excused himself past LAX's cell phones, sunglasses, long hair, tattoos, body piercings, and self-conscious clothes. Carlos stayed hidden in their shadows. Life with Phoenix had taught him the art of invisibility.

Carlos could barely believe it when he walked through the glass automatic doors to the curb outside, immersed in cold morning air faintly scented by exhaust. He had done it! Home.

The red Orbit hydro pulled up to the designated spot at the curb within five minutes, headlights flashing, before Carlos had a chance to panic. The car barely came to a stop before Carlos jumped in, slamming the door behind him. He hiked up the collar of his leather bomber jacket, obscuring his profile.

Carlos's cousin, who called himself Mo Profit, was an indie film-maker living off residuals from a sitcom he'd directed in the 1990s, and he was the only person Carlos trusted to pick him up in L.A. Mo lived in Culver City, only fifteen minutes from the airport. It was 3:00 a.m. Cali time when Carlos had called him from New York to ask the favor.

"Son of a bitch, you know I must love you, right?" his cousin said. He looked sleepy, his gray-streaked 'fro standing as high as Cornel West's.

"Drive, okay?" Carlos said. "Let's get the hell out of here."

Mo squealed in front of a hotel shuttle, racing for the road that would take them to the freedom of the 105. As the car lurched, Carlos remembered an earlier variation of this drive, when Mo had been stranded during a shoot and called Carlos desperate for a rescue from Simi Valley. Police had been involved. Then, as now, no further explanation was required.

"Sorry about Auntie Rosa, man," Mo said, backhanding Carlos across the kneecap.

Carlos only nodded, mute. For the past two weeks, his consolation had been the odd muting of his grief brought on by constant fear. Only self-survival mattered, in the end. When he rented a car a safe distance from LAX, he would have a four-hour drive to remember why he had flown to Puerto Rico. To remember the police and health departments.

And what he had seen behind the glass.

Carlos closed his eyes. *Mami.*

"You look like shit, Carl-i-to," Mo said, emphasizing his accent on his name. Mo was from the Harris side of the family, rooted in Florida, but Mami's nickname for him was a family novelty that followed Carlos across cultures. "Like you've seen a ghost."

Carlos nodded. "Almost," he muttered. The memory of his last glimpse of his mother's face withered Carlos's blood, shrinking him in Mo's car seat.

Carlos's stomach gurgled, and he cradled his midsection like an expectant mother. He tried not to think about the stories linking the infection to stomachaches.

"Pick up a li'l bug down there?" Mo said, glancing him over.

There was only concern, not accusation or fear, in Mo's voice. Poor Mo had no idea.

"Nah, I'm just in a hurry to get home to Phee," Carlos said. "I'm fine."

Carlos Harris prayed that he was right.

Sarge had told Phoenix about Vietnam and how men looked after going to war, but she'd never seen it so clearly until she met her husband's glassy eyes in their doorway.

"Anybody come looking for me?" Carlos said, trying to sound casual while Marcus shrieked and climbed into his arms. Carlos wasn't an actor, so his terror was plain to Phoenix. She just hoped Marcus couldn't see it.

"No one for you," Phoenix said. "A promoter came by yesterday for me."

Relief softened some of the hard lines on Carlos's face, but he had aged in Puerto Rico. She could see where his father's crow's-feet would grow soon.

When Carlos closed the door, he locked both deadbolts and checked the security panel to make sure all the cameras were on. Six cameras monitored their property, and nothing was moving except the Kinseys' pickup pulling into their driveway below them.

The east camera was the one that had shocked Phoenix six

months earlier, when the coyotes came. A pack. She and Carlos had seen the attack, knowing from the frenzied image that it was too late to intervene on sweet old Graygirl's behalf. The coyotes were emboldened by hunger and thirst, the guy from animal control said when he came to the house.

None of them, even Marcus, wanted another dog soon. *Especially* Marcus. He'd stopped wetting his bed two years ago, but he had accidents most nights since Graygirl had died. While Carlos was gone, he'd peed in his bed nightly. Marcus was so excited to be riding in his father's arms, he didn't seem to notice what Carlos was hiding. But how could even a child miss it?

With a loud grunt, Carlos lowered their squirming son back to the floor.

"Jeez, man, you're killin' me," Carlos said. "You grew like a hundred inches!"

"A hundred *thousand* inches, Dad," Marcus corrected him.

"Yeah—feels like it!" Carlos said.

Phoenix wondered about a strange clicking sound from Carlos, moving her ear closer to his chest. With a weak smile, Carlos reached into his inside jacket pocket just as John Wright had the day before. Phoenix noticed his hand's tremor as he brought out three small, clear plastic boxes and gave them to Marcus. The boxes were filled with tiny brown beans.

Clickclickclickclick.

"They're *moving*!" Marcus said.

"Mexican jumping beans," Carlos said. "I got them in Miami. Happy birthday, kiddo."

Through it all, Carlos had remembered missing Marcus's seventh birthday two days after he got the call about his mother's death. During a tearful goodbye at LAX, Carlos had promised to bring him a special present.

Carlos shared a brief, private look with Phoenix: *Best I could do.* She smiled to let him know he'd made the perfect choice, but his eyes stared straight through her. Phoenix didn't see visible bruises, but Carlos's tightly drawn shoulders made her wonder if he'd suffered a beating, or worse. Had he been jailed? Phoenix turned her face away from Marcus to hide her tears as she and Carlos tried to preserve their son's happy reunion.

"These are *awesome!*" Marcus said, already on his knees, scattering the beans to the wooden floor. "How do they *do* that?"

Carlos didn't answer, dropping his backpack and scanning the living room as if he expected to find something out of place. He went to the mail pile on the table, quickly flipping through the letters. Most of it was unopened fan mail, addressed to her. She'd barely noticed the mail while Carlos was gone. Carlos had once faced down a spirit to save her life, but Phoenix had never seen him look so overmatched.

Surviving had mated them before they knew a thing about love.

Phoenix wiped her eyes dry. "Worms inside," she answered Marcus, remembering a lesson from R. R. Moton Elementary school in Miami. "They live in the beans, and they jump when they're too warm. They like to be cold."

"Do they stay there forever?" Marcus said.

"Pretty close," Phoenix said. "They turn into moths sooner or later, but they only live a couple of days as moths. They spend most of their lives tucked inside their beans."

"Sucks for them," Marcus said, trying on his favorite new phrase from Ronny's older brother. No matter how much Phoenix tried to shelter him, the outside world intruded. Phoenix was thinking the exact opposite: *Lucky* them. A hard shell and all of life's needs within touch? Wasn't that her new dream?

Carlos manfully spent as much time as he could playing on the GamePort with Marcus before he told his son he was tired and retreated to the bedroom. Phoenix spent two hours struggling to finish the day's lessons despite Marcus's excitement.

It was a long afternoon.

Phoenix peeked in on Carlos while Marcus finished his math assignment. He was lying on top of the bed fully clothed, staring at the door with unblinking eyes. Waiting.

"Carlos, what happened?" she said, sitting beside him. She held his hand.

Gently, Carlos pulled his hand away. Instead, he laid his palm across her fuzzy scalp. "Later," he said. "After Marcus is in bed. I don't want to tell it in pieces."

Daylight lingered like his two-week absence, but night finally came. Phoenix brought Carlos a plate of chicken and rice, but he ate only a few bites and said he had an upset stomach, maybe later. He pushed the plate far away.

They heard Marcus's music from down the hall, the African lullabies they had played him since he was in his crib. Otherwise, the house was quiet.

"Tell me, baby," she said.

Carlos was nearly hoarse by the time he told her how he'd found his mother in the observation room in the facility outside Maricao. Phoenix covered her mouth with her open palm, afraid she might scream. Mami had been one of her favorite people left in the world.

"I was in a lab coat, so it took a while for someone to figure out I didn't belong," Carlos said. "They were Americans, Germans, I think . . . an Asian man. They were talking about the infection. Something about the family from Hong Kong. They had all seen cases like Mami's. *All* of them. The Asian man said there'd been riots in North Korea. They talked about how fast it spreads, maybe in the air. There's already a name for it in Puerto Rico: *La Enfermidad de Rezo*. The Praying Disease. Because of the hands. The body seizes up—it makes them look like they're praying."

All the words Carlos had been saving for her spilled from him.

"Then I slipped out. No one checked my ID on the way out of the gate. The guard was just a kid. I knew it would be a mistake, but I blogged about it. Not everything, but enough. That was the night I called you, before I changed my mind and deleted the page. But the internet is forever. The history was there. By morning, police were knocking on my door. Cameras had caught me at the facility. I thought I was going to prison.

"My father knew someone in the governor's office. That's the only thing that kept me from being locked up. But they said I had to be quarantined because I'd been exposed. I didn't buy it. The 'quarantine' was just a way to try to keep me quiet. If I had admitted myself to a hospital, I might not have been free to go for a lot longer than thirty days. They're hiding a plague, Phee. Worse than the flu strains. Right in Puerto Rico!"

Carlos went silent, emptied.

A low wind flurried against the house, setting off the cacophony of wind chimes outside their bedroom window. Phoenix wondered if the coyotes were out hunting.

"I know, Carlito," Phoenix said in the hushed voice she saved for ballads. "I know."

That night, she told her husband about the visit from John Jamal Wright. And the websites he had led her to, and the stories being told. And the Glow she had refused, but now wished she had kept.

Phoenix and Carlos talked all night long.

Five

Black roads roll beneath a blind-eyed sky, Phoenix thought, trying out infant lyrics as John Wright's SUV ferried her and her family high up narrow, darkened Mulholland Drive, past the secluded mansions hidden behind gates, sentries, and jungles. Occasional lights twinkled through the foliage to remind her that they were passing homes instead of journeying through wilderness, although roadside signs at every other house proclaimed that the neighborhood was for sale. *Armored in marble, we can't hear the children cry.*

It had been a long time since lyrics appeared spontaneously, and rarer still that lyrics came without chords, so maybe Carlos was right about the gig: once she was on the stage, it would all come back. Like a trained dog. *Thatta girl—sing! Play! Roll over!*

"I must be crazy," she muttered.

Carlos gave her a baleful look, shaking his head. "You're fine. Just breathe."

After she'd vowed to retire from performing, she was doing a *corporate* gig? Even if Clarion World Health was doing the work it claimed, how could she have convinced herself that singing for eight hundred of Clarion's handpicked faithful would have any impact outside Beverly Hills? She would reach more people plugging in her amp at Times Square, if she could get security clearance. At least that would have some integrity.

"Why did I agree to do this again?" Phoenix said.

"You committed," Carlos said. "Ride it out, baby." Slipping into their familiar roles already. Phoenix the fragile artist; Carlos her patient wrangler.

Wright was driving. The young white woman in the passenger seat beside him was stoic, and had barely moved except to tap the keys on her wristphone's keyboard. Her smile when she had introduced herself in Paso had been tight, forced, as if she was as reluctant to take Phoenix to L.A. as Phoenix was to go. Like Wright, she looked like she was barely old enough to be out of college. Was the company run by kids?

Phoenix's mind went back to her new lyrics, which were still missing music. *Waking up is easy if you never go to sleep / Have you seen the soul you promised you would keep?*

Phoenix made a sour face. Those weren't true lyrics, only self-judgment. Damn, maybe that *Vibe* critic had been right when he called her the "self-proclaimed prophetess of self-righteousness." No wonder those kids in Chicago—

Phoenix's stomach gave her a vicious stab.

Carlos squeezed her hand, as if he'd heard her thinking about Chicago. He leaned close to her ear. "Let Marcus see who his mom is."

You mean let Marcus see how his namesake got shot at the Osiris, Phoenix couldn't help thinking, but she squeezed away thoughts of Sarge, too. Marcus had been only a year old when she retired, and he'd never seen her perform. That was the only reason they'd brought him, and part of the reason she'd agreed to do the show at all.

Although it was eight o'clock and just getting dark, Marcus had tired of his GamePort and fallen asleep against the plush leather seat during the long stretch of drive on the I-5. A couple of weeks ago, she would have fretted that he would wet his pants during a long nap, but his recent spate of daytime wetting had magically stopped as soon as Carlos was home.

If Phoenix was honest with herself, she knew that she had come out of hiding for the Glow, already jonesing for a drug she'd never tried. After Carlos's stories about Maricao, she wanted the vial Wright had offered her whether it was legal or not. She wanted it for her breast, now that she'd seen the alarm on her doctor's face, his hurry to schedule a biopsy.

She wanted it for her future. Her son. She cursed herself daily for letting it out of her hand.

So far, Wright hadn't offered the vial again, and the stone-faced young woman with him didn't look like she was ready to extend special courtesies. Her black-dyed hair hung across her brow in a sheepdog cut, nearly hiding her eyes. If she was a fan, nothing in her face had shown it. And Wright was different around the girl—more businesslike, less playful. Phoenix wondered what had sculpted the girl's jaw so hard already.

"Excuse me," Phoenix called to the front seat. "What's your name again?"

Wright turned to glance at the girl, who didn't look back at Phoenix. "Caitlin," she said.

"You like music, Caitlin?"

"Used to," the girl said.

Phoenix and Carlos shared a look. Phoenix had carried this girl's kind of weight after the gunshots that killed her father at the Osiris, and then after three strung-out college kids chewed cyanide pills at her Rose Garden show in Chicago. She knew what weight sounded like.

"Music takes you to another world. Believe me, I know," Phoenix said. "Caitlin, I'm gonna help you remember what music is for."

"Amen," Wright said softly.

Caitlin turned around to look at Phoenix. She gave her head an economical shake to move a swatch of hair out of her eyes: bright blue glass. No smile, but her face was a little softer.

"No pressure, ma'am," Caitlin O'Neal said softly. "But I sure as hell hope so."

The street went from darkness to an unearthly red glow as brake lights lit up the trees within half a mile of the house on Beverly Drive. Wright turned on blue dashboard flashers to skirt the traffic jam, weaving in and out of the lanes. An hour until showtime, and the line for the valet parking was long, with Day-Glo cones set up to bring order to the crush.

Phoenix hadn't realized that Marcus was awake until she saw

him staring at the spectacle through his car window. "Whoa," he said. "All these people are coming to see *you*?"

Phoenix and Carlos laughed at the shock in his voice.

"You know your mom's famous," Carlos said. "Lots of people like her singing."

"Mom, are you a *rock star*? Like Bluefish?" Bluefish was the rage on kiddiecasts, although Phoenix didn't consider the comparison to the costumed teen band a compliment.

Phoenix shrugged. "Something like that. Believe it or not."

Wright spoke up. "Marcus? Your mom is more than a rock star. She's a legend."

Marcus looked at Phoenix, nose scrunched as if to say, *What the hell* . . . ?

Phoenix decided she would put on a show her kid would never forget.

With polite honks, Wright ferried them across an ocean of driveway tiles until they reached the entrance of the palatial home, styled like an Italian villa with windows flaunting enough electricity to bring daylight to a village. Wright drove past porticoes and the crowd huddled at the valet line to a narrow green canopy roped off with black velvet. A security team waited, dressed in black.

Phoenix was trying to convince herself that the gig might be fun when she saw Caitlin brush her hand across her waist, caressing something hidden beneath her long white blouse the way a Catholic might touch her rosary.

Caitlin had a gun. Phoenix shouldn't have been surprised, but she was.

"Are you my bodyguard?" Phoenix asked her.

Caitlin looked back at her with a start, as if she'd been discovered. "No, not officially," she said, sheepish. She straightened her blouse, pretending she'd only been fussing with her clothes. "I'm our boss's personal assistant. But she asked me to take very good care of you."

The security team opened the SUV's doors, swallowing them in lights and sound. What should have been familiar was made dizzying by her lack of practice—circled by staff, rushed past a crowd, doors opened for her in mechanical succession, gentle hands guiding her at her elbow. Carlos, as always, trailed two steps behind her.

Phoenix never let go of Marcus's hand, kept her eyes mostly on her son's pudgy face, finding him grinning, wide-eyed, as if he thought he was the president himself. *Enjoy it while you can, kid,* she thought, remembering why they had decided to raise Marcus away from the noise. An overblown sense of entitlement stunted children's growth.

The only difference between this scene and her old life was the lack of flashbulbs; she'd stipulated *no photos*, except for Clarion's event photographer. She'd never liked seeing spots dancing in her eyes. Besides, she might need to distance herself from Clarion one day. There was a lot of gray area between world saviors and crazed bioterrorists.

"Is this a hotel?" Marcus said as an endless marble corridor spread before them.

"Naw, li'l dude, this is somebody's house," Phoenix said, wrapping an arm around him. Marcus was a tree trunk like Sarge had been, stocky and already as tall as her shoulder. Before long, Marcus would be as tall as Carlos.

"This big?" Marcus said.

"Your mom had a house this big once," Carlos said, as if he hadn't signed the papers, too.

"Our house was a dollhouse compared to this," Phoenix said.

"A fifteen-million-dollar dollhouse," Carlos said, and Phoenix gave him a laser look over her shoulder. Carlos had always hated living in Hollywood. She'd ultimately agreed with him, but she never could stomach his whining about having money.

"*Pobrecito,*" she said sarcastically. Poor baby.

This house would have cost them fifty million dollars. She couldn't guess how much it was worth today, but the sparse furnishings told her it had probably sat empty for a long time until Clarion rented it out. The furniture was sterile, showroom pieces. Through the windows, she could see that most of the crowd had gathered in the backyard by a swimming pool that looked as long as a river.

Inside, at least two hundred people were waiting for an early glimpse. The crowd sharpened into faces, and Phoenix was warmed by their beams of recognition as her family was led past their huddles. "Thanks for coming," she said, returning their smiles. "It's great to see you all here. I'm honored you came."

Her feelings were sincere, but the words were straight from the pages of her reliable script, recited at predictable intervals. She had climbed back into her old skin already. She'd left her costumes in storage, but she wished she'd worn something more than new jeans and her favorite peacock-colored blouse, nearly sheer and fanning slightly at the sleeves. The blouse was elegantly artsy for grocery shopping in Paso, but it was flimsy here. With her head shaved, she felt like a Phoenix impostor. She should have worn a wig!

Most of the people lining the walls were dressed for a special occasion, in cocktail clothes. Like the crowds that had followed her on tour, they were of all races and ethnicities, from teenagers to seniors. The shiny, hairless scalp of a middle-aged white woman in an electric wheelchair reminded Phoenix of her mother. The woman was gravely ill, her floral-patterned dress hanging too loose on bony limbs. *Get that biopsy tomorrow, or that'll be you,* she reminded herself.

Phoenix paused to squeeze the woman's soft, dry hand. She squeezed back, tearful.

"Thank you," the woman said, voice trembling with gratitude.

"Hey, I'm glad to be here," Phoenix said. "And I'm glad you're here with me."

"I'm not going anywhere," the woman said, defiant.

As the security staff encouraged her to keep walking, Phoenix noticed other infirmities—a teenage boy walking with crutches, a hollow-faced black man who could have been Sarge's brother except for his gauntness. The faces were smiling, but many of them were weary.

"We've set up a green room for you," Wright explained, walking beside Phoenix. "Anything you need is in there. I did my research—you don't like chocolate. But we have some fresh tropical fruit and seafood, and pizza for Marcus. If you have any questions . . ."

"Who are they?" she said. "How did they get invited to the concert?"

"They're . . . everyone," Wright said, scanning the crowd. "School-teachers, journalists, bloggers, students, retirees, a couple politicians. The only thing they have in common is . . ." Wright lowered his voice. "They're sick. Even if they don't know it. Or don't want to."

Phoenix went mute as goose bumps traveled across her skin. She gazed at Wright, waiting for more of an explanation, but he only smiled pleasantly. A stocky black man with exotic features whispered in his ear, and Wright suddenly gave Phoenix a Japanese-style bow and then stopped midway, as if catching himself.

"Sorry, I'm needed in the guest house," Wright said. "Can't wait to see the show."

A second black man joined Wright, and the three of them made their way to rear double doors of sturdy oak that opened into the night. Phoenix gazed after them through the rear picture window, unable to wrest her eyes free.

Something about the men captivated her. So striking! Their movements were fluid yet deliberate, like dancers'. Their faces? One of the men, like Wright, had looked like a boy—but he'd carried himself like an elder, a royal. The two men with Wright had seemed barely to notice her, much less recognize her.

Both men were adorned in loose-fitting tunics and pants that glowed bright white.

They might have been the most beautiful men Phoenix had ever seen.

A spotlight shone on the black Steinway baby grand piano waiting for her, lid raised in greeting. An electric hum quivered Phoenix's bones as she walked across the large property, flanked by her family and a team of purposeful strangers. Although the audience had already gathered in front of the stage beyond the colossal lighted swimming pool, Phoenix was blanketed by the expectant hush.

The grounds were at least five acres, free of lighting except for the stage: a silent temple. At this elevation, the air smelled clear as a mountaintop.

Phoenix noticed the guest house beyond the stage, on a knoll to the left of it, wrapped in trees. The smaller guest house had its own thin columns, and there were four men clad in white clustered outside its entrance. Between them, enfolded in their group, was a girl—or maybe a small-boned woman—who had long hair and features hidden by the night.

The guest house was at least twenty yards from her, maybe closer to thirty, and there was no light on the porch where the group stood, but as Phoenix stared at the girl, her view became clear and sharp: the girl's hair hung in dreadlock ropes long past her shoulders, and she was lithe and tall. She looked like a bride dressed in white. Like the other men, the girl was brown-skinned. *A model?* Phoenix wondered, although some part of her knew better.

Was Clarion run by Africans? News to her.

As if her own eyes suddenly had the power of binoculars, Phoenix saw the girl incline her head ever so slightly, the barest tilt of her forehead; a greeting meant for her. Phoenix nodded in return—*bowed* her head, really—to acknowledge the woman-child's greeting.

For that instant, she and the girl alone shared five acres of emptied space. Time crawled.

When Phoenix blinked, the group at the cottage was again a distant huddle in the dark. It was a too-familiar feeling of dislocation, like brushing against her ghost all those years ago. *What the . . . ?*

"You okay?" Carlos's voice said, his assuring hand on her shoulder.

Suddenly, Wright appeared beside her; or maybe she had only noticed him again. The strange telescopic vision had vanished, and her periphery filled with the crowd she had forgotten.

"That's the boss-lady," Wright said, winking. "You'll meet her after the show."

The boss-lady? Phoenix squinted to try to see the girl again, but couldn't make out her features in the haze of distance. In Phoenix's memory, she'd looked barely eighteen.

The crowd parted silently, carving Phoenix's path.

Showtime.

When Phoenix sat, the piano bench was comfortable old slippers, a beach hammock in Carlos's beloved isle of Culebra, the embrace of her parents' arms, and a summertime ice-cream sandwich; every sensation of safety and contentment Phoenix had ever known. She sat still for a moment just to savor it, awed and grateful.

Wright *had* done his research, choosing the same piano that sat in their music room at home, sadly neglected. She touched the shiny keys. Her fingers improvised a chord that filled the night with promise.

Carlos, watching with Marcus at the edge of the stage, mouthed *I love you.*

Phoenix noticed the microphone tilted near her mouth, and she adjusted it the way a guitarist tunes her strings. Wright had offered her a headset mic, but she liked old-school mics that reminded her of the jazz club her parents had run on Miami Beach when she was a kid.

"Do you feel it?" Phoenix said into the mic, gentle breath amplified into wind-song.

The crowd murmured, a church congregation.

"I don't have words for how happy I am to be here tonight," Phoenix said. "I was almost silly enough not to come. Now I'm just sorry I couldn't bring my old band—love you, La'Keitha, Jabari, Andres, Devon, and T." *Love you, Scott. Love you, Sarge and Mom.* Her ghosts. The power of her parents' yawning absence thinned her voice. "They're all here in spirit. Hope it's all right with you guys if it's just me in the flesh."

Carlos began clapping, and the crowd followed in a thunderous wave that stopped as quickly as it had begun, sinking into expectant silence again.

"I think ya'll might know this song," she said. "I've played it a few million times."

Good-natured laughter from the crowd.

"But this time, it's in my heart again," Phoenix went on. "Hope it's still in yours."

Phoenix's fingers relished the familiar, lilting intro to the song that had brought her out of her ghost's shadow. She could remember the exact moment she'd composed it, eating jerk chicken, tired of hearing the gunshots that had taken Sarge—suddenly wondering what it would sound like if Stevie Wonder, Jimi Hendrix, and Nina Simone came by her place to jam.

That day, Phoenix had been born.

Once upon a time, at a long-ago Grammys concert, she and Bono had sung her signature song as a duet, and Prince had surprised them on the stage with his purple guitar's heartrending squeal. Now, alone with her piano, there were none of the subtle *son* and hip-hop undertones, electric guitar flourishes, or funky, stomach-rumbling bass lines. But it was the same song made simple, so sweet on her fingertips and tongue that it was hard to sing without tears.

Phoenix played "Wanna Fly" for the first time—again.

Can you put memories in a jar?
Turn them into marbles
Instead of stones?
Are broken wings just like a scar?

Heal yourself,
Heal the world.

Love yourself,
Love the world.

Wanna fly
Wanna fly

My soul gets cold from standing still.
If I can't test my wings, I'll die.
Don't wanna die for a while.
I think I'll fly for a while.

While Phoenix's tear-roughened voice floated to the treetops, the audience sang with her, clinging to one another's arms.

Phoenix was flying. She couldn't feel the piano bench beneath her or the pedal at her feet. She tasted salt, but she couldn't feel the tears on her face. The substance of her was gone, just like the days when her ghost had taken her on his journeys. Phoenix's fingers

stilled, and she and the crowd sang the a cappella chorus powerfully
enough to shake the earth.

Heal yourself,
Heal the world.

Don't wanna die for a while.
I think I'll fly for a while.

People were hugging. Carlos was closest to her, with moon-eyed
Marcus beside him, so Phoenix hopped from the stage and melted
into her family. Around her, people sobbed and prayed, thanking
Jesus and Jehovah and Olodumare and Allah and Jah, some of them
sinking to their knees. She saw the woman she'd met in the wheelchair on her feet, the chair forgotten, spinning in a circle while her
flowered dress flew above her thighs.

"Thank you," Phoenix whispered, joining their new chorus.

Carlos's body shook with sobs, and she held him to steady him
while he steadied her.

"Mommy, what's happening?" Marcus whispered.

If Phoenix had known which words to use, she would have told
Marcus that a door had opened above them and below them, exposing the core of everything. The music might have led them all to
the door, but Phoenix knew the door wasn't hers any more than the
music was, and she certainly hadn't opened it: she wouldn't have
known how.

No one had to tell her to look back to the cottage on the knoll
beyond the stage. Her eyes knew exactly where to go. All of her *felt*
the source of the power that had swept over them.

The men she had seen earlier were gone.

Only the girl dressed in white remained, arms outstretched
between the columns, upturned eyes seeing straight through the sky.

Six

Washington State
2010
Six Years Earlier

Johnny Jamal Wright had never met the scientist who greeted his father in the packed dirt courtyard, near the huge fountain carved to look like a lion and lioness. All he knew about the scientist was that he was a friend of his father's who had left Tallahassee. He was as tall as a tree, almost seven feet. Johnny couldn't tell his race from his tanned skin.

"Sorry about the blindfolds," the scientist said. "We have these nuisance protocols...."

Johnny blinked into the sunlight, his eyes adjusting since he'd pulled off his blindfold. Trees stood in every direction, mostly evergreens. The limo that had met them at Sea-Tac Airport had been hella cool—the first hour of the ride, anyway—but at the end of a spy mission worthy of James Bond, the limo had dumped him and his father in the middle of the woods. *Not* cool.

His father, surveying the land around them, was beaming. "Look at this, Doc," Dad kept saying, as if trees were his passion. "You've really built it up."

Built what up? They were in front of a large wood-frame two-story house that looked like an antique. Two more cabin-style houses were set farther back in the woods, connected by footpaths. A longer wooden building might have been a church, or a schoolhouse. Some of the boards were uneven. A white domed roof caught his eye inside the treetops.

No basketball court. No baseball diamond. Nobody came here to play.

The scientist stood over Johnny, tall enough to block the sun. He needed to shave. Dad's hand landed hard on Johnny's shoulder, a reminder to smile politely instead of staring.

"Johnny, Doc Shepard is a microbiologist known the world over. I can't wait for you to hear about the incredible work he's doing. He won a major prize called the Lasker Award."

"Pleasure to meet you, sir," Johnny said, although he wasn't sure yet.

The scientist winked at Johnny. "We'll spare you the ancient history. Johnny, I wish my son was here, but he's at summer camp. He's a couple of years older than you. . . ."

Dad asked about the scientist's son in a low, serious voice, and Johnny realized that the kid had been sick once, and the scientist had healed him. Maybe that was why he had left Tallahassee and moved into the woods. Maybe the cure was a secret.

But fugitives also hid in the woods. Mom would scream bloody murder if she heard about the blindfolds, after what her family had been through in Jordan.

"Doc, I swear, you haven't aged a *day,*" Dad said, his voice full of wonder that gave Johnny the creeps. His father's eyes were twinkling merrily, like a department store Santa Claus. Those were Dad's eyes from church, when he talked to God.

Johnny wanted to tell his father he was ready to go home. Only his shyness in front of the scientist kept him quiet.

"I've aged fifty years on the inside," the scientist told Dad, laughing. The scientist steered Dad to the wooden steps to the main house's front porch. The house looked big and airy, the kind where there would be nothing to do, and anything he touched would break. A house that old probably didn't have a working TV.

Johnny started to follow them up the porch steps, but the scientist paused.

"Know what, Johnny?" the scientist said. "Why don't you stay outside for a bit?"

Dad shot him an apologetic look, knowing Johnny preferred AC to outdoors any day. Johnny had just turned fourteen, well beyond his tree-climbing stage.

"I can sit and read in there," Johnny said, remembering his backpack stash.

The scientist smiled pleasantly. "Nah. Look around. Explore. Just stay away from the ax and the woodpile." He pointed vaguely, but Johnny didn't turn to see the woodpile. The trees looked like a maze: a short walk in any direction could get him lost. How could the scientist say he couldn't get in trouble?

"Doc Shepard and I have some catching up to do," Dad said, winking: *Get it?*

"The girls will keep you company out here," the scientist said.

Johnny hoped he hadn't been elected babysitter to a litter of brats who lived in the forest. Before Johnny could protest, the scientist clapped his hands together, excited as he climbed the porch steps with Dad. "Garrick," the scientist said, "I wake up every day and want to pinch myself. . . . You can't imagine how exciting this work is . . . the miraculous strides . . ."

To Johnny, the scientist sounded like the guy in the baggy suit who had sold Dad and Mom their Chrysler. The scientist's voice faded in the foyer. ". . . You can see how it's changed since you were here. There are families now—with children. They just built a school . . ."

The door closed, but Johnny had heard enough. Obviously, the scientist wanted his father to *move* here. Why else would Dad have brought him, too? If Dad was considering moving to a commune in the woods, there was only one answer: Dad had lost his mind.

He hoped this was only an interview for one of Dad's books.

"Hey, what's in the backpack?" a girl's voice said.

When Johnny turned around, he had to squint to hold his eyes steady. A thin, athletic teenage girl with blond hair was sitting astride a mountain bicycle, sweaty from her ride. She was about sixteen, and the sight of her shut down a part of Johnny's brain. He stared at the cigarette dangling from the side of her mouth to keep from gawking.

"Do you speak?" the girl said.

"I've got some comic books," he said, wishing he could have

thought of something less babyish. "I'm . . . really interested in Japanese popular culture."

The girl raised an eyebrow and shot him a look, chuckling. "Relax, anime geek. Lemme see," she said. "You're among friends."

She rifled through his book bag, rejecting or accepting his choices with free-spirited laughter. "Whoa—*Death Note!*" she said, impressed. "This one rocks." *Death Note* was Johnny's favorite manga series, where a high school student named Light Yagami used a notebook from a sorcerer of death to cleanse the world of evil. Light could kill anyone just by writing a name in the notebook. Johnny wondered what he would do with that kind of power.

Caitlin O'Neal introduced herself and gave Johnny a tour of the colony, as she called it: three or four homes, the long schoolhouse, and a laboratory with walls made mostly of glass.

"What's the lab for?" Johnny said. Day by day, it was slowly dawning on him that he could go to medical school.

"Research," Caitlin said, shrugging. "That's what Clarion does."

She explained that the colony was part of a company called Clarion World Health, and her father was vice president. She lived on Long Island, but visited in the summers with her father and sister. She gave him the Clarion pep speech, telling him how thousands of people were being healed of AIDS in Africa, and soon Clarion would be healing people all over the world. Her claims seemed farfetched, but they were impressive if they were true.

"What kind of doctor is your dad?" Caitlin said.

"He's not. He's a writer," Johnny said. "But I'll be a doctor." It was the first time he'd said it out loud.

"Damn right," Caitlin said. "You'll be healing people, anyway."

Still coasting on her bike, Caitlin beckoned him across a path toward the cedar building with a domed white roof. She hopped off the bicycle to wheel it to the rear of the building, waving him to a wall shaded with ferns.

"Your dad must be a big deal, getting the red carpet," Caitlin said, half to herself, pulling down a rolled brown tarp that had been leaning against the wall. She offered him her cigarette. "Smoke?"

Johnny shook his head. "You're really gonna damage your lungs like that."

"Dude, lighten up. You're not the surgeon general. Trust me, I'm not gonna get sick. That's not one of my top ten worries in life."

"Everyone gets sick," Johnny said.

"Not here," Caitlin said. She stepped up onto the carpet-size roll of tarp to peek into a high window near the corner. She whispered down to him, "If we're quiet, we'll hear what they're saying."

Caitlin secured for Johnny the corner of a picture window that spied on a large conference room. The oval table at the center was large enough to seat twenty or more, but only five men were huddled at the end closest to them: Johnny's father, the scientist, a blond guy in Brooks Brothers whom Johnny guessed was Caitlin's father . . . and two black men draped in white tunics and loose-fitting white slacks. Africans? Odd round torches burned in sconces on the wall.

Johnny's heart pounded as if it had split into two, and brushing up against Caitlin made it hard to hold his thoughts together. How could Caitlin sound so sure she would never get sick? What kind of work was Clarion doing?

Johnny strained to hear the voices over his wild heartbeat.

". . . From Florida A&M University . . ." the scientist said, explaining where Dad worked. Dad seemed nervous as he surveyed the men around him. Couldn't he speak for himself?

The next man's voice was clear and close. "You'll have to excuse us, but we're forced to take strict precautions with outsiders . . . *Mr. Wright.*"

Suddenly, the speaker appeared in the window, his face staring straight down at Johnny. He'd been beside the window in the corner the whole time! He was another African, dressed in white. His bottomless eyes looked like hot coals. He yanked a curtain closed.

Caitlin gasped, scrambling away. Johnny was so startled, he lost his balance on the tarp and fell against the house with a clumsy thunk. Dad was going to kill him!

Caitlin was already on her bicycle, pedaling toward the shelter of the trees on a path behind the hall, so Johnny ran to follow her. His heart pounded at him like a mallet. Johnny would see those eyes from the window in his nightmares.

"Stop!" Johnny called after Caitlin, gasping. "Who is that?"

"Fana's father," Caitlin said over her shoulder. "My dad's boss. You never saw me."

"Who's Fana?" But Caitlin melted between the tree trunks as she sped away.

Caitlin's dramatic disappearing act didn't slow Johnny's racing heartbeat, or ease the sour tightness in his stomach since the eyes had chastised him in the window. It was as if the man had known he was there, had been talking to him all along.

Dad wanted to spend the night, but Johnny was ready to go back to the airport. He couldn't live here. And the man in the window . . .

"My dad's bark is worse than his bite," a younger girl's voice said. It wasn't Caitlin.

Johnny spun around to see who had spoken, facing the endless columns of tree trunks.

"Where are you?" he said to the woods.

"Right here."

A tall, skinny black girl came to vivid sight. Dark dreadlocks hung from her scalp, wrapped around her shoulders like a shawl. She was draped in the colors of foliage, browns and greens, standing stock-still, so she'd blended into the tree beside her. The way she appeared, she could have snapped her fingers to bend the sunlight.

Only her eyes moved when he walked toward her. She was trying very hard not to look at him. She smelled smoky, like incense. Her face looked younger, maybe eleven or twelve, but she was nearly as tall as he. Tall for a girl.

"You saw what happened?" he said. "At the window?"

She nodded, her eyes firmly staying away from his.

"Listen, I hope that won't look bad for my father," Johnny said. If she was the boss's daughter, she might have influence. "We were just playing around."

She grinned, and her smile brightened her face. "My father

understands curiosity," she said. "He knows you're not here to hurt us. Or me." She looked like she wanted to say more, but stopped herself. She turned her face away when he stood directly in front of her. Her words sounded old for her age.

"Are you really this shy?" he said.

She smiled again, wistfully. And raised her hand to cover her teeth. "With new people."

"Why do you care about me looking at you?" he said. "You don't even know me."

"Aren't you from outside?" For the first time, the girl in the woods raised her face and brown eyes to his. Her voice echoed in his mind, a stereo effect: *YOU'RE FROM OUTSIDE?* Her eyes spoke so loudly, he swore he could hear her thoughts.

Finally, he saw what a pretty kid she was. Why was her father keeping her hidden here?

"Yeah, I'm from Florida." He wondered if he should explain where Florida was. Or describe a neighborhood. Or a mall. The way she'd said *outside* had made it sound alien. Johnny wanted to rescue her and take her away.

"You've seen a lot of faces outside," the girl said.

"Oh, so I'm at my limit?" he said. "I'm not allowed to see you now?"

She shook her head, her lips curling. "My face isn't me."

Johnny didn't know how to answer that. Was she a philosopher or a mental case?

"I know," the girl said, resigned. "I confuse people when I talk." The girl pulled out a thin white scarf and wrapped it across her head and shoulders until only a sliver of her face showed. She outstretched her hand to him, businesslike. "I'm Bea-Bea. Everyone calls me Fana."

Johnny reached out to shake her hand. When their palms touched, Johnny's skin buzzed. His galloping heartbeat slowed. His scare at the window suddenly seemed funny. He noticed the scent of cooking biscuits from the house, and thought he wouldn't mind staying for dinner.

The day finally fell into place. The trees revealed beauty he hadn't noticed before.

"I'm Johnny Wright," he said. "What does 'Fana' mean?"

Fana started to speak, but Johnny didn't hear the answer from her lips. The knowledge bloomed in his head as he stared at the fascinating girl with the long dreadlocks.

Of course.

Fana meant Light.

Seven

Concert Night
2016

ire. Her skin, her mouth, was fire.

Thin wisps of steam rose as the shower's ice-cold water massaged Fana's naked skin. Her bare soles celebrated cold shower tiles. For a time, her vision had gone completely red, but colors were softening again. Her ears popped open, allowing sounds beyond her rushing blood.

Fana didn't know how long the gentle knocking had played on her bathroom door. She'd thought it was her heartbeat. She'd never felt anything like the concert—floating above the audience, a butterfly knitting together what was weak or broken, flicking sparks of light. Struggling hearts. Overburdened arteries. Damaged livers. Cancer cells. She'd touched all of them, dusting ailments away like motes in the wind. Fana's heart still raced from the pure invigoration of it. Maybe this was what sex felt like to mortals.

"Fana?" Johnny called from beyond the door. Was Johnny in her room?

If Fana hadn't been so exhausted, she might have been angry. Johnny knew better! Her father, Teka, and Fasilidas had all been banned from her room so she could recover after the concert—even Caitlin!—so why was he taking special liberties?

Appearances mattered, whether either of them liked it. Fana wasn't ready to use her voice, so she opened her thoughts to him: *I'm fine. Please go. You shouldn't be here now.*

She couldn't retract her probe in time to preserve his privacy, so she felt him wince at the reproach. Once a mental conduit was open, it was difficult to filter out a busy head.

"I'm sorry," he said. "Do you still want to see Phoenix? It's been three hours, and we promised to drive them back to Paso Robles tonight."

Fana shouldn't have been surprised, but she was. Time evaporated when she tranced.

Yes, I want to see her. Please apologize. Ask her to stay just awhile longer.

"Fana, I really am sorry," he said. "I wasn't thinking."

He waited, hoping for her to soothe him and tell him all right. But she didn't. It was better for Johnny if he didn't fool himself into believing that Michel ever stopped watching him. Michel wouldn't care about the flimsy door that separated them—Johnny was only yards from where his fiancée stood bare of clothes.

Just go, Fana thought sharply.

Their combined pain engulfed Fana as Johnny's footsteps scurried away.

The eyes of Fana's father were heavy on Johnny Wright as he emerged from Phoenix's room into the guest cottage's narrow corridor. Barely a foot between them. To Fana's people, whose vast underground home gave them an exaggerated sense of personal space, close proximity was an insult. In the past year, Johnny had learned that custom the hard way.

"That was childish," Dawit said, and Johnny wasn't sure if Dawit meant his visit to Fana's room or the concert itself. Fana had staged the Glow concert against her father's advice. "Her task is difficult enough without a circus tent."

Did Dawit care about their healing mission? "She changed the lives of hundreds of people tonight, and she did it without using Glow. She manifested her thoughts."

"Don't be hypnotized by her gifts, Johnny," Dawit said. "You'll compromise her path."

"You mean her trap."

She's only engaged to him because you and your people are such cowards, Johnny thought. He immediately wished he could take the thought back, but he couldn't control his thoughts the way Fana could. Dawit was standing too close to have missed the insult.

Dawit's jaw went to stone, a glimpse of a man Fana had told Johnny stories about: a cool killer he hoped never to meet up close. "Fana chose this path—I didn't choose it for her," Dawit said. "Diplomacy is her dearest value, which you would see if you were following *her* vision instead of yours. Whose idea was it to come to Los Angeles?"

"Mine," Johnny said. "Phoenix wouldn't travel." He hadn't let himself think about Michel's proximity in Mexico until later; a cold tickle in his head. Johnny had frozen in place in the mansion's empty yard, expecting Michel's voice in the wind.

Dawit saw the memory in Johnny's face. And in his thoughts. "You and your kind baffle me," Dawit said. "So careless with what little life you have."

Johnny's face burned, and he was mad at himself for his jackrabbit's heartbeat. Was Dawit threatening him, or only telling a razor truth? After last year's terror with Michel, Johnny had vowed never to fear any man.

"I don't have time to be afraid of him," Johnny said. "Or anyone else."

Dawit shook his head, patting Johnny's shoulder as if to give condolences. He moved aside to let him pass. "Enjoy your days, youngster," he said. "Sip them slowly, like honey wine. Fana will remember you fondly." There was no cruelty in his voice.

The immortal's words had the disturbing ring of prophecy.

Phoenix wondered if she would sleep all night, or the next night. Her mind and skin still sizzled from the stage. Each time she heard the swelling of the audience's voices in her memory, her stomach dropped with raw amazement.

The guest cottage smelled like sweet, earthy incense. Marcus had fallen asleep hours ago, curled on a love seat in a corner beneath a sheepskin blanket that looked as warm as a womb. Children could sleep anywhere, after anything.

She and Carlos alternated between pacing the tiny living area and sitting at the round table while they waited, exchanging long gazes but few words. How could they capture it? Carlos fumbled for an explanation for his tears when Marcus asked him why he'd been crying, but he'd finally whispered his confession to Phoenix: *I saw Mami on that stage, Phoenix.* She had envied him. What would she have given to see Mom and Sarge?

"Do you think it was a vision?" Phoenix asked, finally past her envy. "A ghost?"

Carlos shrugged. "I don't know which. She looked more like a ghost in movies, almost transparent. Not like . . ." He didn't say the rest. Carlos didn't like to talk about Scott Joplin, either. "Maybe I saw what I wanted to see."

Carlos squeezed her hand, checking over her shoulder to make sure they were still alone. She hadn't seen the men in white in the guest cottage, except silent shadows passing in the hallway in the rear. Caitlin hovered nearby, in the kitchen, with only occasionally clanking dishes to remind them that she was there.

"What was it for you?" Carlos said.

Phoenix searched for words. "Peace. Flying. Like the flying dreams I used to have when I was a kid. Maybe we're all born with a memory of it. That's why we long for it so much. Maybe it's in our souls."

They both believed in God, but neither of them had a clear picture of what they thought God *was.* Carlos was a Baptist-slash-Catholic, and Phoenix had been raised by a Jewish mother and a father who'd flirted with the Nation of Islam. Their experiences with Scott Joplin's ghost had taught them that there was much more to existence than they could see, but Phoenix rarely spoke of the soul. Tonight, the picture seemed clearer.

"Maybe," Carlos said, muffling his words with his wrist. "And maybe they drugged us."

"Drugged us?"

"*Shhhh.*" His eyes darted toward the corridor.

"Eight hundred people?"

"Think about it. Something in the water. Or the Kool-Aid, more like it. I showed you those articles. Don't forget Clarion could be a cult."

Carlos's theory didn't explain the woman who'd risen from her wheelchair to dance, but Carlos would probably say she was a plant. Phoenix might have believed the cult story once, but not anymore. Something special had happened.

"You're too young to be so cynical, Carlos."

"I'm too old not to be," he said, looking at his watch. "Jesus—it's after midnight. Why are we letting them keep us waiting like this? This is insane." He swore in Spanish.

That was when she emerged from the hallway.

She was dressed differently, in jeans and a faded Phoenix concert T-shirt, but the girl looked the way Phoenix remembered from her earlier glimpse on the porch: brown-red skin like smooth clay, a lithe, willowy figure, and a mane of long dreadlocks. She was slightly taller than Phoenix, about five ten, but she was a teenager. A child, almost. Awkward in her limbs.

Fana came into the room alone, but Caitlin hovered close-by, leaning over the kitchen-bar counter. Two of the white-clad men stood sentry in the hall.

The girl entered the room so quietly that Carlos didn't see her until Phoenix gestured, and then Carlos jumped to his feet, flustered, sweeping an imaginary hat from his head. How had Carlos missed the floating sensation again? The room felt wired with high voltage.

"Hey, I'm really sorry," the girl said, her voice too small and soft for her presence. Her brown eyes were filled with a fan's bright glimmer as she held her hand out to Phoenix. "My name is Fana, and I'm so happy to meet you. I've been listening to you since I was ten years old. 'Gotta Fly' saved me once. That song was in my head when I changed my life."

Phoenix clasped the girl's hand and couldn't let go at first. Fana's hand felt magnetized. Phoenix tried to study the sensation before she slipped her hand away. Strange.

Phoenix watched Carlos's face as he shook Fana's hand next. He felt it, too. Once his hand was free, he glanced down at his palm as if he thought she'd left a mark on him.

"You made a big difference in a lot of people's lives tonight," Fana said. "Not everyone understands Clarion's work. We needed you to bring them here. You helped us give them something to believe in. And now they'll help us convince others."

"Glad to come," Phoenix said.

Phoenix had questions, but most words had fled her mind. Years ago, she'd met Nelson Mandela and the Obamas and encountered the same tongue paralysis, but that hadn't prepared her for the sensation when she met Fana, as if the girl were an eight-foot giant.

"The plague is real," Fana said. "It's worse than anyone has admitted. A whole village has been wiped out in Nigeria. And in North Korea. It's been to Puerto Rico. It's airborne. People have been infected through very casual contact. It kills almost everyone it touches."

"*Yes*," Carlos said, stepping closer to her, as if awaiting a command. Finally, someone willing to admit what he'd seen in Puerto Rico.

"But we aren't helpless," Fana said. "Thank you for helping us heal the world. With your music. With your story."

"What . . . story?" Phoenix said.

Fana was no longer standing five feet in front of her. Somehow, Fana had climbed between her ears, into her mind, filling her: *PLEASE TAKE BETTER CARE OF YOURSELF, PHOENIX*, Fana's voice whispered inside her thoughts. *YOU WERE AFRAID, SO YOU LET IT GROW TO YOUR BONES. THE WORLD NEEDS YOU. I NEED YOU.*

Her heart sailing, Phoenix brought her hands to her chest, wrapping herself as if she were cold. She patted herself, already knowing, but needing to be sure. Tears flooded her.

The lump in her right breast was gone.

Eight

"It's up on HuffPo," Caitlin said.

Johnny raced to peer over Caitlin's shoulder at her window seat, reading the Huffington Post on her notetab. Caitlin tilted her screen so they could both see the color display under the GLOW WARS graphic of a vial. "Phoenix concert puts Glow center stage," by Mike Middleton. Johnny knew his name: Middleton taught biochemistry at UCLA Medical School and was a fierce critic of Glow and Clarion. He had also been one of the first to RSVP for Phoenix's concert when he got his invitation.

He would get a surprise at his next doctor's visit.

"Bet he'll have some nice things to say about Clarion now," Caitlin said.

Johnny's eyes skimmed the glowing screen: ". . . unforgettable experience . . . no easy answers . . . rethinking my assumptions about what is possible in approaches to healing . . ."

Johnny never trusted blind optimism anymore, but he was glad the headlines had started. Huffington Post. MedNet. Even *People* magazine's website! Truth overpowered lies. Glow was becoming a political and social movement, beyond the realm of medicine. People would *demand* access to Glow, the government be damned. Once that happened, vials would be available at drugstores. Hell, the vials would *eliminate* drugstores.

If only Fana could conduct mass healings every night! Maybe she could. The idea made Johnny's heart pound. God's vision manifesting through Fana's Blood!

Fana was staring out her window at the clouds, but Johnny

saw her cheeks dimple in a small smile. Fana didn't smile nearly enough.

Johnny took the empty seat next to Fana, the one he avoided if anyone except Caitlin was nearby. Now that the plane was in the air, only three of them shared the first-class cabin. He wanted to ask Caitlin to leave them alone, but how could he?

Caitlin and Fana had started the Glow movement, so this was their triumph more than his. But he'd persuaded Fana to do the concert, and she had listened to him. If he couldn't at least advise Fana, he had nothing to offer her.

"You're the new religion, Fana," Caitlin teased her. Fana hadn't spoken to either of them in nearly an hour, caught in her head, but Caitlin had a knack for reaching her.

Fana made a face. "And be like him? No, thanks." Fana rarely mentioned her fiancé when Johnny was present. "Why do you think I didn't show myself?"

"Oh, please," Caitlin said. "They knew it was you."

"She'll learn how to mask better next time," Johnny said. Fana was the telepath, but Johnny often finished her sentences or spoke her mind before she did. Fana smiled at him, patting his hand. Johnny's skin sparked beneath her touch.

Johnny almost caught Fana's hand and squeezed it. Almost.

WE CAN'T, Fana said silently, sadly. Johnny moved his hand away.

"Let's see if anybody recognizes a miracle anymore," Caitlin said. She seemed far away; Fana must be carrying him with the current of her thoughts. Caitlin's distant voice went on: "Fana, are you zoning? I never know where you are. . . ."

Fana wasn't listening to Caitlin, her eyes closed.

THANK YOU FOR THIS, JOHNNY, Fana told him. TONIGHT WAS THE BEST FEELING OF MY LIFE. MY GRANDMOTHER USED TO SAY I NEED TO BE WITH PEOPLE, TO TOUCH THEM. I'LL NEVER FORGET IT.

Johnny's heart leaped. Fana seemed barely to see him sometimes, and now she was sharing her mind with him, enfolding them in a private cave.

"Anything, Fana," Johnny whispered to her ear, wishing he could burrow into her thoughts, too. "For you? Anything."

Fana's heart soared as the plane charged the skies.

A year ago, her grandmother had died as Michel's prisoner on this Embraer Legacy 600 jet, one of her colony's planes, and the pain and terror of her family's ordeal still clung like wallpaper. She closed her eyes, acknowledging Gramma Bea in her painful dying place. Gramma Bea had forgotten the pain in an instant, but Fana hated how she had suffered. Now Fana was living the life Gramma Bea had wanted for her, out in the world.

We did it, Gramma Bea! We're doing it!

Fana's father emerged from the cockpit, leaving the others to pilot the plane. Johnny rose from the seat beside her, pretending to check the luggage compartment overhead.

"How's Mom?" Fana asked her father. "Did you talk to her?"

Mom didn't travel, or do much of anything, since Michel's fire had burned their compound to the ground. Mom had folded up her life in the ashes of the Washington woods. Two weeks ago, Dad had retrieved Mom from her dreaming chamber, where she'd been trying to live in her past. Fana knew from peeking into her mother's thoughts that Mom still sometimes burned Dreamsticks to sleep at night, though Mom had sworn to stay away from them. Her dependency was far from behind her.

But Fana couldn't blame her. Mom's life had been uncomplicated before. Since then, Mom had been fighting a war to share the blood Dad had given her.

SHE'LL BE FINE, Dad told her privately in his clipped way, avoiding her question. He didn't discuss anything important in front of mortals, except family.

Dad glanced in Johnny's direction, and Johnny got the hint. He nudged Caitlin, who was reading the report Fana's cousin had sent from Nigeria. Caitlin's heartbeat raced in Fana's ear as she read. The outbreak there was worse than expected, with nearly two hundred villagers dead.

Fana and her father would visit Nigeria next.

Caitlin stood up to leave the cabin. "Party's over," she said.

"Afraid so, hon," Dawit said. Caitlin was one of the few mortals he liked and respected.

Fana was grateful that Mom had raised her with mortals in her family, closest to her heart. Her cousin, aunt, and best friend were all mortals, so she hadn't grown up with the feelings of superiority shared by her Life Brothers, and even her father. She tried not to feel it, anyway. Fana always began her meditations by asking for humility so she would not lose herself.

But her rush from the concert scared her.

After Caitlin and Johnny went to their cabin, Dawit sat beside Fana.

"He's angry," Dad said. He didn't have to say he was talking about Michel. Until now, Fana hadn't been sure Michel knew she'd been to California.

"How do you know?"

"Teka feels it. Michel isn't hiding it—except from you, maybe. It was ill advised to come so close to him on the whims of a singer."

Fana realized her heart was speeding. A visit to California must have looked like she was mocking Michel, or provoking him. He disapproved of her sharing her blood and gifts, so it was all too easy to imagine what he might think about her behavior. If he lost patience, he might take control of her mind. *I could have ridden you like a horse*, Michel had told her once, in anger.

A year ago, Michel had hijacked Johnny's body, and Caitlin's, and made them say and do things against their will. Michel had done the same to other Life Brothers, strong telepaths who were still mortified by their actions under Michel's control—even her powerful teacher, Teka.

And he could do it to her, too. He could have at any time.

"The game you're playing with Johnny is foolish, Fana," Dawit said.

You have no idea what he's done for me, Dad. We're not playing a game, she told him.

"It looks like the oldest game in the world between men and

women," he said. "I nearly brought shame and dishonor to an empress with a game very much like it. You risk much more."

His stories were endless. "Empress Taytu?" Fana said.

"*Shhhh,*" her father said, still protecting his lover's dignity nearly a century after her death. "Yes. She was a miraculous woman—before her time, truly—but she was married to Menelik. We shouldn't have begun a conversation that had nowhere to go."

Yes, but you were sleeping with her, Fana reminded him silently. Whether she liked it or not, she was a virgin who was supposed to be saving herself for her fiancé.

"Johnny is with you constantly. He is more a husband to you than Michel. Why create a foe for Johnny he can never hope to vanquish?"

Michel isn't infallible, Fana said. *No more than I am.*

NOT WHEN WE ARE SO CLOSE TO HIM, FANA. DON'T MAKE IT WORSE. Her father was so angry, his thought seemed to carry physical heat. And surprising clarity.

Michel could probe her at will, no matter what her distance from him, so she'd stopped being afraid he would know what she was thinking. If Michel insisted on marrying her at the end of the decade as she'd promised, at least he would know the woman he was marrying. She would not wear masks for him, just as she wasn't with Dad.

I'll be more careful with Johnny, she said. *But we're just friends.*

"Don't pretend you don't see the longing that's plain to all of us." *AND NOT JUST ON HIS SIDE,* he went on.

I heard you, Dad, Fana said. She wondered if her engagement to Michel might have been what finally drove Mom to her Dreamsticks.

NO, FANA. DON'T BLAME YOURSELF FOR JESSICA.

He'd been sharp enough to hear her thought. Fana's father clasped her hand and leaned close to her. "Emperor Menelik agonized over the question of diplomacy versus war," he said quietly. He always used spoken words for more nuanced communication. "Taytu helped him make his decision: they chose war. They took their destiny in their own hands."

"And which way did you counsel her?"

His eyes brightened with a memory. "I think you know your father by now."

In war, Ethiopia had shocked Italy at the Battle of Adwa. Acting as an adviser, her father had helped Emperor Menelik create an army from disparate tribes, uniting his nation. Later, when her husband was sick, the empress had been Ethiopia's true ruler for a time.

"How would you have counseled me with Michel?" Fana said. "If I'd asked you first."

This conversation was like a bedtime story between them. Fana already knew her father's answers, but she enjoyed the comfort of hearing them. Dawit bumped his forehead against Fana's, the way he had since she was a toddler. "My daughter made the only choice she could—to save lives," Dawit said.

Michel would have killed her father if she hadn't agreed to marry him. Perhaps everyone in her family. The veil of civility over the meeting between their two families had been flimsy, ready to shred. Fana was still surprised that Michel had let them go when he could have kept her with him by force: his one redeeming act. Dad was a great warrior, but he had never faced anyone with mental gifts like Michel's. Even the strongest Life Brothers had been manipulated like puppets by Michel, and from hundreds of miles away.

"You wanted to fight," Fana said. "Take our chances."

Her father's loathing of Sanctus Cruor was generations old. Sanctus Cruor was to blame for Italy's failed invasion of Ethiopia, in search of sacred blood before Michel was born. That same search had uprooted Fana's family a hundred years later—this time at Michel's doing.

"We may still fight," Dad said. "As long as we count the cost."

He's not infallible, Fana repeated, to make sure her father understood.

"Fana, he's a man in love." Dawit sighed. "When you forget that, you underestimate him. I loved your mother, and love became madness. I traded everything I knew for that love. For *her*. Let time judge where love will take Michel."

"Let's see if you can say that after we go to Nigeria," Fana said.

Her uncle, aunt, and cousin had described an entire village of corpses.

Dawit shrugged. "We still don't know if Michel is behind it."

But Fana *knew*. She might even be able to prove it if she meditated long enough. Then what? Would they all have to stop pretending that she and Michel weren't locked in a war?

Fana changed the subject. "What you and Mom have hasn't been destroyed," she said.

"We've never recaptured what we had, Fana." Her father's voice thinned, as it did whenever he thought about how he'd lied to Mom during the first years of their marriage, hiding who he was. Her father's guilt over their first daughter's death always sat with him. "Our lives died in Miami. I can't blame her for wanting to go back."

"You also can't excuse her, Dad. She's using Dreamsticks to sleep at night."

Fana hadn't meant to blurt what she'd learned, but Dad was too blind to notice.

"She told me she's stopped," he said.

"She lied. She uses them to sleep."

"I don't smell it."

"But you're having vivid dreams, aren't you? You must be," Fana said. Even when the smell was faint, Dreamsticks were potent in their creation of lucid dreams. Dawit didn't respond, but she saw realization dawning in his eyes. "She's very good at disguising the smell with incense. That's how she hides it. She was trancing for a month before we noticed, Dad. I'm not guessing about this—I know."

Fana had promised her parents she would never again probe their minds without permission, but she'd broken her promise because of Mom's glassy eyes. There would always be an exception, she reminded herself.

"Leave this to us, Fana," Dad said sharply, annoyed.

Fine. But she needs your help, Dad—not your guilt and empathy.

Her father inclined his head in a half bow, acknowledging the point.

"Should we have done that concert?" Fana said.

"Counsel in hindsight?" he said. "I believe that's called 'too late,' sweetheart."

"Yes. But I'm curious about what you think."

Her father shrugged. "It was a mistake to do it in California. That personalizes it."

"You're right," Fana said. "But what about the rest? The healing?" Even to herself, she sounded like a child trying to show off a crayon drawing, eager for her father's approval.

"Your gift is a beauty to witness," her father said. "The public nature is worrisome, but . . . you dazzle, Fana. You've come so far, so quickly. You're full of love, like your mother."

"And you," she said.

Dad shrugged. "I love a select few. I love my brothers. My wife. And I love my daughter most of all. So be careful about exposing yourself, Fana. Let our blood do the healing. Don't try to turn the eyes of the world on you. Not simply because of the hazards—it all becomes vanity. I've seen it happen too many times to count." His voice went soft. "Khaldun."

He almost never spoke of Khaldun, and certainly never in terms of his faults. The immortal who had created both sects of immortals had claimed to be two thousand years old, the recipient of blood a thief stole from Jesus on the cross. Khaldun had told her father the story more than five hundred years ago, when he passed his blood to fifty-nine men to create the Lalibela Colony in Ethiopia.

To Fana, it was a grand tale from a storybook: her father and his best friend, Mahmoud, had been traders in Ethiopia, and found a Storyteller with wondrous claims of Living Blood. They had each agreed to a ceremony, eating poisoned bread to stop their hearts . . . and the Living Blood brought them back to life. Forever.

Until her father had broken away to be with Fana's mortal mother almost thirty years ago, the Life Brothers had mostly lived secluded underground, studying in Khaldun's five Houses of Learning. Her father loved Khaldun, and considered him a prophet.

But Khaldun had left the Lalibela Colony soon after Fana was born, proclaiming to Dawit and Jessica that their child was Chosen to stand in a coming war between mortals and immortals. Most of

Fana's life, a handful of loyal Life Brothers had treated her like a deity in their own quiet colony in Washington State, virtually outcasts from Lalibela.

Until Michel found her.

Like her, Michel had been *born* with the Blood. Their mortal mothers both died while pregnant, revived by immortal Blood, and their unborn children had gained the Blood and more.

And his sect, which called itself Sanctus Cruor, guarded the Blood as theirs alone. They adhered to a document called the Letter of the Witness with instructions to *Wrest this Blood from the hands of the wicked*—which, as far as Fana could tell, they interpreted to mean anyone who wasn't chosen by Sanctus Cruor. The Letter also described a prophesied mate who fit Fana's description so well that it was hard for her to deny that whoever had written the words— *Was it Khaldun?*—had known that she and Michel would be born two thousand years in the future.

Sanctus Cruor had tortured and killed Glow couriers to get closer to Fana, and Michel had nearly destroyed her family the way he had destroyed their Washington colony. Fana had offered a ten-year engagement to Michel to save her family.

But had Michel expected her to love no one?

Johnny had asked her to give him the Life Gift so he wouldn't age or get sick. And she could do it—she or her father could perform the ceremony on any mortal they chose. But Fana had refused Johnny. She knew his true reason for wanting the Blood: he hoped to compete with Michel, and that kind of thinking would get Johnny killed.

All of them might as well be mortals in Michel's shadow. His abilities were dazzling.

Fana's body and mind were still wide awake from the concert, hungering for the floating feeling again. How much of her elation had been from healing, and how much from the pleasure of her power? She couldn't tell.

The concert had shown her a power source she hadn't known before. Without Johnny to urge her, she might not have learned for years.

Dawit sighed. "Your schoolgirl crush, sweetheart . . ."

Fana flinched. Had he peeked at her thoughts?

"It's not only dangerous for both of you—it demeans you, Fana. You are too many things he is not. Every minute you spend indulging in your stolen joys with Johnny is time spent away from cultivating your gifts. You don't have room for him. Let him go."

Fana didn't blink, but she couldn't stop the stinging of her unshed tears. Her father's words seemed to cut past her skin to her bones.

Dawit leaned over to kiss her forehead before he stood up. "It was a beautiful night, Fana," he said. "I see why you chose the singer. I'm proud to see what you're becoming. But if you love this singer, be careful where you take her. We're very good at hurting the people we love—never meaning to. There may be consequences."

Consequences ruled Fana's life. She had avoided Michel for a year, and now evidence of Michel's anger might be waiting in Nigeria.

"I hoped our engagement would change Michel," Fana admitted, her voice quiet.

Dad's chuckle was sour. "You've denied him even mental visits, Fana. Why should Michel change because he's engaged? But he may one day *be* changed . . . by his wife." The gentle way her father spoke the word *wife*, with tenderness, sounded like a betrayal.

Was he saying she should marry Michel? Fana shivered. "Dad . . ."

"I would not have counseled you to agree to marry this man, Fana," Dawit said. "Like Menelik and Taytu, we could have chosen war against great odds. And if you refuse to honor your engagement, I'll kill anyone who tries to take you to him, or die my last death defending you. But I think Michel feels a strong attachment to you. He gave you ten years to grow up, and we both know he didn't have to. What do you gain by alienating him?"

She couldn't speak to answer.

Dad's advice was even wiser if Michel had already begun the Cleansing that was at the heart of his beliefs; his twisted interpretation of the Letter of the Witness. Michel expected her to help him exterminate most of mankind, saving only a chosen few. She'd hoped a long engagement would delay him, but he might have begun without her. She had to behave more like Michel's true fiancée, or she would lose any influence she had over him.

Fana leaned forward in her chair, bowing to her father.

Thank you for telling me the truth, Fana said.

"It's my birthright, Duchess," Dawit said. "I speak with twin tongues: as your father, and as your war counsel. Don't make provocative gestures unless you hope to provoke."

Teka, her teacher, believed he could help her grow strong enough to stand against Michel one day—but not yet, and not by a long way. Michel was older, so his gifts had a thirty-year head start. She might need more time than she had.

She might have run out of time already.

Nine

Kano
Northern Nigeria

Dawit had flown directly to Kano after depositing Johnny Wright and Caitlin in Lalibela, and by three a.m. local time he had been in the air a full day. Some of his Brothers barely slept, but sleep was a mortal habit he had trained his body and mind to appreciate. He looked forward to joining Fana in the nearby private house they had rented. Dawit avoided lodging in hotels when he traveled with Fana: her rest was too easily disturbed by the dreams of guests.

Was this crisis in Nigeria as bad as it seemed?

Dawit's nephew, Jared, looked shaken as he met him beneath the dripping awning of the Tahir Guest Palace hotel, his T-shirt damp from the rainy season's last warm rainfall. Jared had three days' worth of facial hair and was nearly four inches taller than Dawit, a giant like his father. Jared started to speak, but Dawit patted the young man's shoulder to silence him.

Dawit signaled to a nearby porter who was hovering in hopes of a late-night tip. "*Ya yi. Na gode,*" Dawit told the porter in Hausa, dismissing him. That's fine, thanks.

The porter's smile grew forced as his thoughts slung obscenities. Dawit's meditations with Fana were improving his mind arts so quickly that he could often hear thoughts without trying. Like his daughter, he now heard more than he wanted to.

"I hope you haven't been exposed," Dawit warned Jared, brushing rainwater from Jared's thin back as he ushered him across the hotel lobby's tile floor.

"We wore the hot suits. I'm fine. But it's getting worse, Uncle Dawit."

"More dead?"

"No, thank God," Jared said with haunted eyes. "But I knew one of the victims. Well, I'd *met* her. Do you remember the woman from Oxford I wanted to marry last year?" Dawit had no memory of his nephew having had a fiancée, but he nodded vaguely so that Jared would go on. "It's her younger sister. Gabrielle."

That was too mighty a coincidence! And the largest known outbreak was in Nigeria, where so much progress had been made with Glow, and too close to Ethiopia for comfort. Fana's suspicions about Michel might be right after all. Why doubt her?

"I'm sorry for your loss, Jared," remembering politeness despite his frenzied thoughts. "Did she live in the village?"

"No, she's from Tanzania. She'd been a part-time English teacher out there for a year. We think . . ." Jared swallowed his tears away with great effort. "We think it spread quickly at the school. Issa hasn't heard from me in months, and I have to tell her this." His voice was almost unrecognizable with pain.

"Not now," Dawit said, softening his sharp tone with another pat. "We have work first."

Jared gave him a baleful look over his shoulder and produced a plastic key card at the hotel door at the end of the hall. "We've already been working, Uncle Dawit."

Beside the door, a hotel sign promised twenty-four-hour electricity and water because of storage tanks and backup generators. Inside, the room was filled with bland fluorescent lighting. After the pure light under ground in Lalibela, fluorescent bulbs were an affront to Dawit's eyes.

The large room's hum of activity stopped when the door opened. Dawit was dismayed to find a mortal he didn't know in the hotel room. The young man had features from Southern Africa, wearing gloves and a lab coat. Jared's father, Lucas, was hunched over a too-small desk crowded with three laptops; his wife, Alex, was making a graph with a black marker on one of the large sheets of paper taped to the walls. At the top was a photograph of a lovely young woman, beneath neat red letters: PATIENT ZERO?

Alex walked to David, squeezing his hand. "Hey, Dawit, we're—"

"Who's the boy?" Dawit said.

"That's Dr. Dilebo. Moses! You don't remember him? He used to come play with Fana in Washington. Jess and I knew him before then, in Botswana. He hung out at our clinic, and now Clarion hired him as a researcher. Dawit, we told you we're grooming people."

Alex should know better! The Lalibela Council had strict vetting procedures before mortals could have such close contact. It was bad enough that Alex maintained ties with a South African nurse whose brother and sister had died at the clinic that Alex and Jessica had run in Botswana, where mercenaries hunted them down for their blood. Alex had witnessed the shooting, and had nearly died. Jessica and her sister were painfully slow to learn.

"Are you studying this disease, or trying to spread it?" Dawit said. Privately, he added, *New mortals? Are you mad?*

The young man flashed Dawit a tired smile before resuming his work. Alexis pulled Dawit around the corner of the suite, her voice quiet.

"Only Jared and I went with Lucas," Alex said. "We got sent back after an hour, so don't worry. And we're taking injections. So we're feeling fine—maybe *too* fine. How do ya'll walk around with this stuff in your veins all day?"

Dawit's teeth tightened. How crude it sounded to hear Alex speak of the Blood aloud, even at a hush. And jokes besides! Blood sharing with mortals had been forbidden, and now Alex and Jared were treating the Blood like aspirin. But he couldn't stop Alex's husband, Lucas, from giving his Blood to her. Lucas Shepherd had been a stranger when Dawit passed him the Blood—only because Alex had begged him to save the dying man's life. Dawit hadn't been able to deny a woman whose eyes so closely mirrored his wife's.

Many of Dawit's Brothers in Lalibela still refused to speak to him or make eye contact because he had shared Blood with Jessica and Lucas. Most blamed him for the turmoil with the new sect of immortals that had overwhelmed him in Washington State last year. His role as peacemaker between his family and the Lalibela Council was a daily challenge.

"He's no risk to us, Dawit," Alex said. "He's an epidemiologist, and he was Fana's best friend in Botswana. This has nothing to do with ya'll." *Ya'll* was Alex's code word for his Life Brothers, or anyone with the Living Blood.

She was three years old, Alex! In his anger, Dawit tilted his head close to her forehead. *The* goats *were her friends!*

Alex jumped, startled by the amplitude of his mental stream. She rubbed her temple. "Dawit, chill out with that. I don't need a headache. Fana wants him in our inner circle, so he's here. 'Kay?" Alex patted his shoulder to end the conversation. Jessica and Alex often dressed up their own words or desires as Fana's to get their way. "How did Fana's concert go? Was Phoenix good? Her music is stone genius."

Dawit still couldn't fathom that Fana had staged a concert to promote sharing the Blood at Michel's doorstep, all because the singer didn't like airplanes. Madness! But that was a worry for another night.

"Suppose we talk about the outbreak?" Dawit said tightly.

A spark left Alex's eyes. She nodded.

Lucas Shepherd stuck his head around the corner with a hollow-eyed stare, tall above them at six foot six. His Georgia accent never hurried. "We knew you'd be pissed off six ways to Sunday, Dawit, but come on back to the living room. We've got a full report."

Alex doused her throat with a sip of stale, warm Coke Zero, which had kept her awake for two days straight. They needed fresh eyes— even if those eyes were two weeks late. Maybe two weeks *too* late. And he had the nerve to scold her for bringing in outside help? Waiting for the next reports of infection kept them all awake at night.

Where the hell have you been, Dawit? She hoped he knew what she was thinking.

"It's bad," Alex told Dawit, the point she'd been trying to make in her email reports and sat-phone calls since the first reports from

North Korea. The cold brick that had lodged at the rim of Alex's lower belly since her first visit to North Korea had resurfaced in Puerto Rico and bloated her stomach in Nigeria. She wasn't a hypochondriac, but it was hard not to wonder if she'd caught the bug. Alex injected herself with Lucas's blood once a day, to be sure.

"The mortality rate was nearly a hundred percent after contact," Alex said. "The only survivors were out of the village during the forty-eight-hour outbreak period, or had no contact with the infected. Two hundred dead, but no new reports of the infection in three days."

Alex checked Dawit's face for signs. Anything. He was only nodding as if she'd been reciting ingredients from a recipe book. Yes, yes, go on. Alex knew in her heart that Dawit loved Jessica and Fana—he might think he loved her, too—but he was still The Brother from Another Planet. Dawit's eyes were only mirror panes. How hadn't Jessica seen it before she married him?

Moses walked forward, pointing out the photograph of the pretty young woman who was barely more than a child. "We think the teacher was patient zero in this outbreak," Moses said.

"Gabrielle," Jared corrected, hoarse. There hadn't been any time to console Jared in his private nightmare.

"Yes, Gabrielle," Moses said, apologetic. "She knew the man who ran the school. He was in Jos visiting family the day she arrived, but they spoke by phone. She said she'd had a terrible stomachache for an entire day and would try to make it to the school. She lived alone, and none of her neighbors have tested for the infection. Or reported significant illness."

"Were there reports of illness at the village before her arrival?" Dawit asked.

"Coughs and sniffles, not the stomachaches—as far as we know," Alex said. "But there were only sixty-three survivors. Most of the stories died in that village."

She checked Dawit's face again. Another impassive nod. Death didn't bother him.

Moses went on. "Gabrielle was only at the school for an hour— she called her boss and said she was going to a student's house to rest. That night, the host family also complained of sudden stomachaches. A teenage victim sent an email to a relative in Lagos at eight-thirty. Another student, a neighbor, also complained of stomach pain in a telephone call by midnight. By morning, apparently, dozens in their families were ill. And neighbors. There were emails the next day about a 'stomach flu.' By the next morning, the entire village was dead."

"Might as well have been a bomb," Alex said.

"So here's the part we really don't like . . ." Lucas said. "Seventy-five people died in North Korea, isolated to a village. But only *six* people died in Puerto Rico a month later—even though there were two carriers, not one. And there's no Asian link to Gabrielle. It just . . ."

"Appears out of the sky," Moses finished matter-of-factly.

"Like brushfires," Alex said. "We don't know what's starting the flares. And we don't know what's putting them out."

"But it's the deadliest SOB on record," Lucas said. "It spreads faster than anything we can compare it to. Much more virulent than Ebola. SARS. Dengue fever. Lassa fever."

Finally—a hint of alarm on Dawit's face.

"The bug that wipes us out will look a lot like this one, Dawit," Alex said.

Dawit blinked, seeming to agree. "How has it stayed so quiet?"

"Politics," Alex said. "Just like in Puerto Rico—fear of panic or some other reaction. Here, the new government's scared it'll look like an ethnic clash. It's a Muslim village, past skirmishes with Christian neighbors. At first the police thought it was poison, maybe a chemical agent. Bioterrorist attack, just like the theory in the U.S. An entire village of Muslims getting killed doesn't look good on Al Jazeera. A lot less could set off a killing spree nobody wants. The government is pretending it never happened, so we have to meet our source there at dawn."

"The whole bloody world needs to see it," Jared said, his voice trembling.

The United States had done an even better job of covering up the outbreak in Puerto Rico—if not for a single blog posted for only twelve hours, they might never have heard about it. Rumors of the outbreak in Nigeria were much more widespread.

"Glow had no impact on the outbreak?" Dawit said.

Nigeria had been one of the first nations to make Glow available at dedicated government clinics, which were always swamped with seekers. Glow centers kept the police and army busy. Too often, desperation turned ugly.

Alex sighed. "It's illegal to keep a personal supply, but usually there's somebody . . ."

"Missionaries and witch doctors," Moses said. "Claiming Glow is their magic."

"My guess is, nobody had any," Alex said. "It swept through so fast, nobody had time."

"Then how is it possible to have only six dead in Puerto Rico?"

"Go on and tell him," Lucas urged her.

Alex's stomach ached, spraying a bad taste into her mouth. She had stumbled on the strange significance of Puerto Rico only hours before Dawit arrived, and she still had gooseflesh on her arms. Alex's legs ached to rest, so she pulled up a tall stool and sat with a sigh.

"In Puerto Rico, all of the dead were staying at a little hotel in a tourist town, Maricao. But *no one else got sick*—including dozens of people who had contact with them over the incubation period."

"Fortunate," Dawit said. "But very odd."

"It gets weirder," Alex said. "The dead woman from San Juan was named Rosa Castillo. She had a son named Carlos Harris. His wife—"

"Phoenix Harris," Dawit said, breathless. "I just met them both. Are you sure?" Was Dawit's face growing a shade paler? Alex was almost certain of it. Finally! Dawit got it.

"Damn right I'm sure," Alex said. "Phoenix's mother-in-law died of the same virus we saw in North Korea. Carlos Harris blogged about it! We smuggled out her blood work, and I did the analysis myself. We haven't been able to get tissue samples here yet—we were run off from the village pretty quick—but I'm betting it's the same strain."

Alex pointed out the translucent sheets posted to a lighted panel on the wall beside her, enlarged images from an electron microscope. Dawit leaned close, studying the images. The photos of the new virus reminded Alex of linguini-shaped Ebola, but with coats of spikes.

Alex went on. "It hijacks the immune system, like Ebola. Disables tetherin and turns our immune responses against us to create new virions. *Lots* of them—a flood. That's why the mortality rate is so high. So that's the medical side. But on the personal side . . ."

"Phoenix's mother-in-law *and* a girl Jared knew?" Dawit said. "Statistically . . ."

Lucas nodded. "Right. Impossible. That was our way of thinking, too. Why'd you think we've been so frantic?"

Dawit squeezed Alex's shoulder fondly, a rare affectionate gesture that startled her. A glimmer in Dawit's eyes made her heart race. What did he know that he wasn't telling them?

"Dawit, we've been saying for *two weeks* how grim this outbreak looked!" Alex said. "Where's the support from home?" *Home* was their code for the Lalibela Colony.

WE NEED TO TALK ALONE, Dawit told her privately. *WITHOUT THE BOY.*

The tickling sensation, a whispered breath, always made Alex swipe at imaginary gnats. "Maybe we should talk alone," Alex said to Lucas, as if it were her own inspiration, not Dawit's.

"Looks like we better," Lucas said. He couldn't read minds yet, but he wasn't fooled.

The young man shrugged, standing. "I'll walk to the lobby," Moses said. "Mr. Wolde, please tell your daughter hello from her friend Moses. She was an amazing child. So amazing!"

Dawit didn't answer, staring straight through Moses as if he weren't there. Sometimes Dawit seemed not to see people at all, his eyes bypassing everyone like they had at her mother's Sunday dinners. Everyone except Jessica; you had to work to pry his eyes away from his wife.

The door closed behind Moses.

I'VE SEEN THIS VIRUS, Dawit said silently. *ONE LIKE IT.*

Air seeped from her lungs. Another surprise! The world reinvented itself daily.

"When was the outbreak?" Lucas said. "Where are the records—"

Sometimes her husband's naïveté drove Alex crazy. He reminded her of the way Jessica had been, once upon a time. "What's the rest of the story, Dawit?"

"It may be ours," Dawit said quietly.

"Lord Jesus," Alex whispered, eyes wide. She'd known what he was going to say, but it still hurt her ears.

"Define . . . 'ours'?" Lucas said, still not wanting to face it.

"From the House of Science," Dawit said.

Alex and Lucas had been invited to the repository of technology and scholarship in the House of Science's underground wings in Lalibela, but they had been given very limited access to the treasures. Unrestricted areas only, always under escort. Alex had been waiting for permission to see the colony's HIV research. Lucas blamed their cultural prohibition against sharing with mortals, but to Alex it had always looked like hiding.

"Developed at least eighty years ago," Dawit explained. "Not an identical strain, but very close. There have always been factions . . ."

"Ready to wipe us out," Alex finished. Hot dust seemed to coat her throat.

Dawit nodded. "Only small factions. Our recurring debate." He sounded unapologetic.

Anger lifted Alex to her feet and seemed to raise her height. "Was AIDS yours too?"

"No," Dawit said, his eyes unblinking and impassive. It wasn't the first time she'd asked, and the answer was always the same. She was a fool for having believed him.

Alex wanted to leap on Dawit, to slap at him or pound him with a fist, although she never had before—not even after Dawit killed her niece, accident or not. Now Alex understood what Jessica meant about the past feeling fresh enough to smell and touch: she could *see* Dawit's hands around poor Kira's throat. The coroner's report said he'd strangled her in his badly failed quest to give her immortality.

"Explain this, Dawit!" Alex said. Lucas hooked his arm around her waist to hold her.

"Try right goddamn now," Lucas said.

Dawit blinked with his own anger. "You're making it too simple," he said, struggling to sound measured.

"*Simple?*" Alex said. The urge to strike at him reared again.

"Yes, Alex, *simple,*" Dawit said. "Because if it were my Brothers, we could contain it. But I believe this virus is in the hands of someone outside of Lalibela, which is a significant complication. So we don't have the luxury of raw memories."

Fear curled Alex's stomach into an icy fist. "You think it's Michel?" she said.

As Dawit nodded, Alex's anger at him melted.

"Fana thinks so," Dawit said. "Michel might have access to our research, with or without help. If he's following Sanctus Cruor doctrine, expect bigger outbreaks soon."

Michel.

One man had overwhelmed all of Dawit's people in Washington from thousands of miles away. Lucas had told her he'd been as helpless as a child when he lost his eyesight for a harrowing moment, struck blind by a Life Brother acting under Michel's mental influence.

Alex was as close to crying as she could allow herself. What should she cry about first?

"What was the rationale, Dawit?" Alex said. "When ya'll were back in the lab trying to dream up ways to kill us in large numbers—random men, women, and children. How did you explain it to yourselves? What made it all right?"

Dawit looked wounded. "I can't speak for them, Alex. I pray you know that."

"But you've got an idea," she said, pinching his soft cheek. "Come on, sweetie. We're all family here."

Dawit shrugged. He paused. "The air tastes different now. To us. So much has changed. There are too many of you." His voice was so quiet, Alex barely heard him. Dawit had made the pronouncement without a blink.

"Fana is here," Dawit said. "She's resting from the concert, but she'll go to the village."

Alex felt pained for her niece, who was so young. But her weary heart celebrated for the first time since her stomach had begun its mourning ache.

Ten

6:30 a.m.

Fana realized that this trip was the closest thing she could remember to a family outing. Only her mother was missing; Mom wasn't strong enough for this journey.

The three-vehicle caravan of Land Rovers bounced along the unpaved road in a cloud of dust, undercarriages whimpering. To Fana, their journey was like the replaying of a dream, or a future memory. She had felt this day before. She had seen this dry, rocky land of dying saplings, without a single mature tree in sight across the dusty, arid plain.

The smell of death was everywhere. The air stank of rotting flesh. Fana heard phantom screams, the last echoes of fear and pain to the pitiless sky. Tears burned Fana's eyes. She would no more mourn simple death than she would mourn watching a boatman cross a river—that was all death was—but unexpected passages left so much pain in their wake. Her mother would not have been so shredded by her grandmother's death if not for Michel's hand in it.

Had an entire village suffered because of her childishness?

"We're close now," Jared said quietly, but she had known that from the smell. And the sudden sound of shouting that grew louder as they drove. Jared held her hand, and she held his.

Fana had loved her cousin since before his parents' marriage made them family; before she had met him in the physical world. Their spirits had played together when leukemia ravaged his body, nearly transporting him across planes. His father's search for a cure was what had brought him to Aunt Alex, along with the mercenaries who had almost killed them both.

And Moses was in Kano! She had seen him only briefly when they picked up her family at their hotel, but as he'd leaned into her window, Moses was the same lanky giant she'd known when she was three, and later, when her family flew him to the Washington colony to be her playmate. She had made it rain for him once, and she had hurt him without meaning to. Neither of them had spoken of it, but they both remembered.

Jared's touch and the memory of Moses's smile would carry her through this day.

Hundreds of people waited ahead, crowding in a surge. Army trucks appeared in the road beyond a rise, blocking the growing crowd along a perimeter already fenced with rapidly unrolled spools of barbed wire. Her father and her personal guard in the front seat, Berhanu, coiled with readiness. A year ago, she'd hated living under guard, but she knew better now. The three vehicles' formation tightened as the drivers slowed. In Mexico, the last time Fana's father stumbled into a knot of soldiers, he'd ended up Michel's prisoner. All of them had.

Fana didn't like being nervous, so she tried to reassure herself with logic: Michel had no need to trap them. He could have brought them back at any time.

Her father's gun snapped to his hand, ready.

"How far is the village from this perimeter?" Dawit said.

"Quarter mile," Uncle Lucas said.

Aunt Alex nodded toward the gun. "Dawit, we're supposed to look like scientists."

"Scientists, not fools," he muttered. But he hid the weapon beneath his shirt again.

"How was Phoenix?" Aunt Alex asked Fana suddenly, surprising her. "At the concert?"

Music flared in Fana's mind. She smiled. "Brilliant. Sorry you missed it."

Her aunt smiled. "Me too."

Aunt Alex and her mother had first played Phoenix's music for her, an addictive dance song called "Party Patrol," the first song Fana ever danced to when her physical body was still a novelty. Their shared smile was a balm, but those days were long gone now.

Fana's smile vanished quickly as Aunt Alex pulled a handful of plastic name tags from her pocket and handed them out one by one. "Make sure these are visible," Aunt Alex told them. "As of the last election, Clarion's name is no good here. We're with the CDC today."

Fana glanced at her plastic badge. A recent, unsmiling photo of her sat above a bland name: MARY FIDLER. EPIDEMIOLOGIST, CENTERS FOR DISEASE CONTROL FIELD RESPONSE TEAM.

"The head of the healthy ministry's sharp," Uncle Lucas said. "Dr. Ogunyele. He's mastered the medicine *and* the politics. He alerted Alex, and he's taking good care of us."

Aunt Alex went on. "Chris Ogunyele stepped in quickly enough to stop the spread when the official government line was 'poisoning.' Thank the Lord he isolated the village."

Michel had stopped the infection's spread, Fana suspected. Just as he had in Puerto Rico. To him, it had been like blowing out a match after watching it burn for a time. There was nothing the mortal health minister could have done to make it better or worse.

Rows of green jatropha shrubs began dancing outside Fana's window. She thought they were swaying with memories, until she heard the beating winds of approaching helicopters. She peered up at the sky. One helicopter was flying low enough for her to see inside: soldiers' legs and boots. Guns dangling from the open bay door.

"A riot is coming," Dawit said.

"We'll be in and out before that happens," Uncle Lucas said.

"We better be," Aunt Alex said.

"No—not you, Aunt Alex," Fana said quickly. "You and Jared stay behind."

Her aunt looked at her, defiant eyebrows raised high. "What? We've been there already to lay the groundwork, and we're fine!"

Jared let go of her hand. "*This* again." He hated lines between mortal and immortal.

Sorry, cuz. "It's not just a disease," she said. "Let's not pretend it is."

That was the one lesson her mother always drummed into her head: don't ignore the obvious. Don't be afraid to look at the truth.

"My wife couldn't bear it if something happened to her nephew and only sister," Dad said. His voice was heavy with the idea of it.

Alex's face softened, although disappointment burned in her eyes. "That's the sweetest thing you've said to me in twenty-five years, Dawit."

"Desperate times call for desperate measures, Alexis."

Alex and Dawit laughed, but without joy. Fana smiled at her father's rare joke. She had sensed an earlier argument between her father and her aunt, and she was glad they were moving beyond it. She told herself she wasn't creating the peace, but it was hard to be sure.

Fana scanned the sea of rainbow-colored scarves from the women crowding the barricade, washed in their wails and shouts. Fana remembered that she was wearing her own favorite white gauzy *netela* head scarf, and wrapped the soft fabric across her mouth and chin as she watched the crowd draw closer. Fana had never outgrown the reflex to cover her face when she was away from home. Unwelcome thoughts were louder when others looked at her—or came close to her—and it was hard to filter out the noise. A scarf offered nothing to stare at; it was a relief from being tumbled inside the hurricane. *Like a little kid with a security blanket,* Johnny said.

"Aunt Alex?" Fana said. "We'll bring less attention if you cover your head."

Uncle Lucas muttered, "Told you."

Aunt Alex sighed, but she accepted the mustard-colored veil he pulled out of his briefcase. He had asked her to wear it before. Aunt Alex didn't argue this time, taking the veil without a word and draping it loosely across her graying Afro.

Fana had muted her aunt's thoughts from herself, but she saw the irritation in her eyes. Fana accidentally had left her aunt in a coma a year before, repeating a similar accident she'd had with Moses when she was three. Since the latest incident, Fana tried to speak to her aunt in gentle tones, and Aunt Alex chose her battles.

"There he is!" Aunt Alex pointed at someone through the windshield. "It's Chris!"

The Land Rover ahead slowed as Berhanu, their driver, alerted Fasilidas to stop. The two drivers were powerful telepaths who could communicate mentally beyond fifty yards. Ahead, Fasilidas pulled over toward a waiting army truck. Two dozen young Nigerian soldiers in black berets waited while their fates were decided by others, hands on their rifles.

Uncle Lucas held up his finger. "Remember: we're with the CDC."

STAY INSIDE, Dawit told Fana.

Aunt Alex climbed out of the Land Rover, waving to the civilian.

A man in a dusty office suit walked toward them, flanked by three men in the bright blue shirts of Nigeria Police. Walking at a brisk pace, the man in the suit stumbled in the uneven soil. The man looked forty, with a solid build. His stylish black eyeglasses were almost too small for his square-jawed face. He had not shaved in days. His dress shirt was soaked with perspiration, clinging to his skin.

"Alex, I'd given up on finding you," he said. "We must hurry!"

A man's impassioned voice from a loud radio caught Fana's ear: ". . . is preceded always, always, *always*, by a time of cleansing. Noah's flood cleansed the earth. We cannot walk in fear. Why should we fear death? We must walk with our eyes toward the Kingdom of Heaven and be *cleansed* of fear . . ."

Fana sharpened her focus, clicking a dial in her mind, and knew who the speaker was: Amadi Owodunni, an excommunicated cardinal who had been exposed as a thief. Owodunni's repetition of the word *cleansing* made Fana's heart race. The phantom signal grew faint, lost in the crowd's furor.

"We're here to do whatever we can, Chris," Aunt Alex said, and introduced them all to the health minister's police escort using their phony new names.

Her veil's anonymity worked in Fana's favor. She had been on good terms with the previous president, invited to dinner at his palace once, but Glow distribution in Nigeria had slowed dramatically since the election; the new president was being swayed against Glow by pressure from the United States. Fana had avoided controlling the new president outright. That was what Michel would do. Michel might already have him.

"You're sure no bodies have been transported?" Aunt Alex was asking Dr. Ogunyele. "The virus might live for days in a corpse. It happened in North Korea. . . ."

"Not a single one," Dr. Ogunleye said. "They're still in tents at the outbreak site."

". . . This world is your *prison* . . . God calls you home with *love*, so *do not fear* . . ." The radio sermon went on, quickly drowned out by a helicopter landing in the clearing. The crowd backed away from the thick dust cloud, clasping their clothes flying in the gale.

"Murderers!" a man shouted in Hausa from the crowd. One voice set off an angry chorus, and the crowd surged closer. Fana's eardrums popped from their outrage. The day's light grew dimmer as her mind pulled away.

Someone barked an order, and the soldiers piled out of the truck, shouting for quiet, weapons ready. The troops ran in formation to the barbed wire barricade, which stretched far past either side of the road, patrolled by more armed soldiers.

Dr. Ogunyele huddled closer to be heard over the helicopter. "Relatives of the dead!" he said. "More turning up all the time. Aunts, uncles, cousins. Either crying 'murder' or won't believe they're dead. There are parents who left children behind!"

"You'll need more troops," Dawit said.

"More are coming," Dr. Ogunyele said, resigned. "Many more."

"What's our driving route?" Dawit asked.

"No one drives in or out," Dr. Ogunyele said.

He pointed to the helicopter.

Fana only blinked her eyes, it seemed, and she was flying. Pitching through the sky.

She made out Aunt Alex and Jared below as they stood guarded by Fasilidas and the health minister's soldiers. Aunt Alex shielded her face from the sun with her forearm as she stared up, as if she could meet Fana's eyes.

Below, women's colorful scarves wove like thread through a quilt of dark skin. As the helicopter rose, the babble of furious emotions receded, so Fana lowered her mind's defenses to accept their pain. She saw a panorama of the faces of the dead, most of them idealized in memory. Parents racked with guilt for being away at market or working in Kano imagined their children crying out for them. The children's names came to her, vivid: they mourned Yusuf and Aliyah and Mahir and Jamilah and Hafiz and Ibrahim and Gamal and Safiyah. They mourned Anan and Kubra and Umar and Lina. They mourned Ali and Givon and Fatima.

The parents' grief followed Fana into the sky, her mother's grief reborn.

Fana closed her eyes, hearing Phoenix's music. Phoenix's voice came to her in delicate, feathery strings of golden light, and she showered the crowd below with gentle sparks.

Do not be afraid: they're gone, but they are not hurting, Fana whispered to the mourners. *They knew they were loved. They will wait for you.*

Below her, the crowd seemed to exhale a single, shared breath.

Fana whispered to the soldiers, *Treat them as if they are your mothers, fathers, sisters, and brothers. Have patience with them.*

And felt a succession of fingertips loosening against rifle triggers.

Then came their collective aches, weaknesses, and ailments, and Fana nearly gasped from the weight they carried. Another dusting of golden sparks, and viruses and cancer cells died. They would mourn, but their bodies would live long after the worst of their anguish.

Fana was dizzy, not sure if the floating sensation was from the helicopter or giddiness from her mind's fusion with the mass of people below her. Fana's blood gorged her. Even her earlobes tingled and pulsed. Without wanting to, she remembered Michel's touch. His face.

If Michel were with me, we could heal for miles.

A terrible stench reminded Fana of why she could never unite with Michel.

The lost village appeared below, draped in gray burial tents.

For appearances, the immortals wore the same white protective suits as Dr. Ogunyele and his two staff people, covering themselves head to toe. They were all anonymous behind their plastic masks as they climbed from the helicopter, their feet sinking into muddied soil.

The smell was so thick that it lodged in Fana's throat, a smell from her childhood nightmares.

Dr. Ogunyele led them with a handkerchief pressed to his face to fortify his mask. "The president wants the bodies burned today," he said. "I won't be able to stop it."

"That's outrageous!" Uncle Lucas said. "We'll lose the tissue samples."

"Collect what you can," Dr. Ogunyele said. "We have two hours. Three at most."

Fana walked in her customary formation: her father to the right of her, Berhanu left. Berhanu was mentally scanning the outlying areas for unexpected intruders, so Fana left that job to him. Berhanu rarely spoke a word aloud, nearly as immersed in his thoughts as Fana was. Even powerful telepaths could be surprised, as Michel had reminded them all last year. If they were knocked unconscious, they would be helpless. *As helpless as a mortal,* as the saying went in Lalibela.

The village was small, a collection of only fifty or sixty mud-walled homes. The shell of a nearby home smoldered from a cooking fire left untended, but the fire had burned itself out.

False signs of life lingered everywhere. Bicycles leaned against walls. Clothes on clotheslines blew in a frenzy from the helicopter's propellers, shirtsleeves waving with invisible arms. Somewhere, loud Afrobeat pulsed. The sound of pages turning caught Fana's ear, a book flapping on the ground.

Fana reached down to pick up the book, which was damp, swollen, and smudged. It was a paperback copy of the novel *Kindred*, by Octavia E. Butler. A classic, one of the first books her mother had given her to read. *The desire for freedom is a deep part of human nature,* Mom had said, always knowing that Fana would need to remember the lesson. Fana could see the book clutched to the breast of a sturdy young woman in a white blouse: it had belonged to Gabrielle, Jared's fiancée's sister. Fana slipped the book into her bag for Jared. She would bring back any memories she could for her family.

"Be careful what you touch!" one of Ogunyele's staff warned her sharply. "How old is dis girl?" He made a move to give her a reproachful tap, but Dawit caught his wrist and held it.

"*You* be careful, sir," Dawit said. He held the man's wrist a long time before he let it go. His polite voice was soaked with peril.

The bureaucrat met her father's eyes. Then, hulking Berhanu's. He stepped away. "My mistake," he said. He dropped behind Dr. Ogunyele and didn't speak again.

Fana heard her uncle's pained sigh as they walked into the heart of the village. Ahead, Dr. Ogunyele and his staff members coughed in the putrid air.

There's nothing contagious here now, Fana told her party silently. *It did its job, and now it's gone.*

Most of the homes were empty. The dead had been collected and moved to an area at the center, four long, narrow tents housing fifty bodies each. Despite airtight nets around the tents, the sound of flies' buzzing was like bees', an angry hum that burrowed beneath Fana's skin. She'd had a bad experience with bees when she was three. Bees sowed life, but their song filled Fana with dread. The buzzing was worse than the smell.

Fana was trancing, pulling free. Like mother, like daughter.

"We've slaughtered the livestock. Burned their clothes . . ." Dr. Ogunyele was saying. "Every possible precaution to contain it . . ."

Inside the first tent, which they carefully zipped behind them, the dead were assembled endlessly on tables beneath clear plastic bags, side by side. Nude bodies, almost all of them curled up as if they were asleep. On the table closest to her, Fana looked down at a girl who must have been only ten, still wide-eyed in death, her hands clasped beneath her nose.

The child's pose was mimicked from one corpse to the next. Old men. Young women. Children. Twin boys who looked five or six shared a bag, clasping each other's hands.

Cardinal Owodunni's radio broadcast was far away, but the words came to Fana from the place far beyond her ears: "... *Death is nothing to mourn! Cleansing is a celebration! We should rejoice, for they died with their hands in prayer, calling to their Father. Calling to the Most High to end their suffering ...*"

Most High. Fana's vision swam. For an instant, the dead girl's face looked like her own.

It was he, Fana told her father, uncle, and guardian. *Michel did this. I feel it now.*

Her father and uncle both looked at her with resigned eyes.

SANCTUS CRUOR, Berhanu agreed. *THE SPECTACLE GIVES IT AWAY.*

"This is why they call it the Praying Disease," Dr. Ogunyele said, ignorant of their private exchange. "Look how the bodies are posed. They went into rigor this way!"

Arranged in rows, the praying dead could have been in pews.

"This infection is bigger than one president, or one nation," Dr. Ogunyele said. He sounded muffled behind his plastic mask. "If I lose my job, if I'm arrested, so be it. But the world has to know. If it reaches Kano, Jos, or Lagos, millions will die."

For the first time in a year, Fana truly yearned to find Michel.

Stop this, Michel. Don't hurt anyone else.

"Our people need more Glow ..." Dr. Ogunyele went on, his voice more faint as Fana searched for Michel, far from the physical world. "Faster, steadier supplies ... Enough for every citizen—and in Niger, Benin, Cameroon. There will be panic ..."

How would Michel react if she granted them more Blood? But how could she refuse?

"You'll get more Glow," Fana heard herself say. "We'll work it out with the president."

Dr. Ogunyele suddenly stared at her as if she were a visage. His jaw trembled. Only her eyes showed above her protective mask, but Johnny was right: sometimes, people knew.

"Thank you," Dr. Ogunyele said, grasping her gloved hand.

Leave them alone, Michel. Please. Tell me what you want, Fana said. Begging.

Fana found Michel's presence swinging in front of her like a ripe mango from a tree. She smelled his clove cigarette. She knew his voice as well as she knew her own.

COME TO ME, FANA.

He had never stopped calling for her.

Eleven
Nogales, Mexico

Fana?

Calling her was fruitless, but Michel couldn't stray from her name's song in the quiet of his chamber.

Fana? Are you still there, bella?

The world was emptiness. He had been better off before he knew her, touched her, or smelled her. Michel summoned her perfect scent from memory, but it only shook his throat with a moan. Fana was teaching him the true meaning of pain.

She had been close to him, and still she hadn't come. She had brought *him,* but she had not come to her fiancé. Now her absence rang everywhere.

Ten years' engagement! If he had known that Fana had planned to shun him entirely, he never would have agreed to wait. Papa thought he was a slave to a woman he'd barely touched, and Papa should know about slavery. Michel had released his mother from his father's mental control the night Fana accepted his marriage proposal.

Should he have made Fana his puppet? A mindless bedroom pet the way his mother had served his father for so many years? The temptation came every day.

A whisper to her mind. A fond memory. An instant of longing.

She would never detect it was he. Even if she shut him out, he could find a way in.

But no. He was *not* his father. He was fifty-one, an age when many mortals had been orphaned, freed from the expectations of their parents. He wouldn't behave like a spoiled teenager just because he had a teenager's face.

He wanted *all* of Fana. Her touch must be her own. Her will was her essence.

Michel's bare foot brushed the top of his bedroom's golden curtain rod as his body swung high above the floor, loose coils of hair whipping his face. He lay as if in a hammock, swinging himself in a broad U the length of his room, with the abrupt arcs and swoops that had soothed him since the day, at twelve, when he realized he could. Learning the Shadows had been like riding a wild horse. Just like that—he could fly! The novelty never wore thin.

Michel rocked himself for hours, mulling over the puzzle: Fana both created and destroyed him. She was his fulfillment and his undoing, just as he was hers. Their union was at the heart of the Prophecy: "... *And so a man and woman, mates immortal born, will create an eternal union at the advent of the New Days. And all of mankind shall know them as the bringers of the Blood.*" But why hadn't the Witness written about a long engagement? This terrible test? She was delaying their work!

Time would erase the gap in their ages, but now she was only eighteen, and so sheltered that she could be younger. Papa had separated his mother from her family in Ethiopia as a child, but he could not. So, he had waited.

Fana's youthful face stared at Michel from across the wall on the nine-foot mural he'd painted, styled from her people's murals in Lalibela. Painting was no challenge to him: he could paint without his hands. Michel's paintbrush had followed his memories of Fana's face, the white ribbons crowning her dreadlocks like a nest of butterflies, and the brilliant white Mexican dress she had worn at the engagement dinner with their families, a simple peasant dress made queenly because she had worn it for *him*. Painted her lips for *him*.

In the mural, Fana sat across from him at their engagement table, demure and lovely. A smooth face and tender chin. Shiny ropes of hair. The dining hall was empty except for her ... and him, barely visible except for the sleeve of his white robe across from her. His vestments signified the work they must do; his absent face immortalized his waiting.

His painting had captured her perfectly, except for her eyes. Oh, those eyes! At the dinner, even when she'd loathed him, he had caught her large brown eyes for one startling instant; soft, gentle, wondering. Her thoughtstreams had played in her eyes like gold dust. Those eyes had convinced him that ten years was a small price to pay.

Michel spoke to her eyes in the painting, knowing that Fana would hear him if she chose.

Will I be good to you, Fana? You will be my daily miracle.

Am I sorry for the grandmother I cost you? I grieve for her daily.

Will I help you be strong? I will give you more strength than you ever knew.

Will I steal your body? I will try never to touch you without your invitation.

He made the solemn promises to her eyes every day, but the painting gave him nothing back. He'd captured the color and shape of her eyes just right, but no shadings of shadows or splashes of light could re-create the illusion of *life*.

No, he was not his father. He didn't want a slave. He wanted his wife.

They had made each other bleed and hurt a year ago, but time would heal them. She must be aching for him, too, even if she hated the ache. Destiny was an unforgiving road. When Fana came, she would recognize the mural for the gift it was—homage to her people, a tribute to her father's skills as a painter, a snapshot of the happy moment when he'd shown her Frida Kahlo's *Love Embrace of the Universe*. Before her loathing. An invitation to begin again. In this very room, Fana would gaze at the portrait and tell him it was beautiful.

If only he hadn't broken his word to her!

No matter how he tried to dress his needs with grand justifications, he had struck at her. The disease had forced her to call out to him. To beg him. And for a sweet instant, she had emerged from her silence. Frightened by his virus, she had called his name.

Her presence had been so startling, he'd nearly fallen from his horse when he heard her. Now, her silence thundered. She had flickered to him only to make her plea to end the disease, then had gone. If he hadn't smelled her, he might have thought he'd imagined her.

Now, her absence was as new and awful as the morning he had watched a bus drive Fana and her family away. Physical pain was a trifle; this was a daily horror.

Fana, come to me.

Michel barely heard his bedroom door open and close. Only Gypsy could leave and enter his room without notice. He had sensed her approach in the hallway—he'd sensed the moment she'd decided to come to his room—but she only made him tired. His swinging slowed as Gypsy's scent swept Fana's away.

She stared up, her hands on her hips. A portrait of disdain.

One day, Gypsy would be one of the most beautiful women left in the world. She was a brown-skinned Amazon, thick-bodied and tall, with wide hips and thighs, a stomach and waist so corded they were almost masculine, and breasts that overflowed in his palms. Fana was lovely, but Gypsy made Fana look like the schoolgirl she was.

Like him, Fana might never grow to the appearance of full maturity. He could barely grow a beard! Gypsy was full and complete. She had been modeling lingerie in New York when Bocelli found her. Bocelli knew Michel's tastes.

"You're so pathetic up there, rocking like a baby," Gypsy said with her coarse, guttural London accent. "Really, Michel—you make me want to laugh."

Gypsy could say anything to him, even things his father would hesitate to say. And Gypsy was no actress with a script—she was bright and arrogant and petty. Her arrogance had only multiplied since he had granted her the Blood a month after Fana had left him. Gypsy's envy often made her hate him, but she was a groupie at heart. Loyal enough to kill for him. Or die for him, despite the implied contract of her new Blood.

"Nobody wants to see their gods acting like schoolboys," Gypsy went on while he swung above her. "Look at you, zoned all to hell."

Gypsy's free tongue might have been the finest part of her beauty. She drove Papa crazy despite the opinions of him they held in common—reason enough to keep her. But he hoped he wouldn't surprise them both one day and incinerate her to ash. Gypsy was teaching him restraint—his best rehearsal for Fana, who could hurt him with more than her tongue.

He never wanted to retaliate against Fana again.

"So has she come back?" Gypsy said. "Did she light up your mind?"

"Why would I tell you?" His voice was sandpaper. Did he look as bad as he sounded?

"I know she hasn't," she said. "That's why you're here instead of where you're supposed to be. Everyone's waiting, but you're pissing around. Hoping a pretty girl will come pat your head, maybe toss a bone your way. Sit, Michel. Stay. Roll over. Bloody pathetic."

As she often was, Gypsy was naked. The light from his open window made her dark skin sing, clarifying every hidden shadow. He could spend his day in bed with her. She could train a horde of other girls in her talents. He could blot out the pain of his waiting beneath a mound of wriggling flesh.

Michel gave up rocking near the ceiling and dropped himself to the floor, lighting on his toes. The tile was cold to his bare soles, waking his body's pores. He didn't notice his arousal until she was beside him, a head taller than he in her alligator heels. Gypsy had wrestled a gator on vacation in the Everglades when she was a teenager. She loved deadly teeth.

Gypsy slipped her fingers to his skin and squeezed him.

"Most High," she said. "Is that you, or is it hype?"

He closed his eyes beneath her touch. When he opened his eyes, all he could see was Fana on the wall, a giant above them.

Forgive me, Fana, for what I have done.

Michel stepped away from Gypsy.

"Bring me my vestments," he said.

"What's the hurry now? You're late. Why not remember you're a man?"

Gypsy's smell irritated Michel, reminding him of Fana's mortal lapdog. Had Fana offered her skin to Wright's clumsy fingers? Had she given herself to him? He almost charged into Fana's head to know. He could barely remember why he shouldn't.

My vestments, Michel said to Gypsy's eyes. His temples flared.

Gypsy gasped in pain. Irritation had made the quiet thought a shriek in her head, louder than he'd intended. The pain dizzied her enough to make her stagger. But she had brought it on herself. When he was Michel, she could behave however she liked, say whatever she chose.

But now he was Most High.

Michel reveled in the spark of agony and fear in Gypsy's eyes before she turned away. She stumbled a few steps to the glass case where his robes hung on the wall. One was crimson, one checkered crimson and white, one bright white.

He would wear white today. Fana's people, his cousins, always wore white in ceremonies, which was why he had chosen white for their engagement dinner. His Lalibela cousins were already sharing their finer traditions with him.

Gypsy dressed Michel, fighting tears from the lingering pain in her head. He considered soothing her suffering to keep her hands steady as she straightened his gloves and stole, but he didn't. Why should he deny her the only gift she really wanted?

Michel allowed himself to feel her pain, like running the tip of his index finger across a dancing flame barely long enough to register the heat. It stiffened his back and hitched his breath. No physical sensation could rival it.

"Dress properly this time," he said. "My father will be there."

"Yes, Most High," Gypsy said through pain-clamped teeth.

A bead of blood crawled from her left nostril, peeking out. Michel wiped the blood away with his fingertip. He cleaned his finger by dabbing the blood into the pliant flesh of her cheek. Michel gently cupped his palm against her cheek and whispered in her ear.

"Solo Fana importa," he said. Only Fana matters.

She forced a lie of a smile. Gypsy could hide the prick of new pain from herself, but not from him. It was sharp, deep, and satisfying. Better than blood. This time, he enjoyed her suffering without restraint.

Then he forgot Gypsy, her smell and her pain.

He brought Fana's scent back to his nose. Closed his eyes, as if in prayer.

Forgive me, Fana, for what I have done. Forgive me for what I will do.

Craving forgiveness was another new ritual.

Michel was late to the Cleansing Pool.

Bright candles made the vast hall's light as golden as dusk. Flapping wings overhead sent a tiny white feather floating down from doves that had escaped to the soaring rafters.

As Michel walked the hall at a ceremonial pace, his vestments weighted him like sand packs across his shoulders, chest, and back. He looked straight ahead, ignoring the eyes of the pilgrims crowding the balconies above him. The supplicants watched him in a hush, except for a man's badly stifled cough and a woman's awed whisper in Spanish: *"Alli es."*

He could smell how long they had baked in the sun before the doors opened, and traces of cheap foods they had bought from vendors outside. He filtered them as silently as a brick wall, invisible. Hundreds of pilgrims visiting his home today only sharpened Fana's absence. She should be walking at his side. They were here for her, too.

The music began, just when Michel needed to fill Fana's silence most.

"Lacrimosa," as he had instructed. Mozart's last composition; his own requiem. The strings came first, their sad frolic echoing against the arched ceiling. Then the sixty-member choir he had brought in from Vienna gave chase, voices steady and earnest, filling the church-palace with splendor and gravity. The crescendo misted Michel's eyes. Robed choir members lined each side of the hallway, individual voices caressing his ears as he walked. Where would he be without music? Music might be the only real gift his father had given him.

The tall double doors opened to the Cleansing Pool. No pilgrims would follow him here.

Inside, twenty-five men and women in crimson plumage waited near the door, hands clasped. These were Sanctus Cruor initiates, those who had seen the Letter of the Witness and aspired to see the Blood. They had been waiting in their V formation near the door for two hours, all of them perspiring beneath the heavy regalia his father had modeled from the Catholics.

Their eyes devoured Michel. All they wanted was the Blood. Their offerings to the Cleansing Pool were only their way of trading the lives of others, no matter how much they quoted the Letter or swore their love for him. Given the chance, they would rip off his limbs and bleed him dry. Mortals, like starving dogs, would eat their masters.

The choir's voices and violins were muffled as the doors fell shut. The row of scribes chronicled Michel's arrival, ostrich-feather pens scratching lambskin parchment.

Michel had already decided that he would not travel beyond these walls the way he had on his previous visits to the Cleansing Pool. He would not send his thoughtstreams to Asia, or to the Caribbean, or to Africa, as he'd done when he'd touched Puerto Rico and Nigeria. He didn't want to hurt Fana again. With the virus, he had found his voice; that was enough for now.

Today's ritual was bureaucracy. When Fana came, true Cleansing would begin.

Gypsy was in the gallery, fully clothed for a change. He knew this without seeing her; even a polite glance would have made her ego insufferable. He dismissed an impulse to send her to the Cleansing Pool to join the others, but the irony niggled at him: Mozart had been denied the Blood, but not Gypsy? Eternity forgive him.

Someone was masking in the room, so crudely that the effort glowed above him.

Michel's father stood in the private balcony, acknowledging Michel with a giddy flourish of his wrist. Stefan never missed a Cleansing Pool ceremony, although he couldn't taste the power as Michel did. His father's love for blood had nothing to do with the

Shadows or prophecy; Stefan had learned blood as sport while he was still a mortal.

Beside his father, a surprise: Michel's mother, Teru! No wonder his father was hiding his thoughts. Even a weak mask had kept Michel from suspecting that he was planning to bring Teru. He had never brought her to the Cleansing Pool before. Michel would have forbidden it.

Michel kept his eyes on the Cleansing Pool, although he did not let himself *see*, because he wasn't ready to begin. He filtered out the whimpering, the colliding heartbeats.

Why are you here?

Michel sent his mother a private thought, but he avoided her sweet face, so much like Fana's. Eerie in its resemblance.

After decades of mental imprisonment, his mother wasn't used to direct address, expecting Stefan to answer for her. She was as ignorant as a mortal, but he coaxed her answer from her mind's muddle: *I WANT TO SEE WHO MY SON IS.*

His father bit back a smile. Papa thought he was winning their battle over his mother because she hadn't learned her freedom yet. She never left the grounds. She hadn't left his bed. And Michel wouldn't try to speed her progress any more than he would Fana's. He'd offered to restore her old memories, but she didn't want them. Why remember being a mother watching her son be stolen from her?

Stefan had brought Teru as his prize, but also to show her his life's work.

This is not who your son is, Mother, he told her. *This is the duty he was born into.*

WHO ARE THEY—

Michel's filters failed, and her question was drowned out by the buzzing. The cloying scent that filled the room like thick fog reminded Michel of the choir's music. Beautiful and pure. The whimpers from the Cleansing Pool were a symphony of exquisite suffering. The low hum vibrated in Michel's bones as his mind clouded over with the hum. Finally!

Twenty-five people stood up to their knees in the pool's waters, one selected by each initiate. The water was warmed to body temperature, as if they shared one bloodstream, huddled shoulder to shoulder in nakedness. A boy of nine or ten shrieked when Michel's eyes came to him, clawing his arms around his mother's neck. She was trying to beseech for her child's life, but she had lost her voice days ago, leaving nothing but urgent, teary whispers.

WHY CHILDREN?

Was that his mother's voice buried in the buzzing? Fana's? Or his own?

He had a ready answer for the voice: a child's fear was pure and guileless. And what was the difference, since all mortals were children? The world teemed with children.

WHY CHILDREN, MICHEL?

Michel shuttered away the buzzing, looking away from the boy's perfect terror. He closed his eyes, his face turned to the floor. He panted from the effort of filtering away the Shadows' noise, like trying to balance a heavy table overhead. Heavier with each breath. The air itself was trying to crush him.

"Whose offering is this?" he said. "This boy?"

The question was only ceremony. He already knew.

Louis and Francesca, the married initiates from Paris, had considered themselves clever for bringing the mother and son they had caught stealing from their Las Vegas hotel suite. Children had been offered before. But Michel wouldn't tolerate how Louis had raped the woman, or how Francesca had drugged the boy so she could watch her husband's games in peace. Too many supplicants thought *all-knowing* was only a sales pitch.

Granted, Michel wasn't normally one to judge. They had all fallen short of the glory of the Blood, and so forth. But his mother was there.

In the Cleansing Pool, the whimpers and shallow splashing stopped. Everyone stood still, praying for a negotiation to save them. Their anxious hearts goaded Michel, but he strained against his desire to succumb. His molars ground together.

"I brought him, Most High," Francesca said. She had never been allowed to address him directly, and shyness quieted her voice. He could barely hear her over the Shadows.

"And me," said reedy Louis. "We brought both."

"Why?" Michel said.

"Thieves, my lord," Louis said. His voice shook as he realized he was being challenged.

Francesca's cheeks blushed bright red. " 'The wicked would sooner steal Blood than bread,' " she said, quoting the Letter of the Witness.

In the pool, the boy's mother renewed her voiceless pleas. Water splashed as she tried to run, but Michel's mental ring around the pool made her lose her balance and fall, confused, her limbs tangled with her son's. Michel could feel Gypsy's silent chuckles. And his mother's pain.

Francesca and Louis stared, waiting with pale faces. He enjoyed their fear while the scribes' pens wrote furiously of the unusual delays.

"I reject your joint offering," Michel said finally, his voice raised loudly for the scribes. "You two will stand in the boy's place in the Cleansing Pool . . . and his mother's."

Above him, Stefan couldn't mute his annoyance. He had scouted the French couple himself and had plans for them, since they were journalists with a worldwide audience. Like Owodunni in West Africa, they had been groomed to help steer the masses when the wider plagues came. Untold numbers would rather drink poison from a blessed cup than wait for the disease to take them. But now Michel had no choice but to spare the mother with the boy.

His father would think twice before bringing Teru to the Cleansing Pool again.

"Yes, Most High," Louis said, devastated. His husk of a voice stoked a deeper arousal in Michel than Gypsy could ever touch. Dutifully, Louis grabbed his wife's hand.

"Whatever we must do, Most High," Francesca choked. Her chin struck a noble pose.

The others in the pool screamed their objections, begging. The Shadows roared within Michel, riled by their pleas. Michel distracted himself by counting the sudden nosebleeds among those huddled in the pool: *Uno . . . due . . . tre . . . quattro . . . cinque . . . seis . . .*

None knew they were bleeding. None felt pain yet.

Louis and Francesca didn't resist as they were led to the pool while the mother and son stumbled out. The others clamored and wailed, dumbfounded when the path the mother and son had taken was replaced by a barrier they couldn't see, penning them in. Only Louis and Francesca stood stoically, still holding hands, at peace with their fate.

You were right, Papa, Michel said, unable to resist a jab. *They are loyal to the end.*

GAMES INSTEAD OF DUTY, his father said. *IS THIS TRUE CLEANSING, MICHEL?*

The freed mother shrieked hoarsely and lunged at Michel. He had known what she would do before she knew herself, perhaps before she'd left the pool. His mental nudge made her lose her footing, slipping across the marble floor like an eel. Gypsy chuckled loudly at the ridiculous sight. The boy ran to his mother, hiding her nakedness.

Guns chambered around the room, but Michel held up his hand to calm his guards. Weapons were his father's way. Who could guard him better than he could guard himself?

The freed woman grabbed the hem of Michel's robe, bringing the fabric to her lips. "Thank you!" she struggled to whisper. "Thank you! You are an angel. God bless you!"

He was the vengeance she had prayed for. She had no thought of the others in the pool. She believed that she and her son alone deserved a reprieve. She was a thief, and a proud one, and her son would have grown up to outdo her. Soon, they would be dead of plague.

"There are no angels here," Michel said. "You are pardoned by my mother."

Teru smiled, pleased, and Michel was surprised at how glad he was to please her.

A sarcastic laugh came, as loud as a gunshot in the silence. Gypsy. She covered her mouth, but her eyes still twinkled with the joke of the woman's display. Michel felt sharp disapproval throughout the room, especially from his Lalibela cousins who had joined him willingly, on the promise of decorum—all of them had come on their own, except one.

When he looked at Gypsy, all eyes followed his. His beauty in the gallery; his exquisite mistake. It was time.

Mi spiace, grazie per aver speso i tuoi ultimi giorni con me. He told her he was sorry, and thanked her for spending her last days with him.

Gypsy let out an audible gasp, as loud as her laugh had been. "Michel, *please*—"

He took her quickly to save her from the indignity of public begging. When he dove into her, she was warm, sweet jelly. But there was no time for amusement.

MOST HIGH, I'M SORRY, she called to him. *I MEANT NO OFFENSE.*

He brought Gypsy to her feet. Delicious terror raged within her as her limbs mutinied.

"I have trivialized the Cleansing ceremony," Michel announced through Gypsy's mouth, with her voice. "May I offer myself to the pool and join the others, Most High?"

He nodded his reluctant agreement and gestured with a sweep. Yes, yes, if she must.

Gypsy strode quickly from her seat, her heels clacking on the marble as she walked the length of the room. She stopped before Michel, bowed her head. He raised his hand for a kiss.

MICHEL, PLEASE DON'T. SEND ME AWAY INSTEAD. YOU PROMISED ME—

"Forgive me, Most High," he said, giving her Francesca's dignity as she kissed his ring.

"You are forgiven, and you shall be Cleansed."

Holding her head high with a beatific smile on her face, he walked her to the pool.

The others shouted and clawed at her, looking for escape the way she had come. Michel abandoned his fight then, or lost it. The fabric of his robe seemed to crackle. His ears popped in the Shadows' howl. The light in the room vanished to his sight.

The irresistible chorus of pleas from the Cleansing Pool flooded Michel. He inhaled the sweet scent of the Shadows, the way his father had taught him after he stole Michel from his mother's breast. The buzzing swallowed all.

The last part of him that was still Michel remembered those eyes in his painting.

Forgive me, Fana, for what I will do.

While music played beyond the doors, the pleas in the Cleansing Pool turned to screams.

The water in the pool flushed crimson, stained with blood.

THE CLEANSING

It's the end of the world as we know it.
—R.E.M.

But then I sigh and, with a piece of Scripture,
Tell them that God bids us do good for evil.
And thus I clothe my naked villainy
With odd old ends stol'n forth of holy writ,
And seem a saint when most I play the devil. (1.3.323)
—*Richard III*
William Shakespeare

If I do many godlike things, does that make me God?
And if I do many devilish things, does that make me the devil?
—Khaldun (The Witness)

Twelve

The white Spanish Mission-style church looks like a palace atop the hill. In the bell tower, two bronze bells toll in cacophony, swinging in opposite directions. Roaring winds devour their sour music. A man and woman lean out of the dome's window, only their silhouettes visible in the Shadows.

Below, spread across a vast valley in every direction, rows of worshippers sit on their knees with hands clasped, faces upturned in prayer, as still as tree stumps. Only their clothes move, blowing in the gale. Countless sightless faces are pelted with raindrops.

The rain is the color of blood.

Barking woke Phoenix, faint through her window. She had expected rainfall instead.

Phoenix glanced at her wristphone, which she slept with by habit. It wasn't quite four a.m., long before dawn. *How did Graygirl get outside?*

Phoenix tried not to disturb the mattress when she swung her legs over the side of the bed, but Carlos sat up on one elbow when she stirred. Their bed was a California king, as big as a continent, but Carlos slept lightly since he'd been home.

She'd been dreaming, she remembered. She couldn't remember the dream, but her heartbeat was pulsing in her fingertips. Her tongue was parched. She hadn't felt such a jolt of fright since the visits from Scott Joplin's ghost, which she knew were behind her. But the dream hadn't been about Scott. Phoenix vaguely remembered a sea of the dead.

No more pizza after nine for you, she thought, trying to calm her hammering heart.

"What's wrong?" Carlos mumbled, running his fingers through his hair.

"Graygirl's barking."

"What?" Moonlight captured the confusion on Carlos's face.

Phoenix blinked. Only crickets and frogs outside. No barking. Graygirl was dead. The coyotes had killed her, although Phoenix could almost see her dog's pale shadow floating through the doorway. Graygirl had been dead a month, but Phoenix often heard imaginary barking, most often when she was in the shower. Or half asleep.

"Gotta use the potty," she said instead, the word they had inherited from Marcus.

Carlos grunted and collapsed back to his pillow.

Their bedroom had its own bathroom, but it was the size of a closet—a third the size of Marcus's. Phoenix missed the master bathroom at her old Beverly Hills place. Lately, the bathroom was the only place where she sat still long enough to think. She wanted to be able to stretch out her legs and pick up a copy of whatever book she'd been reading a paragraph at a time. The main bathroom and its lacquered wood walls were her library and spa.

In privacy, Phoenix's pulse slowed as her mind ventured to the night of the concert. Her scalp tingled with the memory of the singing and swaying of the audience, the radiant faces, and Fana with her arms embracing the sky. And her lump *was* gone—her office visit tomorrow would only confirm it. She'd never been so certain of anything.

Glow, she would explain. And then what?

Fana wanted her to tell her story. That was what she'd said.

Why was she hoarding her story in her bathroom? Why hadn't she called a press conference or blasted the internet like so many others who'd been there? A group of six people who had been strangers before the concert were appearing on the newswebs and daytime talk shows as the Glow Messengers. Phoenix's cousin Gloria, the Best Manager in the World, had said that the Glow Messengers had tried to contact her, but Phoenix had declined to join them. Press conferences and interviews weren't her style. Not anymore. But her name would matter. Her story would matter.

The lyrics she'd first heard on her way to the concert sprang back to her, fresh: *Waking up is easy if you never go to sleep / Have you seen the soul you promised you would keep?* The chords were coming, bright and easy. No brooding minors, either. Joyful chords, like the ones her grandmother had played on Sunday mornings. Back in the day, Phoenix would have rushed to her netbook to get to work on her new songs. She would be up working until dawn.

She could lay down new tracks. Call her old band for a reunion. Phoenix's heart quickened at the thought, excitement about her music she'd forgotten. She'd be back on familiar ground, spreading the message of the otherworld. This time, instead of ghosts, she'd be preaching healing. She'd be preaching Glow.

Phoenix's fledgling excitement died.

Then she'd be touring, away from home. Or Marcus and Carlos would be tied to her for a grueling and monotonous life on the road. She'd be lifted up once again on that dizzying pedestal while haters tried to claw her down. She'd gotten death threats after *Joplin's Ghost,* if only because she'd scared as many as she'd inspired. Maybe more.

And with the government so fiercely opposed to Glow, she would be thrusting her family into a drug war. John Wright had led her and Carlos to websites debunking the government's false allegations about Glow: fatal overdoses; high addiction rates; ties to bioterror attacks. The feds were desperate to keep people away from Glow, and if she came forward, she would become a target. The life she'd been trying to give Marcus would be gone.

Phoenix hadn't retired because of the suicides of those troubled kids in Chicago like the media claimed. She remembered her older sister Serena's stories about how much she missed having a father while Sarge was consumed with changing the world. Sarge hadn't known how to be a true parent until much later, when Phoenix was born. She'd promised her newborn son that she would always put him first. No trial runs.

Phoenix smiled at the collection of Marcus's bath toys in a plastic crate near the bathtub. Marcus had stopped playing with toys when he bathed, but she hadn't moved them yet. Grinning red Elmo on a scooter and grotesquely disfigured Mutant Men marked Marcus's journey from toddler to big boy since they'd lived in Paso.

She'd quit show business to take care of her baby. But she didn't have a baby anymore.

"You've got to see about the revolution, Phee," she said aloud in the empty bathroom; her father's words. Sarge had said that to her in a dream right after he died, the last words she'd heard when his voice was fresh in her ear. The words popped into her mind from nowhere.

"You've got to see about the revolution."

Damn you, Sarge. Easy for you to say. You know how I like my peace and quiet.

Phoenix could almost hear her father laughing at her. *Spoiled-ass brat,* he used to say.

When she flushed the toilet, Phoenix thought she heard Gray-girl's bark again.

In the bathroom doorway, instead of turning back to her bedroom, Phoenix shuffled to the living room, where a night-light shaped like a Victorian gas lamp glowed the color of flame near the arched dining-room doorway. She checked the locks on the front door—all three of them—her lingering habit from Carlos's long trip to Puerto Rico. The alarm panel assured her with its cool green light. Armed and ready.

Her last stop before the bedroom was the security system's master control panel. Phoenix had thought the six-screen panel was a hideous addition to the foyer wall when Carlos first had it built, but nowadays she was glad the tiny screens were there; an illusion of control. Each screen showed a different corner of her property: the front door, the back door, the road, the driveway. She looked for coyotes, but didn't see any.

If she'd gotten up only ten minutes earlier the night Graygirl died, she would have seen that Graygirl had drifted from the kitchen bed, squeezing her aging haunches through the doggy door to go outside. Phoenix had come too late, when the coyotes were there.

The coyotes were gone now.

Instead, Phoenix saw a white panel truck, hazy in the darkness. The truck was driving at a good clip despite the bumpy road, so it whizzed past the first camera. Phoenix blinked. For three seconds, she thought the truck had been an illusion like Graygirl's barking. Then, the truck appeared within view of the next camera, passing the jacaranda trees near their driveway.

There weren't any headlights, she realized. Someone who didn't want to be seen was driving to their doorstep in the middle of the night.

The gate was locked at the end of the driveway, but Phoenix ran back into the hall on the balls of her feet. When she got to her bedroom, she closed the door behind her.

Carlos stirred, always on alert. He sat up this time. "What?" he said.

"There's a truck outside. Coming up our driveway."

Carlos vaulted out of the bed. He crouched and went across the room to the curtains, where he peeked through with his head low. "What kind of truck?"

Phoenix hadn't let herself feel scared until she saw how scared Carlos was.

"A panel truck. White or gray."

"*Mierda!*" Carlos said.

"Could it be repairmen?"

Instead of answering, Carlos threw open the closet. He was only in his boxers, but he didn't get dressed. He reached up to the top shelf and pulled down an old black touring bag so worn that one of the zippers didn't work. She hadn't realized she still had that bag in her closet, much less that it was packed.

Carlos thrust the duffel bag into the center of her chest, and she hugged it tight. The bag wasn't heavy, but it was bulky. It wasn't just clothes. Phoenix couldn't quite see Carlos's eyes in the dark, but his face was very close to hers. She smelled his fading cologne.

"Get Marcus," he said.

"What?"

Suddenly, Carlos sounded angry, although his voice stayed close to her ear. "Out back, like we said. I'll stay at the front door. Hurry and get Marcus."

Phoenix's thrashing heart wiped away the fog of sleep. They had a plan they'd laid out carefully since his return from Puerto Rico, and again since the concert. If anyone suspicious ever came to the house, they would steal out the back door to the rear of the property, past the broken wires in the horse fence by the tire swing and down to the Kinseys' house. If necessary, one of them would take Marcus alone.

If was now. Phoenix was almost sure she could hear the truck's engine outside.

No time for pleas, last-minute kisses, or lingering gazes. The bedroom doorknob seemed to fight Carlos, but he flung the door open for her. Phoenix pivoted and ran down the hall, although in her mind it was all for nothing. Just a truck from Pacific Gas and Electric.

Marcus was asleep in bed with both arms wound around his head as if he were trying to shut out a great racket. She shook his shoulder, not worried about being gentle.

"Marcus—it's time. Let's go!"

Marcus kicked off his covers and sprang out of bed as if he'd been waiting for her. Children were always prepared to run and hide.

She saw one of his mud-stained gray sneakers, but not the other. The plan hadn't bargained on a hunt for shoes. Denial peeled away, and Phoenix realized how frightened she was. It was bad enough to be running in the dark, but she couldn't let him go barefoot. And he was too heavy to carry, which had a bigger price now than nostalgia.

"Help me find your other shoe," she said. "Hurry, Marcus."

"What's taking so long?" Carlos said in the hallway.

"Marcus, *where's your shoe*?" Phoenix hissed, as if he were hiding it.

Marcus slid under his bed, retrieving a white sneaker, which didn't match.

"It's for the wrong foot," Marcus said.

Carlos stuck his head in the doorway, a shadow. "Go *right now*."

Neither of Marcus's mismatched shoes was tied when Phoenix grabbed his hand and pulled him into the hall. Carlos gestured wildly for them, urging them on.

"Come with us," Phoenix said. That wasn't in the plan, but she couldn't help herself.

Carlos shook his head. "No time," he said. "I'll catch up."

But that might not be true. The truck sounded like it was on the front porch, a loud rumbling purr that made Phoenix's stomach quiver. It didn't sound like the electric company.

Carlos gave her the barest kiss on the forehead before he veered back to the living room.

We're too late, she thought, but she didn't slow down as she pulled Marcus into the kitchen. Her hip crashed into the corner of the kitchen table in the breakfast nook, but the pain only made her more alert. The deadbolt key was waiting in the lock, exactly where it was supposed to be. The back door opened like a dream.

The cool night air caressed Phoenix's face. Ahead in the darkness lay the fence.

Freedom. Phoenix's relief felt like the flying had the night of the concert again.

"Don't move!" a man's voice said, supernaturally loud, impossibly close.

Phoenix's knees tried to buckle. Her gasp shook her like a blow.

Something tall and pale moved just outside her vision. Marcus wrapped his arms around her waist and let out a scream of raw fright that stabbed her. She didn't want to look at the pale thing, but she had to.

Sleek, shiny skin the color of the moon. More than six feet tall. A misshapen head.

Phoenix almost joined her son's scream, until her eyes focused: it was only a man wearing a contamination suit like someone at a nuclear accident. A large plastic mask hid his face. In his hand, at waist level, he held a shiny gun that was much too big.

Marcus felt weightless when Phoenix swung him behind her with one arm.

"Mrs. Harris, I said *don't move,*" the man said. "Nobody will hurt you or your son."

Phoenix heard noises from the front of the house. Men were yelling orders to Carlos, and Carlos was arguing. He had his problems, and she had hers. Only two rooms separated them, but they were a million miles apart.

"Then why do you have a gun?" Phoenix said. Her voice surprised her, clear and strong.

"Just a trank gun," he said. "It's a precaution."

A tranquilizer gun. Like they were animals being captured in the wild.

"Point that at my son again, and I'm gonna shove it down your throat."

"Yes, ma'am," the man said, full of respect. But he didn't lower his gun. "I need you to slowly put that bag down and put your hands on the counter."

Do you know who I am? Phoenix wanted to say. She'd vowed never to utter those diva's words, but this time the answer was obvious: yes, they knew.

Outside, Phoenix saw the swarm of others wearing identical clothing trampling her squash and tomatoes in the vegetable garden, advancing. Four, five, six. There must have been more than one truck. Someone shone a flashlight into her eyes. Her vision went white.

"Are we under arrest?" Phoenix said. "For what?"

"Mrs. Harris?" the man said again, as if he had not spoken. "I know this is a shock at this hour—but put the bag down."

If she was under arrest, the law said someone had to tell her. Was this worse than arrest?

Phoenix dropped the bag. She didn't know what Carlos had packed, but she felt naked as it thumped to her feet. Despite the politeness of courtesy titles and surnames, or her empty threats, these men could do anything they chose to her and her son. Phoenix hadn't known it was possible to feel so powerless. Pleading words tried to spill from her mouth, but she couldn't pull her lips apart. She heard herself whimper instead.

"There's no reason to be afraid, Mrs. Harris," the man said. "We're not here to hurt you. We work for the Department of Homeland Security. We want to be sure you're not sick."

In the living room, Carlos's shouts were frantic. He was arguing. Phoenix remembered her father's stories about black men arguing with armed intruders. They always led to shooting.

"Baby, we're okay!" Phoenix called out to Carlos. "Don't worry about us—we're fine!"

"*Phoenix?*" Carlos answered, to be sure it was she.

Tears streamed down her cheeks as she gazed at the plastic mask and the gun still trained on her and her son. Phoenix made herself smile so she could borrow some cheer for her voice. Marcus's father would not be gunned down within his earshot. That family tradition would end with her, even if it meant lying to her husband.

"Yeah, baby, *tranquilo!*" she said. "Nobody's hurting us! We're gonna sue their asses! I already sent out the email!"

She almost fooled herself. Marcus's instincts told him not to call out for Carlos; instead, he locked his arms around Phoenix's legs more tightly. She held on to the counter to keep from losing her balance. She wasn't going to fall down and scare Marcus. And she wasn't going to be shot in front of her son, even with a trank gun.

"Come on, Marcus, let's put our hands on the counter," Phoenix said. "You heard what he said. Nobody's gonna hurt us."

Marcus was crying, his grip iron. His tears seeped through the thin fabric of the flimsy track pants she slept in. Phoenix couldn't move him without pulling him away hard.

"He's seven years old," Phoenix said, as close as she could bring herself to pleading. How could anyone with the memory of childhood hurt a child?

"Yes, ma'am, I have a daughter that exact age," the man said. He tried on a more upbeat voice: "Buddy? Stand next to your mom by the counter. I know we look funny to you, but we're just regular folks wearing big, hot raincoats. Do what your mom says, and you can have one of these nifty suits too. See? It's got a light inside."

A dim yellow light went on beyond the plastic. Two eyes stared out at them. Kind eyes.

Marcus straightened, suddenly more fascinated than frightened. The light made him forget the gun. Marcus loosened his grip around her legs and finally let her go.

Phoenix was almost grateful to the man behind the mask, although she knew he was about to take her to a truck and force her away from her home, probably without Carlos. Someone—even this man who claimed to have a seven-year-old daughter—might try to take Marcus from her. That hadn't happened yet, but it could. Knowing that made Phoenix want to break a wine bottle and wield it like a knife. Knowing that made her see blood on the walls.

But that would lead to shooting, too. She would not make this worse than it had to be.

Phoenix needed to believe the man's lying eyes.

Thirteen

6:05 a.m.

The truck smelled of oil and cleanser. The drive took two hours.
Phoenix's wristphone had been politely confiscated, but she had a
good internal clock. The daylight when the truck's rear door opened
only confirmed what she knew: it was dawn, the sky dappled with
unpromising gray light.

Marcus had fallen asleep across her lap, and her arms were
numb from holding him on the lightly padded bench where they
had been strapped side by side. Her shoulder seat belt felt like
chains. Marcus moved only when the truck jostled, but Phoenix
had decided that she wasn't going to let Marcus go. As long as she
was holding on to Marcus, she could handle the rest. The world
wasn't ending yet. Her knees' shaking had stopped somewhere
north of Paso.

If they were expecting her to cry or break down, they would be
disappointed. And anyone who put a hand on Marcus would lose an
eye. Her thumbnails were primed to strike.

Making plans helped Phoenix keep her knees from shaking.
Carlos had been stolen away before she and Marcus were allowed
to leave the house, and she'd never heard a thing. They must have
sedated him somehow, or he would have called for her again.

But Carlos is all right, she told herself when her knees tried to
shake.

Phoenix couldn't wait to call her cousin Gloria and crank up
her machinery: press releases, internet blasts, TV. She would buy a
home-page spread in *The New York Times* online. She would call

the president and shame him into an apology. "This is gonna come down hard."

You've got to see about the revolution, Phee.

Phoenix didn't move after the truck came to a gentle stop and someone pulled open the rear doors. The doors hissed softly on their hinges. Judging by the protective suits, none of the half-dozen people congregated planned to get too close.

They really think we have the killer flu, she thought. One day, it might be funny.

The two men closest to the door held black semiautomatic rifles with both hands, waiting in disciplined silence. She was at a military facility. She might as well be in another country. A mechanical ramp whirred from the back of the truck with a clang onto the asphalt, and Marcus stirred. She wished she could put off his waking, or change what he was waking to.

"Ma'am . . . ?" a gravelly voice began from the open truck door.

"Step back," Phoenix cut him off. "No one touches me. No one touches Marcus."

After glancing at one another, a few of the waiting men took token steps backward. But the men with the guns held their ground. "Ma'am . . ." the lead man went on. "Come forward. Slowly. Step out of the vehicle, please."

Marcus sat up, his body stiffening as he suddenly remembered where he was. His forehead was warm. In the rush to leave the house, she had grabbed him a lined denim jacket that had been far too warm for the truck. All they had were their bedclothes and jackets. Phoenix wasn't wearing underwear under her paper-thin track pants. Or a bra under her T-shirt.

Phoenix pressed her palms to his hot cheeks, which had stopped his crying before he fell asleep. "I'm here, baby . . ." she said, as if they were alone.

"Where's Daddy?" Marcus whimpered.

"That's what we're about to find out." Phoenix stared past the gun's arresting black nozzle to the nearest soldier's eyes.

Phoenix's legs had jellied, so she had to accept a steady, efficient gloved hand to help her walk down the metal ramp from the truck. She held Marcus with her other hand, and he moved like her shadow, so close that she nearly tripped.

As they walked down the ramp, Phoenix was relieved when the men kept their distance, forming a loose ring. They were funneling her toward an open set of double doors at a bland, piss-colored two-story facility with no markings she could see. Mostly concrete, fewer windows downstairs. Around her stretched an empty parking lot, with faded paint lines. She looked for mountains, but no landmarks were in sight. A ring of dogwood trees hid everything else from view. She had no idea where she was.

"Am I under arrest?" Phoenix said. She'd been asking for two hours.

"No, ma'am," the soldier said, the stock answer. A buried southern twang jostled memories of Sarge's stories. "Please walk to the doors ahead."

Her legs wouldn't move. She wanted to stay outside, where she was almost free.

"Ma'am, please walk to the doors ahead."

Phoenix remembered watching the miniseries *Holocaust* with Mom when she was in middle school, the first time she'd cried real tears over anything on TV. The story of the Holocaust in Germany had taught her that sometimes routine was a lie. It was hard for Phoenix to catch her breath, much less walk. Marcus was hugging her too tightly, but she couldn't bring herself to pry him free.

"Ma'am?" the voice said, patient. "Please walk to the doors ahead and we will escort you to the first door on the right. That's our intake office. More personnel will meet you there."

It was the first time she'd been given information in advance, and she was grateful. *Maybe it really is an intake office,* she told herself, and her legs moved again.

But intake to where?

After the dim light in both the truck and the sky outside, the brightness inside the antiseptic facility reawakened Phoenix's headache. The white walls and floors hurt her eyes. She squinted, walking close to the wall.

The space suits ringed her while they walked, some in front, some behind her. Even if running had been an option, she wouldn't have gotten far.

"Here," the same voice said. "The first door on the right. Please go inside."

Phoenix wondered if the same paralysis would meet her in the doorway, but it didn't. The space suits didn't follow her and Marcus into the intake room. The heavy door closed behind them, and a powerful lock whispered to rest.

The room was the size of a large classroom, mostly empty except for shiny metal carts lining the rear wall. It looked like a storeroom with a wall of glass on the other end.

Phoenix was cold, suddenly. The AC was on too high. She felt the thinness of her clothing beneath her light jacket, and her missing socks and loafers. Something whirred loudly above them in the maze of shiny aluminum pipes.

Someone was watching her.

On the other side of the glass, a sole black woman sat waiting at a microphone, beneath a crown of light. The glass was semireflective, so Phoenix hadn't seen her at first. When she walked to the glass, her own anxious, wide-eyed face floated above the stranger's.

The woman was wearing a lab coat instead of a plastic suit. No badge identified her. She was a dark-skinned woman, fit and stern.

Two plain wooden chairs waited on their side of the glass. Only two. Carlos wouldn't be coming here, Phoenix realized, and sadness sealed her throat. He shouldn't have blogged about his mother. Carlos had deleted the page right away, but not fast enough. Not nearly fast enough.

The woman beyond the glass sighed. "It probably won't help . . . but I'm a big fan of your music." She said it as if they could share amusement over the irony.

"It doesn't help." Phoenix barely choked out the words. She wanted to break the glass. She was shaking again, not just her knees. The room seemed colder than when she'd walked in.

"I was afraid it wouldn't. I almost didn't say it. Have a seat, Mrs. Harris."

Phoenix didn't sit. "Where's my husband?"

The woman blinked, and her eyes seemed to dim. Maybe she really was a Phoenix fan. "Do you know that your husband broke into a contaminated federal facility in Puerto Rico?"

Marcus was whimpering, still clinging to her legs. Phoenix decided not to lie to someone who already knew the truth. "He wanted to find out what happened to his mother."

"Your husband exposed himself to a very dangerous virus."

"He isn't sick."

"There may be an incubation period of up to twenty-one days for some carriers," she said. "Were you aware of that?"

It sounded like a lie. Her online research of the killer stomach flu had never mentioned an incubation period longer than a week. A week was bad enough.

"As I said," the woman said slowly, with more authority, "would you please take a seat?"

Phoenix sat, and pulled Marcus onto her lap. His limbs were too large to share the chair with her, but she contorted to make room for him. Marcus would climb back into the womb if he could. For Marcus's sake, Phoenix fought away tears.

"I won't take too long, I hope," the woman said. "I only need to know what your husband told you, and I have a few other questions."

"Why am I really here?"

A hidden emotion tugged at the woman's lower lip. "For the sake of safety—yours, and the public at large. I personally apologize for the inconvenience to you and your son."

Phoenix leaned closer to the glass and her thin microphone. She hoped her voice was loud on the other side. "You're sorry you woke me up in the middle of the night and took me, my husband, and child from our home. You're sorry you won't tell me where my husband is or let me see him. You're sorry I was brought here, with my child, against my will."

The woman's face seemed to shimmer in the glass. "Yes. I'm personally sorry."

"You don't sound a damn bit sorry," Phoenix said. "And no one is going to take my son away from me. Not for a minute."

Marcus tightened his arms around her waist, where his head nestled against her stomach.

"No, ma'am," the woman behind the glass said. "But we'll need to draw blood."

"Fine, as long as the syringes are empty. Nobody's pumping anything in my body," Phoenix said. "The faster the better. My blood is perfect. So is Marcus's. And so is Carlos's. This has all been for nothing."

"You sound very sure about that," the woman said.

"I am."

The woman typed rapid strokes on a keyboard that was just out of Phoenix's sight. "With such a new disease we're still learning about? How can you be so sure?"

"Have you heard about my last concert?" Phoenix said.

The woman blinked. "I've heard reports."

"We were all there. That's why I know our blood is fine."

The woman lowered her voice, as if to caution her. "Are you telling me that you and your husband injected a banned drug, and also injected your son? And that you believe this drug cleaned out the virus?" She was baiting Phoenix with Glow terminology. Glow users called themselves *cleaned out*. Phoenix had learned that only since the concert, from her research.

"You didn't hear me say that. I never said I had a virus or dropped any Glow."

"Then I don't understand *your* meaning, Mrs. Harris," the woman said.

There were no words to explain the concert, even when words might set her free. Phoenix might talk about Fana and John Jamal Wright one day, but it wouldn't be here and now.

"Anyone who was sick before the concert wasn't sick when it was over. Me included. My son and husband too. And we were never infected with anything, so test us and let us go."

The woman looked sad. "I wish the world were that simple."

"The world is exactly that simple," Phoenix said. "You just don't know it yet."

For a few seconds, the woman didn't speak, her eyes gazing at

Phoenix with the same question in most of her fans' eyes: *What did you really see? What happens after we die?* One touch from Phoenix could send some fans fainting to the floor. Her stories from Beyond had inspired those kids in Chicago to race ahead, unafraid.

"Let us go," Phoenix said, woman to woman. Idol to fan.

The woman looked away from Phoenix's eyes with a flash of pain before composing her face. "I'll need the names of anyone you had contact with at that concert. Anyone who might have been exposed. Or anyone who might be distributing Glow. Any names you remember would be very helpful."

Phoenix decided that the woman behind the glass was dressed like a doctor or researcher, but wasn't. Her job was to get Phoenix to talk. She had been assigned this job because she was efficient, fan or not. Under a flimsy pretense, the government had locked her up to question Phoenix about Glow. Others would be locked up, too. Sarge and Carlos had known all along. This *is what this looks like,* Phoenix thought.

"They were just fans," Phoenix said, trying to sound impatient instead of cornered. "No offense, but I have a lot of fans. I don't socialize on a gig."

"Can I make a suggestion to you?" the woman said, like a friend.

The room went silent except for the low hum of the air system and Marcus's whimper.

The woman went on. "Try to start with some of the easy names, like the people we've seen on the internet and TV. The Glow Messengers? Your office contacted them."

"*They* tried to contact *me.*"

"I'm sure you can jog your memory with their names. Easy, right? Let's start there."

It was going to be a long day, Phoenix realized. A hard day for her and Marcus. He would be hungry soon, if he wasn't already. She pressed her hands to Marcus's cheeks and squeezed softly, smiling at him. His cheeks were still hot, although Phoenix's molars trembled in the cold room. Marcus didn't smile back, but he stopped whimpering.

"What are you afraid of?" Phoenix said, meeting the woman's eyes.

The woman blinked, startled.

It was the last time Phoenix would be sure she had heard her.

Phoenix refused to eat or drink all day and all night, although she relented to let Marcus have a McDonald's Happy Meal and a bottle of water for a late dinner. How could she refuse food to Marcus? She tried to have faith that they wouldn't drug a child.

The smell of the fries in the bag a soldier slipped through a tube in the door assaulted Phoenix when the food arrived. For a moment, she was sorry she hadn't put in her own order.

"This is *good*," Marcus said, confirming her mistake. "You should eat too, Mom."

Phoenix only shook her head and lied about not being hungry. Her stomach growled to contradict her, but Marcus pretended not to notice.

Had she been foolish not to get food? Fasting seemed silly, in retrospect. She was on United States soil, a United States citizen . . . and a celebrity! People would notice she was missing, if they hadn't already. Her cousin Gloria was probably having a fit, since they spoke every other day without fail. Nobody was going to drug her food, she told herself. She would have to eat and drink something the next day. Her first chance.

Their room was about twice the size of a standard jail cell, although it wasn't furnished any better. All they had was a bunk bed, a toilet, and a single chair for sitting. Instead of bars, their locked door was made of impossibly thick Plexiglas fitted with a tube and a tray for passing items back and forth. Anyone could peek in at them at any time, and she could see the muddy images of the faceless soldiers ignoring her pounding on the door as they passed. Phoenix wasn't sure they could hear her through the thick glass.

Someone had brought Marcus a SpongeBob coloring book and a box of a dozen crayons soon after they'd been locked in the room, and he'd already worn some of the crayons to the nub coloring furiously on the bottom bunk. He was coloring to forget, Phoenix assumed. She wished someone had brought her a keyboard.

"Dad's gonna be okay," Marcus said, staring at his book. "Right?"

"Yes," Phoenix said. "Of course he will. This is just a mistake. Sometimes when there are new diseases, the government gets scared. But they'll let us go soon."

They'd had this conversation a dozen times, and Phoenix wasn't sure either of them believed her anymore. Why hadn't they been released? Where *was* Carlos?

Her instincts about her first interrogator had been right: the woman had been dressed like a scientist, but she'd been strictly an operative looking for information. The medical aspect of their abduction was pure bullshit. Her captors seemed like military types, perhaps from several different agencies. The soldiers in the hall seemed young. The three people who'd questioned her that day had been vastly different—an officious black woman, a nerd in Clark Kent eyeglasses, and a hairy biker type who looked like he worked undercover.

The last one, appearing with his walrus mustache, mane of shaggy hair, and collection of old scars on his face, had scared the hell out of Phoenix before he opened his mouth. Despite his easygoing smile, Phoenix had expected him to hit her.

Tell me everything you know about Glow. Let's start at the beginning.

She hadn't been denied bathroom breaks, and she'd been offered food and water on a regular basis. She'd been subjected to hours of monotonous questioning about Glow and John Jamal Wright—his fingerprints had turned up at her house, of course— but no one had laid a hand on her or Marcus. Phoenix closed her eyes. *Thank you, God.*

Their blood tests would come back fine, and they would let her go. But if that was true, why hadn't it happened yet? And if the fear of infection was only a ruse, what difference would their blood tests make?

Marcus began dozing off, his empty burger wrapper in his lap. Phoenix had lost track of the time long ago, but she thought it was late. It might be nearly eleven.

"Come on, baby," she said, nudging him awake. "Let's go to bed."

"I want the top bunk, Mommy."

"Why?" Phoenix had planned to share the bottom bunk with him.
"I've never slept in a bunk bed. I want to be up there."

"I don't like sleeping in high places," Phoenix said. She didn't say
so, but if they needed to try some kind of getaway, it would be a lot
harder so many feet off the ground.

"You stay on the bottom, Mommy. You'll be under me, guarding
me. That way, I can go to sleep and I won't be scared."

Phoenix couldn't argue with his point. The blankets were thin,
so she draped hers over Marcus, covering him from head to toe. The
mattresses were uncomfortable.

But we won't be here long, she told herself. *Maybe just tonight.*

Her eyelids tugged together like magnets. She listened to Marcus's steady breathing as long as she could, and then she was asleep.

Hours passed. Phoenix never knew how many.

As soon as she opened her eyes, she knew from the silence of
the walls. She knew from the lethargy in her limbs, and a persistent
drowsiness rocking her head that had nothing to do with normal
sleep.

They had drugged her after all. Had it been an odorless gas
pumped into the room?

"Please . . . please . . . please . . . no . . ." Phoenix whispered.

She pulled herself up by the cold bed frame to see the bunk
above hers. She was so tired from whatever they had given her, peering over the mattress was like scaling a mountain.

Marcus's bed was empty. Even his blankets were gone. Only the
coloring book was left behind. She stared at the empty bed with all
her might, trying to change the sight of it.

Then Phoenix screamed.

Fourteen

Morning. Light. Still here.

Jessica woke as she usually did, breathless and wide-eyed; a swimmer clawing for shore after sleep tried to drown her. She was eager to escape to her bedroom's weak sunlight.

6 a.m., the lime-green face of her digital alarm clock assured her. *Still here.*

Jessica sat up beneath the queenly white canopy of David's antique opium bed. The bed was built low to the ground, smaller than a queen, with regal carvings of dragons in rich teak. The bed and the smell of David's spicy incense evoked an ancient time and place, but the illusion was broken by the shiny metallic CD player on her dresser and her leopard-print bra dangling from the top drawer.

Jessica slipped her bare feet into her waiting white Nikes under the bed, the insoles slick from wear. She wrapped herself in the newsprint bathrobe her mother had bought her during her first internship at the *Miami Sun-News,* when she was eighteen. The hem's loose threads tickled her thighs. *Thank you, Lord. Still here.*

She stole out of bed, leaving David sleeping in a mound beneath the covers. Jessica glanced at her husband's exposed brown shoulder, exquisitely contoured, then forced her eyes away. Contemplating David's skin too long could lure her back into bed, where she might fall asleep staring at his face. David's face could still do that.

No. This was *her* time.

The 1920's-era oak floorboards groaned and creaked in the usual places as Jessica crept to Kira's closed door, beside her bedroom. Jessica smiled at crayon drawings of her orange cat, Teacake, and the black Great Dane, Princess. Jessica pressed her ear to the door and heard the music of her daughter's breathing.

Still here.

Jessica took the knob with a practiced, silent touch and cracked the door open to see Kira's sleeping face. Coiled black curls rested on Kira's forehead beneath a lone pink barrette. Last night's shampoo smelled like honey. Kira's tiny nose, which mimicked her father's, was slightly crusted from the cold she had finally fought off after a week.

But Kira's breathing was clear and strong. No asthma today.

Sweet relief came, a fresh taste in Jessica's mouth. *Still here.*

Her relief dizzied her. Her daughter Kira, her daily miracle, was safely asleep in a cocoon of silent toys and dreams. She watched Kira's nose twitch above the rumpled pink face of Ariel from *The Little Mermaid* on the sheets rising and falling with her clear, even breaths. Sometimes Jessica stood in Kira's doorway and watched her sleep for hours at a time.

"She's beautiful," a woman's voice said behind her.

The voice cleaved Jessica in half; a voice she both knew and didn't know.

Already, Kira's nose was swimming, blurry. The entire room would wash away.

"No," Jessica said to the woman behind her. "Not now."

"When?"

"Not *now*, dammit." She almost said *damn you.*

Jessica waited without turning around, to be sure the voice was gone. She inhaled deeply, bathing her lungs. *It's 1997. I'm still here.*

But it was too late. Jessica had blinked, and now Kira's bedroom door was closed. Quickly, she tried the doorknob, but it wouldn't turn, much less yield. She was locked out. Jessica pressed her ear to the door, listening for Kira's breathing. Silence.

And the door wasn't a door. It was a stone wall as smooth as marble.

Jessica was in her bed again, but it was a different bed. A different place. She was hugging the wall as if she could melt through it. Her cheek, pressed against the cool surface, was slick with tears. A tide of hatred welled inside her, with nowhere to go.

Jessica wiped her face dry with her shirt. She hoped never to cry in front of Fana again.

"What do you want?" Jessica said.

She turned, expecting to see her adult daughter. Instead, there was a horrific, stunted figure draped in bees standing only as tall as her waist in the center of her room. The bees scuttled over one another in a wriggling mass, impenetrable.

Jessica's heart knocked against her rib cage, but only for a breath. She blinked, and the horrific image was gone. Her memories were confused, remaking Fana as a toddler on their worst day together. Some part of her might always see Fana draped in bees.

The disorientation sometimes lasted for hours. Hallucinations. Voices.

Was Fana really in the room with her? Maybe not.

"I wanted to let you know we're back," Fana said.

Yes. Fana was standing over the bedside table, stubbing out the Dreamstick in the clay platter that served as Jessica's ashtray, scarred with tar and soot. Fana politely kept her eyes down, although her face seemed tight with disapproval. Or was that Jessica's imagination, too? Maybe she wanted to see a teenage daughter's pout, something she might recognize. Once the thin wisps of smoke were smothered, Fana pocketed the Dreamstick in her jeans like a magician.

Jessica almost told Fana to keep her hands off her property, but she had four more sticks in her desk. Those would last two or three days, and she could get more. In some wings of the colony, her status as Fana's mother gave her access to anything she wanted. Beautiful men who looked young enough to be her sons were eager to bring her food and gifts, enchanted by the novelty of her. Some of them hadn't laid eyes on a woman in decades, or longer.

But Jessica steered clear of most of the colony. She steered clear, period.

She was thirsty, as she always was when she woke, so she poured herself a glass of water from her crystalline decanter. No matter how long she'd been back in the Lalibela Colony, she never tired of how fine the water tasted. It was as thick as apple cider, rolling across her tongue with a vague whisper of sweetness. So crisp! Each gulp was like tasting water for the first time. One of the Life Brothers upworld was bottling the stuff and selling it, she'd heard.

"How was the concert?" Jessica said, remembering. Proud of her recollection.

"Fine."

"Phoenix came?"

"Yes."

Jessica tried to say *Good for you, Fana,* but she was beyond empty praises or the glories of her daughter's gifts. Fana had healed people at the concert, no doubt, using her mind as a conduit for the Blood's healing.

Khaldun would be proud. Fana, his pet project, was everything he'd prophesied.

Jessica stood up, shaking feeling back into her legs. How long had she slept? Her limbs were awkward and unwieldy. In her dream world, there were clocks in every corner: her nightstand, her wrist-watch, the microwave, her car. Here, she was always wondering about the time. *So like a mortal,* Fana's guard Berhanu said when she asked him.

Their sole clock was in the bedroom, a cheap plastic wall clock she'd bought at the last minute from an Addis market when she remembered that the Life Colony had none. But Jessica practically lived in the smaller room adjacent to the bedroom, separated by a door Dawit had built for her. She'd christened the room her study. She'd planned to start writing a book, her vow for years, but she spent most of her time on the spongy pallet beside her table, half sitting, half reclined, fleeing the terror and monotony of her new life.

Dawit must be back, too. He'd decided not to disturb her, sleeping alone.

So she was busted. Fine. It was silly to lie to him. Why bother?

She and Dawit hadn't lived apart since their first reunion in Lali-bela when Fana was three, but maybe it was time. She'd felt that way for at least five years, not so much out of anger or boredom, but because she was wrung out. She was dry to the bone. She'd shared this new quarters with Dawit in Lalibela only because she'd been too intimidated to set up her own space in the vast, foreign colony where she was a stranger.

Jessica didn't have a good history with the Lalibela Colony. During her first visit to see Dawit, she and three-year-old Fana had been attacked by two Life Brothers. But no one dared to stand up to Fana directly now: if you were supposed to kill the dragon while it was small, that day had passed. She and Dawit had reunited to raise Fana, and Lord knew Fana had been raised.

Jessica still sometimes enjoyed Dawit's touch, but she preferred making love to him in the dream, where she still called him David and didn't know anything about his Blood, his violent history, or his alien people. Physical sensation under Dreamsticks could seem more vivid than life. When she wanted David, he was always waiting in her memories. Why did she need Dawit when she could go back to the man he'd manufactured to fool her into marriage?

It was his fault. He was the one who'd split himself in two. Split *her* in two.

Jessica walked to the red marble washbasin on its contoured marble stand and splashed her face with the constantly replenishing water. The colors in her room jumped from dull gray to a sharp rainbow: red-tinged walls, Fana's mustard-yellow T-shirt, a shiny orange at her bedside. Dawit must have brought the fruit for her. At least some of him was still David, thoughtful and doting—most of him, if she was honest with herself.

She wished his best gestures felt like anything more than penance.

Jessica's stomach stabbed her with hunger pangs. She ate vivid meals in the dream, but her stomach never got the message. She might have been dreaming for nearly twenty-four hours. She didn't need food as often as she had before the Blood, but breathing in misty nutrients like the Life Brothers who meditated for months didn't do the job for her. Jessica shoved orange wedges into her mouth while juice dripped down her chin.

"You should look at yourself in a mirror, Mom." A ring of judgment from Fana.

Jessica only grunted as she chewed. When the wall beside her glimmered with light, Jessica ignored it as a hallucination. Sometimes the whole room rippled like a waving flag.

"Please look," Fana said.

A square patch of her wall was a mirror now, like a clear liquid pool upright. Jessica glanced at herself. Her hair hadn't been combed in as long as she could remember, so it was in disarray across her forehead. Her T-shirt was stained with old meals eaten equally as hastily. And her face seemed gray instead of brown, even in the natural light from her open ceiling that stretched up at least a hundred feet. If not for the Blood, she might have thought she'd aged five years.

Fana stood behind her in the reflection, tall and unknowable.

One glance was all Jessica could take. "I get it," she said. "I need a bath."

The liquid mirror froze and solidified, shifting until it was only the wall again.

"You need more than a bath," Fana said quietly. Gently. Fana seemed to float above Jessica, gazing at her with a blank pity that Jessica couldn't stomach.

"I've told you about that zoo in Miami called Metro Zoo, right? It's mostly designed so it doesn't have cages. Just these wide ditches. The animal are supposed to think they're free. I'm taking Kira there today. Feel free to drop in, if you'd like to meet your sister."

"I've made a decision," Fana said, ignoring her invitation. "I wanted to tell you first."

Jessica wasn't clairvoyant—Teka had judged from her aura that she was still fifteen years away from even rudimentary telepathic gifts, *if* she kept up her meditation, which she hadn't in at least three months—but she knew what Fana was going to say.

Maybe she'd known since the shock of seeing blood on her daughter's clothes and face in Mexico. He wouldn't let her go.

"You're going back to him," she said.

"To ask him to stop the plague."

Of course. Jessica had avoided most conversations with Dawit and Alex about the new illness, but she should have known it was Michel. What else could Fana do, except follow her mother's path straight to the man who could destroy her?

Jessica shrugged. "He's got you, baby."

"It's not like that, Mom."

"Oh no, he's got you good and tight, like a fly in a honey jar," Jessica said. She sounded more like her own mother, probably because she spent so much time with Bea now. "The sticks mess with my memory, but I remember even if you don't: you came to this room a year ago and said, 'Mom, if I try to go back there before the ten years are up, you know I'm not in control. It's him.'"

Fana's placid expression wavered as Jessica grazed one of Fana's doubts. *Stick around, baby girl, I've got a million of 'em,* Jessica thought. The first days after their return to Lalibela had been better, when Fana had needed a mother again. Finding friendship with Fana hadn't blunted the pain of losing her mother, friends, and world in one horrible night, but it had been a shiny trinket in the rubble.

Now that was over. Fana had her world of meditation and instruction with Teka, and Dawit was happy to surf the havoc with Fana when she needed him. Havoc was his specialty.

Jessica was fine with her quiet world in the dream. Years ago, Dawit had warned her that she would lose everyone she loved, but people always lost themselves or everyone they knew; the Blood didn't change that.

"Seems funny," Jessica said. "Here you are stressing about me and a little smoke in the air, and look at you headed straight to Hell. You need to think about your own choices, Fana."

"It's not a happy choice, Mom."

"What Michel does or doesn't do isn't your responsibility. But you know that. And you didn't come for my advice, so I won't waste it." Was she so short with Fana because that was who she had become, or because she was searching for a way to reach her?

"You don't think I should go?" Fana said. "Even to prevent suffering?"

"Stop it," Jessica said. "If all he had to do was spread a little misery to get you back, why did you bother to leave him?"

"Five hundred dead already," Fana said. "Phoenix's mother-in-law. Issa's sister."

Fana's voice was at the end of a tunnel. There was enough resi-
due from the Dreamsticks in the room's sweetly scented air to make
the colors fade when Jessica tried hard enough. Bees crawled errati-
cally across Fana's face, wings flitting; gone when Jessica blinked.

"You've done worse by accident," Jessica said. "People die, Fana.
Now they're home."

The hurricane once had been a taboo subject, a primal wound
between them. Maybe Fana had grown beyond her trauma, but Jessica couldn't forget witnessing her toddler daughter's transformation into a terrible, foreign entity with power over the sky, riding
the Shadows.

Michel swam in their stink, and Fana would go back to the
Shadows, too, one day. Jessica had known that since Fana was three.
It was too much power to ignore.

"What happened to the woman who raised me, Mom?" Fana
said. "Who taught me that it was worth risking everything to help
people?"

Jessica tried to feel hurt, or pain, but all that came was a weary
laugh. For all Fana's gifts, the girl was still so blind sometimes. "I
wouldn't sacrifice you for five million people, Fana. Or five billion."

"I can't just hide from him."

Talking to Fana was hard work. Jessica looked for a watch on
her wrist, found none. Day or night, what did it matter? *This* world
was the dream, this place without clocks where time fled and peeled
everyone away.

Kira should be up by now. Time to knock on her door and see
if she was dressed. Since Kira had turned five, she preferred to dress
herself. David was going to drive them to Metro Zoo in the minivan
after they picked up her mother from church. Jessica could almost
taste the cheesy arepas at the concessions stand. Her mouth watered.
Kira loved arepas!

"Mom, don't," Fana said. "Forget your ghosts for now."

A surge of anger made the edges of the room sharp and clear.
Jessica stepped closer to Fana, almost lashed out to slap her daughter's face. Maybe she was only afraid to hit her, because she wanted
the contact so badly that her fingers were unsteady.

"You stay out of my damn head!" Jessica said between gritted teeth.

Fana's face gave way to a tiny, childlike alarm. How could Fana stand against Michel if she couldn't control her impulses at home?

"I'm sorry," Fana said. "I didn't mean to . . ."

"You better learn how to keep out of places you don't belong," Jessica said. "You hear me? Learn fast. Screw around with anyone else you want—but not me. And not your father."

"Dad doesn't need you to speak for him. He isn't the one who's hiding."

The slap came before Jessica realized her hand had flown free. Fana's cheek rang brightly beneath Jessica's palm. The old cliché was true: the slap hurt her more than Fana. Once, there might have been tears from both of them. One of them. But their locked eyes were mirrors, dry as bones. Fana's hand brushed her cheek, as if to wipe away a gnat.

"I'm very sorry," Fana said, as placid as her teacher. The deeper Teka took Fana into her mind's ocean, the more she sounded like she was reciting lines from a script. "I didn't mean to trip over your feelings about Dad."

"Stay out of my head," Jessica said. "Find your way back into yours."

Fana breathed a small sigh, a rare display of impatience. "Like I said, I wanted to tell you first. I'm going to Michel. I'll have guards, so I won't go alone. I'd like you and Dad to come, but that's your decision."

Jessica closed her eyes, withering at the mention of guards. What could guards do?

This is not my child, she told herself, the mantra that had helped her survive the night of bees and shadows. Back when being Fana's mother was all the power she needed to save her.

When Jessica opened her eyes again, Fana was gone.

Kira's door waited for her, halfway open. Kira's cheerful, melodic voice was singing "Stormy Weather." Her daughter's unspoiled voice invited her inside.

Fifteen

Dawit waited for a challenger in the Circle.

Berhanu and Fasilidas sometimes sparred with him, but they were tending to Fana. Besides, Dawit had faced them too often in the woods of their lost Washington colony. They had physical weaknesses—Dawit was faster than most of his Brothers—but their mind arts made them nearly impossible to best because they predicted his movements.

Worse, Berhanu's mind was strong enough to deflect blows! He was a menace.

But their tutelage had sharpened him. Dawit had improved his mind as quickly through fighting as he had by meditating with Fana while she guided him. He needed no less focus in the Circle. His patience had been decimated in the mortal world, but he was learning again. His senses must be sharp for what lay ahead.

But Dawit was an outsider, invisible. Even Brothers who would take pleasure in dismembering him did not honor him in the Circle. To his Brothers, he and Fana had split the colony apart and brought a wolf to their doorstep, and Dawit couldn't claim otherwise.

Dawit stood at the Circle's center, waiting in the bright ring of light. After five hundred years, wearing a mask in the Circle was only a tradition. They knew one another too well. Their bodies were static, resisting new muscle or fat, so they easily recognized one another despite the semisheer, skintight white masks that hid their faces and eyes. Originally, Khaldun had used the masks to train them to fight without personal animus; rage should not guide them, he said. But, like everything else in the Lalibela Colony, the practice had outlived its inspiration.

"What a heartbreaking sight!" the voice boomed from the darkness behind him. "A bride all dressed up, left alone at the altar. And quite comely! Was your father's dowry so meager?"

Dawit smiled inside his mask. Not only did he have an opponent—but one of his most reliable, and the Brother he loved most. When had Mahmoud returned to the colony?

"I'm too high-spirited, I think," Dawit said. "I castrate every groom-to-be."

Mahmoud's laugh was hearty as always, echoing in the empty upper circle, where spectators might gather to watch the matches. The Circle always reminded Dawit of a beehive.

Mahmoud strode to the Circle's periphery. He was already dressed for combat, in a matching white lambskin waistcloth. Mahmoud was masked, but even if Dawit had not known Mahmoud's voice, the olive skin and onyx ponytail would have betrayed him. Like him, Mahmoud was most at home in a fight.

Mahmoud carried a carved mahogany staff in each hand, tossing one to Dawit, who snatched it from the air. Dawit closed his fingers around the staff, a tight grip. The challenger chose the initial weapon—but *he* would choose the next one, as the winner.

Mahmoud removed his mask with a swift gesture, and Dawit followed his example. Good. He had questions for Mahmoud, and there would be no thought of conversation once Mahmoud entered the Circle.

Dawit could remember few times when Mahmoud's beard had been so full. Dawit would never tell him so, but he looked like Khaldun.

"How goes the search?" Dawit said, the customary greeting to a Searcher.

Mahmoud's grim sneer made Dawit wish he had chosen another greeting.

"How fares the father of the bride?" Mahmoud said.

Touché.

Mahmoud had been in Khaldun's disciplined cadre of Searchers who were responsible for bringing home Brothers who had stayed upworld too long. In flight from Mahmoud, Dawit had suffered a living death when he lost his old life in Miami. Dawit refused to blame Mahmoud for that heartache—*he* had made the choice to love a mortal woman and try to pass Kira the Blood—but Jessica might never forgive either of them.

No small miracle that he counted Mahmoud as either a friend or a Brother.

"Michel has unleashed a plague," Dawit said.

"Oh, I know well what he has unleashed," Mahmoud said, chuckling.

Dawit's back went rigid. He probed at Mahmoud, but his friend's thoughts were hidden. He did not believe Mahmoud had a hand in the infection, but Mahmoud had surprised him before. "You know this how, Brother?"

A sarcastic smile. "As you reminded me, Dawit, I am a Searcher. It is my duty to know. There are twenty-two of us upworld. The monkeys are lucky that only ten have gone to Michel. Always bearing gifts, I might add. One of those gifts was a plague."

Ten! Dawit had suspected that Wendimu and Alem were with Michel, given their long tutelage in the House of Science and their vocal disdain for mortals, but so many others?

"You jest," Dawit said.

"I never jest so near the Circle. It's the worst of luck."

"But Teka has perceived nothing of it. Or Fana."

"Teka!" Mahmoud laughed like a schoolboy. "Michel protects them, Dawit. Teka is blinded to Michel. And Fana apparently shares her teacher's blindness."

"Yet, you see more." Skepticism soured Dawit's voice. Mahmoud's mind arts were crude, beyond masking and basic projection. Where would Mahmoud gain the insight? Dawit tried another probe, failing again. Mahmoud did not want his thoughts known, even to a friend.

"Wendimu tried to recruit me," Mahmoud said. "He couldn't contain his glee over the disease. 'The Cleansing has begun!' He expects me to join him at Shangri-la any day."

Mahmoud's silenced thoughts worried Dawit. The mask for the Circle was only a costume; cloaked thoughts were far more troublesome.

"Will you join them?" Dawit said.

Mahmoud shrugged. "Michel's plans for the monkeys don't disturb my sleep. But why would I lie with that pompous tyrant? Wendimu! All of them are fools eager to give up their minds to another, hoping to find Khaldun again." In one breath, he condemned both Michel and the two-thousand-year-old man who had created the Life Colony.

Once, Khaldun had been their God.

Khaldun's offenses were myriad: he had built the Life Colony out of a selfish wish to have captive students. He had used his advanced mind arts to keep them placid in the Lalibela Colony, denying them their rights to the world above. He had spawned a second family of immortals, never revealing that there were others like Michel who might challenge them.

And he had created Fana as a mate for Michel! Even if Khaldun himself had stolen the blood of Christ in the burial cave instead of the unnamed Storyteller he always claimed, Dawit was angriest at Khaldun for the treacherous path he had laid out for his child. Had Khaldun allowed him to remain with Jessica in Miami so long only to create Fana? Had Khaldun always planned to sacrifice Dawit's first child to create his second? What if the madness that had overcome him in Miami had been Khaldun's doing all along?

He would never truly know.

"If the girl were my daughter," Mahmoud said, "Michel would be ash."

Dawit laughed a bitter laugh, though laughter was far from his heart. "If Fana were your daughter, you would never have met her." He and Mahmoud had sired dozens of nameless, faceless children. "Michel may yet be ash. But I have learned patience, Mahmoud."

"What you call patience is only enchantment, Dawit. You believe Khaldun's nonsense in that Letter, a prophecy that ties her to him. When will you free yourself from his lies?"

"Fana believes she's the best match against him. Her gifts bear it out. Let us see."

"You're like the others scurrying to Michel—a believer in search of a prophet!" Mahmoud said. "I never thought I would see you leave your battles to a child."

Mahmoud's blows with the staff would carry far less sting than his indictment. Dawit hoped he would not one day wish he had heeded Mahmoud. Fana had unpredictable weaknesses, and Michel's mind arts far outmatched hers. Yet, she had nearly killed Michel when she saw through his mortal disguise and realized how he had tricked her. Fana could protect herself. He prayed so.

"Where did you see Wendimu?" Dawit said, choosing a softer topic.

"I was looking for Khaldun in caves in Pakistan. A mystic's dream led me there." Mahmoud might be more a prisoner to Khaldun than any of their Brothers, fueled by rage as he searched for answers from the man he had once worshipped.

"So remote?" Dawit said. "Wendimu came to lay a trap for you, then."

Mahmoud twirled his staff and pounded it on the floor with a *crack*. "I dearly hope so."

Mahmoud yanked on his mask. He was ready to enter the Circle.

Talking to Mahmoud before the match had been a mistake. Mahmoud's combat arts sharpened with strong emotions, and his claims of the defections might be a ruse. No weapon was illicit in Mahmoud's mind. His strategies began well outside the Circle.

"How many have gone to Michel?" Dawait said again, to be certain.

YOU WILL BLEED, BROTHER, Mahmoud's thought came. Mahmoud bowed low, his chin to his knees. Dawit returned his bow, accepting his challenge.

Their staffs would speak for them.

Time passed slowly in the Circle. It might have been a mortal's twenty minutes, it might have been an hour. Dawit and Mahmoud glistened with perspiration and blood, grunting beneath each teeth-jarring blow across his shoulders, knees, temples, and knuckles. Dawit's arms were raw from the effort of absorbing the impacts of Mahmoud's sure staff.

They blocked more blows than they landed. Mahmoud was Dawit's mirror.

When Dawit swept left, Mahmoud's staff was there to meet it. If Dawit ducked and thrust, Mahmoud parried. Neither of them was fluid enough in mind arts to trust mental cues as much as they trusted their eyes, or their years of history in the Circle. They leaped at each other from the large ascending blocks at the Circle's rear, landing blows as they flew from the perches.

They had fought together too often, either as adversaries in the Circle or allies on the battlefield. At Adwa, the first time they had faced the Sanctus Cruor sect that had birthed Michel, they had used their emptied rifles like staffs, bedazzling mortals with their speed before they split their skulls. They had made a game of it, one hypnotizing an Italian soldier with theatrics while the other swung from behind. Italian Cricket, they had called it.

This match was less a game. Dawit's hands sopped with perspiration as his staff rang against his palm with each *clack*. Dawit was attuned to Mahmoud's darting and ducking, every successful strike a victory to race his heart. Blood ran into his eye from a cut above his forehead, but he barely felt the sting.

Spectators had arrived. Mahmoud was as popular a Circle warrior as Dawit had once been. Above them, hisses signaled displeasure when Dawit struck a blow, and cheerful clucks when Mahmoud bested him. At least a dozen of his Brothers must be in the upper circle.

For the first time since Michel had driven his family from Washington State, Dawit's spirit sang.

He was home again.

Then, the instant of perfection was over. A gong sounded from the edge of the Circle.

"I call a draw!" a voice said. Hagos.

At first, in the fever of battle, Mahmoud didn't hear the gong's low call. Dawit ceremoniously dropped his staff, raising his hands, and Mahmoud's staff stopped its swing only a centimeter from Dawit's nose. Mahmoud's control was impressive, as always.

There was loud hissing from above.

"Nonsense!" Mahmoud roared, breathless. He ripped off his mask and strode to Hagos, who stood a head taller. "You've no right! Why did you stop the match?"

Matches might last at least a mortal's day before a restless spectator called a draw. Dawit had strained with every moment, but to his Brothers the match had just begun.

Their traditions were now ghosts, to be honored or ignored as they chose.

Hagos was masked and armed with gloves and slippers fitted with customary seven-inch blades on the backs of his palms and at each big toe. A Gloves and Slippers match meant lost digits, or limbs. Dawit knew that Hagos meant to punish him. Hagos had railed that Dawit's family should be expelled from the colony.

Hagos's bald head gleamed in the light from the Circle. When a Life Brother was beheaded, he lost his hair and memories when his head re-formed on the stump. Memories returned with coaxing, but not hair. Hagos had undergone the beheading ritual twice.

Hagos's eyes smoldered as he stared. "Dawit." He named his opponent.

"Dawit has no obligation to accept!" Mahmoud said.

"I accept." Dawit squeezed Mahmoud's shoulder. "Another day for us, Mahmoud."

Mahmoud glanced at him with surprise and anger. But he understood. To refuse the match was cowardice, though it was a match Dawit would rather avoid. He and Mahmoud rarely sparred with Gloves and Slippers. But Hagos relished pain, and would relish inflicting it more.

WEAR A COLLAR, Mahmoud whispered to Dawit, his head close to pass the thought.

Dawit left the Circle to suit up in the rows of weapons in a compartment beyond the Circle.

The collection held most handheld weapons except firearms: spears of all lengths, Zulu assegai knives, and dozens of variations of rods, blades, and batons.

The blades in Gloves and Slippers were an alloy created in the House of Science, three times sharper and stronger than carbon steel. Double-edged and serrated. A wondrous weapon. Dawit considered a small shield and iron wrist guards, but decided not to carry the extra weight. He would risk Hagos's blows. He did not glance toward the cumbersome metal neck guard Mahmoud called a collar. He would not give Hagos the satisfaction.

Hagos stood close behind him, breathing hot breath as Dawit fitted on his pointed slippers. His rudeness made Dawit want to kick back and stab him in the gut. In time.

"Will you call your girl-child to protect you?" Hagos taunted.

"Ease your nerves, Brother. We will be alone in the Circle."

He saw the strong image in Hagos's mind: crimson oozing from Brother Kaleb's eyes, nose, and mouth as he lay dead in the pool of blood Fana had drained from him. Fana had acted reflexively; she'd only been three, after all. Kaleb had provoked Fana by attacking Jessica with a sword while a horrified Fana stood witness.

Dawit couldn't help his glow of pride in the power Fana wielded.

Aside from Khaldun's Ritual of Death—a mental practice he claimed to have used only twice in a thousand years—Kaleb had been the first with their Blood to die. His Brothers were still smarting from their newfound vulnerability in Fana. But most feared Michel more.

"You have too much hair, Dawit," Hagos said. "I will see you bald."

Dawit ignored the taunting as he walked back to the Circle, instead sifting through his memories of Hagos's past matches so vividly that he could see them. Hagos had great agility and speed, but he was not as ambidextrous as Dawit, or as fast. He favored blows and kicks from his right side. And Hagos was lazy in his mind arts.

Dawit would have to trust his mental skill as much as his eyes, or he might lose his head today. He had no time for a long debilitation. Fana needed him.

At the edge of the Circle, Dawit bowed low to Hagos.

Hagos pushed past his bow, slicing Dawit's upper right arm on his way, drawing a bright string of blood. Dawit had not been cut so deeply by a knife in years, and the pain startled him, flaring when he flexed his arm.

The spectators hissed at Hagos. Some rituals still mattered, apparently. Without his meditations with Fana, Dawit might have been angry at such an insult. But, unlike Mahmoud, anger was not his friend in a battle; he had suffered his worst heartaches and defeats when his emotions roiled most. Dawit smiled instead. *I am the better fighter,* he told himself, holding the thought close.

He hoped so, anyway.

Dawit met Hagos in the Circle's bright light.

Facing Hagos, Dawit remembered Khaldun's first lesson when he and his Brothers had awakened with the new Blood in their veins: *Your Blood makes you longer-lived than ordinary men, but you are still men. You are not stronger than ordinary men. You will hurt and bleed like ordinary men. You will heal, but healing takes time. Do not expect to be gods.*

He wished he had not fought with Mahmoud first, or with such vigor. Dawit was alarmed at his own sluggishness. At first, he seemed to be only watching Hagos spring around him as he tested for weaknesses, his gloves' blades pinwheeling close to Dawit's face and belly. Hagos's sweeping kick toward his groin came within two inches of slicing Dawit's most tender region, an indignity he had avoided in five centuries of life. Dawit's legs and arms were leaden, and Hagos was fresh. Even the wound on his arm throbbed enough to distract him.

His mind arts were a disappointment, too. Most of Hagos's thoughts were incoherent, and the signals often came too late. Hagos fought by instinct, not strategy.

NECK, a thought came through, and Dawit ducked in time to avoid an assured swipe with Hagos's right hand that might have been strong enough to behead him. The spectators clucked, excited, another distraction. Their thoughts would attract others, and Dawit was already struggling to stay focused on Hagos. How did Fana tolerate her heightened sensitivity?

Dawit's mental clumsiness cost him. While he fumbled with Hagos's thoughts, a blade suddenly pierced him to the bone just above his knee, unheralded. The pain was so dazzling that his leg nearly buckled.

Dawit yanked his flesh free from the blade, slashing an X across Hagos's bare chest before he leaped away with the strength of his uninjured leg. When he landed several meters away, the soles of

Dawit's slippers whined against the blood spotting the Circle's floor. His pierced leg was numb in places, afire in others.

Hagos charged.

Finish him, Dawit thought. His mind went as placid as the waters of Miami's Biscayne Bay, which he imagined during meditation.

The approving clicks and clucks from his Brothers vanished as the room went silent. Hagos's chaotic thoughts, too, went silent. All Dawit heard was his own steady heartbeat, slowing even as it strengthened. His flesh vanished, too, taking his pain away.

Images appeared in sudden flashes of bright light: Hagos's right arm hooking toward him. The flash of the sinister blade on Hagos's right foot.

Dawit watched Hagos's spectacular, spinning midair flip, as if he had taken flight. Saw the luminous tip of Hagos's blade nearly rake his eyes.

Dawit rolled, springing and leaping as soon as his feet found the floor. Calmly, he noted that he was behind Hagos when he landed. His eyes fixed on the brown skin at the nape of his opponent's neck. To Dawit's perception, Hagos stood as still as a monument.

No one will harm my daughter, Dawit thought. *No one will harm my family again.*

Dawit did not recognize the yell that spilled from his lips. He spun toward Hagos with both arms outstretched, his twin blades blurred as he snapped them like scissors.

A wet *thunk* at his feet, like a tumbled melon, told Dawit that the match was over. He saw Mahmoud's delighted grin beyond the Circle, through the void between Hagos's hulking shoulders. Then Hagos's headless torso slumped to the floor.

This time, Dawit mused, his Brother might be luckier.

Perhaps he would wake up with a full head of hair.

Sixteen

The tires of Johnny Wright's ATV whirred over a pile of gravel on the winding, polished-stone path, skidding, and the Lalibela Colony sprawled above and below him as he drifted toward the ravine. The vehicle righted itself with a tap from Johnny's thumb on the handlebar controls, as sensitive as a nerve-controlled artificial limb.

The colony had three levels, each two or three stories high, and the oval courtyard below was at least the size of a football field. Like a giant beehive, or an ant colony, but without the activity, Johnny thought. It always looked deserted, most of the immortals out of sight.

The lighting was bright, like midday sunshine, so Johnny slipped on his shades. The colony never had night, and he had never missed the dark so much. Johnny's watch was still set to Southern California, so it was the middle of the night for him.

Like an immortal, Johnny didn't sleep much these days. He was bone tired, but the nightmares in his waking hours kept him from going to sleep.

Dawit had warned Johnny to stay away from the House of Science, but they needed news about a vaccine or an antidote. Then they needed to pray there was time to flush it into the Glow network. Suddenly, the Glow network seemed to exist for no other reason than to give people a chance to survive the Big One.

He and Caitlin didn't rely on anyone else to make sure the House of Science was cooperating, and not in immortal time. Fana vanished into meditation for six hours straight, trying to be ready for Michel one day.

When Johnny rounded the bend, he saw two men approaching in animated conversation. Amharic? Arabic? Their voices were too soft to tell. Dawit had advised him to avoid direct contact with immortals he did not know.

These two men quieted as they neared him, but they didn't slow their pace. Johnny coaxed his ATV to a careful stop on the narrow path, brushing his knee against the smooth, blood-colored stone wall to allow them to pass. His heart sped as he pasted a polite smile on his lips. If one of them decided to give him a friendly shove over the side, it was a long way down to the rock garden, where a clawlike stone spindle would skewer him.

Like all the immortals here, they walked nude. Johnny averted his eyes as the two men approached him in a cloud of thick cologne. Scented baths were a religion here.

One man seemed to return his smile when he glanced at them, so Johnny grinned more widely. Damn—a mistake. They stopped walking, towered above him; one in front of him, one behind. Their gazes were heavy enough to carry weight.

"Good morning," Johnny said, a nervous reflex. Who knew if they spoke English? And that greeting was meaningless in a place with no day or night.

The man in front of him looked like a pro wrestler, squat and thick-muscled. Johnny gripped his handlebars. He kept his smile, but he would mow over this guy if he made a sudden move. On such a narrow path, he didn't have room for diplomacy.

Just try it, Johnny thought. Johnny hoped he was a HiTel, and he'd gotten the message.

The squat man wrinkled his face and made an exaggerated sniffing sound for his friend, and they both chuckled. Johnny didn't need a translator to tell him they thought he stank like a mortal. They walked on, still laughing and almost surely talking about him. They hadn't been taunting him—he could have been an animal at the zoo.

Glad to entertain you, Johnny thought. *At least I don't smell like I fell into a vat of Polo.*

The immortals seemed to laugh more loudly. Johnny tapped his accelerator and raced on.

Only a few more days, he told himself. Fana wanted to spend some time with her teacher and her mother, and then they would all go up to the real world to get back to healing. Johnny didn't think he could get used to the Lalibela Colony if he had a lifetime.

It had been a year since Fana and her family had first brought him to Lalibela, but the immortals had never let him and Caitlin forget that they were mortals. Caitlin hated the word "mortals"— she said it was like "nigger." Almost every immortal they met, even the ones in Fana's circle, gave him and Caitlin looks as if to say, *What are* YOU *doing here, monkey?*

Now *that* word, *monkey,* had more than a ring of "nigger" to it. Johnny had heard it only once, muttered under Berhanu's breath, but once was enough. And Berhanu was on *his* side. Caitlin said she got it worse because she was a female, and no woman had lived there in more than five hundred years. And Fana's last visit with Jessica had been a disaster.

The founder of the colony had forbidden female immortals, Fana had told him, because he didn't want them to reproduce and dominate mortals. But why create Michel and the others?

The Lalibela Council had chosen his housing, so he and Caitlin had two large, spare rooms at the end of West Hell while everyone else got to live one level higher, closer to Fana. His room was twice as big and airy as a New York loft apartment, but it was empty and lifeless. It looked like a cave; all it was missing was real bats.

That's why he'd gotten himself a Batmobile. Dawit had built it for him, probably because Fana had pressured him—and it looked like the real-world version of an ATV, except it didn't use gas. The Batmobile was always on, and never made a sound. Dawit had explained the intricacies of the power source, which was the same as that which powered the globe that perpetually shone above them, something Dawit had called "solar transfusion." Although Johnny had been premed at Berkeley and thought he knew his science, he'd mostly nodded his head and felt stupid. The Life Brothers kept technologies lying around like spare change.

He could learn so much, if he could slow down. If the immortals would share more.

Why wouldn't Fana give him the Blood? Sometimes, Johnny's frustration emerged as anger. He had asked her on two occasions, even if he'd pretended that the first time had been a joke. Fana did everything in her own time and way, but she should have offered him the Blood a long time ago. There was a ceremony that could turn mortals into immortals. He shouldn't have had to ask, and she'd been selfish to deny him. Fana didn't have to care what the Lalibela Council thought, or anyone else—even Michel.

Especially Michel.

Hadn't he proven himself? Like Doc Shepard, he had risked his life to help heal with the Blood. And he wasn't confused about the Blood like Doc Shepard and his wife, Alex, who were always bent over a microscope, looking for answers in the red cells, platelets, and leukocytes. *Because they seeing see not, and they hearing hear not,* just like it said in Matthew.

Johnny and Fana's mother prayed together and talked sometimes, when Jessica was in the mood for praying or talking. And that's when she'd told him: Fana wasn't sure she believed her blood was from Christ, or that Christ had been anything except another immortal.

If Fana wasn't a believer, she couldn't recognize Michel, either. But Johnny didn't need to meditate his days away to know who Michel was. Maybe Fana didn't *want* to see it, because then she would have to remember the Book of Revelation:

Who is like unto the beast? Who is able to make war with him?

Johnny felt a chill despite the colony's temperate air.

When he saw the narrow cavern that housed the steps, he stopped his Batmobile again.

Time to start walking.

Johnny could smell the House of Science long before it was in sight. Unlike the rest of the colony he'd toured, the House of Science smelled *green.* Damp. Alive. A bird's subdued warbling reminded him to turn left at a fork in the passageway, so he trudged on, his way lighted by glowing globes on sconces.

The walk took a solid hour. Johnny's shirt was wet with perspiration from climbing the steps. He'd tried to pace himself, but three hundred steps were three hundred steps. Thank God the passage was saturated with oxygen from the foliage growing ahead. Johnny gulped at the air.

The passage opened up, and suddenly Johnny was in the folds of a jungle, moist soil sucking at his shoes. Doc Shepard had nicknamed this space the Rainforest, saying it reminded him of the rain forest in Peru, where he'd studied plants years ago.

Johnny was dwarfed beneath fifty-foot trees and colorful, big-leafed plants that were a botanist's paradise. One had broad, waving leaves that looked like human hands in startling purple, snapping shut at intervals like a Venus flytrap. Rust-orange shoots of grass stood ten feet tall. One neon plant draped itself over the trees like netting, as delicate and intricate as a spider's web. Like the animals he sometimes spotted in the House of Science, the plants were a combination of known breeds, past and present, and hybrids unique to the Lalibela Colony.

Something rustled near him, and Johnny tensed. He never knew what kind of creature would come crashing out of the brush here, but a glint of silver told him that it was only a tiny mechanical camera on legs, shooting up the tree trunk to broadcast his arrival. The immortals called them Spiders. Once he noticed one, Johnny counted a half dozen scurrying within sight. Spiders seemed to follow him, especially in the House of Science.

The immortals treasured their secrets.

The Rainforest was only the foyer in the House of Science, the equivalent of potted plants and a magazine rack in a doctor's waiting room. Doc Shepard and Alex had been invited beyond this area twice, but Johnny never had. Returning, they had described an amazing information system that was part voice, part holograms. Antigravity chambers. And an arsenal that would give the DOD nightmares. The House of Science was one more benefit he would receive only after he had the Blood.

"Hello?" he called out. "Is Yacob here?"

Doc Shepard had told him to speak only to Yacob, not that anyone else would respond. Yacob was one of the few Lalibela immortals who treated them with courtesy, since he'd lived among mortals and was a self-proclaimed "mortalphile."

A sharp tug at Johnny's right pant leg and a blur of gray fur made him cry out, panicked. The creature was small, but it was fast. Johnny's eyes could barely track the furry tail as the creature flew to a branch on a tree five feet from Johnny's face.

It was only a chatter monkey, he realized when he took in the animal's bony limbs and wide, childlike eyes. But this wasn't a monkey from the real world: this was a genetically engineered monkey with a squirrel's full, plumelike tail and a human's opposable thumbs. They were roughly the size of squirrel monkeys, or lemurs. Johnny was partly enchanted by the creatures, partly repelled. The furless, oval faces looked far too human.

And then there was the talking.

"Yacob!" the creature chattered at him. Almost perfect speech. A newcomer might not hear the distinct sounds forming the word, but Johnny did.

"Is Yacob here?" Johnny said. He always felt foolish talking to the bright-eyed monkeys; they seemed to have the mental capacities of a four-year-old. If not for Michel and the virus, he would have been awestruck.

"Yacob come!" the monkey said, and bounded into the treetops, vanishing.

"Tell him it's . . . urgent." Johnny's voice trailed off. Judging from the swaying treetops ahead, the monkey wasn't listening anymore. And they did only what amused them, so he'd learned the hard way that they weren't reliable receptionists.

The talking monkeys reminded Johnny of the singing frog from the old Warner Bros. cartoon. He imagined himself stealing one to get rich, only to be humiliated when it refused to make a sound after the curtain rose. He'd had a similar experience when he tried to coax one to talk for Caitlin: silence and those big *who, me?* eyes.

Hell, the chatter monkeys were better off with the immortals. Would their lives improve once they were introduced to the world outside? The thought made Johnny shudder.

Immediacy was a foreign concept at the Lalibela Colony, so it might be a long wait. Johnny was looking for a dry stump on which to sit down and rest when Yacob appeared from a shadow, as if from nowhere, dressed in a white lab coat. A tangle of hidden passageways beneath the surface gave the illusion that immortals could teleport themselves. Maybe they could.

Yacob looked about thirty, an older appearance than most immortals', with a handlebar mustache that reminded Johnny of a sheriff in a bad Western. He had full cheeks and large teeth. Johnny took a step toward Yacob.

In more light, the illusion shattered.

Johnny was face-to-face only with Yacob's visage, lifelike except for a mild haziness that obscured fine detail. He should have known that Yacob would never wear a lab coat; he'd only made himself appear that way as a courtesy. Yacob didn't smile as he usually did. Maybe it was only a lazy projection, but his face didn't look friendly today.

"You should not be here," Yacob said. "I've told you this, John. The council—"

"Doc Shepard said you would help me," Johnny said. "Help *us*. I'm sure you've heard."

Yacob, through his visage, sighed. "I'm so very sorry. We are aghast at Alem."

"All due respect, but we don't need hand-wringing. We need allies." The sharpness in his own voice surprised Johnny. "Do you have a cure? A vaccine? Doc Shepard and Alex are still waiting to hear something in Nigeria. It could flare up anywhere, Yacob."

"Dawit has spoken to me," Yacob said.

"It started here," Johnny said. "So you can fight it."

Yacob spoke in a frustrated rush. "Some records are missing, it seems, and the tissue samples Dawit brought are useless to me. The virus mutates once it reproduces, to prevent decoding. Michel has altered it. It's a damnable puzzle, which leaves me with millions of viruses to study in virtual darkness. I am extrapolating what I can, but I can only report my findings to Dawit and Fana. You cannot envision the furor you cause every time you leave footprints here, John. Our science is sacrosanct to us."

Johnny's teeth tightened. "Your science is about to exterminate us."

Yacob's visage went silent. He couldn't deny it. No wonder Yacob had sent his visage—Yacob didn't want to be seen with him. Yacob's figure was already growing fainter. Johnny could barely see Yacob's eyes anymore.

An invisible creature shrieked from the treetops, a sound that was half laugh, half crazed scream. Not one of the monkeys.

"Yacob, please wait," Johnny said, but the visage was gone. *Damn.* He hadn't climbed three hundred steps to talk to a monkey and an optical illusion.

The side of Johnny's belt vibrated, and he reached for his video pager. Caitlin's face waited for him on his four-inch video screen. Caitlin was always pale, but her face looked painted in white chalk. Had she overheard?

"Have you seen CNN?" Caitlin said before he could ask. "The newswebs?"

Johnny's bones froze beneath his skin, and his heart's hammering dizzied him. He didn't want to guess, or his words might make the worst happen. "Another outbreak?"

Were those *tears* in her eyes? Johnny had seen Caitlin cry only once.

"Phoenix and her family are missing," Caitlin said. "Her kid, too. It's our fault, Johnny. I knew that concert was a bad idea. Your music star's been ghosted."

The video screen clicked dark.

Caitlin was outside Fana's antechamber, hugging herself as she leaned against the wall, waiting. Johnny smelled the last of the cigarettes she'd been smoking. Several crushed butts ringed her feet on the floor. Johnny was breathless from running most of the way. The stitch in his side was a knife's blade.

"I don't understand," Johnny gasped to Caitlin. "The security guys emailed last night—"

"I got the same email, but someone's gaming us," she said. "The neighbor said she's been gone *two days*. I just called the lady on my sat phone to confirm it." Johnny looked at his watch, which displayed six time zones. It was four a.m. in California.

Caitlin went on. "Their kids were supposed to go to a movie the day before yesterday, but nobody's home. The house is empty. She has a key, and she said it looks like they left in a hurry, a huge mess. And a bunch of weird tire tracks. Like trucks. Phoenix's cousin was the one who went public. I saw her on CNN. She said Phoenix would never take off without letting her know. She's scared shitless."

An image assaulted Johnny's memory: a blood-painted wall. Johnny had made the gruesome discovery in Arizona last year. The last family that had tried to help them distribute Glow had died, drained of their blood in their sleep. Murdered by Michel.

"Caitlin, was there—?"

Caitlin waved her hand to cut off his question. "The neighbor didn't see anything else." She didn't want to talk about the blood or the dead family.

Thank God. Maybe Phoenix was still alive.

Grating stringed music floated from inside Fana's antechamber, where a musician always played for her. Fana said the music helped her meditate, but the monotonous, high-pitched plucking pecked at Johnny's temples, tightening them into a headache.

"Does Fana know?" Johnny said.

"I doubt it. She's with Teka."

"Why are you still out here?"

"Why do you think?" Caitlin said, gesturing with her chin. "We're on IT now." Immortal Time. Johnny followed her gesture until he saw the profile of Fana's guardian, Fasilidas, posted inside the doorway. "I can't find Dawit to get past him."

"What about Fana's mom?"

Caitlin's face clouded. "What about her?"

A knowing gaze passed between them. Johnny had volunteered at Tallahassee Memorial when he was in high school, and he'd recognized the same vacant look in Jessica's eyes as he saw in the eyes of hard-core meth and freeze addicts. Part manic, part walking dead. Maybe she'd had a nervous breakdown.

"I'll go try to talk to her," Johnny said.

"Don't bother. Maybe Fasilidas will listen to a man."

Not likely. With a sigh, Johnny tugged on the woven silk rope to ring the bell posted outside Fana's chamber. The discordant sound echoed around them. The bell was a formality—Fasilidas was only yards away, and as a HiTel he could hear their thoughts anyway—but maybe it would help. All official visitors to Fana were expected to ring the bell.

Fasilidas stepped outside to face them, nude except for a baton-like weapon strapped to his solid thigh. His head was shaved bald, and his skin was midnight black. Johnny saw Caitlin's eyes appreciating Fasilidas despite herself. Fasilidas looked like a model and an Olympian in one, smooth skinned and ripped. Caitlin had once joked that if she ever decided to try men again, Fasilidas was at the top of her list.

Johnny envied Fasilidas for his proximity to Fana day and night, his mental powers, his Blood—even his looks and obvious physicality. If not for Michel, would Fana choose Fasilidas? Despite the way Fasilidas worshipped Fana like a queen, they were more equal. More kindred. Sometimes Johnny's envy felt so much like hatred that it filled him with shame.

Johnny hoped his worries about the plague and Phoenix buried the feelings Fasilidas brought out in him, but he couldn't hide such strong emotions from a HiTel any more than he could from himself. And why should Fasilidas care? Johnny was just a talking monkey.

"We must see Fana right away," Johnny said, trying to muster the firm indignation he had with Yacob's visage. "We have news she would want to know."

"Fana already knows all she *must* know," Fasilidas said. His voice was barely above a whisper. Johnny had to strain to hear him. "She *wants* to know nothing more. She is taking no visitors except her teacher. Her instructions were clear."

Caitlin chuffed with annoyance. She'd had this conversation before.

Fasilidas's voice came to Johnny's head: *YOU CANNOT PROJECT THOUGHTS, BUT I MUST ASK YOU TO SPEAK SOFTLY SO*

CLOSE TO FANA'S CHAMBER. SHE HAS ASKED FOR PEACE . . .
AND PEACE SHE SHALL HAVE.

Irritation sparked in Fasilidas's steady eyes.

Johnny's throat closed in on itself, dry and tight, and the feeling calcified to his chest. He couldn't sway Fasilidas. He couldn't fight him.

Caitlin was rubbing the back of his arm with unusual gentleness. Her touch reminded him of their days at Berkeley, before Glow. He suddenly missed his life, his ignorance. He wondered what his parents were doing at that instant. Had they heard about Phoenix yet?

He and his parents had seen a Phoenix concert when he was a kid, about ten, the one time they had all enjoyed an artist with equal fervor. He'd missed a day of school so that they could drive two hours to Jacksonville to see her show, and they had sung "Party Patrol" all the way home. It was the first time he'd seen his mother laugh since her father had died in Jordan.

You see? She touched a ghost, his mother kept saying, passing her certainty to them like delicate whorls of cotton candy. *Death is only a new beginning.*

The music in the antechamber stopped abruptly, and the silence made Johnny turn again. Fasilidas was in a deep bow.

At first, Johnny thought the mighty immortal was bowing to him.

Seventeen

How could I not have known? How could I not have noticed?

YOU ARE NOT A RADIO RECEIVER, FANA, Teka said. *YOU DO NOT KNOW ALL.*

Fana and her teacher were face-to-face on her meditation pillows, their usual pose. She could always travel farther when her teacher was close enough to lead her with his breath.

Even with the soft pillow beneath her, Fana's body felt weighted down after such an abrupt release from Teka. His streams were a gentle trickle, and now Fana had been yanked to the rapids outside. The noise.

At least it was pleasant to wake to Teka's face. Her teacher was the only person Fana knew whose face captured his essence: a perfect mirror for his wisdom and kindness. He had never killed anyone. He seemed to have a thousand-year-old spirit, but he was only half that old, the same age as her father. The one deception was his youth: Teka looked only eighteen.

Fana closed her eyes.

How will I face him if I can be so easily surprised? Fana asked her teacher.

EXPECT SURPRISES, Teka said. *HE WILL SURPRISE YOU IN EVERY WAY.*

Maybe her father had been right. It had been a mistake to involve Phoenix, no matter how much more healing she could spread on the wings of Phoenix's music. She never should have agreed to hire a mortal security firm to protect Phoenix. She should have sacrificed Berhanu for Phoenix, or Fasilidas. A Life Brother would not have failed.

UNLESS MICHEL TOOK HER, Teka reminded her.

Why would Michel take Phoenix? Only to get her attention again?

"Hel-lo?" Caitlin's voice said, harsh and grating to her ears. "Come back to us, Fana."

Vaguely, Fana saw Johnny and Caitlin standing over her, their features obscured in too-bright light. "Sorry," Fana said, shielding her eyes. "I trance out."

She expected Teka to still be sitting with her on the mound of pillows, but her teacher was now far across the room, his eyes appraising her potted palms as he stood with his hands behind his back to wait for an end to the interruption. When had he gotten up?

Teka had been helping her learn how to lift her physical body from the floor with her mental stream, a basic levitation, maybe an inch or two from the ground. To Michel, that would be child's play. The last time she'd levitated had been a year ago, when he'd fooled her into kissing him. Their feet had floated effortlessly from the floor.

Fana wanted to learn how to float. It was one more thing he knew that she didn't.

In meditation, Fana had been floating in an empty space, alone except for Teka's whispered presence, feeling herself rising toward a warm, pulsing light. But hazy, sometimes hidden in mist. Then Fana had seen the bright, oval orb—so, so far above her, but in sight!—when she'd heard Caitlin and Johnny pleading with Fasilidas to let them into her room, something about Phoenix.

YOU'RE VERY CLOSE, Teka had said. IGNORE THE VOICES.

But how could she?

Fana had felt herself falling, the light gone long before she had touched it. Her body had not moved from the large spongy pillow, molded to her shape. She realized that six hours had passed since the start of their meditation! Teka argued that Fana's nearly infallible internal clock worked against deeper meditative states; a part of her was always marking the time.

Peculiar hot electricity shuddered through her as Johnny grabbed her hand to get her attention. Startled, she pulled her hand away. She'd felt something like it only once before, with Michel. Johnny had learned that a touch could pull her from her mind's hypnotic song.

"You back now?" Johnny said. His eyes were close to hers. He must have just come from the House of Science; she smelled exotic plants and flowers on his clothes. His skin was perfumed with rich, fertile soil.

"Sorry," she said to Johnny's eyes. "I was under pretty deep this time."

"Yes," Teka said, a mild rebuke in his voice. "Fana's lessons are of paramount importance before her journey, wouldn't you agree?"

Please let me tell them in my own way, Teka, she told him.

But Johnny and Caitlin were too agitated over Phoenix to wonder what Teka meant. Besides, they didn't understand the true stakes—Teka was trying to light her way through the Rising so she would be armed against Michel and the power he drew from the Shadows. The Rising was like carrying water, using her will to gain power. The Shadows were more like *being* carried, where will was easily lost.

Michel had been nursing on the Shadows for fifty years, and she'd been hiding from them since she was three, afraid of their power over her. She didn't know nearly enough. But she would have to reach out to Michel. Find his thoughtstreams. Today.

Suddenly Fana understood why her mother would not trade her daughter for millions of lives. Fana had postponed contact with Michel to visit her mother and spend time with her teacher, even with many more lives at risk—but for Phoenix, she would not wait. Were some lives more important than others? Who should have the power to choose?

Johnny and Caitlin were speaking to her in what sounded like staccato gunfire.

"Three employees are missing from the security company," Caitlin said. "They were posted near Phoenix's property, and they're gone too."

"It sounds like the government took her," Johnny said. "DHS snatched my mother the same way, to pressure my father into giving me up last year."

"If that's true, they're using her to try to get to us," Caitlin said. "Why else would they risk ghosting someone with such a high profile?"

"And she doesn't even know anything," Johnny said, his voice weighted with sadness.

"They don't know that," Caitlin said.

It was time to tell them. She wished she had told Johnny sooner.

"It may not be the government," Fana said. "Michel might be sending a message to me. Like he did with the outbreaks. He's reaching to his fiancée."

She looked directly at Johnny's eyes when she said *fiancée*, knowing that her status pained him, hoping to prepare him. Caitlin would not accept her plan any more than Johnny or her mother, but Fana would be sadder to leave Johnny. With Johnny, she was not leaving their past—she was erasing their future. Her own future.

She said none of it aloud, gave him no whispers in his thoughts. But he knew. The horror of his knowledge flamed in his eyes.

"Fana . . . ?" Johnny said. She felt the thrumming of his heartbeat, with no idea if the air was stirring between them or if she was creeping beneath his skin without trying.

"I need quiet now," Fana said. "I'll try to see if Phoenix is still alive."

"What will you do about Michel?" Johnny prodded. "If it's him?"

Fana stared at her lap, at her calmly clasped hands.

"Wait," Caitlin said, stepping closer to her. She crouched to try to meet Fana's eyes. "You're not . . . communicating with him, are you?"

IT'S BEST IF I LEAVE YOU FOR A WHILE, Teka said.

Johnny and Caitlin didn't notice her teacher slip discreetly out of the room.

Fana remembered her father's cool logic, his stories of diplomacy between kingdoms. She thought of the pain blanketing Michel's village of the dead, and the bewildered left behind. She even thought of the Letter of the Witness, written by the two-thousand-year-old man who had paved the way for her unlikely birth: *And they shall be known as the bringers of the Blood . . .*

"I have to go to Michel," she said. "I can't wait ten years. His plagues won't wait."

Fana expected them to explode with arguments, but only silence filled the room. And what a silence! Their thoughts, which had whirled in the room like mosquitoes, were so focused that they were nearly silent, too. Their silence landed on her like heavy bricks.

Caitlin hugged her stomach, tears streaking her red face.

Fana could not look at Johnny at all.

So Fana closed her eyes instead, remembering Teka's uplifting presence so soon before, and felt her mind fly high above the constraints of her room, high above the Lalibela Colony, upworld and beyond. She sought out the light of the Rising, a mere pinprick above her, a half-formed starburst, but it was in sight. Despite the haze, she was getting better at finding it.

The squall of noise as she tried to follow the light nearly took her breath away. How could she find Phoenix in the storm of the world?

Don't wanna die for a while
I think I'll fly for a while . . .

The music lifted her, carrying her probe like a balloon flying in the wind, just as it had at the concert. Fana heard tinkled strains and a voice almost soft enough to be her imagination. Almost. Singing! Somewhere, Phoenix was singing, even if it was only in her sleep.

Fana opened her eyes to Johnny's somber face, only a foot from hers. She smiled for him, sharing her joy. "She's alive! I feel her. I don't know where yet . . . but she's still alive."

Johnny accepted her report, nodding. He was sitting cross-legged in front of her, in Teka's place on the pillows.

To the others, ten minutes had passed, Fana realized. She smelled Caitlin's cigarette smoke, but Caitlin was gone. She and Johnny were alone.

"Where's Caitlin?" Fana said.

"Went to find your father. She doesn't believe you're you anymore." Johnny's voice might have been dug from a deep, grimy well.

Fana finally realized that her cheek was stinging. Or, rather, that it *had* been. She touched her face, confused.

"She slapped you and cussed you out first," Johnny said. "She thinks you're Michel. Or he's in there somewhere pulling your strings. She took it badly when you zoned like that."

"Oh," Fana said. "I was looking for Phoenix."

He nodded with the same blank acceptance. "I tried to tell her."

"Do you still think I'm still me?" she said. Fana didn't think she could bear it if Johnny thought Michel had taken her over, that she was gone already.

Johnny shrugged. Then he sighed, wearied from the effort of lifting his shoulders. "I guess so." His eyes were glassy red. He'd done his crying while she was gone. "Sounds like something you'd do. A crazy idea about helping other people no matter what."

"There's no other way, Johnny."

"Yeah there is, Fana," he said. "You know there is."

For a fleeting instant, Johnny's thoughts were so focused that a formless murmur congealed into crude, growling words: *FIGHT HIM.*

"I heard that," Fana said. She couldn't help smiling. "You've never done that before."

"Done what?"

"You just projected a thought to me."

"What was it?" Johnny only wanted her to say it aloud, where she would hear its weight.

"You want me to do something I can't do," she said. "The last resort."

Johnny's jaw hardened. "If not now . . . when?"

When there's nothing left, she told him. *When I'm ready to die and lose everyone I love.*

"Isn't going back to him the same thing?" Johnny said.

Fana shook her head. "If I believed that, I wouldn't go. Just because we can't see the whole path doesn't mean it isn't there, Johnny. Faith is a hard walk. You know that. You came here on an act of faith, leaving your family. Your whole world. I have to do the same thing."

"I came here to heal," he said. "He wants you to help him kill."

"I'll stay in control of my beliefs, Johnny."

"Most of the time? Some of the time? Maybe," Johnny said. "But not always. You're lying to yourself about who and what he is."

Johnny's doubts lanced Fana so deeply that she had to take a breath. Knowledge was hiding in her that she still wasn't ready to see.

But she couldn't keep living with paralysis in the face of Michel's superior gifts. Michel didn't *want* to control her the way he had ridden Johnny and the others, or he would have already. Michel's memories had shown her how he hated his father's control of his mother. The Shadows had devoured much of Michel's conscience, but not that. *Not* that.

Fana wanted to pass her belief on to Johnny as a gift, but she couldn't. He would never give her permission to massage his mood, and she wouldn't do it in secret. If she did, how could she expect Michel to respect the sanctity of her thoughts and will?

Instead, Fana leaned closer to Johnny, brushing her face against his scent of life from the garden. Before she realized it, she'd pressed her lips to his, kissing him. Her kiss lingered.

Fana had often thought about kissing Johnny. In her imagination, his lips were not so dry. So firm and unyielding. And the beating pulse in his lips would have been from desire, not the steady drum of fear. In her imagination, his lips hadn't tasted of salt water.

Johnny pulled away. "Don't," he said, his voice agony.

"Wisely spoken," her father's voice said.

Another surprise. Dawit and Fasilidas were watching from her doorway. Fasilidas was muting his disapproval, but not her father. Johnny stood abruptly and walked away from her, hands deep in his pockets, his head down. Johnny's anger was bright and hot.

"Does Michel have your singer?" Dawit said.

I don't know yet, she told her father silently. *But I'll find out.*

Johnny whipped around and took three quick strides to Dawit, giving his shoulders an abrupt shove. "You call yourself her *father*?" Johnny said. "A warrior? She's giving herself to that monster! What the hell are you going to do about it?"

Her father tolerated Johnny's push the way he would have humored a toddler.

Fasilidas bristled at Johnny's disrespect toward the man he considered the Blessed Father, but Fana sent him a mental pulse to keep his distance. This was a private argument.

"I respect my daughter's choice—do the same, youngster," Dawit said. As Fana had hoped, there was compassion in his voice. "Who besides Fana has cause to loathe Michel more than I do? I trust her intuition. Life's machinations are bigger than you or me."

Johnny . . . Fana called to him, but what else could she say to him? She felt such a strong compulsion to massage his emotions that it frightened her. She couldn't interfere with the minds of the people close to her, especially Johnny's. Wouldn't Michel feel the same compulsions with her? He would not treat her better than she treated others.

Johnny did not look back at her before he stormed out of her room.

Fana's mind was blank. Stripped.

Dawit took Johnny's place on the pillow, sitting gently. He held Fana's hands.

"This is grief—what we feel after a death," Dawit said. "Loss. Leaving. I would bear it for you if I could, Fana. It's the bitterest taste of all. I believe this is why Khaldun tried to protect me and my Brothers here. We would lose nothing. Risk nothing. But now we'll never know what we would have been."

Thanks, Dad, Fana said.

Why hadn't she realized how much it would hurt to leave Johnny behind?

Eighteen

A canopy of conifers' spindly needles blotted the sky in deep, soothing green. Filtered light painted crisscrossing mazes against the stoic trunks gathered around Fana like sentries. Remnants of new rain sparkled in the trees, crowns of jewels.

Fana knelt to touch the damp soil's blend of earth, pebbles and dead leaves and twigs melting back to their beginnings. She held the soil to her nose. Breathed it.

Home.

"You miss the woods," he said. Directly behind her.

Fana had allowed herself to forget why she was back in her woods in Washington, in the five-hundred-acre backyard of her childhood home. A year ago, she had made herself forget the sound of his voice, which had been one of his best instruments. His dash of an Italian accent, which sometimes sounded more Hispanic, depending on his mood. The mature, seasoned timbre. Michel's voice was hard to listen to.

She had found her fiancé.

"Yes." Fana answered quickly, even brightly, hoping to compensate for her unwillingness to turn her head and look at him. "I told you, I grew up in the woods. Until I was seventeen, this was all I knew."

There had been her mother's clinic in Botswana, of course, but there wasn't much about those days she wanted to remember. Forgetting was a mercy given the very young. She remembered enough.

"But I don't have to tell you that," Fana said. "You've seen."

"A glance." He sounded closer. He was only a yard behind her. "Too quickly."

Michel had chosen the meeting place because Fana had called for his thoughtstreams, and now Michel had merged them seamlessly, like warm fingers slipping into a glove. He might have allowed her to pull away from him, but she didn't try. She had shut him out too long.

He had found her woods. Fana recognized the pathways in the gaps between the trunks, the fallen branches that smelled like sap, the rings of saplings. In the periphery, she saw the faint lances of orange light that fenced the property, the firefence that should have kept her and her family safe. But not from him.

He was roaming inside her. He saw everything he had burned to the ground.

"I did not set the fire," Michel said. Then he corrected himself. "But, yes, I caused it."

To him, an admission was an apology. He sighed, and this time he sounded farther away. Fana was glad when he retreated. He had promised not to touch her—to *try* not to, she recalled—but he might forget his promise if he was too close to her. She could feel how much he wanted to touch her hair.

"I could appear to you as one of your chatter monkeys," Michel said.

"Too silly," she said, almost smiling. Already, she might think about Michel every time she saw a chatter monkey now. An unwelcome association.

"I don't mind being silly for you," he said.

"No. But thank you for offering."

Would she be this painfully polite in life? Maybe all of Teka's meditation had only been preparing her for banter with Michel. She could have done this a long time ago! If she'd believed she could face him sooner, the plague victims might not have died.

But it would not be this easy in Mexico. Nothing was quite the same in the physical world. The world below was so far away already! No wonder the dead forgot where they had been unless someone called for them, and often even then.

"I won't show myself to you here," he said. "If you prefer."

"Thank you," she said. "That would be helpful."

Fana quickly turned her head, testing him. He kept his word—he was nowhere in sight. Only the trees lined up behind her. The creek bed was swollen with gurgling rain racing toward her house. She could almost see her house's wood planks through the maze of tree trunks.

"Shall I change my voice?" he said on the breeze. "You can hear any voice."

"I'm used to your voice now," she said. "It's all right."

Red hibiscus flowers appeared in the branches, Michel's own creation. She loved hibiscus plants, but they had never grown wild on their property in Washington. Michel gave her a sea of blooms in red, pink, gold, and orange, the colors of dusk.

"I love hibiscus flowers too," Michel said. "But there is sadness in them. The blooms last only a day, and then they die. Fiery beauty for a gasp of time."

Yes. That was how their meeting had been. Beauty destroyed by lies. She wouldn't let his flowers make her forget why she had come.

"Stop the outbreaks, Michel."

Michel didn't answer. For the first time, she wished he weren't invisible, that she could see his thoughts on his face. Nothing stirred in the wind to show his mind.

While she waited, Fana followed the creek, walking down the path. Toward the knoll.

Fana stopped at the edge of the woods, still sheltered by trees. She was fifteen yards from the wooden steps to the kitchen's back door. The kitchen light shone brightly through the closed curtains, and purposeful shadows moved beyond the curtains. Gramma Bea's biscuits were baking in the stove, a perfection of scents. If Fana had been alone, she would have gone to the kitchen to sit with Gramma Bea and talk for a while. Yes, Fana knew why her mother loved her Dreamsticks—but too many memories were a distraction. It was so taxing to live in two places at once, shuttling between realms.

"Please stop the outbreaks, Michel."

"I heard you," he said gently, as if it pained him to hear her beg.

A breeze blew through the treetops, whistling in the pine

cones. The whistle seemed to call for her, from her left. Behind her again.

"Come," Michel said.

Fana followed the song in the wind. When they climbed over the knoll, they saw that the woods had been replaced by a wide river the color of mud. They stood at the center of the bridge, looking at the city spread before them on both riverbanks. Apartment buildings that were hundreds of years old stood crowded on cobblestone streets.

At the corner marketplace, a loud bidding war for a large goose broke out, a dozen men and women shouting over one another. Glass crackled as something broke beneath them. The cars and mini-scooters looked like they didn't belong near the ancient buildings, their exhaust misting the air. Cars' honks dueled with the seagulls' wails. And beyond the physical sounds, the mingled thoughtstreams sounded like shrieking. Like a creature in pain, or in a panic.

"I always lived near cities," Michel said. "Such a racket. Especially at night."

Fana was glad she hadn't grown up in a city. How would she have tolerated the noise? Her own house had been hard enough, with her mother's nightmares about her dead sister keeping her awake. Mom had been facing down her regrets in her dreams long before she'd rediscovered Dreamsticks in Lalibela.

A bright royal-blue curtain blew like a flag from a second-story balcony just beyond the bridge. Michel's squat shadow walked toward the billowing curtain, so Fana followed him in the bright afternoon light. The building was better kept than its neighbors, its white paint new. The curtain was gilded with gold that gleamed in the sunshine.

Boys' conspiratorial giggles sprayed from the open window.

Suddenly, Fana knew the place, the river, the corner market, and the bright blue curtains. She had seen this place in Michel's memories before.

Two boys in short pants playfully tussled over a soccer ball on the balcony. One child was pink skinned, the other the color of bronze. The darker boy's hair grew to his shoulders in a mound of springy black curls. Both boys were beautiful.

The soccer ball fell to the street twenty feet below, and the boys rushed to the balcony in time to see it crushed beneath a truck's tire. The truck spat out black smoke. They cursed at the driver in Italian. Then they went back inside.

"On weekdays, Papa brought me with him to his apartment where he met his women disciples," Michel said. "Twenty at a time, sometimes. But there was one in particular he liked, Constanza, and she always brought her son, Nino. When we ate our rosemary bread or *ricotta e cioccolato*—oh, that wonderful cake!—Nino dutifully said 'Bless the Blood' over his food while his mother communed with divinity, or so she hoped. But Nino was my first good friend. I didn't think of him as a mortal. There was no prophecy, no Letter. Just boys playing."

He sounded mournful.

"Yes," she said. "I had a friend like that—Moses. When I was three."

The streets suddenly fell utterly silent, even the seagulls near the river.

Then a cry pierced the quiet. A child's shriek of terror, or agony, or both.

"I let him see me fly," Michel said. "Just to the ceiling fan, I thought. To amuse him. Papa had told me never to show off to the *mortali*, but boys love showing off. 'I can do this,' or 'I can do that.' Boys play that game in every language. But Nino was shocked. He went as pale as the dead. He cried out as if he'd seen the devil himself."

Wind kissed the nape of Fana's neck, and she couldn't tell if it was Michel or the storm brewing just north of them, where the sky brooded dark. Were the clouds hers, or Michel's?

"He threw a lamp at me," Michel said. "The way one would at an insect, or a bat. Only when I was angry, *really* angry, did I let myself feel how much I enjoyed his fear."

The shrieks in the room changed tenor, the pitch rising. More pain than fear. A child's cry of *Per favore! Per favore!*

Fana did not want to see Michel hurt his friend. She turned away.

"For me, I put my friend in a coma when he teased me," she said. "Then, a storm. A hurricane. People I'd never met . . ."

Cold rain fell on them. Michel's warm breath huffed against her cheek as he instinctively pulled her closer, giving her a canopy against the rain. Gently, he steered her back to the bridge.

"Yes, I know," he said. "But others before that, no? All when you were three. You must have been confused, to have been so young. I'd had an accident with a nanny before Nino, but that was different. I didn't really understand. After Nino, I had an appetite." The wind whispered the last word, *appetite*. "Papa told me my appetite would make me strong. So he fed me—and it did."

Fana did not remember having an appetite, but maybe that was why she'd shut down for so many years as a child, fleeing to her head. Maybe Khaldun had joined her thought planes to help her forget the appetite the Shadows had shown her. But why hadn't Khaldun ever told her about Michel? Why hadn't he helped Michel, too?

They had reached the center of the bridge again. The city now looked more a life-size painting, everything frozen, the colors brightened. Instead of storm clouds, the sky was awash in strokes of light like Van Gogh's *Starry Night*. The two boys were leaning over the balcony, frozen in solidarity as they waved their fists at the truck. Michel was a painter, she realized.

"No further outbreaks," he said, "until you come."

"And after I come?"

"I have conditions too," he said, ignoring her question.

Fana waited. He had waited a year, so she could be patient with his conditions.

"Stop defiling the Blood," he said. "No more concert spectacles."

"Until I come."

"Yes," he said, reluctant. "Until you come. And . . ."

He didn't have to say Johnny's name. His voice told her.

"Were you watching me?" Fana said.

"I smell him on you."

The waters below them rippled as if from a school of feeding fish: Michel's anger.

Fana wrestled with embarrassment. "A goodbye kiss," she said. "You've had others."

"When you come, there won't be others," he said. "How could there be?"

"I promise you, Michel—no one will touch me." In the physical world, her voice would have been shaking with unmistakable resolve.

The wind sighed, far from satisfied, and the waters' rippling spread to a bigger ring. Nothing would be gained by talk of touching. Still, she pleased him every time she spoke his name. Naming him was a small enough courtesy.

"I shouldn't have kissed him, Michel," Fana said, and the waters calmed.

A confession *could* sound like an apology. Kissing Johnny had felt like a mistake from the moment their lips touched—because it had been so unfair to Johnny. Unfair to her.

"I don't want to think about him when I'm with you," she said. "If that's all right."

"That would make me happiest, Fana. If you don't think about him, I'll forget him too." He spoke gently enough, but the threat hung in his words.

The woods reappeared on the other end of the bridge. He was inviting her to return to her own thoughtstreams. Light glowed from the kitchen window, where the curtain had been pulled back. Someone inside was watching her.

"You can show yourself now," Fana said.

And so he was there—standing beside her on the bridge, three inches taller, his smooth hands folded across the railing as he stared down into the calm waters. She had made herself forget how handsome he was, too. His honey-colored face was hairless, his lips faintly pink, dark eyelashes as full as a child's. Shiny black ringlets of loose, springy hair cradled his ears. The sight of him also brought scents: clove cigarettes and mango.

His face pricked her, hard. He was Charlie.

Despite everything, he still seemed to be the persona he had created for her to love when she had run away from the woods: a brave teenage mortal risking his life on the Underground Railroad. Her beloved phantom had been molded in Johnny's image, but she had loved Michel's face first. Michel had known whom she wanted before she did, fooling her the way her father had fooled her mother. History repeats, she remembered.

Fana glanced at him sidelong, careful to move no closer. "Hello, Michel."

"Hello, Fana." His eyes swallowed her before they skipped back to the water. "I'm sorry I was so . . . *terrible* . . . to you. To your family. I became the creature Nino saw when he threw the lamp at me. I will not be that creature again. Not with you."

Michel's voice was so weighted with shame that the wind could barely lift it.

His idealized painting of Tuscany faded in the rising mist. A joyless castle appeared before them on a mountaintop, the sole structure visible in the fog. She had dreamed of it once.

"Let Phoenix go, Michel," Fana said.

"I never sent for her," he said. "A network is a living thing, with a mind of its own."

"Then don't interfere when we find her," she said. "I won't come to you until Phoenix, her husband, and her son are free."

"She'll be free," he said. "As long as you don't use her to defile the Blood."

"Until I come," she clarified.

"Yes," he said. "Until you come."

"And after?"

Michel stared toward the waiting castle hidden in rising river mist.

"We begin," he said.

Nineteen

Although the late-afternoon sun is still bright above them, the zoo is unusually empty for a Sunday. Jessica is tired, but Kira won't rest until she sees the white Bengal tiger. The tigers will be their last stop, Jessica decides. Then she'll be ready to go home.

It is daylight, but Kira is amusing herself by reciting her nighttime prayer in singsong: "Now I lay me down to sleep . . ."

The day is so bright that Jessica's vision is clouded, forcing her to blink to see more than a few yards in any direction. All the animals must be hiding from the sun, because the grassy hills, ponds, and trees beyond the fenced-in ditches are empty.

Is the zoo even open? How did they get in?

Bea is walking ahead of her, never far out of sight. Jessica reaches out to grab the sleeve of Bea's lilac batik blouse, her favorite Sunday-outing clothes, to slow her down. When Bea turns around, her face is nearly washed out in the brightness. "Lord, I'd forgotten about this sun," Bea says. "Kira and I shouldn't be out here today, Jessica."

Bea looks younger every time Jessica sees her. The wrinkles that lined her face have smoothed out, and her arms' muscles are springy again. *This* face is the one Jessica remembers from her parent-teacher meetings and Sunday-school programs and Girl Scout campouts.

Jessica is holding Kira's hand, all warm stickiness from Kira's ice-cream cone. Kira grins at her with a wide smile, showing off her missing bottom tooth that fell out last night. Her tongue is coated with light brown chocolate. Jessica hoards the details.

"Mommy, where's the tiger?" Kira says.

"We're almost there. Pinky swear." Jessica hooks their free pinkies together, but Kira unhooks herself. She doesn't like childish gestures in public. She also doesn't like Jessica holding her hand, but that's the rule: Kira always has to walk right beside her.

Loose strands of Kira's hair are escaping their barrettes, so Jessica lowers herself to one knee to smooth out her daughter's soft curls, clipping her two pigtails back into place. Jessica wipes a dab of dried ice cream from the corner of Kira's mouth.

Kira's brown eyes, so much like David's, take on an adult aspect. "You shouldn't look at me so much, Mommy," Kira says. "You should look where you're going."

"I know, baby," Jessica says.

Bea sighs, impatient. "Well, I don't care if it's a tiger, a bear, or a flying dragon, I need to head back," Bea says, fanning herself. "You two go on."

Jessica searches the zoo's empty pedestrian walkways for David, but he's nowhere in sight. She is sure that David was with them, but she can't remember where he went.

Jessica holds tightly to Kira's hand. "Mom, let's not separate now. We'll get lost."

Bea laughs, smoothing Jessica's hair away from her forehead the way Jessica fixed Kira's. "Pumpkin, you can't get lost when you always know where you're going." Her brown eyes are flecked green near her pupils, a detail Jessica had nearly forgotten. How can she remember it all?

The growling sky steals Jessica's gaze. Not far from them, the bright light is cleaved by a bank of heavy, dark clouds. In Miami, summer storms appear from nowhere.

"Whatever you need here, better hurry," Bea says. She covers her head with the loose pages of the *Miami Sun-News,* which flap in the cooling breeze, hiding her face. "You hear me? Better keep that girl out of the storm."

"She wants to see the tiger, Mom!" Jessica calls after her, but Bea is already hurrying away. Bea takes the path that forks right, but a sign reading BENGAL TIGERS steers Jessica left. Jessica fights tears as she watches her mother go.

But at least she is still holding her child's soft, warm hand.

"Come on, sweetie," Jessica says. "Let's hurry, before it rains."

They run together, giggling like playmates. Breathlessly, Kira sings "I Am the Hare that Stays in the Road," a children's song from Botswana. The song isn't in English, but Jessica understands her daughter's words. Where did Kira learn it? Where did *she*? Neither of them has ever been to Africa.

The shaded tiger enclosure ahead is so big that Jessica forgets that it's a part of the zoo; she is hypnotized by the temple set against the shade of palm trees. The temple is Khmer architecture, modeled after Cambodia's famed Hindu temple Angkor Wat. Like a holy place.

But none of the tigers is in sight.

The singing stops. Jessica feels her daughter's pace slowing beside her.

"Don't worry, baby," Jessica says. "The tigers will be way over there, and we're way over here. They can't hurt us."

"Where's the white one?"

"Maybe it's hiding," Jessica says. "That's my favorite, too. One-of-a-kind, like you."

Her daughter giggles again, but she still sounds nervous, pulling closer to Jessica.

More thunder above them. The sky is growing darker. Trees sway, leaves and fronds hissing and rustling overhead. Jessica hadn't realized that there were so many trees around her, a jungle. The path behind them is wrapped in shadows.

Jessica studies the temple's intricate carvings, waiting for a tiger to emerge. Nothing.

She looks for her watch, but her wrist is bare. What time is it?

Jessica sighs. "Sweetie, I don't think we'll see the tiger today."

The growl that comes from behind her, low to the ground, turns Jessica's skin to ice.

Jessica whirls around to see the snowy striped tiger, massive sinews gliding beneath white fur, as it winds toward them at an angle ten yards back, herding them. The tiger's paws are heavy, bigger than baseball mitts.

Jessica looks for zookeepers, for anyone with a gun, but she and her daughter are alone.

Tigers give chase, she reminds herself between the violent knocks of her heart. She clutches her daughter's hand tightly enough to crush her bones. "Stand still," she whispers.

The tiger's attention snaps to them with alert, cool blue eyes. A hunter's eyes. The tiger's massive jaw falls open; impossibly sharp, yellowed teeth. The tiger's eyes stare through to Jessica's soul, and he issues a sound midway between a growl and a roar, close enough for her to smell the beast's rancid breath.

Our Father who art in Heaven . . . hallowed be Thy name . . .

Armed with nothing but prayers, Jessica lifts her daughter into her arms. A tiny, terrified heart patterns against her bosom. But it isn't Kira! Her daughter's face is smaller and rounder with baby fat than before, familiar features mismatched. All her tiny teeth are intact. Her hair is wound in thick dreadlocks.

"I'm scared, Mommy," Fana whispers, clinging tightly.

I know you're scared, baby. It's hard for you to say it, but I know. I'm scared too.

Jessica won't let Fana feel her body's tremors or see the fear eating her heart. She will be strong for Fana, just like when she stole her back from the Shadows.

"Mommy's here, Fana," Jessica says. "Mommy's here."

The tiger springs just as the clouds open, drenching them with rain.

Jessica sat up with a strangled cry just short of a scream. She curled herself into a ball, expecting to feel the tiger's hot breath before his teeth ripped at her neck.

"It's okay," a man's voice said. "You were dreaming."

Jessica looked up and saw him standing over her with her drinking glass, his fingertips damp from the water droplets he'd sprinkled to her forehead. It was hard to see him in the room's light, in the spinning walls.

"David?" Jessica wiped her forehead with her forearm. Still no watch. "What time . . . ?"

"There's no David here," the man said. "It's just me."

Jessica sat up so quickly that she bumped her knee against her table, and the jittering pain snapped her back into focus. *Dawit,* not David, she corrected herself. But the man above her wasn't Dawit. He was much younger, with a thin mustache, a small cross dangling from his ear. His golden cross winked in the room's light.

Johnny Wright.

At any other time, Jessica would have been pissed that Johnny had come into her room without an invitation, but she was so grateful that she wanted to hug him. She'd never had a bad trip on sticks. *She* was supposed to control her dream!

Jessica held in a deep breath of air. Real air. From the real world. *Thank you, God.*

"There was a . . . tiger," Jessica gasped, trying to explain what she'd seen.

Johnny Wright nodded. The wretchedness on his face told her he already knew all about the tiger. His voice was hollowed out. "Fana . . ."

Jessica covered herself, realizing that she wasn't wearing a bra beneath her oversized T-shirt. She wouldn't want to see herself in a mirror. "Give me a few minutes," she told Johnny Wright, her voice still hoarse from dreaming. "We can't talk here."

An hour after she'd bathed and changed, Jessica was still looking for the tiger. Her eyes searched the colorful rock garden and its unpredictable, coral-like formations that reminded her of her dream zoo's jungle, expecting a blur of white fur to leap at her. It might be another hour before her fingers stopped shaking.

No more Dreamsticks, Jessica promised herself as she splashed her face with warm water from the garden's soaking pool. She had promised to stop burning the sticks before, but the tiger might help her keep her word. Her fears had tracked her into her haven. She wanted dreams, not nightmares.

"Michel won't let her go again," Johnny said.

No. Michel would not let Fana go. Maybe Fana couldn't see it, but that had been plain to Jessica in his white silk robe, his languid eyes. Jessica had known he would not let Fana go since she first saw the blood on her clothes. Since she'd seen the look in Fana's eyes—the look every daughter's mother dreads—saying she had been *touched*. Jessica's pupils narrowed with rage as she thought about the way Michel had played with Fana, sowing lies to trap her.

Jessica couldn't answer. She stared at the towering stones.

"But I know a way, Mrs. Wolde," Johnny said.

Johnny's face came into crisp focus, down to his razor stubble and eyes swollen from half-mad tears. Something irreparable was about to happen between her and Johnny Wright, a moment that couldn't be backed away from. Ideas became plans. Plans came to life. She glanced around again, this time looking for listeners hidden among the wonderland of stones.

"Go on," Jessica said.

"I shot two of Michel's men last year. I rescued Caitlin." Johnny's voice as calm as the garden's pools. "Michel thought he was control-ling me . . . but he lost me for at least ten minutes. I was myself again. I had free will. I've been praying, Mrs. Wolde, and God told me a secret. It's a secret I already knew from Mexico, when I fired the gun, but I'd forgotten. . . ."

Suddenly, Jessica knew the secret, too. Like Johnny, she had only forgotten.

"Fana distracts him," Jessica said. "When she's with him . . ."

Johnny finished, his voice hushed, "He's vulnerable."

Jessica assessed John Wright with new eyes: he wasn't the fright-ened, confused child fresh from Hell. The oft-told story about Johnny Wright shooting his way past Michel's men hadn't fit the jittery young man who had first come to Lalibela. But now, *this* was the Johnny Wright who risked instant arrest every time he went upworld to help spread Glow. This was the Johnny Wright who'd faced Michel in Mexico and fought his way free.

God help them, was Michel listening to them now? Jessica was too weary to be afraid.

"He would take precautions," Jessica said. "It might not happen again."

"But what if it can?" he said.

"Fana won't help you," Jessica said. "Or Dawit. They're both dead set against a direct confrontation. But there might be others."

"Who?" Johnny said.

"They would never confide in a mortal, Johnny. A stranger."

"What about Teka?"

Jessica smiled weakly. What a waste! Fana's teacher knew enough about the weapons in the Life Brothers' arsenal to wipe Michel from the planet. "Teka would never go against Fana's wishes," Jessica said. "Don't even approach him—he'll see through you."

"Who, then?"

"Mahmoud," Jessica said. Mahmoud's name tasted like burnt dust in her mouth. She rolled her tongue in the caverns of her cheeks to feel moisture again. Was she fully awake, or still dreaming? Jessica checked her reflection in the water, one of the tricks she'd had to learn after too much time on Dreamsticks: in her dreams, she couldn't see her reflection.

But she was there. She splashed her face again, trying to forget how Mahmoud had tried to kill her and Kira in her old life, and then Fana, too. Mahmoud had tried to destroy her family from the beginning. How could she speak his name?

Jessica dried her face on her shirt, forcing herself to go on. "Mahmoud would want to see Michel dead, and he wouldn't care what Fana says. Or Dawit. Mahmoud always does what he thinks is right for the colony."

Jessica's stomach gurgled, so she walked to the orange tree a few paces beyond the washbasin. The oranges were as big as grapefruits here, all of them ripe for months at a time. More decoration than food. Jessica chose an orange at random, since they all looked and tasted the same. She buried her thumb in its heart to peel it.

"Then let's talk to Mahmoud," Johnny said.

"I can't *know* about this, Johnny. Fana wants me and Dawit to go with her to Michel. I could hide from Fana, I think, but Dawit can't filter as well. And I couldn't hide from Michel. Once we're near Michel, he'd be a fool not to know us inside and out. Assume they'll all know we've had this conversation."

"That's not a problem," Johnny said. The determination in his eyes didn't dim.

"Michel doesn't have to be near you to kill you," Jessica said. "Remember?"

"We're just talking," Johnny said. "I'm not worried about anyone except Fana."

Jessica remembered when her sister, Alex, brought her the idea to open a clinic in South Africa to distribute the blood Dawit had forced into her veins. In one glorious instant, the world had opened itself up, and Jessica finally understood why Kira had been taken away from her: Kira's death was her daily reminder of loss, so she could help others heal. Now, Jessica understood again. She might not be able to free Fana from the tiger, but she had to try.

Sometimes a mother's power wasn't enough, but Fana needed her.

Jessica clasped the young man's clammy hand between hers. "There's no such thing as true immortality in the body. Evaporation. Incineration. Telepathic exsanguination; I've seen Fana do that, when she was only three. If Michel even loses consciousness . . ."

He can be killed, she finished to herself, hesitating to speak the words.

"I need your blessing, Mrs. Wolde," Johnny said.

Jessica's heart pounded the way it had when she'd seen the tiger, flushing her veins with adrenaline. Johnny was still a kid, no more prepared than Fana, who could be so impulsive and childish. But children always fought for the future, full of imagination, uncorrupted by doubts.

"*Only* Michel," she said. "If Fana is in danger, you have to stop it. Give me your word."

"I promise never to do anything to hurt Fana," Johnny said. "But I need the Blood, Mrs. Wolde. I need to be one of you."

The Blood would not keep Johnny alive if Michel went after him, but it might save him once. Or twice. It might buy him enough time. Jessica's heartbeat sped.

"Lucas and I don't know the ceremony," Jessica said. "I've asked about sharing the Blood with you all, but Dawit doesn't want to bypass the council. He's a pragmatist deep down, Johnny. There's only one person who might do it for you."

"Fana?" Johnny said.

"Yes. You'd have to convince her. And you won't have much time."

"I've asked her before."

"Why did she say no?"

Johnny sighed. "She said I didn't know my reasons yet."

"Give her good reasons, then," Jessica said. "As much as you can, tell the truth."

Now it was Johnny's turn to look sick to his stomach. "I'll need time alone with her."

"I'll get you the time. You have a chance, Johnny. She's in love with you."

Johnny Wright's wide eyes swept her like searching floodlights.

From the way he looked at her, Jessica might have thought he didn't already know.

Twenty

Bells tolled somberly throughout the colony to signal the Lalibela Council meeting, one of the colony's few acts of spontaneity. The courtyard before the entryway to the Council House was crowded and giddy, everyone barefoot and dressed in white.

Fana had never attended a meeting, although she'd held an honorary seat on the council most of her life. In the year since she had moved to Lalibela, Fana had missed three meetings while she was upworld on Glow business or meditating, leaving Dawit to speak on her behalf.

Not a great record, Fana realized. She'd kept away from colony politics, preoccupied with her race with Michel; meditating for strength through the Rising and building her Glow network so she could fight Michel's agencies' work to slow them down. It was exhausting.

But Fana wanted to win over her own people before she could work on Michel. To most of the Life Brothers, she was an enigma; to others, a stain.

It was time to make her mission official.

Fana walked the wide corridor, trailed by her teacher, Teka. Beyond Teka, her guardians Fasilidas and Berhanu walked in formation. The Life Brothers' intense curiosity nibbled at Fana as she passed them. Her presence elicited extreme feelings, from bright-eyed worship to hot loathing. Which was worse? How could she deserve either?

Fana was wearing a ceremonial white robe from the House of Mystics, with three intersecting rows of cowrie shells sewn on the hem, brushing her bare ankles. The shells represented past, present, and future, all interwoven. Many of the Mystics believed they had been prophesying her birth for four hundred years.

Three wiry dancers from the House of Mystics cleared a path for her, singing the prophecy in flawless harmony while drums and shakers played at a frenetic pace. Each drum had a different pitch, the voices eerily human, in dialogue with one another as well as the dancers.

"And her name shall be called Light!" one Mystic sang, waving his arms to the sky.

"And she will bring rains from the sky!" another sang, scooping imaginary water.

"And she shall be born with the Blood!" The third leaped to show the Blood's strength.

The Mystics were as enchanted by the Letter of the Witness as Michel, and they considered her the rightful heir to Khaldun—his Chosen. Even the Brothers who didn't believe in the Letter as prophecy respected Khaldun's special presence in Fana's life.

The flea thinks it is the camel's master, Fana remembered Khaldun telling her, and they often had debated whether Fana was the camel or the flea. As a child, she'd been sure she was the camel. Today, she seemed like neither. Or both.

Or was Michel the camel, and she the flea?

The twenty-foot statue of Khaldun stood prominently in the courtyard beyond the Council Hall's archway, and Fana followed tradition by stopping to reflect on the colony's creator. The statue's marble shone like new, but Dawit said it had been built before he and his Brothers arrived in Khaldun's underground kingdom more than five hundred years ago.

Despite its height, the statue looked puny. The rendering was stylized, Khaldun's facial features heavily lined, his beard cropped, so he didn't resemble the man Fana and her parents had met in Lalibela. He looked nothing like the dreamlike figure who had guided her when the world overwhelmed her, when even her parents had been locked out.

Her father said that Khaldun had spoken through this statue in years past, with a greeting for every Brother. But Khaldun's statue had gone silent when he'd left Lalibela. Fana reached up to wrap her palm around the smooth marble hand, three times the size of a man's. She dropped her chin to her chest, eyes closed.

Khaldun, I need your guidance as much as I did when I was three, she said.

The statue was lifeless stone, cold to the core, as if Khaldun had never touched it. Had Khaldun found a way to die? Freed himself to his Rising? That would explain why she'd never been able to find his thoughts, and a part of her was always searching.

Fana understood why the Life Brothers felt abandoned. Khaldun hadn't prepared her for Michel, or explained the prophecy he'd saddled his two Bloodborn with. The silent statue almost made her as angry as it did many of her Brothers, but what was the point of anger?

Fana moved beyond the statue when she thought a respectful time had passed, but she noticed several glares from council members who thought she had not lingered long enough.

PATIENCE, FANA, Teka said, walking closely beside her to share his thought privately.

But I knew Khaldun, she said. *What's the point of pretending I found him in the statue?*

THE POINT ISN'T TO FIND HIM. THE POINT IS TO SEEK HIM.

The stares and riot of speculations made Fana lonely, so she was glad when she saw her family huddle—Teferi's wives Abena and Sharmila, Teferi's boys Miruts, Natan, and Debashish. Her aunt, uncle, and cousin were still upworld, but where was her father?

The women showered Fana with hugs, draping her in beads and flowers. Fana ignored the nearby thoughts, wondering why a gaggle of mortals congregated so near the Council Hall, and the complaints exaggerating their smell.

Abena's eyes danced. "Today you are taking your throne, my daughter," she whispered.

"It's only a courtesy call," Fana told her. "I'm not here to lead Lalibela."

"And yet you will. You do!" Abena said, and kissed her cheek.

Fana wondered when she would see them again. She'd been upworld only a week for the concert and Glow visits, and Natan already seemed three inches taller, past her shoulder at only ten. Natan's ocher face dimpled when he grinned and handed Fana a sewn doll with three heads with nests of black hair. Each head was shorter than the last, but the doll shared a single body.

"See?" Natan said. "That's me. That's Deb. And Miruts. For good luck."

"Yes, you'll always be with me," Fana said, hugging him. Children's energy was like no other, floating straight through her. No masking. So few regrets. Bright and vigorous. Fana knew she could never be a child again, and wouldn't want to—but if she had a child of her own one day, would she be a Bloodborn, too?

"Best good-luck charm ever made," Caitlin said.

Caitlin was at the edge of the huddle, dressed in white jeans and a white tank top—her nod to ceremony. Fana hugged Caitlin a long time. The spike in her Brothers' thoughts sharpened as they watched her with Caitlin—hugging mortals! This one not even an African! And Caitlin was helping her spread the Blood, which was controversial in Lalibela, too. Fana had already scandalized her Brothers without a word.

"He's a mistake," Caitlin said to her ear. "A really big, awful mistake."

"I think you're wrong," Fana said. "Waiting was the mistake."

"I sure as hell better be wrong," Caitlin said bitterly.

Fana tugged on the ends of Caitlin's hair, their game since childhood when either of them needed to be pulled out of a bad mood. "Am I still me?" Fana said, not entirely teasing. Caitlin would know if Michel was riding her.

"He couldn't be you for a day if he tried, Fana," Caitlin said.

Fana realized she might not see Caitlin again before she left Lalibela, and she owed her so much! Without Caitlin, she might never have had the courage to spread the Blood and create the Underground Railroad for Glow, beyond her parents' more cautious efforts. Glow had brought Fana to Michel's attention, but she and Caitlin had saved tens of thousands of lives. Hundreds of thousands.

And Fana had told Michel that she would stop healing until their meeting! The networks were running, but she wouldn't intervene the way she'd promised the health minister in Nigeria. As Fana gazed at Caitlin's sad smile, her truce with Michel felt like a betrayal.

"Caitlin . . ."

The confession almost came, but Fana's father's strong presence radiated behind Fana the instant before he tapped her shoulder from behind. Dawit was dressed in a warrior's loincloth and ostrich feathers. With her father beside her in Mexico, she could face Michel.

But her mother hadn't come. Fana was surprised at how deeply her disappointment burned, like anger. Fana wanted to lash out a probe to find Jessica, but the memory of her mother's angry slap reminded her not to. They were beyond each other's guidance now. And where was Johnny? Fana scanned the Life Brothers, and Johnny wasn't in sight, either. She felt that Johnny and her mother were bound up together, and something was badly wrong.

YOU SHOULD TAKE YOUR SEAT IN THE HALL, FANA, Teka said.

The throng thickened as she neared the door. Everyone seemed to want to enter the Council Hall with her, brushing uncharacteristically close. The clumsier telepaths needed proximity to glide through her.

"Where's Johnny?" Fana called to Caitlin as the crowd pulled them apart.

Caitlin waved her off. "He'll survive!" she said.

Make sure he's all right. I have a bad feeling, Fana told Caitlin.

Caitlin tapped her temple to signal that she had heard. Her empty eyes haunted Fana.

Dozens of thoughts amplified as Fana waded toward the hall's archway with her Brothers. Walking within their furious streams was like trudging through thick mud. She hadn't planned to veil herself at the council meeting—Teka had warned her that Higher Brothers would find it rude, as if she were hiding—but she might not have a choice. So much noise!

An intriguing melody issued from the strange instrument one of the Brothers was playing outside the archway, stringed like a lute but held like a clarinet, with a reed embedded in its neck. The musician was a master with the bow. The instrument sounded like three being played at once. Had she heard a hidden strain of Phoenix's "Gotta Fly"? Fana would have thought she'd imagined it, except for the twinkle in the musician's eye.

A hand grabbed Fana's arm and held on so tightly that Fana almost snapped it away. *How* dare *someone!*—

Then Fana's irritation melted. Joy came instead.

Her mother was a beautiful sight. The broken woman from the dream chamber was gone. Jessica smelled sweet from her bath, and Abena had carefully braided her cornrows. Jessica was wearing a white sun dress Fana had never seen, a simple design from a market.

Fana hugged Jessica tightly, and they breathed together within their hug before her mother pulled back. Jessica was always conscious of having her head too close, letting her thoughts loose. But she hadn't pulled away fast enough: Jessica was thinking about Johnny, too, worried about him. Excited for him. Fana clipped off the stray thought as quickly as she could, but she'd felt it. And there was more that Jessica didn't *want* her to see. As always.

Fana concentrated on her mother's smile instead, which was weak but genuine. Faces were far less complicated than thoughts, even if they left too much unsaid.

"I'm here, Fana," her mother said. "I hate the reason like hell, but I'm here."

You've done this before, Fana said privately. *You never wanted to see Dad again. But you needed something from him, so you came here on faith, with no idea what to expect.*

"I needed somebody to teach me who you were," Jessica said.

"That's how it is for me now, Mom," she said. "I have to learn."

Jessica's eyes fluttered with a flash of pain at the idea of Fana learning anything from Michel. "And teach," Jessica said. "Don't forget to *teach.*"

"Every moment," Fana said. "I promise."

Jessica crossed her hands across her chest in an X, clasping her own shoulders. A sigh shuddered through her. "I'm tired, Fana. But I'll come wherever you need me."

Dawit hesitated before he kissed Jessica. The hurried, tentative kiss reminded Fana of her impulsive kiss with Johnny; wondering if it was welcome, hoping it wouldn't hurt them both. Jessica touched Dawit's cheek with her fingertip, tracing a message to him in their secret language. Fana shut out the courtyard's noise, watching her parents rediscover each other, finding the new paths around old pain. Fana heard her parents' whispers.

"Thank you for coming back, *mi vida*." Dawit held out his hand to Jessica.

"Thanks for waiting."

They clasped hands, holding tightly, as if one of them might float away.

The first six hours of the council meeting were a test, because Jessica wished she could escape the dimly lighted chamber. She kept herself awake by counting and recounting the thirty Life Brothers sitting in the semicircle of floor pillows, cataloging their clothing, their gestures, trying to remember their names: Jima. Demisse. Yacob. Ermias. Almost all the remaining Life Brothers were here, more than she'd seen gathered in one place. A few were bleary-eyed, fresh from meditation.

Tiny metallic Spiders scurried across the tabletop, racing between the council members as they spoke. "For Teferi and the others upworld," Dawit explained when she asked about the devices. "So they can watch too."

The eyes of the world's immortals were on her child.

Dawit gave Jessica translations while each of the twelve council members offered greetings, rebukes, or warnings. Some spoke only to Dawit, some only to Fana, others to Fana and Dawit. Jessica, so recently a mortal, was ignored. Many of the Life Brothers refused to look at her, so Jessica relieved herself of her phony smile.

The Life Brothers rarely ate meals as a ritual, but the council meeting was treated as a banquet, the tables arrayed with baskets and platters of food. Few of the Brothers were eating, but Jessica helped herself to whatever she could reach, remembering to steer clear of the spicier pastes unique to the colony. Ethiopian injera.

Boiled eggs. Figs. Grapes. Pastries. And there was more than enough coffee to keep her awake, richer and sweeter than the Cuban coffee she and her friends in Miami had called rocket fuel. Her mind still foggy from Dreamsticks, the taste of Miami was fresh on her tongue. Here, she could be eating lumps of soil. Her racing mind made it hard to eat. *Can Johnny find a way? Can any of us?*

Jessica closed her eyes and tried to practice the breathing that Teka and Fana were teaching her, tied to her heartbeat. Her heart was excited from thoughts about Michel and Johnny, but she willed her heart to slow. Peace. Stillness. Another pastry. More coffee.

Finally, it was Fana's turn to speak.

Jessica was mesmerized as her daughter took her place before the council. The ease of her walk. The way she threw her head back, high on her shoulders, her back erect. Fana walked to the center of the circle that separated the council members from the spectators. Weighted by cowrie shells, the back of Fana's robe dragged on the floor. Spiders clicked after her, climbing the wall on thread-thin legs to document her words.

A hush followed her.

Jessica glanced at Dawit, and found tears in his eyes. She didn't dare let herself cry, or she would be a spectacle. How could Dawit sit there and watch Fana like a proud father at a high-school graduation? Jessica squeezed Dawit's knee, and he rested his steady hand on hers.

"She's extraordinary, Jess," Dawit whispered. "You'll see."

I know, Jessica thought. *But so is he.*

"My name is Fana."

Fana didn't have to raise her voice. The Council Hall was silent as stone.

Nothing had prepared Dawit for the feeling.

During rare moments after his return to Lalibela, he realized a weight had been lifted from his spirit as he was no longer forced to choose between life with his family and life with his Brothers. There was still dissent about the Blood mission, but Lalibela felt like home again. Perhaps he had always imagined a day when Jessica could sit beside him at the Council Hall, and they might hear the laughter of children in the rock garden.

But *this*! His child addressing the council!

Fana's presence swept Dawit back to his own beginnings with the Living Blood, awe-filled as Khaldun's floating visage had addressed this same hall. Khaldun's voice had filled his life before he'd found Jessica, a voice so vast that Dawit had never questioned Khaldun's Covenant: *No one must know. No one must join. We are the last.*

Had Khaldun been the tyrant Mahmoud now believed he was, or simply a teacher trying too hard to keep his students close to him? To keep them from lording themselves over mortals? Fana would bring a new way to his Brothers, like Dawit's favorite passage in the I Ching: "When the way comes to an end, then Change. Having changed, you pass through."

They would not want to listen to her. But they had no choice, because she was there.

Fifteen years ago, it had been impossible to see this woman in the fat-cheeked, impetuous baby Fana had been, barely able to walk, driven by a toddler's rages. But Khaldun had seen Fana's future. Or, had he and Jessica created Fana's future based on Khaldun's words? That was the snake eating its own head, the question with no answer.

If Dawit ever found Khaldun again, he had only one last question for his teacher: *Did you write the Letter, Father?* If so, Khaldun had created Michel as he had created Fana, and they had been destined to meet thousands of years before their births.

Michel's telepathic attack on their Washington colony had shown Dawit that Michel could easily overpower them all, and Michel had let them go. Michel was haughty and spoiled, but he had respected Fana's mental dominion in ways he didn't have to. Michel's "plague" had been exercised only mildly, with so few deaths. It was only a message, a communication. Dawit wasn't willing to trust Michel, but he studied Michel's actions to judge him.

Even if Michel didn't deserve Dawit's faith, Fana did. Now his Brothers would see it.

"I've spent my life with mortals," Fana said. Her Amharic and

Arabic were fine, but Fana chose English so that her mother could understand her.

"My father chose a woman who did not share our Blood to make his wife. She was pregnant when he shared his Blood with her, and they created me. It is the oldest and simplest of stories in the history of humankind. A man and woman fell in love, and made a child."

Fana's gaze came to Dawit and Jessica, and she bowed low.

Dawit and Jessica inclined their heads. They did not publicly bow to their daughter.

His Brothers' tension came in silent, angry waves. Dawit had been ridiculed for taking a mortal wife—more than one! Sharing the Blood had violated Khaldun's Covenant. But there were other Brothers, like Yacob and Teferi, who'd felt the same call. Most of the Brothers who had gone upworld since Khaldun's departure had gone to seek a mortal's life of fleeting passions. *Except for those who have gone to Michel*, Dawit reminded himself.

Fana went on. "You have forgotten grandmothers and grandfathers, mothers and fathers—but I was raised in my grandmother's bosom. I tasted my grandfather's last breath. I have grieved, as all of you have, even if it was so long ago that you've nearly forgotten grief. Not everyone who shares my blood—my family blood—has the Living Blood. But now I must twine my two families: the family of my heart and the family of the Blood."

LOVELY! Teka told Dawit. But the room was warm with his Brothers' agitation.

"There is much we can learn from mortals . . ." Fana went on. "The world over, men, women, and children know their mortality. They are driven by this knowledge. They move quickly. They build and build. They hope for immortality through their children. They choose a few pieces of the world to learn before they're gone. They sing and cry for each other. Sometimes they mate for life. They live on memories. They have no time to waste, Brothers."

"Yes," Jessica whispered, clutching both hands to her chin as she leaned forward in her chair, rapt. Warm hums of affirmation from some Brothers clashed with impatience from others.

"I know I'm young," Fana said. "I've only seen eighteen rains.

I'm more like a mortal than I'm like you, my longer-lived Brothers. I count time like a mortal. I eat with a mortal's cravings; breakfast, lunch, dinner." She gestured in the air with a rigid chopping motion.

There was laughter, but Fana's next words cut the laughter short.

"Yet, of all of us here, I am the only one who was not born to mortals. I'm the only one who was born *with* the Blood," she said. "Me . . . and one other."

The mental hums grew more anxious. The only subject more sensitive than Dawit's upheaval of the colony, or Khaldun's disappearance, was the existence of Michel. For five hundred years, they had not known there were others like them, who woke again after death.

"Yes . . . his name is Michel," Fana said. "And although Michel doesn't have a seat at this table, he is a member of our Blood family. And it is time for us to know him."

The Brothers broke out with vocal cheers and dissent. The council was debating its position on Michel, but the Cleansing clearly had support within the Brotherhood.

"Do not mistake me: I am opposed to Michel's Cleansing!" Fana said, raising her voice. "I can't sit by while he implements plans for depopulation. And I will not tolerate members of this colony aiding his efforts. Michel has agreed to withhold further outbreaks until we meet."

Fana's language triggered objections. "Won't *tolerate*?" Jima said, on his feet.

Now she had lost them, Dawit thought.

Jessica whispered in his ear, "She's talked to Michel . . . ?"

"She must be negotiating with him," Dawit said. "Through their thoughts."

"Then she's already let him in," Jessica said, almost to herself. A panicked whisper.

Dawit had long ago given up lying to Jessica to comfort her. "Yes."

Fana spoke over the din. "I will take a delegation with me from Lalibela to see Michel. Everyone in my delegation must come resolved to protect the world population."

"*You* will lead the delegation?" came the outcry.

"*Protect* the population? Lunacy! We're infested! They fight for food—"

"We *will meet with Michel on* our *terms.*" Demisse's voice, shaking with outrage.

"Fana won't find allies here," Dawit muttered to Jessica, translating. "If they have political reasons for avoiding Michel, it won't feel like cowardice."

"They'll still be here debating after millions are dead," Jessica said, a realization. Again, Dawit could not deny it.

A voice called loudly, "How will Michel receive us?" Rami, his Brother from the House of Music, stood in the rear. He, too, had taken wives and raised mortal children in years past.

The hall quieted, waiting for Fana's answer.

"I don't know," Fana said. "We can succeed . . . but Michel is unpredictable."

Jessica locked a grip on Dawit's hand, silent. Her face was hardening to the pose she wore when she craved her Dreamsticks. Her terror and misery made Dawit ache for her.

"It *is* possible that Khaldun wrote the Letter of the Witness," Fana said, and her pronouncement deepened the hush in the room. "Our father may be Michel's father. If Khaldun gave birth to all of us, he envisioned our meeting one day. But is it prophecy? I only believe in a prophecy that preserves life. This is the purpose of our Blood. Any other interpretation of Cleansing runs against my deepest beliefs."

"Then I have another proposal!" a too-familiar voice called out. Until then, Dawit had not seen Mahmoud among his Brothers. Had he slipped in during the speeches?

Mahmoud wore his Searcher's skullcap, a visual reminder that, once, he had forsaken all mortal life for Khaldun's wishes to bring straying Brothers home. Mahmoud walked far too close to Fana, so insolent that Fasilidas stirred. Mahmoud was close enough to strike her.

Mahmoud had tried to kill Fana when she was three. He had nearly been in tears when he begged Dawit to let him kill Fana after she exsanguinated Kaleb. Mahmoud once had believed that Fana would destroy their Brotherhood. Did he believe it any less now?

"I apologize, but I don't know your courtesy title, Your ... Excellence?" Mahmoud said, addressing Fana from arm's reach. "Queen Empress? Or, like him, shall you be Most High?"

"I am only Fana." Dawit could hear the brooding three-year-old still inside her.

Gently, Brother, Dawit warned Mahmoud.

"Then hear me out, O Light," Mahmoud said with a hint of sarcasm and a shallow bow. His voice roughened. "These arrogant dogs, Sanctus Cruor, encroached upon Ethiopian soil in war to search for our Blood. I fought that sect at Adwa, as did Dawit." He jabbed, pointing. "And Berhanu, and many of us who loathe mortals' schoolyard skirmishes—but we defended our Blood. And now here is Michel and his self-righteous gibberish. I shun mortals for *my* own reasons, heeding *my* council's opinions. So my proposal is this, O Fana: kill Michel as you killed our Brother Kaleb. Drain him of his Blood. Chop off the head of the beast, and the beast dies."

Mahmoud leveled a gaze at Dawit when he spoke of beheading. Mahmoud apparently had forgotten that the beheaded do not always die.

"Remember who she is, Brothers!" Mahmoud finished, and took his seat.

Lively shouts rained on Mahmoud, support and denouncement. Fana stood stoically, her hands at her sides. Dawit probed to find out Fana's mood about Mahmoud's theatrics, and she pushed his probe away with her veil. Fana was laying none of her thoughts bare.

Jessica's hand squeezed Dawit's, hard. The bright red burst in Jessica's aura told him how much she wished Fana would kill Michel. Or kill Mahmoud, perhaps. Fana was hidden, but Jessica was practically shouting.

You're projecting loudly, Jess, Dawit told her privately, and Jessica looked mortified. She inhaled deeply, and the angry red glow began to fade from her aura.

Fana's gently knowing eyes gazed directly at Jessica. "A child killed Kaleb with a child's ease. I'm not that child anymore. And Michel isn't Kaleb." Fana spoke to Jessica alone.

"And that child hurt," Jessica whispered through tears. "I know, sweetheart."

Dawit gave Fana an encouraging smile. *At least it will be over soon,* he told her. Fana pulsed a heartbroken laugh to him, but she did not smile for the council.

So. Fana would not have time to unify the colony before she went to Michel, but what had she expected without planting the thoughts herself? She had begun her work with the council too late, preoccupied with the worlds above. She really was half a mortal. Khaldun had once said the same of Dawit.

"We should raze that mad prophet to dust!" Demisse cried. "You choose your course, girl—we'll choose our own."

"*Course?* You have no course!" Ermias said. "Fana knows—tell them what no one will say! Michel is the Most High, and the prophecy calls Fana his mate. What more shall be discussed? Read the Letter of the Witness. *Read Khaldun's own words!*"

Dawit had never known Ermias to be a zealot who quoted prophecies, even Khaldun's. The possibility chilled him: was Michel influencing his Brothers? What of Alem, who had gone to Michel with his knowledge of viruses? What of Fana? Teka had confessed that Michel could elude him, and Michel had fooled Fana before.

Yacob, the councilmaster, called for quiet. An angry hush swallowed the storm.

"Tell us why you came to us," Yacob said gently to Fana. Yacob had loved as many mortals as Dawit, one of the few council members who wasn't an avowed separatist.

"I'm taking a delegation to see Michel," Fana repeated, although her voice had lost its spirit. "I've come to the council to find any among you who agree that we must preserve lives with our Blood. My parents will accompany me. So will Teka, Berhanu, Fasilidas, and Teferi."

A low hiss from a darkened corner. "Fanatics!" And baffled whispers.

Fana finished. "Would anyone who wishes to join us please rise?" Her voice was full of youthful hopefulness.

Dawit rose first. Then Jessica, slowly, beside him. And Fana's four guardians.

In a room of nearly thirty others, they stood alone. Fana's beloved Mystics did not rise, though Dawit could feel their deep regret. Mystics never traveled far, at least in body. Yacob pursed his lips, clearly torn, but remained on his sitting pillow.

I'M SORRY, DAWIT, Yacob said. *I DO NOT TRUST HIM TO BE A GOOD HOST.*

When spiders unite, they can tear down the lion, Dawit reminded him, the old mortal proverb. Yacob's grim laugh sounded like a sigh.

Finally, a Brother stood up in the very rear. Rami, the musician. Fana smiled as if the entire hall had leaped to its feet.

Twenty-one

Even with so much to say, Johnny could only stare at Fana. She already looked like a memory in the thin vapor filtering the light in her mother's dreaming room. Fana stood frozen in midstep with her hand on the door frame, literally dressed like an angel. *Be patient,* Jessica had told Johnny. *She'll come looking for me sooner or later.*

Activity flurried just outside Jessica's room. Fasilidas was there, and probably other attendants. Maybe Dawit, too, who wouldn't be happy to find him in his family quarters.

"Close the door," Johnny said.

Fana paused as if she wanted to slip back outside. Instead, she closed the door. "I'm glad she's not in here burning sticks," she said. "We're about to leave for the airport, Johnny."

That answered the only question Johnny had about the council meeting. Fana hadn't changed her plans. His last hopes died with a sharp pain in his stomach.

"I tried a stick once," Johnny said. "It just gave me nightmares."

"You were creating the nightmares," Fana said. "Lucid dreaming takes practice."

"I'd rather stay awake."

For a time, they ran out of conversation.

"I won't be staying here," Johnny said. "Not much point, I guess." As mortals, he and Caitlin wouldn't be safe underground without Fana and Dawit. The Washington colony had fallen apart as soon as Fana had run away from home, and Fana was running away again.

"You shouldn't stay," Fana agreed. "Go to your parents."

Johnny swallowed back his irritation. Was he supposed to hide in his parents' house? Go back to med school and forget what he knew?

"Just like that," Johnny said.

"For a while."

"How long?" he said.

"You know I don't know."

Fana seemed to shimmer in the room's hazy light, already vanishing. She'd barely moved a foot from the doorway. He took a step closer to her, wishing he didn't feel so much like he was trying to corner her.

"I want to hear you say it," he said.

"Say what?"

"You don't want to go."

"Of course I don't want to go." Fana's brow furrowed, her voice raw. "I *have* to go."

Johnny was immediately sorry. His pain churned in hers, fresh.

"He knows you're coming?" Johnny said. "You're talking to him?"

Reluctantly, Fana nodded. "Once."

Johnny almost didn't ask any more questions. He dreaded the answers too much.

"Did my name come up?" Johnny said.

Fana gave him a desperate look. "Johnny . . ."

"That means yes," Johnny said.

Fana's face said it all: Michel knew about them. He knew their feelings for each other. There were a dozen practical reasons why Johnny wished he hadn't tumbled down this impossible tunnel, in love with Fana. Now, Michel seemed like reason enough. *The* reason.

Johnny hated being afraid, but he was. His stomach wriggled from cold adrenaline as he remembered Michel's face swarming with bees, a veil over his human disguise. Michel had put a gun in Johnny's hand and made him shoot himself. Johnny still had nightmares about watching his own limbs defy him while his mouth parroted Michel's words. *YOU ARE WEAK, AND THEREFORE NOT A WORTHY DISCIPLE,* Michel's unearthly voice had growled in his head. *THROUGH SUFFERING, YOU WILL BE CLEANSED AND LEARN OBEDIENCE.*

Why couldn't everyone else recognize Michel on sight? Why couldn't Fana?

"Then I guess I'll sleep with my lights on," Johnny said. "Not that it'll matter."

Disappointment soured Fana's face. Maybe she had hoped he had come to bring her strength instead of weakness. "If that was a problem, you'd be dead already," she said. "Go see your parents, Johnny."

Basic survival concepts were hard for Fana and the other immortals to grasp, except Fana's mother and uncle. Fana's unsympathetic lapses were typical immortalitis.

"Why would I inflict this on my parents? My enemies have big budgets and high positions, Fana." Johnny lowered his voice. "One of them is the antichrist."

Johnny knew his mistake as soon as the never-spoken words tumbled out. Fana's face colored, blood pooling beneath her skin as her eyes blazed. Johnny hadn't wanted to reveal so much, but he couldn't leave it unsaid. He stopped himself from quoting Paul's warnings about the Man of Sin in Thessalonians. Having the passages on his tongue made him dizzy.

"That is *not* true," Fana said. "What would that make me?"

"That makes you God's most beautiful gift to humankind," he said. "To me."

Fana couldn't have looked more miserable if he'd slapped her. She walked away from him, pacing. Johnny heard Dawit's voice outside the door, asking Fasilidas about her.

YOU SHOULDN'T HAVE COME, JOHNNY.

Johnny blocked Fana's path when she tried to walk past him. He slid his palms beneath her fanning sleeves to hold her slender arms. Fana's skin was electricity itself.

"I don't want to die of an aneurism in the middle of the night," he said slowly. "Or drive myself off of a bridge. I won't be a sacrifice like Phoenix."

"We're leaving right now to save Phoenix," Fana said.

"Save me," he said. "I want the Blood, Fana."

Fana's face didn't change. She'd known what he wanted as soon as she had seen him waiting for her. Her long silence was her only answer.

"Then you're a damn phony," Johnny said, and they both flinched from his words. "You think you're so revolutionary, sharing drops here and there, but it's only for a chosen few, Fana. 'Give me your reasons, monkey.'" Johnny's mouth was dry. "You told me to always keep it real, right? Tell you the truth?"

Had he hurt her? Made her angry? It was harder now to tell anything from Fana's face.

Fana spoke softly. "Johnny, you would live hundreds of years, or thousands—and you won't take a short breath to weigh this? Why make this decision in an emotional moment? Of course I want to share the Blood. I'll work with the council—"

"Stop acting like you have to give a damn about the council! *Show* them the way, Fana. What good is a gift you won't use?"

It wasn't easy to make Fana cry, but her eyes dampened. Did he have her?

"I don't want to make any more mistakes," Fana said.

His hands shook because he couldn't press his palms to her face and kiss her, only for fear that she would pull away. Johnny caressed the electric skin on her arms. "You *will* make mistakes," he said. "But leave your Blood—our mission—inside me. Please, Fana. Don't leave me with nothing of you—nothing of yours."

Her eyes gently melted into *yes*, and Johnny's flesh tremored.

"You have to die, Johnny," Fana said. She stared earnestly, to be sure he understood. "It's not like a dose of Glow. For the Blood ceremony, your heart has to stop. It's real death. You'll feel it."

Johnny's heartbeat shook his knees. He'd known his heart would have to stop, but he hadn't thought about what it would be like to die.

Fana was right. He wasn't ready.

But Fana wasn't ready for Michel either. She needed him.

"I want you to share your Blood with me, Fana," he said. "Whatever it takes."

Fasilidas, do not disturb me, Fana said to her guard beyond the door. *Tell Teka and my parents I need to be alone.*

YES, BLESSED FANA, he said, but she heard him wondering why Johnny was with her. Fana had promised a wall of privacy to her parents, Johnny, and Caitlin, but Fana knew her teacher's thoughts, and those of her guards. Fasilidas constantly probed Johnny for clues that she was sharing her bed with him, roiling with envy and disgust. But Fasilidas wouldn't dare probe Johnny while he was in her presence.

She and Johnny were truly alone. It was a small act of magic.

Johnny was rubbing her bare arms beneath the folds of her robe, a simple gesture that rocked her. She and Johnny had decided not to touch long ago, so Fana hadn't known how much she enjoyed his warm, calloused hands. It was clear to Fana now: her mother had orchestrated the meeting to bring them together. Fana was as irritated as she was grateful.

With Johnny standing in front of her, their unfinished story in his eyes, she couldn't ignore her grief. If not for Michel fooling her heart with lies, she might have loved Johnny first. The Blood would be her goodbye gift to him, but he deserved so much more.

Now she had to kill Johnny, just when she wanted to savor his love the most.

"You have to be sure," she said. "There's no going back."

His nervousness filled the room; the flood of his perspiration, the flurried whisper of his racing heartbeat. "I'm sure."

Was Michel watching? Fana remembered her promise not to defile the Blood, but she had never agreed on mutual language, a definition of terms. He had only mentioned the concerts. Still, Michel wouldn't like it; she couldn't lie to herself about that. They would argue about whether or not she had broken her word. There would be consequences. Fana's heart sped, waking. Maybe Johnny's nervousness was contagious.

"Are *you* sure?" Johnny said, reading her thoughts from her eyes.

"If this is what you want—I'm sure," she said. "Lie down. We don't have much time."

After a quick glance at the door, a reflex, Johnny rushed to the spongy pallet where Jessica had dreamed so many months away. The pallet still smelled stale and sharp, but Johnny might not notice. Mortals couldn't smell scents and odors the same way.

Fana sat beside Johnny like a nurse at his bedside, slipping so easily into the pose. She had never before visited the room he called his Bat Cave, but now she saw how ridiculous the pretense of distance had been between them. No wonder Fasilidas could see it, and everyone else. Fana was a virgin, but she and Johnny had been lovers all this time.

"I won't let him change me into his image," Fana told Johnny, a promise.

"He's telling himself the same thing. He's ready for you."

Fana laid her finger across Johnny's lips: *shhh.* Would talking about Michel conjure him? *The ground shook when we fought,* Fana whispered. *We both nearly bled to death. I'll talk to him this time. And I'll listen.*

"Will he listen?" Johnny said. His hands were clasped across his chest, his nervous fingers locked. Fana rested her hand on top of his. Johnny's skin shivered beneath her touch.

"He might," Fana said. "But I don't know the future, Johnny."

Sometimes she could find a piece of the future in her dreams and visions, but hindsight made clues clearest. Aside from her visit to Michel's thoughtstreams, Fana hadn't dreamed about him in a year, when she had imagined them inside the beautiful Frida Kahlo painting he had used to seduce her, *Love Embrace of the Universe.* While Mom had been lost in her dreams, Fana had been exiled from hers; even in meditation, her visions were hazy now.

Teka said it was her price for blocking out Michel.

Fana stared into Johnny's brown eyes, overflowing with anxious life. She could always tell a mortal by the eyes: their hunger to engage, to confront, to find language for their thoughts.

"Once you have the Blood, don't run out into the world like you think you're invincible," Fana said. "Find a safe, quiet place to sit with it. Don't draw attention to yourself. Uncle Lucas can help you transition, since he's been through it. Go to him right away."

Johnny only nodded, barely listening, fogged with fear. Fana fought a strong, sudden urge to probe him, to peel him open. Her awareness licked at a glaring omission in his thoughts.

"You haven't told me everything," Fana said.

"Then you'll have to live with that," Johnny said. "Like the rest of us."

Did Johnny mean to try to kill Michel? Even without a probe, Johnny's fondest hope seemed to leak from his body language, his eyes. Johnny expected the Blood to solve far too much. But how could she deny him? Her blood was Johnny's, too, and always had been.

"Give me a chance to do this my way," Fana said. "The Blood won't protect you from him any more than it could protect you from me. Even less."

She saw a quicksilver flicker in Johnny's eyes. He didn't like remembering how easily she could kill, how different and dangerous she was. She would give him the Blood—but she would show him everything that lay underneath it, her true face. And Michel's.

She owed him that.

Fana rooted around her mother's desk for something sharp enough to make her bleed. The search took longer than she expected; her mother didn't keep sharp objects within easy reach. Fana checked the sturdy length of her right thumbnail and decided that should be enough for the thin skin at their wrists.

She would stop his heart with her thoughts, then cut them both to give him a drop of her Blood, in the ancient way. She might not need the ceremony's incantation, but she knew the words from her father's memories. Only her father had heard Khaldun's words the night he gave fifty-nine men the Living Blood.

BOOM BOOM BOOM BOOM BOOM BOOM.

Johnny's heart was beating so hard, he might be shaking the walls. Or was it hers?

"You'll be awake," Fana said. "If you're strong enough for the Blood, you're strong enough to die. But I'll try to be fast."

Johnny blinked, his eyes red. "Okay." He sounded brave, but he looked ready to vomit.

"Now you'll see how easy it is for me to stop your heart."

"I always knew that," he said, his voice feeble. He tried to smile.

Johnny's pounding heart called to her, a perverse music. Her hands stroked his, mapping his throbbing pulse. Fear had a smell, she remembered. Pungent. Terrible at first, and then . . .

"Close your eyes, Johnny," Fana said.

Fana's probe dove into Johnny's warm body, past his skin and pores. His essence blazed around her, and she surfed the brightly strobing stream, yanked and flung through his pores, riding on his blood. She was inside him.

She imagined the quivering mass that was his heart, finding its thunder. She'd never tried to burrow inside a body before—she'd been afraid to try to heal Johnny with her mind a year ago, after Michel had made Johnny shoot himself. But now she'd gone in with ease. She could have repaired him herself! Her mind brushed the bullet's lingering damage, pieces frayed and shredded that the first drops of her healing Blood had kept alive.

But now she would *give* his blood Life, forever replenishing.

Johnny's heart was powerful in its youth, but it was already dying, a little each day. Fana ventured a glancing touch across Johnny's heart. Her presence sent his heart flailing, its warm throbbing suddenly frantic, disordered.

Johnny's heart bucked so strongly that it brought a cry to his lips. Outside the door, Fasilidas misunderstood Johnny's cries for pleasure.

Fana leaned over Johnny's wide-open, wondering eyes. She could have spared Johnny more pain, but then he would have lost the lesson.

You're dying now, Fana whispered.

YOU'RE DYING NOW.

Fana's voice: outside, inside, everywhere. Johnny didn't need the voice; the pain told him, making him forget everything else.

Johnny clutched his chest, trying to claw his way out of his dying body. His chest, his back, his neck, everything radiated blinding pain. He arched his back, trying to escape, and bands of agony enfolded him. An invisible tank had pinned him, slowly flattening him.

Johnny tried to pray, but he couldn't catch hold of words.

Stop, he tried to say. His inability to speak made his limbs shake. Johnny had lost control of his body, a too-familiar horror. His arms and legs wouldn't obey. His body flung itself to the floor, but he barely noticed the impact. The weight on his chest was crushing him.

Just one more breath! The air was too hot, too thin. Johnny heard himself gasp to the depths of his lungs, and he still couldn't find air. He was drowning in himself.

stop stop stop stop

Johnny no longer knew whom he was begging, or who might be listening. He was alone.

He begged the void, *Stop. Please.*

TOO LATE, the void said in a voice he did not know.

Johnny's heart would not go gently. It had cowered from her at first, but now it was fighting her with surprising strength, suddenly slippery. Fana was hurled away from his heart, and she scrambled to find it again.

If she lost Johnny's heartbeat, she might lose her moment to give him the Blood. Sometimes the ceremony failed, or was interrupted. Her father had failed with Kira. Fana didn't want to break her promise to Johnny. He had expected to live again after he died.

Just when Fana needed to concentrate most, she felt her attention tossed in so many directions—to Fasilidas, by her door; to her father, packing his bag in the next room; to her mother, praying in the rock garden. Even to Michel, a growing throb in the distance.

She was losing Johnny, hurting him more than she wanted to. *Too long.*

Fana tried to visualize the bright light of the Rising, but none of the floating sensation that guided her in meditation came. Johnny's cries sounded like a distant kitten's mews. He was so far from her! Fana was drowning with him as doubts assailed her. Was Michel sabotaging her? Was she working against herself?

Then, she understood: she had never stopped a heart with the power of the Rising! What had made her so certain she could? Why was she so surprised when she couldn't do anything she chose?

There's another way. Fana's own voice cleared her thoughts.

When she was three, Fana had thought the words *bye-bye* and stilled a soldier's heart. She had drained Kaleb's blood while she scribbled pictures. It had been easy! But she'd had help from the Shadows then; their humming was always waiting to be unburied. She needed to practice, or how would she learn to use the Shadows instead of only being used?

Like Michel, the Shadows were always waiting for her. Since Michel, she'd had to keep them at bay in her sleep, in her meditation, in her waking hours; it was less work to let the Shadows in than it was to shut them away.

Fana's vision dimmed, a blanket over her. Light fled the room. Had the sound always been there? The walls vibrated with buzzing, as if they were covered with bees.

Fana remembered what she'd forgotten about the smell of fear: yes, it started out pungent . . . but then . . . Fana inhaled, her nose brushing Johnny's face, and his waves of fright caressed her skin. Fear baked from him like hot bread.

Sweet. After a time, fear smelled sweet.

A scream came. Fana held on to the fascinating sound, savoring it, falling into it, climbing in and out of it. A playground to her senses. The Shadows roared with bliss.

But that's Johnny, someone reminded her. Or maybe she reminded herself. Still, the scream rocked and dizzied Fana, whirling inside her. Filling her. Tickling her.

Don't wanna die for a while. I think I'll fly for a while.

The singer's voice. A memory even the Shadows couldn't hide.

Slowly, too slowly, the spinning stopped.

Johnny's fear seeped away, replaced by a tide of euphoria that swept out his pain as his body settled to die. Fana heard Johnny's last thought: *THANK YOU, LORD.* Her thoughtstreams almost followed him, caught up in his euphoria. The Rising, so elusive before, swept her high. Through Johnny, she heard music somewhere in the blinding light. . . .

But Fana steadied her awareness, blocking out the music and the lights, forcing herself back to the physical world. She pressed her feet against the hard floor to bring herself back.

Johnny's heart was still. Slick, limp warmth.

"Fana, *no!*" her father shouted, so commanding that Fana

almost left Johnny's heart again. But she held on. She hadn't heard her father come in. All she knew was that Johnny's heart lay still, and his pain was gone. "You're *killing* him—"

"Give me your knife," Fana said.

Wildness churned in Dawit's eyes as he understood. "Use my blood, Fana—not yours."

"We want it to be mine." With her thoughtstream, Fana squeezed Johnny's heart to circulate his blood. Once. Twice. Not enough to bring him back; just enough to prepare him.

Hurry, Dad!

A sharp blade appeared before her, and Fana glimpsed her own face, elongated and distorted. Fana took her father's knife and poked at Johnny's wrist, opening his vein in a stream of bright crimson. Her pain when she cut herself was an insect's pinch. Her wound bled far less, tingling to heal right away, but she needed only a drop.

Fana pressed her torn skin to Johnny's, washing herself in his blood. Washing him.

"The Blood is the vessel for Life . . ." she recited, although she was certain that she and Michel didn't need to use an incantation like the others. "The Blood flows without end . . ."

Dawit's whisper joined hers, their last words in unison.

". . . Like a river through the Valley of Death."

Fana stroked Johnny's warm forehead. His corpse was curled in a fetal position on the floor beside the pallet, his struggle absent on his calm face. *I'm sorry,* she whispered. *I didn't mean for it to hurt so much.*

Johnny was still dead. His body would start to cool. Rigor mortis would set in.

Then, in a few hours, he would grow warm again. His heart would stir. He would wake.

Dawit paced the room slowly, rubbing his face with both hands as if he were trying to scrub off his skin. His thoughts rang with his disappointment and anger.

WHY? WHY NOW?

He asked me, Dad. The Blood belongs to him, too.

"Fana, this was the worst possible course with Michel!" This time, he spoke aloud.

She had just traded something away. Something awful, maybe. But her father couldn't say he didn't understand.

"If you want your singer, we can't stay to see him wake, Duchess," Dawit said.

Fana nodded. They should have left long ago.

Fana stood above Johnny, enjoying his peace the way the Shadows had savored his suffering. The kindest gift would have been to free him, but how could she have made him understand that? *Safe journey,* Fana told Johnny. *I'll find a way, Johnny. Trust in me.*

Fana raised her palm to her nose and smelled the warm, damp oils from the skin on Johnny's forehead. Even as his face grayed, she could imagine his boyish dimples when he smiled. She looked at him for only an instant, but she made the instant last.

Fana turned away from Johnny.

Phoenix first. Then, to Mexico. To Michel.

She was a year late for her wedding.

Twenty-two

"**W**ake up, you selfish son of a bitch."

The voice made Johnny stir.

He opened his eyes, and saw only a white sheet of light. *Am I dead?*

The woman's voice sounded mousy and faraway. Not Fana. Somewhere outside him.

"I can't believe you would go over without me. I hope you have a really, really bad hangover. Worse than a hangover. But you better wake up and stop scaring the crap out of me."

Johnny was awake, suddenly. His heartbeat rang in his chest, *thump thump.* He could hear it without trying to. His bloodstream was swollen, all his nerve endings tingling. His lungs drank in the air, and oxygen flooded him. Had he gained ten pounds? His back chafed against his soft bed because he felt so heavy. His blood was glowing as it charged through his veins.

Glow. They had named it right.

He opened his eyes and saw Caitlin leaning over him.

"You jerk—thank God!" she said. She grabbed his hand, then flung it away as if it had bitten her. "What the hell were you thinking? She could have killed you, Johnny!"

"We knew she wouldn't." Johnny's throat was so parched that it hurt. He glanced around the room for water and found none within easy reach. When he sat up, the room whirled. His heartbeat was louder in his ears.

You did it, he reminded himself. *It's done.*

The simple words stilled Johnny's thoughts, paralyzing him.

He didn't have to ask Caitlin if he had died and come back. More than his blood was new; he had new skin, too, taut and lively across his bones. He barely recognized the room because his vision was so much brighter, everything vivid and crisp. Johnny stuck out the tip of his tongue, and his tongue lapped up the flavors in the air: citrus and incense and rich oxygen. Had the air had a taste before? He closed his mouth when he noticed the bed's odor. The bed smelled rotten, as if that scent was on his tongue, too.

Johnny had been tired when he first heard Caitlin's voice, but after a minute he was ready to leap to his feet and run. It was hard to imagine ever feeling tired again.

"She did it?" Caitlin said, hushed. "She gave it to you?"

Slowly, Johnny nodded. His head rocked up and down, fluid. Johnny thought about the Tin Man from *The Wizard of Oz*, and how oil made him a new man.

"How do you feel?" Caitlin said.

Johnny wished his throat weren't so parched. Talking hurt. Johnny rolled his head on his neck, testing every angle of himself. No twinges, pops, or pain.

"Weird. Wired. No wonder they don't need much sleep."

"You," Caitlin corrected him gently. "*You* won't need sleep."

Her unblinking blue eyes made it real again. He was one of them. Immortal!

"We should be recording this," Caitlin said, awestruck. "Documenting it."

Johnny leaped up and paced, ignoring her. Caitlin was missing the point "Is she gone?"

"They left about four hours ago," Caitlin said. "You've been out for nine."

Fana was four hours closer to Michel, and four hours farther from home. She was gone. That idea stunned him almost as much as his strange new awakening. His pacing stopped cold.

"She needs help, Caitlin," Johnny said.

"I swear, I thought he already had her," Caitlin whispered. "But Michel wouldn't let Fana give you the Blood. *She* did that. Right?"

"Yes," Johnny said. "Definitely."

Like him, Caitlin was craving assurances. But Johnny remembered that Michel had been patient when he first found Fana, humoring her by allowing her to give Johnny a drop of blood to heal the gunshot. Michel's air of kindness had drawn Fana straight to him.

Caitlin sighed. "I'm scared for you, Johnny. And I hate you deeply right now, so imagine how scared I must be."

"I'll give you the Blood, too. As soon as I figure out how."

"Thanks, but screw you," Caitlin said. "You should have given me a chance."

"Do you even want it?" Johnny said. "You always said you weren't sure."

"I would have wanted the choice!" Caitlin said. "The power to say yes or no. I never would have done it without giving you the chance."

Johnny had never heard such envy from Caitlin. She was nearly whining. When had he become the adult and she become the child? He'd always felt two steps behind Caitlin. Something had changed already.

"You could have asked her if you wanted it," he said, irritation creeping into his voice.

"She wouldn't have done it just for me," Caitlin said. "Stop playing dumb."

Caitlin had warned him about his pattern of falling for women he couldn't have, starting with her at Berkeley. But this was different—far different. Caitlin had tried to help him keep his sanity when he was near Fana, but no one could have. How had Caitlin avoided falling in love with Fana, too? Or had she?

"I wasn't thinking straight, Caitlin. I just wanted . . ." Johnny's new heart of brick pounded at his sternum. How much should he tell her? Caitlin might be the only person he could truly trust, unless Michel was hiding somewhere inside her. "I wanted to feel less helpless. We're not helpless, Caitlin. I'm not. I won't let Fana face this alone."

Slow horror unfurled in Caitlin's eyes. "That's why you did this?" she said.

"Anyone can die," Johnny said. "Even Michel."

Johnny looked for a spark of fire in Caitlin's eyes, but there was only fear. Michel's men had butchered Caitlin's girlfriend to learn about Glow. Michel had stolen control of Caitlin's body to walk and talk inside her, too. Caitlin might not know it, but Michel had broken her.

Rare tears crept into Caitlin's eyes. "Fana stopped your heart by *thinking* about it. If we're worried she isn't strong enough, what makes you think you are?" she whispered.

"I may not be," he said. "But how can I not try?"

Johnny took a step toward the door, but Caitlin leaped in front of him. "Wait!" she said, her anxious face reminding him of how he must have seemed to her at Berkeley: naïve and excitable. "Johnny, one of the immortals is coming to talk to you. Yacob, I think. Fana asked him to orient you. She made me promise you'd talk to him, and then I'd get you to Doc Shepard. We're meeting them in Lagos."

"You tried, Caitlin. I have to go."

"Why? She gave you the Blood, so you think you can fly now? Walk on water?"

That whininess again. Caitlin was the first soldier he'd known, so it hurt to see her so afraid. Fighting for Glow had taught him how to think like a fighter. All he needed was a plan.

"I'm going to kill him, Caitlin," he said. "Or maybe I'll die trying. You know why I have to. My beliefs don't give me a choice."

"Because you think he's the antichrist?" Caitlin said, exasperated.

"Don't you?"

"I don't know if I believe in the Bible—how can I believe in the antichrist?"

"We saw what he wants to do, Caitlin," Johnny said. "Both of us saw."

He recognized the memory in her eyes. She had seen Michel's projections of the Cleansing, too: a planet stripped of most of humanity, exclusive to those who remained. She had seen the photos from Nigeria and North Korea, and how his virus posed the dead to pray to him.

More than that, Caitlin's fear of Michel was personal. Michel's men had touched her while she lay pinned under his mental paralysis. Caitlin's terror at that moment still swam in her eyes. She didn't want to face Michel again.

"How?" Caitlin said anyway. "How would we stop him?"

Johnny's chest shook with the aggressive thumping of his reinvigorated heart.

"With help from my new Brothers," he said.

UPWORLD

Learn or die.
—Earthseed: The Book of the Living
Octavia E. Butler
Parable of the Sower

The price one pays for entering a profession or calling is an intimate knowledge of its ugly side.
—James Baldwin

Twenty-three

Phoenix was nearly hoarse from singing, but she didn't stop. She sang more softly, pacing herself, taking long breaks, sometimes only mouthing the words. Singing worked better for her than screaming, and screaming was all her body wanted to do.

Phoenix sat with her back against the door, her tailbone sore from the frigid floor in clothes so thin they were like tissue. Since Marcus had been stolen, her room was too cold. Phoenix had never gotten used to the cold after growing up in Miami. Her teeth chattered while she shivered violently. Her palms and the backs of her hands felt numb. She missed the blankets, but she'd given up asking for them back. She'd come to terms with begging long ago, but begging hadn't worked.

Phoenix's nose had plugged up the same day as Marcus vanished, an illness invading her when she was weakest, and she had to breathe through her dry mouth. Sometimes phlegm walled her throat, and she couldn't breathe. Phoenix couldn't sing during her coughing fits, so she waited for those to pass. She felt her lungs constrict with each hacking cough. Maybe bronchitis. Maybe pneumonia. Whatever had happened at the Glow concert had killed her cancer cells, but her body could still be attacked.

Whatever had happened. Phoenix hated her ignorance. If she knew exactly, she would have told everything. Her defiance had vanished with Marcus. She'd answered every question as well as she knew how, wishing she knew more:

Her name is Fana. F-A-N-A, I think. No, I don't know her last name. John Jamal Wright came to my house and tried to give me a vial of Glow. I refused it. He had access to more. I don't know why they came to me. I asked them to try someone else. I was worried about the stories I'd heard, but I thought one concert would be okay. They offered me money for charity. Something happened to us at the concert: Fana raised her arms and healed us.

But what she knew wasn't enough, apparently. They wanted something else from her. She only wished she knew what.

Phoenix was enraged at Fana and John Jamal Wright for the trouble they'd brought her. Sometimes her anger at them dwarfed her rage for the captors who watched her freezing to death and carefully avoided her eyes when they brought her scraps or ice-cold water to drink.

Phoenix sang of forgiving her captors so she would not scream.

She sang of seeing Marcus again so she would not scream.

She sang of Carlos so she would not scream.

And when she was half asleep, Phoenix sang about the palace on the hilltop she dreamed about, and the man and woman who held dominion there.

The Lioness meets the Lion
In the place where love collides.
Keepers of agonies and wildest dreams
Draw blood from shadowed skies.

Phoenix woke to hear herself singing and didn't recognize her own words. Sometimes her song about the palace terrified her—*blood from shadowed skies?* And yet . . . Sometimes her strange songs brought her indescribable comfort, transporting her far outside her cell and the faceless facility that had stolen her life from her.

Those moments were always over too soon.

A tall, wide man was approaching her cell door to open it. Harley. She didn't allow herself any feelings about Harley's coming, since there was nothing she could do about it.

Phoenix moved away from the door. As she scooted back, her

palms flopped against the floor like dead fish, numb. Today she would tell him about her dreams and songs!

Harley wasn't his real name, but his large Harley-Davidson belt buckle made Phoenix imagine him in leather chaps. The bridge of his nose was crisscrossed with old knife scars. Phoenix didn't like being close to his heavy black boots, so she tried to pull herself to her feet. Her hands rebelled, useless. Her fingers were numb, too.

"You'll piss me off if you make me do this the hard way," Harley said.

The first morning after Marcus was gone, he'd had to literally drag her to the interrogation room. She'd been out of her mind that day. She was still out of her mind, but she'd learned how to hide it better.

Harley didn't seem like himself. He was the only one who scared her, who shouted at her and stood close enough to pose a physical threat, but Harley was a professional. He didn't start out in a bad mood.

"No," Phoenix said. "I'm up, see? I'm ready. I thought of something I forgot to tell you—it's the whole thing. I can't believe I didn't think of it before now. And then you'll bring Marcus back? And let us go?"

Phoenix didn't recognize her own voice anymore. A blathering jellyfish.

"That's what you said yesterday, Mrs. Harris," Harley said, shrugging. He cuffed her hands behind her back, too tightly. That wasn't like Harley either, using such a low street cop's trick. Harley was *yes, ma'am* and *no, ma'am* even when his eyes had a different message.

Phoenix realized she could smell the sour spice of Harley's day-old deodorant. He was standing too close to her, a mound of body heat. Harley ran his palm across the top of Phoenix's head, lingering at her neck. It was an intimate touch, one she saved for Carlos.

"You know, your cold's not getting any better," Harley said. "You need to get out of this hellhole before you really get sick." His words were tender, but his voice was not.

"Carlos is all right?" she said, hoping to tempt him to say the words. Waiting for Harley to answer made Phoenix so anxious that she started coughing. "There's a palace, maybe a church, high on a hilltop . . ." she began, breathless. A wheeze.

"Save it for the room," he said, leading her into the hall. "Let's get it on tape."

Until then, Phoenix hadn't been sure they would leave her cell, with Harley's mood so strange. Relief quivered her knees. She didn't want to be locked in her cell with him.

As he pulled her into the hall, Harley ran his hand across her scalp again, and farther down her neck. Caressed her shoulder blades. He always touched her in ways she didn't like, subtle taps on her kneecaps now and then, but his hand felt heavy and purposeful now.

"There's a valley below the church, or maybe it's a palace . . ." Phoenix said.

Harley's hand slid casually across her lower back as he walked her briskly down the hall.

"You'd say anything to get out of here today," Harley said.

"All this time, I was looking in the wrong place," she said. "It's the *dream* I should have looked at. I've had the dream more than once. I had it the first time the night of the raid, when I was brought here. I should have realized . . ." Her teeth were chattering.

Two soldiers were waiting in the elevator. The dark-haired one had a mustache, the one who brought her oatmeal and stale bread occasionally, making jokes about room service. She had never seen the younger soldier, who was about twenty-four, badly sunburned, his carrot-colored hair shaved into a crewcut. The new soldier was husky, but he watched Harley with trepidation, taking a step back. Neither soldier met her eyes.

Harley led her inside the elevator, his hand pressing harder against her back. Phoenix despised Harley's touch, but at least his hand was warm.

The elevator door opened, and Harley's hand guided her out. The last door on the right loomed at the end of the hall. Would they be alone? Was there a camera in the interrogation room? His two hundred fifty pounds could crush her.

It didn't matter, she tried to tell herself. Nothing Harley could do to her body was worse than Marcus being away from her.

"No time to drag your feet now," Harley said.

"I'm not dragging," she said. "Let's get this done quick, real fast, so I can go. I'll tell you all about the palace. It's . . . Spanish, maybe. . . ."

"This isn't a good day for you to jerk me around, princess. Don't say I didn't warn you."

Her feet *were* dragging. He lifted her by her armpits every few steps to keep her walking. Her weight was nothing for him to carry, but she knew that if she didn't walk faster, he would fling her over his shoulder the way he had the day they took Marcus. *And then he'll rape me as soon as he closes the door.*

It was more than a premonition; it was just a hard fact. She'd never had those thoughts about Harley, who was stern and loud, sometimes, but always professional. Harley had changed.

"Just—just give me a chance to tell you," she said. "It's all in my dream."

"*Walk.*" His grip around her arm was a clamp. The suddenness of the pressure made her realize he could snap her arm in half.

"*Ow!*" she said. "There's no reason to hurt me. I said I'll tell you all about it!"

Phoenix saw moral outrage in the younger soldier's eyes. He was scared for her.

Phoenix's own fear caught in her throat, and she started coughing again. This time, Harley shoved her. She flew ahead three steps, nearly losing her balance against the wall.

"Uh, sir . . ." the younger soldier began, before he'd planned out what he would say.

"Mind your goddamn business," Harley said.

As if to punish Phoenix instead, Harley leaned against her, pinning her to the wall with his weight while he pulled out his key card for the interrogation room. He was so big, he smothered her light. Her insides gave a spasm from the effort of coughing against his bulk.

Through the crook of Harley's arm, Phoenix saw the soldier

staring at her, flinching as his instincts told him to help her. His jaw was shaking, he was so mad. Or scared. Phoenix didn't know which. Maybe, like her, his rage and fear were tied together so closely that they were impossible to pull apart.

"You think you've got the guts for my job?" Harley said to the soldier.

"No, sir," the soldier said quickly, and the second soldier shot him a cutting glare. The soldier with the mustache had never had a problem seeing Phoenix as a prisoner. Maybe he'd seen worse. Maybe he had done worse to Carlos.

"You think we should sit back and let this spoiled, crazy bitch open our doors to bioterrorists?" Harley said. He leaned harder, and one of Phoenix's joints cracked. The soldiers heard it, too. Phoenix's body was too compressed to feel new pain. Harley had never called her names before. He sounded as if he were talking about someone else. *Becoming* someone else.

"No, sir," the soldier said in a small voice. "I don't think that at all."

The panel glowed green with approval. Phoenix heard the door click open.

"Got any other quandaries you want to chat about, dogshit?" Harley said.

"No, sir."

Phoenix gave the soldier a smile that she hoped was more than miserable. "It's okay," she wheezed through her cough. "I'm stronger . . . than I look."

The pep talk won her a punch in the stomach with an impact like being hit by a car, ramming her spine against the wall. Phoenix had never been punched so hard. She sucked in a long gasp while her lungs tried to remember how to breathe. Red and black spots cartwheeled before her eyes.

Her legs were gone now, or seemed to be. She couldn't move, much less walk.

"Still feeling strong?" Harley said, his breath hot and full in her ear. His gums smelled infected and his breath stank of coffee, but Phoenix inhaled his odors, hoarding the air.

He dragged her beneath her armpits, clawlike fingertips digging. Instinct made her feet scrabble against the floor. The orange-haired soldier's apologetic eyes were the last thing Phoenix saw before Harley pulled her into the interrogation room and closed the door.

This door was metal, not glass. No one could see in or out.

Phoenix braced for another blow, or Harley's hands tearing at her clothes.

Instead, Harley gave out a strangled grunt, and melted to the floor at her feet. To Phoenix, it looked as if someone had pulled a plug and deflated him. His huge palm, which had stroked her back only moments before, flopped open. His key card skittered under the table.

Phoenix stared at him in confusion until she saw the ring of blood across his neck.

Two masked black soldiers stood behind her in green fatigues, out of sight from the doorway. One of the men was nearly as big as Harley. The other man was slender, holding a bloodied knife. The big man raised a gun, pointing toward the empty wall beside the door. Phoenix realized he meant to shoot at the other two soldiers through the solid concrete.

"No!" she said. "He—"

But her call came too late. The gun made a sound like two puffs of air, virtually a whisper. Two holes appeared in the wall, three feet apart. Chest level. The masked man had aimed directly at the soldiers' hearts.

"The lioness and lion meet . . ."

Phoenix sang instead of screaming.

DON'T BE AFRAID, Fana's voice said in her head. THEY WON'T HURT YOU.

The voice made Phoenix's eyes snap open. She was still being carried over the big soldier's shoulder, her sore stomach and bruised ribs chafing against him with every jouncing step. The men spoke to each other in a rapid-fire language she didn't know. Despite their uniforms, they weren't American.

Where was Fana? How could she hear Fana's voice? Was she dreaming?

The big man called out a warning in a commanding basso. The man leading them, the one with the knife, dove across the floor, reaching the end of the hall in time to surprise a man rounding a corner in a three-piece suit. The soldier plunged a knife into his neck, once on each side, so efficient it was like an illusion. Blood spurted in twin fountains. The dead man didn't have time to make a sound before he was on the floor.

No! Phoenix tried to say. *Not for me. No more killing for me.*

DO NOT BE AFRAID, Fana's voice said. *YOU'LL SEE MARCUS AND CARLOS SOON.*

Red lights were flashing in the hall, silent alarms. More urgent whispers from the soldiers, and she was jounced in yet another direction. The soldiers were running up the stairs, talking back and forth, increasingly agitated.

What if she was sent to her cell again? What if these men were worse than the last?

Phoenix felt herself swooning, her consciousness fading into a wave of panic. Each jolt up the steps was a new blow to her stomach. She wanted the soldier to put her down on her feet so she could stumble some kind of way on her own. She wriggled, but his iron arm held her.

DO NOT BE AFRAID, Fana's voice said. *LET ME HELP YOU BE LESS AFRAID.*

Yes, yes, yes, Phoenix thought. *Please. I'm hurt.*

It was as if Fana's voice was the voice she had been looking for when she tried to talk to God. Time had taught her to be satisfied with silence when she really needed to think God was there—in the cell downstairs, and when her mother had been screaming in pain at the hospital. But sometimes she'd thought the silence meant that no one and nothing was listening. Deep down, she'd wondered if it was foolish to believe anything else.

Not anymore. Fana was listening.

Phoenix asked Fana to take away her fear, and fear receded like a Miami Beach tide racing away so quickly that the loss of it made her woozy. Alertness and euphoria filled the void: Fana was rescuing her! She was free! The pain from Harley's punch was still there, but it wasn't nearly as bad without her fear.

The two men navigated the stairs in silence. Phoenix watched over her shoulder, missing nothing. The soldier in the lead took Harley's key card and swiped it on the lock panel at the top of the stairs.

"I can walk," Phoenix said as they waited for the card to register.

The soldier turned to look at her, only his eyes visible through his mask. She had met him before, she realized. He might be Fana's father, almost too young for a teenage daughter.

"But can you run?" His English sounded American, but with an arresting exoticism.

"I . . . I think so."

The light on the panel flickered in yellow. Quickly, he swiped the card again. This time, the panel glowed in green. The door clicked loudly, ready to open. The taller man gently rested her on her feet, holding her steady.

The man who might have been Fana's father reached out to her. "Hold my hand," he said.

Phoenix grabbed his gloved hand, grateful for his steady grip. The bigger soldier spoke quickly in their language again, but this time he seemed to be addressing someone who wasn't in the room. A radio? The bigger man nodded to him, and Fana's father opened the door, pushing hard against the sudden wind.

Outside, the sun shone as brightly as the star it was. Phoenix couldn't see anything except brightness as she charged ahead, following the soldier's sure grasp. The unearthly beating of wind whipped her T-shirt against her skin. A helicopter, she realized.

"Hurry!" Fana's father said, pulling her along.

Phoenix's tight stomach slowed her more than she'd expected, but she ran as fast as she could make her legs move. The slate-gray helicopter hadn't quite landed, but the cabin door was wide open. Inside the cabin, a child beside the window was wrapped in a blanket, peering out.

Marcus? Hope took the rest of her breath away.

"Yes—we have your son too!" Fana's father shouted to her, urging her along.

Ten yards to run across the rooftop. Loose gravel tried to steal her footing as she craned to see the child better. Five yards. Phoenix couldn't believe her son was there until—

The toothless grin came. "Mommy!" Marcus cried. She couldn't quite hear him over the helicopter's propellers, but she knew even slivers of her son's voice.

The larger soldier hoisted her by her waist from behind, and suddenly Phoenix was tumbling into the cabin, the soldiers careful not to trample her as they climbed in after her. The cabin door slammed shut behind them, and Phoenix's ears popped.

"Mommy, Mommy, Mommy!" Marcus was chanting, half laughing, half crying, his arms reaching out for her as he fought his seat belt. Phoenix collapsed into the middle seat beside him, blanketing him in her embrace. She sobbed as she touched his warm face, pressed her ear to his beating heart. No noise, no fear, no pain—only Marcus.

Fana's father shouted something to the pilot. The helicopter lifted into the air, racing away. The cabin tilted sharply.

It took more than a minute for Phoenix to notice that the woman sitting in the seat across from her was Fana. Her face and dreadlocks hadn't changed since the concert. Fana's eyes were as sad as the soldier's who had been shot outside her door.

Biting back another sob, Phoenix reached to clasp the girl's hand.

Fana squeezed tightly. Her voice floated into Phoenix's head, ethereal.

I'M SO SORRY THIS HAPPENED. I DIDN'T WANT TO SEE YOU HURT.

When Fana touched her, a tingle cascaded through Phoenix's body. The cramping in her stomach loosened. Her ribs stopped complaining. Her lungs cleared. Healing. Phoenix's next tears were ecstatic, the only release for a feeling too big to hold all at once.

Yes I knew you at the concert when I saw you standing between the columns I knew you when I saw the ropes of your hair I knew you

when you raised your arms to the sky and you rained down I knew you
I knew you I knew you

NO, Fana said. *I KNEW YOU. I NEED YOU, PHOENIX.*

"Carlos?" Phoenix managed to say, struggling to think past her euphoria to remember her heartaches, so much left undone.

Fana didn't answer at first. Her eyes had drifted into a private space.

"Your husband was being detained at a separate facility," Fana's father said. "He's already safe on the plane. We're taking you to him now."

Twenty-four

As the helicopter sped due north for San Francisco, Dawit could only shake his head while the singer comforted her child. True, their joy was touching, and he hadn't minded slicing the throat of the singer's captor, who had been ready to brutalize a woman under the guise of duty. But at what price?

A DEBACLE! Berhanu complained, staring out the windows for aircraft in pursuit. Berhanu was seeking out thoughts of approaching pilots; Dawit and Berhanu would never have made it into the building without Berhanu's ability to monitor remote thoughts.

If they were being chased, they would divert away from the others. Their waiting jet was well armed, but Dawit wasn't looking forward to skirmishes with the air force.

Dawit leaned back to call to Teka in the pilot's chair. "Have we triggered a war?" he said in Amharic. He didn't need to tax his telepathy for private conversation. Teka was intercepting military radio transmissions, listening on his headphones.

WE HAVE NO AIR PURSUIT AS YET, Teka said. *THERE IS CHAOS WITHIN, BUT FANA HAS MASKED THE HELICOPTER.*

Fana was the only one of them with the power to hide such a large object, manipulating the appearance of its mass to make it virtually invisible. She alone could alter the sounds for multiple listeners, dimming the racket of the helicopter's blades.

Fana had practiced the skill on automobiles, eluding police before. If not for that, Dawit would have preferred to leave Fana on the plane with Jessica in San Francisco.

Their plan for a nighttime raid had been scrapped after their sources in the DHS and NSA had reported that nightfall would be too late. Since Fana could conceal only one vehicle at a time, Fasilidas and Teferi had gone by car to find the singer's husband fifty miles north, without Fana's protection. Luckily, the singer and her child had been only two floors apart.

Teka had corrupted the facility's surveillance cameras. The flimsy cover wouldn't survive scrutiny, but they might have carved a clean escape. It was a pity they'd killed so many personnel—at least five. Two of the dead had worn military uniforms, and one had been from a covert branch that wore no uniform. Three more had died trying to keep the boy, including a female bureaucrat who had believed she was protecting him.

Made public, it would sound like war on U.S. soil. If they were forced to ask Glow loyalists in Washington, D.C., to intervene, it would be a civil war. All for a singer!

SHE IS MORE THAN A SINGER TO FANA, Teka said.

"I pray we can leave the airport with our precious new cargo," Dawit said.

AIR TRAFFIC CONTROL IS AN EASY MATTER, Teka said. *IF WE GET THAT FAR.*

Dawit turned back to Fana. Camouflaging the helicopter was a monumental mental task for Fana, but Dawit had learned that he could trust her to answer when she was able.

"Michel did not keep his word," Dawit told Fana in Amharic, leaning toward her. "She was on the disposal list, Fana. She would not have survived until nightfall."

All men, regardless of power or station, could be judged by the chasm between their words and deeds. If Michel had promised Fana that he would free the singer, he had lied to her. If Michel was still lying to her, they could not trust him to receive Fana with honor.

Fana seemed not to have heard him. Her eyes fell closed.

Dawit persisted quietly. "If Michel believes the circumstances of this rescue were favorable, he is lying to himself. That is the worst kind of liar."

WE HAVE ALL THREE OF THEM, Fana said. *THAT WAS HIS PROMISE.*

"She was on the disposal list. Her husband, too. We reached them by chance."

HE EXPECTED US TO BE EFFICIENT.

"He gave us nothing, Fana."

Dawit realized that his one-sided conversation with Fana must look strange to a mortal in any language, but Phoenix was too intoxicated by her son to look their way. The helicopter veered again. Without pursuit, it was safe to proceed directly to the airport.

HE MAY BE PUNISHING ME FOR JOHNNY, Fana said. Finally.

His dear Fana had inherited her father's foolish, destructive heart.

"Then we might wait and judge how much you have offended him," Dawit said gently.

HE KEPT HIS PROMISE BETTER THAN I KEPT MINE.

She was right, of course. In Michel's eyes, she might have broken trust first.

Mahmoud had teased Dawit for his perfectionism in battle, which was, of course, an oxymoron. Plans were only the beginning of a long and arduous conversation between expectations and circumstance. They had emerged without injury or capture, so far, but he could not be at ease. They nearly had been overmatched already!

Dawit had banished his doubts about Fana's visit to Michel— and *visit* was the word he stubbornly clung to—but the doubts had reappeared. How could Fana trust him?

Dawit had prepared for the worst with the rescue, but he had hoped for courtesy. Even with internal sources, a technological advantage, and access to the facilities' computers, the rescues had been dangerous. They would be lucky to lift off from San Francisco without F-14s scrambling behind them.

Dawit closed his eyes and took a breath. If he was quiet, he heard his own wisdom.

"They can't cry war over prisoners they never had in official custody," Dawit said, assuring himself aloud. "If the public knew she'd been detained, it would cause an international outcry. Her music is beloved. Bureaucracy will keep it contained."

MICHEL WILL KEEP IT CONTAINED, Fana said.

Dawit hoped Fana wasn't relying on the same intuition that had driven her to share her Blood with Johnny Wright, passing him the Life Gift from her own veins. What good was their tortured celibacy if Fana offered Johnny the one thing Michel treasured so much more than the body? And on the eve of her arrival, no less.

Dawit could see the child in her, unchanged.

"I have to ask you . . ." the singer began, addressing Fana. Gently, so gently.

Fana opened her eyes.

"Where are we going?" the singer said. The poor woman's ordeal stamped her face: dark pits under her eyes from lack of sleep, lips flaking and bleeding from dehydration. Fana had visited a typhoon on her, and Phoenix was gazing at Fana as if she were the face of the sun. The rescued were always eager to follow.

Fana smiled. "Right now, I want you to have some time with your family," she said. "We're about forty minutes from the plane, and the three of you will have a private cabin tonight. I want you to hold each other. And you should rest for tomorrow."

"What happens tomorrow?"

Fana closed her eyes again, smile fading. "You're coming with me to Mexico."

The plane seemed to stretch for a city block.

Phoenix had hoped Carlos would be her first sight, but instead she was in a galley with a marble floor and fully stocked bar. And then a cabin full of the Africans she had first seen at the concert, who still looked like nobles even in unremarkable street clothes.

Then a long conference area with a sofa, plush leather chairs, long desk, wide-screen TV, and another stranger, an American woman: Fana's mother, Jessica. The woman's face was fresh from the memories Fana had shared with her. Jessica pampered Marcus like an aunt, but she wasn't Carlos. "Let's go see your daddy," Jessica said, and led them to yet another door in the rear, only half open. "He's in here. I'm so sorry about—"

A shadow moved inside the cabin, and the door flung open. Carlos stood there wearing a towel, dripping from the shower, freshly shaved. He looked like a snapshot from their life in Paso on an ordinary day. Judging by the pain in his face, she looked like a nightmare.

"*Daddy!*" Marcus shrieked, and leaped into Carlos's arms.

Marcus's exuberant weight was a burden. Phoenix saw Carlos lean on the door frame to keep his balance, his knees nearly buckling. Like her, Carlos was weak.

"Phee?" Carlos said between kisses to his son's neck and cheek. "Are you okay?"

He reached for her hand, pulling her closer.

"Fine, baby. I'm fine now." Phoenix folded herself behind Marcus, taking some of their son's weight in her arms.

They sank into the cabin, and the door closed behind them, the privacy she had been promised. The compact bed by the window was just big enough for the three of them to rest without having to let go. Once they were wrapped inside each other, remembering and forgetting, Phoenix heard her own wailing sobs and Carlos's muffled ones, and Marcus was saying, *Why are you crying? We're back together now.*

But that only made Phoenix cry harder, until she had to clamp both hands over her mouth so she wouldn't worry Marcus on his celebration day. How could she explain to either of them? How could she destroy their homecoming?

They both quizzed Marcus on his time away from them.

"I cried a lot and said I wanted to be with my mommy and daddy," he said matter-of-factly. "They gave me pizza and ice cream, though. And DVDs." As if it were a fair trade.

Marcus had not been mistreated, thank God. Phoenix had told God flatly that if she had to choose between her husband and her baby boy, please let her baby boy be safe. Carlos would have said it, too. But she had both of them. *Both* of them. Phoenix sobbed from joy.

Each new sob brought questions to Carlos's eyes. He asked in Spanish, but she just said, "I'm fine. I was hurt, but Fana healed me." Then he wanted to know how she had been hurt, who had hurt her, and how. She heard the question *violado*, a word that made her remember Harley's hand. But Harley was far behind her now.

"Nothing happened," she said. "My room was cold. I was hungry. What about you?"

Carlos didn't want to talk about his experience, either. She fumbled through her Spanish to ask if he'd been beaten. His shrug alarmed her. *"Agua,"* he whispered. *"Agua."*

"I know that means 'water,' Daddy," Marcus said, proud of himself. Blissfully oblivious.

Phoenix's next sob was for Carlos. Her mind flashed images from the news, documentaries and protest signs, and her limbs seized with horror for him. She imagined his face smothered with a wet towel while he gasped for air.

"Shhhhh. Don't cry," he said. "I survived."

She hugged him around his neck, and they rocked together. "That didn't happen to me, baby," she whispered. "They didn't do that to me. Hear me? Nothing like that."

Happy tears came to his eyes. "I kept seeing you drowning. . . ." Carlos's hand trembled as he grabbed hers to anchor him against his memories.

Phoenix kissed his hand, but it took his trembling a long time to settle. Phoenix decided never to tell him about Harley's hand on her back. Dawit's knife had washed away the need to tell her husband that story. Fana's mission made Harley irrelevant.

"Please forgive the intrusion," a pleasant male voice said from the loudspeaker above their doorway. He also spoke exotic English. "We have been cleared for takeoff, so please stay seated in case of mishap."

Phoenix had forgotten they were on a plane.

All three of them huddled at the windows by the bed, watching as the jets and rampways passed in a blur. It was still daylight, but the fog was as thick as smoke. How had the pilot ever gotten clearance to take off? Could he fly blind? Phoenix thought she saw the flashing red light of a police car, but it was only a luggage cart on the tarmac. They all held hands as the plane gathered speed, shaking the wall. As the plane rose, an ocean of ghostly fog unfurled beneath them, swallowing the city except for the tips of the Golden Gate Bridge.

The rising fog banks could have followed Phoenix from her dream.

"I'm . . ." Marcus mumbled. Then his chin bobbed to his chest, and he was asleep. The motion had rocked him to sleep, just like when he was a baby. Phoenix rested her cheek against his forehead, feeling him breathe. What would she give to be Marcus, safe in his parents' arms with no idea what was outside?

For a time, Phoenix and Carlos watched Marcus sleep. They each held one foot to take off his black sneakers, which were a size too big, someone's best guess. They curled him in the upper corner of the bed, beside the plane's gently humming wall, and smothered him in blankets.

A knock at the cabin door. One of the men brought a tray: baked salmon, mashed potatoes, freshly steamed broccoli. Garlic bread. Phoenix didn't think she was hungry, but she ate voraciously. Despite the generous helpings, she could have eaten more. She kept eyeing the minipizza set aside for Marcus, wondering if pizza had been ruined for him by his captors.

Carlos ate purposefully, slowly, trying not to rush. They had both been hungry for days.

While Carlos finished his plate, Phoenix followed his example and took a shower. The sky wasn't bumpy enough to make her delay cleaning herself, since she hadn't been allowed to bathe. The shower was surprisingly large, as big as a shower in a budget motel room. It had been a long time since Phoenix had flown on a private jet, and none had been as big as this one. This was a queen's quarters.

The hot water dancing on her skin ignited her gratitude.

Thank you thank you thank you Fana.

Phoenix could have stayed in that shower for days. When she came out, Carlos was holding his head in his hands at the edge of the bed, where Marcus was sleeping.

"I never could believe it," he said. "The worst moments, it was all that kept me sane: 'This can't be happening. I reject this.'"

Yes, Phoenix thought. She'd had to do that, too.

Carlos sighed. "And then . . . I was thinking, 'They won't let us go. How can they?' I thought you were gone, Phee. All of us. Just gone."

In separate cells, she and Carlos had been making the same hard contemplations.

"They were afraid of me," Phoenix said, one of the lessons Fana had taught her during the helicopter ride. "If I preached Glow, I would reach too many people. They tried to shut me down for the same reason Fana came to me. They're fighting Glow with everything they have."

"*Screw* Glow!" Carlos whispered fiercely, his teeth gritted. Carlos didn't believe in anything easily, and captivity and torture had soured him. "It's not our fight."

"The healing is real," Phoenix said. "I got punched in the stomach today—I was hurting." Carlos winced, feeling her pain with her. "Fana healed me by touching me. I had a bad cough too, maybe bronchitis. It's gone because she touched me."

"Phee, I know you believe that's true . . . and maybe it is . . ."

"None of this would have happened to us if the healing weren't real."

"Healing you is the least she could do!" Carlos said. "Phoenix, they have *destroyed* us. Everything we had, everything we were . . . everything *you* were . . . it's gone."

Phoenix's grief mounted. So much more could be gone soon.

"Yes," Phoenix said. "You're right, Carlos. It's all gone."

"We have to tell the public what—"

"You can't go public now," Phoenix said. "This is wider than the government, Carlos."

"Then now what?" he said. "We can't go home. We can't . . ."

"Fana's people are taking you to a safe location outside of the country," Phoenix said. "South Africa. It's Glow friendly, and they're sheltering other families there."

Carlos's eyes squinted, confused. "What?" he said. "We're going to South Africa?"

"Not me," Phoenix said. Her voice broke. "You and Marcus."

Carlos had begun to slouch against the enclave's wall, but he sat upright, his eyes locked on hers. "Phee . . ." he began, already begging.

Phoenix's jaw quivered. She stared at her sweet baby, safe and warm beneath his blankets, but she had to look away immediately. Her grief scorched her insides. "She needs me, Carlos."

"You have a seven-year-old son who just went through hell," Carlos said. "Please forgive me, Phee, I hate saying this . . . but you're not in your right mind. Maybe what you're saying makes sense in your head, but you sound crazy right now. Remember when we talked about how they could be a cult? This is what cults do—they twist reality."

"Your mother didn't die by coincidence," Phoenix said.

Carlos looked stunned, his eyes glimmering. "What?"

Phoenix told him the story, starting at the beginning, choosing her own words. Fana had offered to walk Carlos through her memories, too—that surreal sensation of being immersed in someone else's place and time—but Phoenix wanted to bring Carlos along herself, the way she had convinced him that she had to settle her debt to Scott Joplin's ghost in her own way.

As hours passed, she told him about Fana's incredible powers, and how her people had created the drug the world knew as Glow. She told him about Fana's engagement to Michel, who had abilities beyond hers. She told him about the prophecy, and Michel's beliefs that the world should belong to only a few. She told him how Michel had spread the Praying Disease as a precursor to his Cleansing. Carlos had already seen his mother's corpse in Puerto Rico, but Phoenix described the images Fana had shared with her from Nigeria. The ten-year-old girl.

While she talked, Carlos paced the cabin and occasionally interrupted her with sighs and questions. Carlos had known ghosts before she had, so he couldn't ignore her stories just because they were extraordinary and inconvenient.

"She wants all of us with her—her mother, her father, her teacher. And me. My music . . . helps her because she loves it. It opens up something in her," Phoenix said.

Carlos stood over Phoenix where she sat on the bed, holding her shoulders, trying to rub his message into her muscles. "They all love you," he said. "Your music. They want pieces of you, Phee. Remember what you learned? They'll eat you until there's nothing left. You told me you would give yourself to Marcus first. You promised me. You promised yourself."

"That was before I knew about *this*. Don't you understand? This isn't a story she told me—she *showed* me. I walked with her. I saw what she saw, heard what she heard. This man, Michel . . ." Phoenix had never met him, but his name felt like bad luck on her tongue.

"Scott's ghost nearly killed you, and he loved you," Carlos whispered. "It was . . . the nature of your interaction with that realm, playing with the lines between life and death. I understand that Fana is special. But if you die for her, what do we get? What does Marcus get? An apology? A plaque?"

"I wouldn't be dying for her," Phoenix said. "Marcus deserves a world to grow up in."

Carlos knew then. He could not change her mind. Hope left his eyes.

"I'll go instead," Carlos said. "He killed Mami. I'll go, not you. Not you, Phoenix."

One last try. Phoenix only shook her head. For the next hour, the two of them cried and clung to each other, trying not to wake their sleeping son. The light through their windows flared bright orange with dusk as the plane veered, changing course.

She was in the air, but she was not free.

She was away from her cell, but she was not free.

Phoenix had been a prisoner from the moment John Jamal Wright had come to her door.

Jessica stood near the doorway at the top of the jet's metal stairs as Vancouver's crisp morning air tickled her scalp. The private airstrip where Teka had landed overnight was deep in the woods, déjà vu. These Douglas firs and maples had grown all over their property in Washington, a short drive south of this Canadian border city.

Jessica could barely look Carlos Harris in the eye as he passed her to walk down the plane's gangplank with Phoenix, holding his son's hand. The man was a zombie.

"We'll take good care of her!" Jessica called, trying not to feel like a liar.

Carlos turned over his shoulder to give Jessica a broiling glare.

Ugh. Jessica already felt like she was carrying rocks in her stomach, but her worries about what waited in Mexico seemed small compared to separating this family. How could they justify bringing Phoenix with them?

The boy, Marcus, was in unnaturally high spirits as he listed everything he would do while his mother was gone. ". . . And I'm gonna get up to five hundred points on my GamePort . . . and I'm gonna learn how to whistle really good . . . and I'm gonna learn how to pop a wheelie on my bike . . . Oh! And I'm gonna read a book to Daddy every night." He had an angel's piping voice.

"You're going to do all that?" Phoenix said, hugging him with one arm.

"Yeah, and I'll do it quick, Mommy, 'cuz you'll be back soon."

Phoenix tickled him under his armpit, and the boy shrieked with laughter.

Marcus's laughter gave it away. Fana must have adjusted the child's mood! Jessica glanced back at Fana in the leather reclining seat where she was drinking orange juice, waiting for an end to the goodbyes.

A CHILD'S HAPPINESS SPREADS TO THE PARENTS, Fana said, answering Jessica's look. *I SHOULD MASSAGE HER HUS-BAND, TOO.*

Jessica shook her head and wagged a finger: *No.* It was hard to argue with making a child feel better about leaving his mother, but where did it stop? Fana invented her boundaries according to the moment's whims. Not everyone would be able to slap her out of their heads.

While Phoenix and her husband hugged goodbye, Jessica left the ramp to return to her seat. She didn't want to spy on them, and it hurt too much to watch. Phoenix's love for Carlos Harris was beautiful; the kind she'd had with . . .

Damn. She'd been away from her Dreamsticks for forty-eight hours, but the loss of David was still sudden and new. Kira and Bea weren't the only ghosts in her memories. The man wearing David's face was with her on the plane—and she loved that man, too—but

David was gone. And, like her, Phoenix might never see the man she loved so purely again.

"They're in the car," Dawit reported, bounding into the cabin from the gangplank. "Their flight to Jo'burg will leave in thirty minutes." He sounded relieved. When he caught her eyes, the smile he gave her was David's. That never changed, at least.

Phoenix came next, and Fana jumped to her feet to meet her in the galley doorway. Marcus's laughter had left Phoenix's face already. Jessica remembered a rainy winter day in Washington she'd brightened by playing a Phoenix music video in their living room, dancing in a circle with Fana and Alex. Fana, who would barely speak to them during her trance state after the hurricane, dancing!

Had Fana been seven? Eight? She'd been about Marcus's age.

Jessica knew why Fana had chosen Phoenix. She had been there at the beginning.

The woman walking past Jessica on the plane looked nothing like the energetic girl who'd been dancing with her keytar in the "Party Patrol" video a decade ago. All joy had been peeled from her. Fana held Phoenix's hand and walked her to the rear of the plane, her head leaning against Phoenix's. Was it consolation, or was Fana massaging Phoenix, too?

Dawit closed the cabin door, and the plane whirred to life. Jessica liked the Lineage 1000, if only because she hadn't wanted to fly in the plane where her mother had died. The luxury aircraft had a new-plane smell that made Jessica wonder if Dawit had bought it especially for the trip, to spare her the heartache.

When Dawit cracked the cockpit door open, a small brown ball of fur raced out with a laugh that sounded eerily like Marcus's. Jessica gave a start. The monkey had been hidden while Carlos was onboard, and she had forgotten that the creature was with them.

Having a chatter monkey in the cabin had burned off Jessica's enchantment with the creatures fast. God had been wise not to create him. Adam, as Fana called the monkey, had scratched most of the countertops with his sharp nails and shattered a TV screen in the main cabin with a metal tray. He jabbered constantly, senselessly.

"Fana, wait for me!" the chatter monkey called, scurrying after her. The monkey's voice sounded like a tiny old man's.

Teka was piloting with Berhanu in the cockpit. Fasilidas, Teferi, and the musician named Rami were in the first cabin, and the music from Rami's collection of instruments was constant. Jessica hoped the music would be a comfort to Phoenix, but much of it, especially in the higher register, was an acquired taste.

By custom, Jessica's family was given the rear half of the plane, the large conferencing area with reclining seats and a long leather sofa, and the separate bedroom that Fana had left for Phoenix. The large conference cabin was empty when Jessica returned. Fana, Phoenix, and Adam were in the back, behind a closed door.

Jessica turned on the TV that still worked, which was mounted on the wall facing the cockpit. She'd been playing a satellite news channel earlier, and the story hadn't changed: POP LEGEND MISSING, the screen's banner headline read; ". . . say the pop icon is a recluse. Phoenix retired from the stage after the deaths of—"

Quickly, Jessica hit Mute. Reporters had invaded her life after Kira died, and Jessica wouldn't wish it on anyone. When she'd been a reporter herself, she'd hated interviewing tragedy victims. Suffering was hard enough without spectators.

Dawit joined her in the cabin, closing the door behind him.

"Nothing on the military channels about the singer and her family," Dawit said. "Their strategy at this point seems to be, 'Let's pretend this never happened.'"

"Lord knows it's worked before," Jessica said.

"Once again, Fana gets what Fana wants."

Dawit's light tone irritated Jessica. "Her name is Phoenix Harris," she said. "You call her 'the singer.' She's brought joy to people all over the world, not just Fana. Her husband is Carlos Harris, and their son is Marcus. They all have names."

Dawit kissed the top of her head, sitting beside her on the sofa. "I'm sorry, *mi vida*. I'm lazy with names. The curse of having seen too many faces."

"We may be about to get her killed," Jessica said.

Dawit nodded. "And I worry about her husband being discreet—

Carlos. If I'd had my way, Teka would have cleaned his memory by a week."

Jessica winced. One of her best friends, Jared's godmother, no longer had any memory of her; that fourteen-year friendship was another of Michel's casualties. Teka had wiped the entire family's memories for their own protection, but mostly to protect the Life Colony. And Jessica had sanctioned it, unable to persuade a family to choose their memories over their freedom.

"Carlos would lose more than a week," Jessica said. Fana had tried to wipe a small part of Alex's memory to cover running away from the Washington colony, and she left Alex in a trance state. She might do better now, but it wasn't laser surgery. "Let's leave these people alone."

"Fana refused," Dawit said. "So you two are agreed."

Good. Jessica exhaled. One battle at a time.

The plane began its slow taxi, building up speed on the runway. Jessica's stomach rattled. She leaned against Dawit, resting her head on his shoulder. "What are we doing?"

Dawit stroked her hair. "Believing," he said.

The door from the bedroom opened, and Fana came out with Adam on her shoulder, his long tail wrapped around her neck. Gently, she closed the door behind her.

"Phoenix is resting." Fana glanced at the television news. A blond white woman identified as Phoenix's cousin and manager was a tearful wreck on the screen, begging viewers for information about Phoenix. GLOW CONNECTION? the headline above her read.

Fana quickly looked away from the TV.

I DIDN'T CONTROL PHOENIX'S DECISION, MOM. SHE MADE THE CHOICE.

Jessica spoke quietly. "Of course you controlled her, honey. Put yourself in her place—you blew her mind. She didn't have a real choice."

Fana looked to Dawit for his opinion. He shrugged his agreement. "You led her, Fana."

I NEED HER, Fana said. *WITH MICHEL, I NEED EVERYONE I HAVE.*

"What you think is best isn't always what's right." Jessica's voice was hushed. "Own your decisions, especially the ones you're not proud of. We might as well be kidnapping her."

Fana inclined her head, a bow. *I KNOW SHE'S IN SHOCK, BUT I NEED HER.*

The speeding plane rocked, and Fana stumbled. As she tried to step forward, the plane pitched her back. Adam squealed and leaped, swinging away by the curtain rod.

Dawit was suddenly on his feet, catching Fana's arm. "You see we're taking off, Fana," Dawit said sternly, at the same time Jessica said, "Girl, sit down."

Sometimes Fana seemed as awkward in her body as she had been when she was three, as if her limbs were in her way. What was it Fana had said when they flew to Lalibela that first time and she stared out her window? *See, Mommy, I can touch it! I can reach out and touch the sky!* Jessica heard the pealing echo of her little girl's voice.

Fana sat between them on the sofa, burrowing between their hips the way she had when she was young. For that golden instant, Fana was just her daughter, and she and Dawit were exactly where they belonged. Sweeter than any dream. Jessica breathed in deeply, the way Fana and Teka had taught her, filling her lungs with the moment.

Jessica wrapped her arm around Fana and offered her daughter a place to rest her head.

Twenty-five

"**Y**ou must take her quickly," Stefan said. "You understand this, *sí?*"

Their horses were walking so slowly that they barely moved along the rocky path above the valley. Below, Michel spotted a wedding party snapping photographs in a clearing between tall Mexican fan palms and jojoba shrubs.

The wedding party was courageous to come so close to the church palace, with so many of his soldiers nearby, but word was spreading quickly throughout Sonora State and northwestern Mexico: because of Sanctus Cruor, there were blessings in Nogales. No more cartels in Nogales. Peace in Nogales. Healing in Nogales. An oasis in the vast Sonoran Desert.

Michel could not abide street shootouts and disorder so close to the place where the Cleansing would be born. The repetitive sirens and sporadic gunfire had been intolerable. Narcos and kidnappers had been the first to visit his Cleansing Pool.

A table full of narcos was plotting against him even now, Michel realized, twenty kilometers southwest, in a cantina near the beach. They had called his name, so their blustery voices were as loud to Michel as they would have been if they were standing in front of him. Three of them: one from Tijuana, another from Mexico City, a corrupt city official from Ciudad Juarez, all of them incensed because of the interference of El Diablo, who lived in the grand new church in the mountains outside Nogales. They spoke of storming the church with an army, tearing down its walls with grenades.

Michel sent a mental message to Bocelli and Romero: *Bring them all to me.*

They would be his next offerings to the Cleansing Pool, with Fana at his side.

In the valley below, the wedding party had no thoughts of war. The couple stood between two massive, wide-trunked palm trees. Michel admired the young bride in her vintage cream-colored wedding dress, her sun-browned skin peeking through eyelets in the crocheted lace. Perhaps Fana would wear a dress like hers soon.

BE STRONG, MICHEL, his father said, intruding in his thoughts.

"Leave it to you to spoil my good day, Papa," Michel said.

"Am I the one spoiling your day?"

"It doesn't give me pleasure to think of hurting her."

"Taking pleasure is your choice, Michel. It's not the point."

A contact in Lalibela, Ermias, had reported what Michel would have considered unthinkable after his last encounter with Fana: She had given her Blood's eternal gift to the Wright boy. Could she have thought he wouldn't learn of it? He had nearly announced another Cleansing ceremony—and this time, he would not have contained the killing.

Perhaps Miami was due for an outbreak. Or the mortal village of Lalibela itself.

But Teka, Fana's teacher, had sent him a mental pulse to let him know they would arrive *today!* The party would land before nightfall: Fana, her parents, and her retinue. His constant headache eased when he imagined her arrival.

"She's bringing her parents," Michel said. "That demonstrates trust, no?"

"Trust! Her father should be barred at the door. He's a barbarian."

Stefan and Dawit had met twice before—once at Adwa more than a hundred years ago, and again only last year, after Stefan had tracked the Glow network to Fana's doorstep. Both times, Dawit had stopped Stefan's heart and believed he was dead, unaware of his Blood. Stefan complained incessantly about Dawit's cruelty with his knife, an irony that amused Michel. Stefan, who trafficked in cruelty, would complain about the sport in another?

"I should meet her at her plane," Michel said.

"Michel, ludicrous! And look like an enchanted schoolboy? She's a heretic, and each day she tempts you to weakness and makes a mockery of the Prophecy. Your sacred purpose!"

Stefan was not Most High, and yet he never wavered from his purpose. Stefan would have begun the Cleansing in earnest by now.

The wedding party lost its allure. Michel turned away.

"You know why she has come," Stefan said.

I know, Michel said.

He spurred his horse, racing faster down the mountainside's horse trail. Michel wished Fana were coming to him because she had accepted her role in the Cleansing, or because she could not resist her Blood bond to him. But she had shown herself in her mental visit, laying herself bare. She meant to stop the Cleansing.

"And you talk about meeting her plane? Will you carry her bags too? *Rallenta!* Slow down!" Stefan called as he sped after him. He sounded breathless, as if he were the one running, not his mare. "She wants to impose *her* will on *you*. She expects to mold and shape you, Michel. Or kill you, of course. That's the root of this entire farce!"

After his bloody clash with Fana the year before, Michel had forced her to promise that she would never try to kill him again. But she had also promised not to defile her Blood, and what had come of that? When she had opened herself to him, he had seen no plans to harm him, and he had none to harm her. But they both held convictions that made plans and desires irrelevant.

"I'll never forget the sight of you in those bloodied clothes!" Stefan shouted. He was falling too far behind Michel's horse, so he abandoned his voice.

YOU ALMOST LET HER KILL YOU, MICHEL.

She could only have killed me by killing us both, Michel said.

AND DON'T THINK SHE WOULDN'T.

She will not have the opportunity, Michel said.

THEN TAKE HER! YOUR HESITATION CONFOUNDS ME, Stefan said.

Does it?

Michel reined his horse, suddenly bored with his ride as well as his company. Nogales was spread beneath his perch, crowded and energized. In time, this city would belong to his most faithful, the others swept away. Poverty would be gone. Suffering would be gone.

Stefan rode beside him. "Michel . . . if I made mistakes with Teru . . ."

Don't speak of my mother, today of all days.

"Let's discuss it like men!"

Papa, you ignore my wishes at your own risk.

"Yes, I took her from her family. *Stole* her. You know what I am. We have no secrets. I didn't have your advantages, Michel, so my methods were uncivilized. I butchered her mind, I admit it. But I gave her the Blood! Don't shy from sacred duty because of my weaknesses. Don't you see that I was trying to make Teru hap—"

Stefan stopped in midsentence, clutching his throat with his palm. His face turned bright red as iron fingers tightened across his windpipe. In his surprise, he fumbled and fell from his horse. The Shadows celebrated within Michel, tasting Stefan's pain as a stone cracked his upper arm. But he did not release his neck. Stefan had no breath with which to cry out from the fracture.

If you were sincere, I might almost be moved, Michel told him.

MICHEL, YOU'LL BREAK MY NECK—

Stefan's thought was snuffed as oxygen fled his body, diminishing his brain function. Michel watched his father's mouth falling open like a fish's as he tried to draw air. Michel considered snapping Stefan's neck entirely, or sweeping him over the ravine. That would teach him to pollute his ears with false remorse over Teru. Let him wake bleeding on the rocks.

But there was no time. Fana was on her way, and Stefan had to be there to greet her. Perhaps Dawit might entertain him by cutting his father's throat. Michel released his mental hold on his father's windpipe. Then he yanked his reins to ride back.

Behind him, Stefan gasped and choked from the ground. "You've broken my arm!" he coughed. "Has she driven you insane already?"

Michel would have been happy to let his father suffer his injury for a few hours, but he didn't want his arm broken when Fana arrived. She would know he had done it, and he didn't want her first impression to be a display of the violence he wanted to avoid.

As Michel rode away, he fused the shattered bone in his father's arm with half a thought. An hour's walk wouldn't hurt Stefan, so Michel bade his father's horse to follow without its rider. The beast trotted obediently behind him.

The solution could be that easy with Fana, too, he reminded himself. All his distress could be stilled by a simple mental exercise, and Fana would be his in mind, body, and soul.

I'M NOT THE ONE YOU SHOULD BE ANGRY WITH! Stefan called after him. *YOU KNOW IT AS WELL AS I DO! BE STRONG ENOUGH TO DO WHAT YOUR DESTINY DEMANDS OF YOU BOTH!*

Michel was glad his father could not see his tears.

The cathedral was his classroom.

In the silence of his private cathedral, Michel studied the Letter of the Witness. If his heart was weak, the Letter would prepare him for Fana.

Michel imagined himself as a boy when he visited the Witness's classroom, about twelve, dressed in the short blue cotton jacket he had envied so much on the afternoons he watched the mortal boys streaming home from school when he was at the apartment in Tuscany, his happiest times. Papa had never permitted him to attend school with other children; Stefan had not wanted Michel to grow overly fond of the *mortali.*

His father had discovered the Letter while he was running guns in Ethiopia in 1894, and his first act had been to slay the houseboy who translated it from Ge'ez. The Witnesses had told his remarkable story of Blood stolen from the cross at a momentous time in Jerusalem, leaving the last page damp with a drop that never dried.

Michel sat in the front row of wooden pews. Michel was the Letter's student, and the Witness himself was his teacher. Passages from the Letter were written in gold paint covering the walls, twinkling in candlelight, and his eyes traveled the words he had memorized as a child.

Michel created the visage, a man who appeared as flesh and blood, embodying all the knowledge from the Letter. The Witness stood before him at the altar, in his teacher's robe with the crest of Sanctus Cruor. After meeting Fana, he had incorporated her memories of Khaldun, whom he was certain must have written the Letter: skin as dark as midnight, a long black beard.

"Wickedness is cunning, and hides in the hearts of men," the Witness said.

"Yes, and we must wrest the Blood from the hands of the wicked," Michel said.

"And who are the wicked, Michel?" the Witness said, a merry glimmer in his eye. Stefan was stern enough for ten men, so Michel created the Witness's persona as jovial.

"There is wickedness everywhere," Michel said. "Children are wicked to each other. Parents are wicked to their children. Lovers carry out small acts of wickedness toward each other every day. Wickedness roams unspoken in everyone's thoughts."

"If all have the capacity for wickedness, then who shall be Chosen?"

"The Chosen are merely those I choose," Michel said. "Those *we* choose. And the Blood shall cleanse them of wickedness."

"As it cleansed your father?" the Witness said.

"Certainly not." Michel almost laughed.

"Then . . . who are the wicked?"

The Witness gave a mysterious smile. The Letter did not specify how to identify the wicked, and the visage would not answer questions that were not found in the text. Instead, he offered a question: "Would an act of kindness make a wicked man kind?"

Michel sighed, washed in the painful memories of Fana's last visit and her loathing for him. "Fana believes I am wicked," Michel said.

"As others believe *she* is," the Witness said. "Would not the thousands left homeless and hundreds left widowed or orphaned by her typhoon call her wicked?"

"Fana is not wicked. Misguided, yes. Naïve. But not wicked."

"When the two Bloodborn unite, their Blood shall cleanse the world," the Witness said.

"And if we fail?" Michel said. "If there is no Cleansing?"

The Witness paced, pointing out the gold lettering on the wall above his head. "You know very well, Michel. Wars shall flourish. The air will be choked with smoke. The sun will scorch the earth like fire. The oceans will turn to poison. The very world itself will die."

Michel mouthed the two-thousand-year-old words as the Witness spoke. Michel could already see it unfolding! He had wasted too much time. New tears stung Michel.

"And if she will not unite with me?" Michel said.

"She will," the Witness said. "It is in the Prophecy. Her name means Light. Your union signals the advent of the New Days. You are the Bringers of the Blood."

Michel did not want to utter his true question aloud: *Am I destined to become like him?* Instead, he whispered. "Will she choose to unite with me . . . or must I force her?"

Perhaps there was an interpretation of a passage he had overlooked or misremembered, hiding the truth from himself. Somewhere in this chapel, was his answer plain?

But the Witness was silent, offering only his empty, imaginary smile.

Twenty-six

Phoenix had stepped back in time: the private jet, solicitous handlers waiting at the gate in suits and ties, the caravan of shiny white vintage Rolls-Royces racing through anonymous, foreign streets. She could be back on tour, chasing magic she had never found.

Was she bringing magic this time? Or only witnessing it?

Their party split up between three cars donning small white flags with crests Phoenix had never seen before, with a crimson teardrop in the center. SANCTUS CRUOR, the letters read. Before she climbed into the lead car with Fana and her parents, Phoenix saw the same crest on a large white flag flying above the red, white, and green Mexican flag on an official administration building. She could be riding in a presidential motorcade.

Nogales was a modern border city of busy storefronts; the Mexican kitsch of touristy bars and craft shops alongside professional pharmacies and dental offices. Pedestrians, minibuses, bicyclists, and cars competed for space on the freshly paved roads lined with rows of tall, decorative palm trees. The hillsides were crowded with a frenzy of new housing developments. And churches! There was a church on every corner, it seemed, although they were missing their crucifixes. Nogales's churches flew the Sanctus Cruor flag where a cross might have stood.

Phoenix noticed children everywhere: a husky boy being led by his mother's hand in front of a massive Coca-Cola mural, twins being pushed in a stroller, a thirteen-year-old girl riding a bicycle. They all stopped to return her stare.

Phoenix missed Marcus the same way she'd missed him when

she'd been locked in her cell. Her tongue curled, ready to ask the driver to take her back to the airport. She felt claustrophobic in her seat against the window, with Jessica beside her, in the middle, and Fana on the other end. Phoenix's neck tingled.

A panic attack. She'd had them often in detention. Phoenix thought about asking Fana to hypnotize the despair out of her, but Fana had her own problems. As much as missing Marcus and Carlos hurt, her pain reminded Phoenix of why she was here. Her reason to stay.

Every streetlamp was adorned with a Sanctus Cruor banner in alternating colors: white, crimson, white. At a courtyard near the freeway, the car passed a giant bronze statue of a man spearing a winged beast that looked like a cross between an eagle and a giant bat. Beneath the massive statue, an impossibly old woman was holding up a hand-written placard: ¡La Sangre es aquí! The Blood is here.

Phoenix gasped when a man in black tuxedo pants whose white dress shirt was soaked with—blood?—ran up to their car, just shy of her passenger-seat window. The man was trembling, but Phoenix saw rapture on his upturned lips. The stain on his shirt was only paint, she saw as they passed; too pink to be blood.

"The first who come are saved!" he screamed after their car, in English.

The driver spoke up. "I'm so sorry," he said. "The faithful sometimes lose decorum."

Dawit muttered in the front seat, "One can hardly blame them, with so much pomp."

"The faithful?" Phoenix said, embarrassed by her ignorance.

"The Most High," the driver said. "He does so much for Nogales, the people cannot contain their gratitude. These new roads, the new schools, the hospital annex—all at the beneficence of the Most High. He has cleaned out the cartels, stopped the violence on the streets. The city has just elected a new mayor representing our movement. These are very exciting days. New days!"

The back of Phoenix's throat went sour. The city belonged to Fana's fiancé.

Phoenix stared back at the paint-spattered man to see him sub-dued by four police officers, two on either side. They had brought him to his knees, his hands behind his head. One officer pulled out his baton and raised it to swing at the man with both hands. Phoenix had to look away, her insides turning to stone as she imagined the blow.

"He hasn't changed," Fana's mother murmured.

Ahead, a festively colored banner waved high across the road, strung between palm trees: BIENVENIDO, FANA—LA REINA.

In this city, Fana was a queen. Fana didn't glance at the banner as it flapped above the car. Her face looked frozen.

The car slowed, turning. CALLE DE SANCTUS CRUOR, a decora-tive street sign on a post said.

Spectators lined the streets, and excitement stirred as the cars pressed on. Two thousand, maybe three thousand, people stood on either side, their faces hungry for a glimpse through the darkly tinted windows. Children, young women, and grown men ran through alleys and side streets to see the cars. The crowd was restricted from the road by velvet ropes strung to poles adorned with bunches of white gardenias. A mariachi band dressed entirely in white and gold, down to their gold-tasseled sombreros, played on a raised stage. The trumpets rang of love.

Phoenix experienced the crowd's wonder—*She's sitting so close to me*—melting into worship, until she remembered the crowd in Tokyo that had choked the street, and a young American serviceman who had danced on top of her car, shouting, *I can't believe you're here!* All Phoenix had brought was a sore throat and the same old songs, but they worshipped her.

Fana sat with her eyes closed, either steeling herself or taking herself away.

"You never get used to it," Phoenix said. "I don't think we're sup-posed to."

I HAVE A HARD TIME WITH CROWDS, Fana told her. *BUT I'M GETTING BETTER.*

"It's like my dad used to tell me—they all have to go home to whatever's wrong with their lives," Phoenix said. "You help them take away their pain. Open your window. Wave."

Fana opened her eyes, realization relaxing her face.

"I'm not sure that's a good idea," Jessica said.

"No . . . I'd like to do that for them," Fana said. "Will you sing, Phoenix?"

"Just for you," Phoenix said.

The backseat windows whirred down, and the cool air blew through the car, with the smells of car exhaust and fresh paint. Fana leaned to her window, showing her face. The crowd erupted, waving handkerchiefs and newspapers and anything their hands could hold. The sound of joy. Women thrust their babies above their heads to see her, or for Fana to see them. "*Por favor, Fana,* look at us . . ." came their calls, asking for her eyes' validation.

Softly, just loudly enough for those in the car, Phoenix sang the lyrics that had first come to her on her way to the concert, in a melody she pulled from the air: "*. . . Waking up is easy if you never go to sleep. Have you seen the soul you promised you would keep?*"

When Fana waved, the crowd's roar engulfed the car.

Nogales had changed in the past year. So many people!

Frenzied noise from their thoughts came in a blast, so much like the first time Michel had touched his thoughts with hers; when he first showed her what she'd shut away.

Riding on Phoenix's song, Fana discovered so many others behind walls, cooking at their stoves, typing on computers at their desks at work, sick in their beds. More still were crowded in half-finished apartment buildings, tents, or alleyways after trekking from Juárez and Chihuahua and Oaxaca, or Tucson and Yuma and Corpus Christi, because they had heard stories of Sanctus Cruor and the Most High and the *Sangre de Vida.* Blood of Life.

The people around her prayed for the souls of those who would die in the plagues, but they welcomed the Cleansing because they and their families might be saved. They dutifully attended sermons at Michel's churches, where they learned how they could serve the Most High. Their children sang folk songs about the Most High at their schools, with the lyrics written carefully, painstakingly, by their teachers' hands on chalkboards. The most popular song, "Las

Flores," called on the Most High to pull up the weeds so that flowers might grow.

The faithful tossed roses to the paved street in time for Fana's tires to crush them.

REMEMBER HIS VANITY, her father said. *IT IS A WEAKNESS.*

Fana did not answer. Their driver, Romero, was one of Michel's most trusted guards, and although her probe had bounced against his pliant mask, she was certain Michel was lingering close to him. Romero probably could intercept thoughts with her father's level of skill. She had sliced easily past Romero's mental defenses, and much of what she had seen turned her stomach. The man was a psychopath, a killer in search of a calling.

But Michel had given him specific instructions: No one was to touch her or harm her party. That was a good start, so she would keep faith on her end, too. She remembered how Johnny had shot Romero and stopped his heart a year ago, but the thought was gone in a blink.

A full-stemmed white rose flew in through Phoenix's window and hit her face, an accident of the breeze. "Ouch!" Phoenix said, touching her cheek. One of the thorns had scratched her. Phoenix stopped singing, and the day grew slightly grayer. Less light. Fana wished she had felt the rose coming, but she wasn't all-knowing, like Teka said.

"Put the windows up now," Dad said, and Romero obliged obediently, despite the enraged obscenities in his head because Dawit had bested Michel's father, Stefan, twice.

Jessica fussed over Phoenix's face, dabbing it with a tissue from her large woven purse. Phoenix told her she was fine, but Mom needed to have someone to fuss over. Jessica sighed heavily at Fana.

That was an accident, Mom. I wouldn't have brought her if I couldn't keep her safe.

Fana had considered the Blood Ceremony for Phoenix when she first found her, but she hadn't had time to prepare her. Besides, since Michel had forbidden concerts, how would it look if she gave her Blood to Phoenix, too? She would trust Michel not to hurt Phoenix. Offering trust might help him trust her. Michel liked to live up to his word. His life had been shaped by words since infancy.

Their side of the freeway had been cleared, so the cars sped on the empty road. They drove away from the city, toward the mountains.

On the opposite side of the freeway, the crowded lanes toward central Nogales were clogged to a standstill, cars twinking like diamonds in the bright sun. Only bicycles were moving. Roaming drivers milled in conversation beside their vehicles. Vendors strolled between the paralyzed lanes, selling bulls' horns and bags of fruit.

So many people! Fana had to shut out their noise.

The smell of the Shadows came unexpectedly, so acute that Fana's knees trembled. For the first time since she was three, she longed to swim in the Shadows, if only because of the smell. She had forgotten that any smell could be so strong, flowing through her veins like blood.

She didn't ask Phoenix to sing for her again, because she wouldn't always have Phoenix with her. Instead, Fana directed a thin veil toward the Shadows. The smell softened, but not by much. She wouldn't be able to filter out the smell without losing other perceptions. And she didn't want to arrive at Michel's wearing an ironclad mask, no matter what Teka said.

"Dear Lord," Jessica said, her voice soft. She'd closed her eyes. "We know the journey ahead is a difficult one. Only our faith in you gives our legs strength to walk this path. Please bless us as we work to carry out healing in your name. Please bless the Blood, Lord."

Exactly what Gramma Bea would have said. Or Johnny.

"*Benedetto sia il Sangue*," Romero echoed her blessing, voice trembling with sincerity.

"Amen," Jessica whispered.

The road climbed into the mountains, winding steeply. Concrete gave way to green thickets, and a new road sprinkled with dust. No other cars passed them, or followed from behind. Military vehicles appeared on the wooded borders, trucks full of disciplined soldiers with shiny boots and perfect haircuts. The troops fell into line and stood at attention as her caravan approached.

Fana remembered a time long ago, almost in the time before remembering, when she'd wanted to be a princess in a fairy tale. And

then Teferi and Teka had come and begun bowing to her—only a
little girl! She thought she'd wished it true, and maybe she had. But
in her fantasies, she'd imagined a different kind of prince waiting
for her.

They were a mile away, and she had underestimated Michel
already.

His presence loomed taller than the mountain. He shook the
leaves in the treetops.

How would she stand in a room with him?

YOU'LL DO FINE, DUCHESS. Her father's constant assurance.

No one spoke the rest of the drive.

Peace. No strangers' thoughts. None.

As she climbed out of the car, Fana heard only frogs, the ebb and
flow of the cicadas' calls, and the gurgling of a massive fountain with
life-size marble sculptures of a man and woman astride horses side
by side. Water sprayed a shower above their heads, rainbow halos
in the last daylight. The woman on the horse was she, Fana noticed
when she saw her mane of dreadlocks. Michel's likeness carried a
medieval-style Sanctus Cruor banner on a tall pole.

Michel's face on the statue felt like a slap. Fana blinked away,
startled.

No wonder she had stayed in Lalibela. No wonder she had
blocked him for so long.

The massive courtyard was empty except for their cars. Lush
bougainvillea hedges twenty feet tall ringed the courtyard, crowded
with bright blossoms. The manicured grass was dotted with sago
and pygmy date palms, the ones she kept in her room. The grounds
were as well kept as a painting.

Berhanu, Fasilidas, Teka, Teferi, and Rami surrounded the three
women as the group followed Romero toward the dozen marble
steps. Dawit walked behind Romero, and Rami fell to the rear. Even
Adam hushed his chatter, his bright eyes darting among the new
sights as he sat perched on Rami's shoulder.

Fana wished they had brought Michel a gift beyond the chatter
monkey. But what? She'd been confused about courtesies when she

met with health ministers and presidents about Glow, but it was too late to think of better gifts now.

She was the only gift he wanted.

The air in front of the palace seemed to shimmer. Michel stood at the top of the palace's steps, between statues of Vulcan and Venus. Or, they might have been Shango and Oshun. Fana smelled his mental scent, nearly impossible to separate from the sweetness of the Shadows.

To keep from looking at his face, Fana concentrated on Michel's bright clothes: white linen slacks and a peasant-style white shirt with crisscrossing laces across his chest. His thick gold Sanctus Cruor ring.

Michel jaunted down the steps. A large white German shepherd trotted down behind him at a well-trained distance.

Fana hadn't expected Michel to meet them at the door, much less alone. He'd been in full regalia the last time she'd seen him, infatuated with ceremony. Now he looked like he was on his way out for a walk. Fana felt overdressed in her silly business skirt and jacket. She wished she could climb back into the car.

Instinctively, Phoenix began humming "Gotta Fly," almost under her breath. The song helped Fana escape to other details around her. A man and woman stood in the wings on the steps behind Michel, hanging back—Stefan's parents. When Fana stared at the woman's face beneath her white Ethiopian head scarf, she was startled to see herself. Michel's mother was her twin sister in every way; Teru might be a vision of her future.

And Teru's mind was as close to blank as anyone's Fana had ever come across. Adam's head was busier than Teru's! Most of Teru's mind was still, like someone deep in meditation . . . but hovering, not listening. The woman's face was mostly empty, too, except for a tiny smile of anticipation. She watched her days unfold like a dream.

No one could have scared Fana more.

Beside Teru, Michel's father gave Fana a warm, actor's smile. Stefan's thoughts were carefully concealed, but Fana could guess what was in his mind. Stefan was a sick man. There might not be enough time to undo his damage to Michel.

Dawit stopped walking within five yards of Michel, and Michel stopped, too. For a moment, standing in silence, they looked like they might duel. Her father's smile was thin.

Fana still could not make herself look at Michel's face. She stared at the Mediterranean tiles at his feet, as close to him as her eyes would go. Michel was wearing suede loafers the same copper color as his eyes.

Dawit gave Michel the deep bow he would have given a Life Brother. "Michel Gallo," he said, pointedly avoiding Michel's preferred title. "We represent the Lalibela Colony. Thank you for agreeing to host us." Teka had suggested a longer speech, but Dawit had said no.

"I'm honored to receive you at my home, signore," Michel told Dawit, appropriately grim. "You are my treasured guests. I'm sorry for our unfortunate beginnings."

Her mother's temper surged in a hot red shimmer. Michel must have seen it too.

"I'm especially appalled at my role in the terrible loss of your mother, signora," Michel said to Jessica quickly. "I've shed many tears over her death. If it takes eternity, I intend to prove to you that I'm not the monster you think I am."

Michel was really talking to *her*, but Fana still would not look his way. Her mother's thoughts were churning so furiously that Fana wondered if she would slap Michel. Jessica's lip trembled, and she gathered a deep breath before she gave Michel a nod.

"Thank you for your apology," Jessica said. "You didn't mean for it to happen."

The visit was already a miracle, if only Fana could look at him just once.

Adam squealed, suddenly bounding toward Michel's dog. The German shepherd towered above Adam, but the dog didn't move as the monkey circled him. The dog looked to Michel for guidance.

"I hope your monkey doesn't bite. My dog is shy. Aren't you, Caesar?" Michel joked, and his men laughed. Chatter monkeys were clever, but Michel's dog had sharper teeth.

Teka pulsed Fana a query: *FANA?* She had planned to present Adam to Michel.

When Fana didn't answer, Teka bowed to Michel. "Please accept Fana's gift from our House of Science. The breed is unique to Lalibela."

"Your colony's House of Science is unmatched," Michel said. "I accept Fana's gift with humility. You and Dawit are greatly respected by your Lalibela Brothers here, who are eager to see you." He didn't remind them of the Brother, Alem, who had brought him the virus.

Adam bounded to Michel, practically at his feet. He stood on two legs and bowed as he had been trained. "My name is Adam, Most High," the monkey said in his reedy voice. "I promise to be good, I say the words, but I tell lies lies lies!" Adam had improvised the end of his speech; chatter monkeys were proud of their lies.

Michel laughed, genuinely amused, and Michel's parents and guards laughed, too. Any gift that brought laughter was a good one. Michel held out his arms, and Adam leaped to him. Fana knew that fickle Adam wouldn't have jumped to Michel without a mental prod.

"Adam is a lonely name for you," Michel said. "We must find you an Eve!"

She knew how much he wanted her to look at him for the sake of his faithful who were watching. She tried, but she couldn't make herself raise her head or address him, even to send him an apology. Would she destroy her mission over such a simple thing?

Michel snapped his fingers sharply, and Fana nearly jumped, expecting his displeasure. Two girls who looked fifteen came scurrying out of a shadowed corner, dressed in long aprons.

"I've made a promise to some of the girls who cook for me," Michel said. "You have fans here. They begged for a chance to shake Phoenix's hand. I hope you don't mind."

To Michel, asking his followers to shake Phoenix's hand was the same as an apology. Phoenix managed a bright smile, keeping her thoughts about her family's abduction and detention off her face.

If Phoenix could smile for Michel, why couldn't she? Wasn't she as strong as a mortal?

Michel had never met the girls before—they'd been chosen by his kitchen matron—but their titters as they approached Phoenix were touching. Both girls wore their hair in prim buns. They were more awestruck by Michel, to be in *His* presence, but they loved Phoenix, too. As Phoenix shook their hands, the taller one said she was Consuela, the stouter one Pilar.

"*Mucho gusto*," Phoenix told them. "What's your favorite song?"

"'Party Patrol'!" they cried in unison, and dissolved into shy giggles.

The girls' giggles made Fana forget that she was avoiding Michel's eyes, and a careless gaze brushed past him. Their eyes caught.

The dusk sun amplified Michel's black eyelashes and honey face, showering every ringlet of his springy dark curls with gold dust. The sky careened out of place, dizzying her. Fana nearly lost her balance, her legs fighting to stand upright.

I HAVE MISSED YOU MORE THAN I KNEW WAS POSSIBLE, FANA, Michel said.

If her thoughts hadn't felt as empty as Teru's, she might have said the same thing to him. She couldn't answer, spoken or silently. She had been so angry with him, so hurt and confused, that she had made herself forget.

Michel's splendor filled Fana's eyes with tears.

Twenty-seven

At Jessica's insistence, dinner had been cut short.

Jessica prayed she was only dreaming again. Maybe she had dreamed the tears, speechlessness, and nervous fever that had gripped Fana since she had first seen Michel. Please, God, let her have dreamed what she'd seen in Fana's eyes when Fana stared at him.

Jessica had seen those same empty, glassy eyes when Fana was three.

Why had she let her daughter come back to him?

Jessica flipped open the small oval mirror she kept in her purse, checking her reflection. Her eyes stared back at her from her mirror, panicked and red rimmed. No dream.

Berhanu and Fasilidas were posted outside Fana's door, but Fana needed guards inside her head, instead. Jessica hadn't seen Fana cry since right after she had first met him.

Fana's strange mood had continued at dinner with Michel's family. Fana and Michel had sat at opposite ends of the table, but the room had been invisible to them. Fana had been too absorbed by Michel to touch her food.

Jessica wondered if she was the only one still in her right mind.

Fana and Teka stood at the window with their eyes closed. He was guiding Fana back to a familiar mental landscape, he said. Strains of rapid stringed music floated into the room through the open doorway, where Phoenix was learning a violin duet with Rami.

Jessica wanted to leave, but Fana had said she preferred to meet in a private room. And Michel, of course, already had rooms made up for them. The room intended for her and Dawit was adorned with a wooden opium bed identical to the one they had shared in Miami. Leave it to Michel to use stolen memories as decor. Dawit noticed the bed, too, and they shared a painful glance. Did Michel expect her to spend her days in a haze like his mother? Like Fana?

"Let's get her far away from him," Jessica said to Dawit. They had been through this test before, and they had failed. He'd given them their bed to remind them.

Dawit's eyes were sad. He couldn't give up on Fana. "If she will go," he said.

Teka opened his eyes, excusing himself from Fana's side. "She wants to stay," he said.

"I need to hear *her* say that," Jessica said.

"Do not assume Michel is exerting influence on Fana," Teka said calmly. "Remember, Jessica, these are two unique beings with extraordinary mental skills. They react to each other on a physiological and psychic basis. Her thoughtstreams are faster now, but they seem to be hers. I warned her that her response to him would be significant."

"I *saw* him go into her," Jessica said. "I saw her eyes change."

MICHEL'S RESPONSE TO FANA MAY BE NEARLY IDENTICAL, Teka told her privately. He was shy about speaking about Michel aloud in his house, not that it mattered: Michel could hear everything anyway. *HE WAS PROJECTING—*

"He could project himself as my grandmother," Jessica snapped. "It's a movie screen, Teka. He'll show you what he wants you to see."

"Michel was much more composed than Fana," Dawit said, agreeing.

"He has had a year to train himself for her," Teka said. "I believe—"

"Stop believing anything about him!" Jessica said. "*All you see is what he lets you see.* What's wrong with you, Teka? You know better! Does he have you too?"

Compelled by Michel, Teka had been piloting the plane where her mother had died, refusing Jessica's pleas to answer Bea's chest pains. How could they trust Teka's advice? How could any of them believe their own words? Their own minds?

Please help Johnny against him, Lord, Jessica thought, hardly realizing she was praying.

"Mom," Fana's voice said sharply. Fana's eyes were suddenly wide open and clear. She stood directly over Jessica. *TURNING ON TEKA WON'T HELP ME. OR WISHFUL PLANS AGAINST MICHEL.*

Jessica's racing heart rocked still. How could she have been so careless?

"Stay out of my head," Jessica said.

"We have to work *not* to hear your head," Fana said. "Your thoughts bleed everywhere."

"Who's we?" Jessica said. "You and him?"

Fana looked startled by the question. "Yes. Me and him. Me and Dad. Any of us who are higher telepaths." Fana was pulling farther away from her, wading more deeply into the fog where Jessica had lost her. If Jessica had known that Dreamsticks would cost her Fana's trust, she would have let Kira and Bea die long ago.

Jessica held Fana's face between her cheeks. "Fana, even if he doesn't want to . . . he could be pulling you toward him. Maybe he can't help it any more than you can. How can you expect him to resist leading you if you make it so easy? At least look at the possibility."

"Of course I've looked at it, Mom."

"Then what's your strategy?" Jessica held up her mirror for Fana to see her reflection. "How do you check in with yourself?"

Fana turned her face away from the mirror, as if her image pained her. "Stay with the mission," Fana said. "Remember my goals. Nothing else matters."

Fana was wrong. Plenty else mattered. But at least that was what Fana would say.

"We all saw it," Jessica said. "You're not ready, Fana."

Now Fana laid her hand across Jessica's cheek. "I wasn't ready before, but I'm ready now," she said like a schoolteacher. "I've adjusted. Just being here makes me learn so much faster. I should have veiled the way Teka advised me, but I wanted to show Michel I had nothing to hide."

Fana sounded satisfied to feel that she shared a pull toward

Michel that even Teka didn't have a vocabulary for. And it might be only Michel's ruse.

"I'm not surprised, dear Fana," Teferi said. "Khaldun's Letter of the Witness says you are 'mates immortal born.'"

A cold needle pricked the base of Jessica's neck. "You sound like you're ready to join Sanctus Cruor," Jessica said. "Like your Brothers."

"No, of course not," Teferi said quickly. "I'm horrified by Michel's methods and interpretations of the Cleansing, but the Letter—"

"Not now, Teferi," Dawit said, impatient. There wasn't time enough to debate the Letter.

"We have to go," Jessica said. "Fana, you can always come back when you've had more time to adjust. If he feels it too, he'll understand." She searched for the most complimentary lighting for Michel: the lighting Fana saw him in.

Dawit nodded with agreement. "Caution costs us nothing," he said. For the first time since she had seen Fana's tears, Jessica thought it might not be too late. Fana still trusted Dawit, and Teka would follow. Relief made Jessica's joints tremble.

"This first dinner was tremendous progress already, Fana," Dawit said, wrapping his arm around Fana's shoulder; the reasonable man Jessica had married again, the man she had chosen twice. "We know we're welcome as his guests, but there's no need for such close proximity. Continue your meetings with Michel tomorrow, but tonight we should fly as far as Los Angeles. This is my most deeply held counsel, Duchess."

Jessica was so eager to leave this room, this building, this city, that the soles of her feet itched. All of her skin itched. She could already see the plane gathering speed on the runway, breaking Fana free the way they had freed Phoenix.

Slowly, sadly, Fana shook her head.

"I can't go," Fana said, resigned. Only her resolve kept her from sounding helpless. Tears peeked out, but stayed hidden. "I have to see him alone."

A sixteen-year-old mortal girl, Inez, led Fana to Michel's studio at the opposite end of the hall, walking in practiced silence on the balls of her slippered feet. Fana was relieved to be in the company of a mortal, to loosen her mask for a dozen more steps down the hallway.

Fana probed Inez to learn if Michel treated her well, sifting through the girl's thoughts: paid well, and barely had contact with Michel, whom she worshipped. Fana couldn't find evidence that Michel had a reputation for sleeping with the women who worked for him and worshipped him. A *santo*, the housekeepers called him.

Fana let her mind rest for a few steps.

The floor was already vibrating beneath her feet, so she would need all her mental energy to filter out Michel. The fight against his brightness was giving Fana a terrible headache, but her mind was starving for him, a new kind of wanting. A new appetite.

Fana was still chafing from the shared gazes at dinner, which had rubbed her until she felt bruised, but she was already sinking into his scent again as Inez knocked on the oak door.

"*Veni!*" Michel's voice came, in Italian. His earlier joviality was gone. He sounded like he had a headache, too, or worse.

The large studio was crowded with paintings on easels, and splashes of brown skin and woven black dreadlocks made her realize the art was about her. The five-by-five-foot canvas closest to her was painted in an Ethiopian Coptic style—giving her wide eyes and an oval face as she gazed toward the heavens in a cathedral adorned with gold script. Or rode a gray horse in the countryside. Or cradled a golden infant to her breast. His images of her future.

Fana didn't see him until the vibrations told her to look *up*. Michel was bobbing thirty feet above her, painting a fresco across the ceiling while he floated on his back. He dabbed at the green and brown flecks of the fronds on his palm trees, nearly real enough to sway.

"No closer, please," Michel said.

Fana stopped walking beneath him, only a few steps from the doorway. Yes. Thank goodness he didn't want to be closer. A new space behind her ears was burning. Beneath her forehead. Soon, her desire to fuse their thoughtstreams would feel like fire.

Was it worse for him? The same?

"I'd rather speak only verbally, Michel." She couldn't trust herself to receive Michel's thoughts, or she might try to burrow into him.

"*Sí, sí,* if that's easier for you," Michel said, waving his brush hand.

"You've always felt this," she said. "You knew."

He had muted his presence more than she'd realized when he visited her thoughts in Lalibela. If she'd known how he would thunder through her, she might not have come.

"Our union lies at the heart of the Letter, and you would expect our meeting to feel ordinary?" Michel said, chastising her. "Did you think this was a boyish infatuation, Fana? The only thing worse than being away from you is having you here. So close, but . . ."

Fana knew. The hour she had spent comforting her family had passed impossibly slowly, but her time with Michel fell still. The ceiling where he floated warmed the room. She was dizzy again, inching to the border of the necessary gulf between them.

"It must have been terrible when I left," Fana said.

"Waiting since dinner has been terrible," Michel said. "Your leaving was indescribable."

He fell silent, painting with his careful strokes.

"Will it help us be close to each other?" she said. "Talking like this?"

"Of course," he said. "But not long. I'm not good at restraint, Fana."

"You're wrong about yourself," Fana said. Now that she had tasted his suffering, she was amazed that he had delayed his virus by a year. "Thank you, Michel."

Michel made a sudden swoop, as if to come down to her, and the air flared around Fana like the heat of blue flames. The burning behind her ears reached for him. Michel flew upward again with a cry of frustration. "Don't thank me yet, *bella,*" he said softly.

"I needed to see you," she said. "To understand." There was no reason to lie.

Michel landed on the floor far across the room, nearly hidden behind a row of canvases. Seeing his face in the courtyard had opened mental portals she had sealed, nearly swallowing her inside him. Was Michel hiding his face for her sake, or his own?

"I'm happy beyond words you're here, Fana," he said. "But there's something I have to tell you now—right now—so you won't think I'm cruel for raising your hopes. Once you hear what I have to say, I'm sure you'll be sorry you've come."

"That sounds ominous." If not for her pounding heart, she could have made it a joke.

"You won't convince me to stop the Cleansing." His voice was stern, the Most High, the one she could not negotiate with.

If she couldn't reach Michel, she was lost.

"Do you see the future?" Fana said. Her feet tried to take her closer to him, but she held on to the wooden easel to keep her place, to avoid setting herself ablaze in him.

"I see that much, Fana."

"What else do you see?" Fana said, to know the worst.

"Three days from now, the Cleansing will begin. With you at my side."

"I would never do that," Fana said.

"But you will. I can't wait, Fana. I won't. Three days may be too long for me."

He was being honest, too. *Or seemed to be,* her mother's voice reminded her.

Fana was hurt, blinking away tears. "This is our fresh start, Michel? Threats?"

"It's not a threat." His voice said he wished that it were. He walked along the easels, farther away from her. "You lied to me."

Now she would learn the cost of sharing her Blood with Johnny.

"I didn't see it as a lie," she said. "That had nothing to do with the Cleansing."

"Our Blood has everything to do with the Cleansing!" he roared. A paint-spattered tarp hanging near her flapped with the power of his anger, falling to the floor in a heavy heap. Michel softened his voice again. "To rub salt in my daily misery, you've given me *this* now. Why did you do it, Fana? Why him?" Michel's voice hissed with pain.

"He's earned it through service to me . . . just like Romero and Bocelli have with you."

"Don't insult me! I would scatter them like dust if you asked me to. Let's trade, Fana: my two acolytes for your one."

The ring of triumph in his voice made her heart flutter, nervous. Johnny could be collapsing dead somewhere already. Michel wouldn't have to fumble to find his heartbeat.

"Michel, don't," Fana said. She almost said *please*. She might have to.

"Then how can you compare them?"

"It wasn't fair to compare them, and I'm sorry. But he earned it, Michel. It's a mistake for us to talk about him. We said we wouldn't. See how much harder this is for us now?"

Us. We. Us. She comforted him with the rhythm of her language.

Michel peeked at her from among the canvases. She saw lightning in his eyes before his face winked away, gone. Her instincts warred to rush toward him, but she stepped away from his slow, careful footsteps as he circled her.

"You're beautiful, Fana," he said. "No other woman will feel like a woman to me again. You're the most precious being I know, and I don't want to touch you. I don't want to steer you. It's agony. I'll never forgive myself for how I hurt you before . . . and how I will again."

Fana was silent, more frightened of herself than of Michel. Her head was pulsing as if it had been chopped in half. She wanted to press her face into Michel's and melt her pain, vanish into him. Quickly, Fana took three steps away from Michel, until her back was against his door.

"How did you stay away so long?" Michel said. "How did you tolerate it?"

She noted the wariness inside his curiosity. She'd had an advantage over him.

"I was so angry," she said. "That made it easier to shut you away, like a hole in my memory. Just like shutting away the Shadows. But it created a weakness. It blocked my growth. And when I got here . . . I was surprised."

Michel chuckled loudly, without mirth. "Anger won't help me with you. I *want* to stay angry, because I'm tired of this *ridiculous* pain in my head!" Rage soaked his voice, volcanic. Then it was gone. "Learning how to be good to you has been the struggle of my life, Fana."

"Thank you for fighting for me, Michel."

"Stop thanking me," he said. A whisper.

"This headache—"

"The headaches get worse," Michel said. "I hope yours are easier than mine."

Michel flew high once again, rising as if he were on invisible parachute strings adrift in a wind. Moving away from her. Her headache eased, but a different throbbing emerged at the base of her skull. One pain was sated by distance, another created. Fana studied every sensation, racing to learn and grow.

"Why couldn't you have been someone else?" Michel said.

"Why couldn't you?"

Silence burned between them.

"Make your peace with the Cleansing, Fana," Michel said. "I'll study the Letter with you. I'll help you understand. Take comfort in choosing the saved. You can choose each one."

She wouldn't have time to reach him if his mind was full of the Cleansing.

"I'm here to marry you, Michel," Fana said.

Michel held his breath. He waited, expecting her to take back the words.

"I'll marry you tomorrow," Fana said. "If that would make you happy."

Joy lighted his face before he threw his head back, snapping himself from the spell of her promise. "You'll marry me *if* . . ."

"If you admit that you don't know the future."

Impatience creased his brow. "But I know the Prophecy, so I do know the future."

"I can't marry you if you think everything is decided," Fana said.

He swooped away. "So you'll agree to marry me only if I dismiss what I know is true?"

"You're not dismissing it," she said. "Only testing it."

"Everything about you is a test!"

"For me too."

Their promised marriage was all she had to offer him. Michel knew it as well as she did. If he refused, she had failed already.

"What kind of marriage?" Michel said. "You open your dreams to me once a year? Even if I could stand it, I won't. Never again."

"Not just an empty wedding—I'll give you our union," Fana said. "Like in the Prophecy, Michel. We'll join in every way, fuse without masking. We'll stop this pain. We'll see what we become next. Both of us. Together."

Fana surprised herself with the eagerness in her voice. Blocking her mental ties to Michel had clouded her meditation, her Rising. Hadn't she always wanted to learn to fly?

Michel was so startled by her offer that he landed clumsily, stumbling behind the easels. A can of paint nearly hit the floor before he caught it with his mental stream, setting it upright on the counter. His longing surged, a furnace blast. He couldn't refuse her.

"Thursday," he said. "The day after tomorrow. I need time to give the people a proper wedding. Friday, we join in the Cleansing."

Every time Fana thought she was with Michel, he became the Most High again.

"No," she said. "I won't marry you if you plan to make me a slave, Michel. Why should I? I'll marry you by *my* will, but my will has to last beyond our wedding day."

"Fana . . . do you want me to lie? To speak against my knowledge, against my heart? If I ever say there won't be a Cleansing, you'll know I'm lying. I'll say it now, but it's a lie."

"That's not what I asked you to say, Michel," Fana said. "You want to marry me on Thursday, but we might wait until Sunday or Monday. *You don't know the future.* I have a voice. We have to start there."

Michel gave an exasperated sigh. "Go," he said. "*Per favore.* Leave this room. Your mother knows best, Fana, and she wants me dead. You're safer in Los Angeles or Santiago, if you're safe from me anywhere. But . . . I'm begging you to stay in your chamber tonight. I hope I can sleep a full hour now that you're here."

Longing and weariness radiated from Michel. He was fighting himself with all his soul. If he lost his fight, who would she be when she woke up?

"If you try to take me, I'll kill us both," Fana said. "I'll find a way."

"For the Cleansing, I will take you," Michel said, near tears. "I have no choice."

Suddenly, they were back where they had begun.

Fana watched Michel's shadow glide across the floor as he flew overhead, a moth trying not to burn against her flame. She needed to be away, too, but not too far away. Her mind was raw from him and famished for him.

"Will I stay near you tonight?" she said. "Or will I listen to my family and go?" She wasn't sure herself, thinking aloud. Either decision would rend a part of her. "Tell me, Michel."

I DON'T KNOW OUR FUTURE, FANA, Michel whispered. *MARRY ME.*

His single, gentle thought blew through her like a gale, snuffing the old fires and igniting new ones. Her headache dimmed, but it would be back soon, as long as she was waiting. He had broken their agreement to speak only verbally, or maybe he couldn't help himself. His essence vibrated through her.

Now she wouldn't sleep, either. Her mind would sing from his mental scent for hours.

Yes, she said, giving him the words he craved most. *I choose you, Michel.*

Fana fought Michel's fire with hers.

Twenty-eight

Addis Ababa

Johnny Wright lingered outside the coffin maker's shop, scanning the noonday marketplace crowd under the bright orange awning. The shop was packed with upright, colorful caskets with too few buyers. Not enough people were dying. Glow was ruining the funeral business, as the saying went through Ghana and Botswana and South Africa. Who would need these coffins of paisley and quilt patterns, or carved from dark wood? Feeling prideful, Johnny used to joke with the coffin makers about their struggles. The boom was over, he'd said.

Soon, there would not be enough coffins, or enough survivors to build them.

Johnny wished he could set up his own shop with his arm hooked to an IV to give his Blood away like bottled water or canned food before a coming disaster, but he'd seen enough riots at Glow centers even if Fana hadn't told him about her childhood at the clinic.

He hadn't realized how hard it would be to walk near the sick and aging with the Blood in his veins, every stranger suddenly a personal responsibility. He'd felt the same way when he was transporting Glow, but he had never carried so much guilt.

We can't save everyone, Fana often said, a saying from her father.

"You!" the lanky coffin proprietor said in English, recognizing him. "Get away from my shop with that Glow rubbish!" He was half joking, or maybe not. His sneer might be a smile.

"Don't worry—Glow doesn't bring back the dead," Johnny said. He was itching to tell everyone he met. He couldn't stop flexing his fingers to feel his blood throb in the fat veins on the backs of his hands.

"No kidding, the U.S. says there's a virus in it," the coffin seller said. "Get a bad batch and your whole family dies. It happened in North Korea. You should read the newswebs."

Johnny saw Michel's work every time he checked the news. Michel's machinery was seeding its false history of the virus, ready to blame the outbreaks on Glow.

"Then I guess you'll have a good year," Johnny told the coffin seller.

Johnny had been lazy about disguising himself in Addis, but he would need to be more careful outside Ethiopia's borders. He could be arrested at any airport. He slipped into the crowd so that his face wouldn't draw stares, flipping up the hood of his light cotton jacket.

Johnny dodged the path of five burros walking with sacks of feed and boxes tied across their backs, prodded by three boys who looked twelve. One of the boys swatted the rear burro too hard with his stick, and the animal whined in pain while the boys laughed.

Johnny was ready to tell the boys to treat the animal more kindly, but he accidentally walked into a woman in a scarf bent over a cane, nearly knocking her over. He grabbed the woman's stick-thin arm to hold her upright, careful not to crush her.

"I'm sorry! I mean—" Johnny tried to remember his Amharic. He'd learned ten phrases in at least ten languages by now, and he often confused them.

She turned to look at him with a toothless reprimand. Her face was a nest of wrinkles deep enough to make shadows. Johnny stared, his English suddenly gone, too.

The woman looked like she could break, except for her active eyes. Walking through the crowded market must be awful for her, Johnny thought. Did she cook her own food? Was she hungry? What ailments were killing her slowly? How did her body feel when she settled in to sleep at night? Did she have a bed, or did she sleep on a pallet in an alley?

He was horrified by her, heartbroken for her. He wished he had an emergency Glow packet in his shoe, but he was traveling without Glow for the first time in a year.

What about your Blood? he reminded himself.

But the woman yanked her arm from him, annoyed. Johnny watched her walk slowly away, half sliding her right foot after her left. Was he supposed to pull her into an alley, cut himself, and force her to let him cut her? Johnny was paralyzed as he watched her walk away.

She would die soon, and so would the bearded old man driving his white truck through the packed crowd, honking when he was stuck. And the six-year-old girl in cornrows and a *Princess and the Frog* T-shirt singing a song with her brothers. And so would the endless parade of beggars, men and boys who looked malnourished and desperate. All of them would die.

The street seemed to melt into a black-and-white photograph like the ones in his college history books, a crowd captured before they were ghosts. Johnny stood lost in the flock of the dying, his heart hammering in his chest. He was suddenly drenched in sweat across his back. He had forgotten to eat before he left Lalibela—he had forgotten to eat before he tried to sleep, too—and now he was sick to his stomach.

He was zoning. Damn! He'd had Fana's Blood for two days, and he was still freaking out. Johnny closed his eyes. *We can't save everyone,* Fana's advice reminded him. He could barely tell the difference between his memories of Fana and the gentle sound of her thoughts.

No, he couldn't save them all. He couldn't heal them one by one. But he could try to stop the Cleansing.

Johnny's heartbeat slowed as he remembered why he was in the throng, how important his task was. His eyes skated past the faces.

He only needed to find Mahmoud.

Mahmoud wasn't in the colony. After Johnny had searched for Mahmoud all day, Yacob had finally told him that Mahmoud had gone upworld to look for Khaldun. And there was a mortal woman in Addis he often saw for a day or two, Yacob had added with a smile. He'd told Johnny as a joke, looking forward to Mahmoud's irritation if Johnny found him with a lover.

Yacob's advice to check the fresh-fruit stands at the markets had seemed too broad, a fool's errand, but it was Johnny's only lead. As Jessica had suggested, Johnny hadn't confided his plan to the other Brothers, even Yacob. He didn't know Yacob's feelings about Michel, and Sanctus Cruor had a strong foothold in the House of Science.

Michel might have swayed them all.

Johnny would look for Mahmoud until nightfall. If he couldn't find him or get his support, he would go on his own. Catch a red-eye, if he could. He didn't like the candidate that he and Caitlin had come up with during their all-night brainstorm, but the benefits outweighed the cost. They didn't have time to be picky.

"Any luck yet, gorgeous?" Caitlin's voice came to his ear from his radio. She'd begun flirting with him, an old, familiar feeling to make Fana's silent absence less horrifying.

"Not yet," Johnny said. "Still looking."

The earpiece's microphone could pick up a whisper. Their conversations might or might not be private, since the universal radios had been built in the House of Science. Teka had proclaimed their radios clean months ago, but Johnny wondered now.

"Just thought you'd want to know . . ." Caitlin said. "We're in."

Johnny's heart thudded. "What does that mean?"

"He'll do a meet-and-greet," she said. "We got his attention. Told you it would all work out if the call came from the right person. One of our Camelot guys reached out."

Camelot was their code for Washington, D.C.; someone who owed Glow a favor, often because of a personal healing from Fana. Johnny's heart pounded with a blend of excitement and deep paranoia. The more people they reached out to, the bigger the chance for leaks.

Were people staring at him? Was Michel watching him in a dream?

"That's big, Caitlin," he said, shielding his mouth with his palm.

"Everything better be big from now on."

A broad-shouldered white man walking toward Johnny in a baseball cap made his mouth freeze. Romero! Johnny had shot Michel's personal guard a year ago, but Romero was an immortal.

He was awake, striding toward Johnny through the crowd, hardly five yards away.

Johnny didn't run. If Michel knew what he was planning, there was nowhere to go.

Then the man passed, and Johnny realized the man was five inches shorter than Romero. A tourist!

"What is it?" Caitlin said. She must have heard him stop breathing, and start again.

Caitlin was in Nigeria with Doc Shepard and the others, but she might as well have been standing beside him on the open street. He had put Caitlin at risk. Had he neglected giving Caitlin the Blood because he'd wanted to be alone with Fana? If so, he was making the kinds of mistakes he was hoping Michel would make.

"Cat, you better jump off," he said.

"I booked you on this train, remember? Underground Railroad to the last stop."

Even over the radio, Johnny heard the soft fear clamping her bravado. They were alone with it. So much depended on how Fana did with Michel, and they hadn't heard anything. Neither of them wanted to go back to being alone with their waiting.

Just when Johnny was deciding he didn't need Mahmoud, he spotted Mahmoud's pale forehead at the mango stand across the street. He was wearing a white guayabera, blending into the river of white fabrics at the market, but Johnny recognized his beard and long ponytail. His only disguise was a pleasant grin.

"You won't believe this," Johnny said. "I see him."

"Handle it, cowboy. Love you."

"Love you longer."

He heard her begin to laugh before she clicked away, so he laughed, too. Better than crying or zoning, even if it was nervous laughter.

Mahmoud was squeezing fruit for a tall woman in chic office attire and gleaming black heels beside him. The woman wore her hair long, maybe a wig, and she looked like a newscaster or a politician. Or a model. Johnny took a precious few seconds to cross the street and get out of Mahmoud's sight. If Mahmoud thought he was being tracked—

But Mahmoud was gone. The woman, too.

Johnny ran to the corner table, weaving through bystanders to gape at the empty spot where Mahmoud and the woman had stood. Was he delirious? Had he convinced himself that he'd seen Mahmoud out on a date? *How likely is that, exactly? What if this is a diversion?*

Johnny felt himself sinking again, his heartbeat speeding to catch up with his thoughts. His own mind could become a weapon against him. Maybe it already was.

Johnny went to the fruit stand and studied the customers and sellers, craning to see around the corners, measuring the footsteps to the nearest alleyway. He tried running a few steps in each likely direction, but he didn't see the woman's short skirt or Mahmoud's ponytail.

Johnny leaned against the corner of the squat, unpainted concrete-block building behind the fruit stand. The market around him seemed to swirl. *You're just zoning. Close your eyes and ride it.*

A fiery sting across his face snapped Johnny's dizziness away. His ear!

Before he could cry out, a hand clamped over his mouth and he was flung through the air, as if he were weightless. He was suddenly out of the sun and in the dark, pressed against a wall with an iron elbow against his chest. Maybe it was Romero after all. Or Michel, swooping from the air itself.

Johnny had been in public, in broad daylight. Now he was neither.

Hot blood ran across Johnny's right cheek from his right ear.

"You cut my—" Johnny started, but he was quiet when he saw Mahmoud's eyes and felt the sharp, pressured prick deep in his navel. Mahmoud still had his knife, so the cutting might not be over. Despite Fana's warm Blood, Johnny's pores went as cold as ice water.

"Why are you following me, monkey?" Mahmoud said in a voice of quiet death. His knife's tip had already drawn new blood. All it needed was Mahmoud's weight to impale him.

"I want to kill Michel!" Johnny blurted.

Mahmoud pulled back, surprised, and the knife's tip retreated.

He assessed Johnny for a breath that took an hour, then he laughed. The more he laughed, the farther he stepped away.

Johnny raised his hand to his ear, which was radiating hot pain. His ear was misshapen, and blood painted his fingertips. "You really cut off my ear!" he said.

"Don't be a child—just the lower lobe," Mahmoud said. "You don't need it."

It didn't matter, Johnny realized, stunned to remember.

His ear would grow back.

They chose the kitchen of the closest restaurant, steamy and uncomfortable, huddling near the ice machine beside the back door. An army of waiters and cooks passed them. Mahmoud never seemed concerned about being overheard, but Johnny studied every face.

"So you want to kill him?" Mahmoud said. "Congratulations. Bring an army with you."

"I can," Johnny said. "Sixty men."

Mahmoud studied him, probing his thoughts. "A rancher?"

"He's not a rancher by choice," Johnny said. "His family was running a major cartel out of Sonora State. His brother was the king, until Sanctus Cruor came. Michel let them know they weren't welcome. Blood on the walls, cryptic messages—you know their methods. The younger brother lived. He's left Mexico, but he could put together an army on short notice. He can get fifty fighters, maybe sixty. With the right backing . . ."

"You've studied him," Mahmoud said.

"We've had to study everyone," Johnny said. "The enemy of my enemy is my friend."

Suddenly, Mahmoud laughed loudly. "Your face! So much hellfire."

"I think people are worth fighting for," Johnny said.

Mahmoud doubled over, laughing harder. "You still stink like a mortal, but your wit! I shall call you Hannibal. Are you ready to march over the Alps with your elephants to save humanity, Hannibal?"

Johnny didn't answer, but Mahmoud's mocking smile made his stomach sink.

Mahmoud swallowed his laughter. "Son . . . dear sweet boy . . . poor fool . . . how can I put this?" Mahmoud put his hand on Johnny's shoulder, sighing paternally. "She has agreed to marry him Thursday. Is this any way to talk about your beloved's husband?"

"What?" Johnny said. It was the only word he knew. He wasn't sure he'd said it aloud.

"They've been engaged for a year, Hannibal. You didn't expect them to marry? I imagine you weren't invited to the wedding, but they set the date right away. I've heard from Teka. As far as we know, he's still an adequate source."

Johnny blinked, trying to clear his head. Why would Fana agree to marry Michel so quickly? Would Fana *ever* agree to marry Michel? He saw Fana in bed with Michel, and his stomach tried to wring itself. Did Michel already have Fana? He must!

Johnny would have wept if not for Mahmoud. His insides were weeping.

"It takes some of the sport out of it when you look so miserable," Mahmoud said. He glanced out the open doorway behind him, lighting a cigarette. "If my lady friend isn't waiting for me, Hannibal, we have unsettled business. Don't spread your misfortune to me."

The air cleared, and Johnny smelled the fish and incense from the market.

Fana always said to remember the mission. Anything else was a distraction.

"So you do care about the monkeys," Johnny said.

Mahmoud chuckled, not looking back at him. "Don't presume so much. The females amuse me from time to time. When these are gone, there will be others."

"And the Cleansing?" Johnny said.

"I've never seen the logic in healing the perpetually dying," Mahmoud said, "but then again, I'm unclear about who would be left to clean up Michel's ghastly mess."

"You're against it, then."

Mahmoud's eyes still studied the crowd outside.

"I'm against the Cleansing the way I'm against all forms of madness. I'm also against overcrowding. Look at them all. The famines!

Endless conflict! I have to admire Michel's willingness to take a stand. If he weren't a raving lunatic, I might shake his hand."

"And when he's marching you over there to join him? Like Fana?" Johnny whispered.

"Is that the version you like best?" Mahmoud said, winking over his shoulder. "He compelled her? It's a pity you didn't know Fana when she was a tot, Hannibal. She gave a whole new meaning to the term *enfant terrible*. They're a perfect match."

Johnny was too sick to argue with Mahmoud. He suddenly vomited into a metal sink beside him while kitchen workers scowled. Quicky, Johnny rinsed the mess away.

"As you can see," Mahmoud said, "the Blood doesn't heal maladies of the mind, like overpowering fear of the truth." He leaned over Johnny, pointing out bloody handprints on the sink. "You'll want to clean up. We prefer not to leave it in the open, since it never dries. It tends to leave a trail."

"I'll remember that," Johnny said. He rinsed his mouth in the tepid water and spit.

"Your vision of an army is ambitious, so I admire your conviction. But before you cast your lot against Michel with druglords and other ne'er-do-wells, I offer you counsel as a new Brother . . ." Mahmoud said, and paused. "Make sure your damsel in distress wants rescuing."

There was no humor in his face or voice. Johnny felt foolish for holding his breath, hoping that Mahmoud might offer him something worth hearing.

"This isn't about Fana," Johnny said. "Michel is about to let loose a pandemic outbreak, and nobody's willing to stand up to him. Either that matters to you or not."

"Point well taken," Mahmoud said noncommittally.

"Any other advice, Mahmoud?" Johnny said, sarcastic. Before today, he hadn't had the nerve to say more than three words to Mahmoud. "What else can I learn from your vast wisdom? We monkeys don't usually get the chance to live hundreds of years."

"I wouldn't rely on that timetable, considering your circumstances," Mahmoud said casually, leaning over him. The tobacco on his breath reminded Johnny of Michel. "The most important thing to remember? Expect pain."

Johnny cried out as steel fire lashed his left ear. Mahmoud had sliced his other earlobe so quickly that Johnny hadn't seen him move. Fresh droplets of his blood had sprayed to the kitchen's tile above the sink, a progression of small dots.

Both of Johnny's ears flamed with pain. "You son of a—"

"Watch yourself heal," Mahmoud said. "That's all the fun, the first days. Earlobes might take three to five hours. After that, there's day and night and day again. Most days and nights are exactly the same—only the faces change. Or they don't. Now you know the secret."

Mahmoud pivoted away, vanishing through the open doorway into the crowd.

Twenty-nine

Mahmoud had expected to be on his way to the Qinghai region of China, following another Mystic's dream to search for Khaldun in the mountains, but life had gotten in the way.

He had been delayed in Addis. Selam had surprised him by cooking him dinner after his impolite disappearance at the market, and he'd surprised them both by refusing Selam's invitation to spend the night in her bed.

Instead, Mahmoud flew his prop plane back to Lalibela.

"You're not as clever as you think," Mahmoud told the councilmaster.

"I'm thinking the opposite: I may be too clever by far," Yacob said.

"He's a perfect disaster," Mahmoud said, half to himself. "These mortal boys are like girls, with soft hands and delicate sensibilities, trained to sit at desks. He nearly pissed himself when I flicked his ears. How did he fire that gun?"

Wright was one of the remaining puzzles from their disastrous visit to Michel a year ago when Mahmoud had first understood what a hazard Michel was to them. Even Teka had not been able to wrest himself from Michel's mental stream! But Wright had escaped bondage to shoot Michel's guards. Or had Michel allowed it?

IT MAY BE TRUE THAT FANA DISTRACTS MICHEL, Yacob said. *WEAKENS HIM.*

Yacob spoke silently, not wanting to be overheard. Mahmoud

wished he had the skills for refined silent discourse, but he needed his meaning to be clear.

"I want to be free of Teka," Mahmoud said. "He is linked to me. He woke me from sleep with news of Fana's wedding. I can't have him so close."

HE MAY NOT CONTACT YOU AGAIN.

Mahmoud shook his head. "No. Nothing must escape to him. If he attempts to reach me, I might bleed. I do not want Wright's plan known to him."

Yacob raised his eyebrow, surprised. *YOU HAVE DECIDED A POSITION.*

"Can you sever him?" Mahmoud said, impatient.

For a moment, Yacob's thoughts were silent as he meditated for his answer.

I CAN IMPLANT THE ILLUSION OF A MASK FOR YOU, Yacob said finally. *TEKA WILL KNOW IT'S BEYOND YOUR CAPACITIES, BUT IT MAY GIVE YOU A BIT OF TIME.*

"A bit of time is all I need," Mahmoud said. "If anything is to be done, it must be done quickly. That much Wright says is true. Put up the mask."

I ALREADY HAVE, BROTHER. FOR MY OWN SELFISH REASONS.

Another silence. Now that they were free to speak, what would they say?

"What is the council's position on the Cleansing?" Mahmoud said.

Yacob closed his eyes and sighed. He'd dreaded the question. "Mahmoud . . ."

"No more debate, Yacob. Does he debate? We must learn decisiveness from Sanctus Cruor and the mortals. What is *your* position?"

HOW CAN YOU ASK? I AM AGAINST THE CLEANSING, OF COURSE.

No surprise. Over time, Yacob had collected enough mortal offspring for his own nation. Mahmoud had brought Yacob back to the colony three times in fifty years, and each time he'd begged for more time with his mortals. It amazed Mahmoud that it had been Dawit, not Yacob, who first broke from Khaldun over his ties to the mortal world.

"Their herd needs thinning," Mahmoud said, testing Yacob's rationality. "Never mind their destructiveness. If you love them, how can you watch them starve?"

THEN LET US INTERVENE. BUT MICHEL'S INTERPRETA-TIONS ARE MORTIFYING. WHERE DOES IT END?

"Perhaps it ends here," Mahmoud said.

The air in the room was hot. Mahmoud realized his heartbeat was jogging, increasing his blood flow. His heart rarely stirred—not since Adwa, when Dawit had persuaded them to join the Ethiopian forces to repel Italy and Sanctus Cruor. If Khaldun had told them they had immortal cousins in Sanctus Cruor's ranks, they might have vanquished them a century ago. And Michel would never have been born.

In last year's skirmish against Michel's men, he and Dawit had been cut down far too soon when they came for Fana and Dawit's family. Michel had known they were coming.

"How was your visit to Addis?" Yacob said, as if to change the subject.

"Addis is a congested bore," Mahmoud said. "But Selam was the new flower to take my breath away."

Yacob's knowing smile drove Mahmoud mad, but he couldn't deny the reason. He had seen Selam's shade of skin countless times, and legs that mirrored hers, and faces her ancestors could have worn—and yet his eyes feasted on her. She barely knew her own body, much less how to please his—but her nakedness excited his loins. She was ignorant of history, her mind was cluttered with trivia and politics, and she knew only three languages—and yet he was fascinated by everything she said. There was a kind of music in her voice. In her face. If he sired a son with Selam, how would he look?

Mahmoud shuddered. "Dawit has poisoned me," he said. "Or you did, perhaps."

"Wait until you love a child, Mahmoud. *Your* child."

"'The disease of attachments,'" Mahmoud said bitterly, quoting

Khaldun. " 'As the sun shuns the night, so too shall we be separate.' "
He had treated them all as children.

"Will you spend all your days searching for Khaldun?" Yacob
said. "To what end?"

"To tell us why!"

"Forgive him without knowing why, Mahmoud. Walk free."

Mahmoud had often wished he could.

"There are millions of Selams upworld," Yacob said. "Others,
men or women, who would intrigue another as she intrigues you.
You came for me when I was so happily married in Paris—"

"You can't possibly call *that* happy," Mahmoud said, remembering his cow of a wife.

Pain quivered on Yacob's face. *RESPECT MY MEMORIES,
MAHMOUD.*

When Mahmoud bowed in apology, Yacob went on. "You
asked me, standing outside in my garden, 'What do you love
about them?' I love the homes they make for themselves. So
many needless kindnesses toward each other. Their cleverness—
like Fana said, they learn so much so fast. Their laughter—we
have too little here."

"Laughter! We have known different mortals, Yacob."

"I don't deny I'm no warrior; you've tasted more war. I know
how they destroy—"

"They would cage us, given a chance," Mahmoud said. "Their
envy alone—"

Yacob held up his hand to bat away conflicting politics. "But
there's an essence about them. Look at Wright. So frightened and
ill-prepared . . . and such lofty goals! It's stirring."

And Johnny Wright might have pulled himself free of Michel
once. There *was* that.

"Yes," Mahmoud said. "Wright is a promising piece of fortune."

Mahmoud opened himself to Yacob so he could hear the details
of Johnny Wright's plan. Yacob hadn't realized that the rancher had
already agreed to meet with Wright. The boy was silly in a dozen
ways, but he had use of Fana's network. The Glow network was
effective.

"If Michel is distracted, he might be surprised," Mahmoud said. "Overwhelmed."

NOT BY US, Yacob said. *HE EXPECTS IT. LALIBELA CANNOT STRIKE.*

"But an army of *vaqueros* dispatched by a druglord . . . at the behest of Wright," Mahmoud said, imagining cowboys charging the mountain on horseback. The sound of the plan alone was ludicrous. "If Michel heard of it, he might only laugh. He has too much pride."

HUBRIS SLAYS THE GODS, Yacob said.

Mahmoud felt the strange heavy thump in his chest that he'd felt when Salem opened her door to him and the streetlamp caught her smile. He had seen that same smile hundreds or thousands of times before, he was certain, and yet . . .

"If we use our weapons and fail to kill him, he'll drain all of Lalibela in his Cleansing Pool," Mahmoud said. "You've heard the atrocities. Don't tell me you think Alem suddenly woke with the idea to go to Mexico and join Sanctus Cruor!"

Yacob's grief shone in his thoughts. Michel had chosen Alem because of their Brother's sharp mind for viruses.

"The theft of Alem was an act of war," Mahmoud said. "We cannot declare war on Michel. But we can help end him, Yacob."

THERE ARE MORTAL WEAPONS ENOUGH. FROM MORTAL HANDS.

If Wright's attack was effective enough to disable Michel and create disarray, perhaps Mahmoud would incinerate Michel to ash. And his new bride, if he must.

Mahmoud's racing heartbeat slowed, and dimness fell over him. Dawit might be stirred to join an attack, or would Mahmoud and his dearest Brother be poised as foes again? He might face worse than Michel in Mexico.

WHAT OF FANA? Yacob said.

"She gave Wright our Life Gift! With her own Blood. Would Michel engineer such a comic sacrilege? *She* chose to go to Michel, and now she will marry him. The obvious speaks best for itself. With Michel, she may feel at home at last. Dawit has never seen what she is."

*AS A FATHER, I CAN TELL YOU WHAT DAWIT SEES—HIS
CHILD.*

Mahmoud had faced Fana in the Lalibela tunnel with a gun
when she'd been small enough to be carried in her mother's arms.
He'd seen her eyes wake with effortless power, and heard her siren
song to a wall of howling, angry bees.

"Fana," Mahmoud said, "has never been anyone's child."

Thirty

Nogales

2:30 a.m. Wednesday

Jessica couldn't find a flashlight. Instead, she'd resorted to the sturdy white votive candle from her night table. As the flame withered and grew, mammoth shadows frolicked along the marble walls on both sides of her. She wasn't sure she'd slipped past the others, but it didn't matter. Nothing they could say would change her mind.

Jessica nurtured the fragile flame with her palm, walking past darkened doorways and stairwells, some winding up, others straight down. She softened the sound of her footsteps while her eyes raced along the walls. Jessica was sure she would turn a corner and find herself in her own doorway again, or see Fasilidas striding the hallway. Or Michel.

The lavish, well-staffed palace was surprisingly dark and still at night, as if it had stood empty and abandoned for years. Jessica couldn't find the white door she'd noticed behind a partition during the walk to dinner, when she had already been looking for a way out.

The flame dimmed, collapsing toward the wick. She was moving too fast. "No, no, no . . ." Jessica whispered, standing still, and her flame breathed again.

A large space had opened above her, Jessica realized. Banners gleamed in gold in the dark, hung from the rafters where a hidden bird cooed softly, the only sound except that of her heartbeat. She realized she was in the main foyer and public cathedral of Michel's palace—she would never call his home a church. Empty pews sat next to her, brooding in dark wood. If she kept walking straight, she would end up at the palace's massive double doors.

But the doors won't open, she told herself. *You're a fool if you think they will.*

The surreal moment swamped Jessica. It was too dreamlike; the pews, the banners, the palace itself. She yanked her mirror out of her back pocket, flipped it open. The mirror gleamed an empty space at her, and Jessica gasped.

Where was her face? *Was* it a dream?

Then she blinked, and she saw her eyelids' movement in the dim flicker. No dream, only dark. Jessica wanted to sit on the closest pew, but where would her prayers go here?

Mom and Dad, I've offered to marry him Thursday morning, Fana had told them with her hands folded in front of her, businesslike. She'd said it as if marrying Michel Gallo was right and necessary, as if she expected congratulations. *Once we're fused, I'll sway him against the Cleansing,* Fana had said, sounding like every doomed woman who had married a man to change him. *My path won't take me around Michel—I have to go through him.*

This was not her child.

This was not the girl who had sobbed in her arms over Michel's lie named Charlie, finding solace in a mother who had fallen in love with a fiction, too. This wasn't the girl who had vowed she would not lay eyes on Michel for a decade, if then. Fana hadn't been herself in so long, she might not know her own face in a mirror.

But Jessica did, so far. She was still here. She rushed ahead, grabbing the large brass handle, venturing a prayer. "Please please please . . ."

The door clicked and fell open, an inch's width of moonlight. Jessica smelled gardenias

Dear God, he was going to let her leave!

Regrets came. Why couldn't she have found a way to bring Fana? Or Phoenix, who never left Fana's side? Or Dawit? Leaving alone filled Jessica with new wretchedness, but she slipped out of the palace.

Moonlight painted the empty courtyard gray. Even without

man-made light, it was so bright outside that it looked like dawn. No chorus of frogs, crickets, and cicadas; everything holding its breath. The woods beyond the courtyard were still.

Jessica raced down the wide steps.

In the moonlight, Jessica saw a ghostly animal in the center of the pebbled driveway, thirty feet from where she stood frozen. It sat Sphinx-like across the stones, staring into the woods. Jessica's hand was water suddenly, and she dropped her candle.

The tiger from her dream!

Her heartbeat rioted. She tried to check her mirror again, but her hand couldn't fish its way inside the back pocket of her jeans, fumbling and patting. The creature didn't move.

Wait—

Jessica stared long enough to realize that the tiger was only Michel's dog, Caesar. Was the dog sleeping in that strange pose? Caesar was a big dog, but he was no tiger. He might not have seen her yet. Or smelled her.

Jessica veered away from the front path, walking gingerly toward the long, vine-draped carport on the side of the palace near the kitchen entrance, where the three majestic Rolls-Royces were parked shining in the moonlight. She had thought about those cars after Dawit left their room to meet with Teka, realizing she had a plan.

Jessica pulled the door handle of the car closest to her—it was unlocked!—and met the antiseptic scent of overcleaned leather when she opened the door. An odd blue light from the dashboard made her check the rearview mirror for her wide-eyed face. Still here. No dream.

Jessica bent over the steering column. She nearly swooned when she saw the gleam of a single key on a golden key ring dangling for her, waiting. Jessica reached over to touch the key, to make sure it was real. It was.

Caesar had better get the hell out of her way.

Jessica saw herself climbing into the car, slamming the door shut, turning the key. But a sudden riffling in dry leaves above the carport made her realize she was still standing in the open doorway. A shift in the breeze whipped her head around to look back at the palace.

Michel was standing just beyond the awning. Five steps from her. The moon brightened above him as clouds drifted free. He looked like a fresh-faced boy, nineteen at most. His face seemed too smooth to grow hair, obscene in clean handsomeness. He was barefoot, fresh from bed. His silken crimson pajamas shone on his legs. He had a woven white poncho slung over his pajamas, wearing it open like a cape.

Jessica's hand closed around the car key, and she pulled it free, hoarding it in her palm. She wouldn't give up the key. As long as she was hanging on to the key, she knew she was herself. Jessica propped the door between herself and Michel.

He might still let her go.

Michel crackled in front of her as if his poncho were static-filled. Jessica hadn't experienced anything like the way the hairs on her arms pulled toward Michel. Poor Fana! Something like *this* was pulling Fana to him. Worse than this.

"You're up late, signora," Michel said. He sounded concerned.

Words tumbled out of Jessica's mouth so quickly that she wondered if they were hers. "I was doing an experiment to see if I could get up and walk out of here," she said. Having Michel so close made her tongue heavy, hard to move. "I see I have my answer."

"I don't lock my doors," Michel said. "Or my cars, as you see. No one steals from me."

Jessica heard Caesar rise and shake himself in the driveway, rows of thick fur snapping. *He's going to kill me now.* What was the point of trying to hide thoughts from someone she couldn't hide from?

"Where will you go?" he said, still playing the worried host. She heard his soft Italian accent in the singsong of his voice. "The roads are dark."

"It doesn't matter," she said. "You'll know when I get there."

He took a step toward her, and Jessica recoiled although she didn't try to run. She still had the car door. She could hit him with it if she had to. She could try to. Her breathing was accelerating. She could feel it, and he must have, too. She turned the key over in her palm, comforted by its slickness and warmth.

"You don't have to be afraid of me, signora," he said. "You're Fana's mother."

As if that explained everything.

"I'm not afraid for me," Jessica said. She hated the sound of tears in her voice; she wanted to sound like Judgment Day. "Do you love her, Michel?"

Michel was silent. Maybe he didn't always lie.

"If you love Fana, or even think you do, let her go," Jessica said.

"You've tried," Michel said. "You know she won't leave."

"*Make* her go, Michel," Jessica said. She almost choked on his name.

In a long silence, Michel seemed to consider it, or Jessica's frantic hope said he was. Caesar trotted up to Michel, his tail wagging weakly, and sat beside him. Waiting.

"I cannot," Michel said in a long sigh. "Only Fana controls Fana. I think you may have learned this once or twice."

"For how long?" Jessica challenged him.

Michel didn't answer. The woods and courtyard slept, silent.

Jessica's rage surged. "How *dare* you!" she said. "How dare you stand there and say Fana is in control, you pompous hypocrite. She wants to *heal* the sick. She won't do the horrible things you want from her, and *she never will.* Then who's in control?"

Jessica was close enough to see his pleasant expression peel away as his jaw flexed. Michel stayed silent so long that Jessica was sure she had severed their communication. Her heart's drumming started again. She eased herself toward the leather driver's seat, ready to slide in. The key was hot in her hand.

Michel walked in front of the car's grille, leaning. He planted his palms on the hood.

"I understand your anger. Believe me, I do," Michel said finally. "Neither of us wants to find ourselves here."

"Yes, you're so helpless, aren't you? You poor, sweet thing." Her coo had thorns.

Steel crept into Michel's voice. "I'm far from helpless, signora. You were not helpless when your husband told you he was a liar, he wasn't quite human. He said you and your little girl were in danger because of him, no? You wish you had gone, but you chose to stay."

When Jessica heard the car door slam, she was shocked to find herself still standing in the carport. Had she slammed the door? She had the key in her palm. She was so senseless with anger, her sight blurred. Michel was roaming in her mind and memories. Of course he was!

But she had weathered taunting from Fana's demons before. Michel could tell her nothing about her mistakes that she didn't already know.

"I see," Jessica said. She stepped toward Michel, an arm's reach from him, ignoring the way he made her skin vibrate. "You like to hear begging, don't you, Michel? You won't be happy until you see me on my knees, will you . . . Most High? Is that what you want?"

"Often, I like begging very much," Michel said, with unashamed candor. "But not you."

"Let's try it anyway. You might enjoy it," Jessica said in a seductive whisper. She was ready to kneel, to pour her hatred into wailing tears, but Michel held her arm to keep her standing. His slender, gentle fingers on her bare arm gave a warm shock. She yanked away.

"*No*," Michel said forcefully. "You will not beg. My men are watching. So are yours."

Appearances mattered to him. Jessica looked around, trying to find onlookers. The courtyard was empty. She couldn't see any lights on in the palace, but a window on the third floor was conspicuously open, a white curtain floating on the breeze.

"My, my, my," Jessica said. "I never would've guessed you're so shy. Am I embarrassing you?"

"You would embarrass yourself," he said. "Fasilidas followed you. Do not make me harm him. Fana would like him to stay with her."

"Oh, I see your little game now. We all get a comfortable room, nice meals, every courtesy. That's how you'll justify violating her."

She had chosen the right word. Now that she was closer to Michel's eyes, she saw them wither. He pursed his pink lips tightly.

"Yes, Michel," Jessica said. "Call it what it is. That's what I always tell Fana."

Jessica heard wind gather in the treetops, rolling around them. An unnatural wind.

"She's free to go. I have not touched her," Michel said. "You are also free to go."

"If I'm free, why are you here?" she said.

"I'm here to ask you to stay."

"What a surprise."

Michel's poncho flapped as he knelt to the ground in a sudden motion. She instinctively moved away from him, expecting him to become the tiger, but he was only bent on one knee. He bowed his head to her.

"I am the one who came to beg *you*," he said, his words falling in a breathless flurry, as if in prayer. "On Thursday, I hope you will become a kind of mother to me, but I understand if it asks too much. My mistakes will take time to mend. But Fana wants you here . . ."

"Don't tell me what Fana wants."

Michel didn't raise his head. "Signora, she chose each one of you, each voice. She loves all of the others, but she needs you here too. She needs your voice close to her . . . even if you tell her she should try to destroy me."

Adrenaline swept through Jessica's pores as Michel looked up at her suddenly, his eyes revealing how much he knew. "*Si*, you want me dead. Of course you do! It's all you're praying for. You think I'm the devil. Any mother would! Tell Fana all of your thoughts. Don't hide them. She won't always do as you ask, but your voice will stay with her. She must have all of her voices. If she doesn't, I can't know . . ."

"You?" Jessica said. She was angry at herself for feeling moved by Michel's plea, straining to make out his whispered words. Of course it was about him!

"I must be sure she is choosing me," he said. "That I haven't moved her. Her choice is very important to me. It's all *I've* prayed for. We both want the same thing for her, signora."

If she'd had the strength, Jessica would have laughed until she cried.

He did think he loved her. God help them all.

Michel raised himself to his feet. A light had gone on behind the third-floor curtain, someone making his presence known. Michel glanced up at the palace. Flurried footsteps from the darkness sounded like armed guards scurrying into position on the palace's rooftop.

"Now my father is worried," he said. "He's never seen me kneel to anyone, so imagine the sight. He forgets I don't need a guardian."

"Everyone needs a guardian," Jessica said. "Especially you."

The double doors to the palace opened. Dawit, Berhanu, and Fasilidas appeared with flashlights. "Jessica?" Dawit called, anxious. His gun might be in his hand. "Are you all right?"

"We're fine!" Jessica called back. "Michel and I are having a chat." Their voices ricocheted through the courtyard.

Dawit and the others stopped short at the top of the stairs, watching. Fasilidas and Berhanu were close enough to probe her. Why had they stopped?

"Let's walk to them," Michel said, extending a genteel elbow to her. "Please stay."

Jessica shook her head, her jaw trembling with shame at how much she wanted to give up her escape plan and go to sleep. How much she missed her Dreamsticks.

"I may be the only person who ever says no to you, Michel," Jessica said.

FORGIVE THIS INTRUSION, BUT I WANT YOU TO UNDERSTAND . . .

"Get out of my head." She didn't shout or scream, or Dawit would have tried to shoot Michel for her right to go. A single gunshot might be the end of the world.

Jessica tightened her fist around the key hard enough to cut her palm.

Michel leaned to Jessica's ear, his hand on her shoulder. He whispered, his breath sweet with cloves. "What do I know of love, signora? I'm not blaming love. Please forgive me in advance. Teka couldn't put it into words for you, but I can show you in an instant. I want you to know what Fana is suffering. Both of us. I want you to know why she's stayed . . ."

Before Jessica could say no, a flash of white heat swallowed the night.

Michel was standing over Jessica in the shadows of the moonlit carport, an unnatural sight. *SHE IS TERRORIZED,* Berhanu reported, confirming what Dawit saw.

Michel had a hundred men within thirty meters; twenty on the rooftop alone. A hundred more beyond the gate, and those were only the ones Fasilidas and Berhanu had told Dawit they knew about. But Michel was an army unto himself. The rest were only for show.

If she wants to go, let her find her own way. Those had been Fana's instructions to Fasilidas when he reported that Jessica was slipping out of the room. Fasilidas had only followed her instead of alerting Dawit and Berhanu in time. Fasilidas's first loyalty was to Fana.

Where was Fana now? Dawit was ready to end the mission, his gun in his hand. But weapons were impractical in Michel's house, like paper toys.

Dawit called out to her. "Jessica? Are you all right?"

"We're fine!" Jessica said. "Michel and I are having a chat."

The forced casualness in her voice bloated Dawit with enraged adrenaline.

Then Dawit nearly doubled over from a sudden impact across his midsection, a mental barrier at the top of the stairs. Fasilidas and Berhanu grunted, also barred. Across the courtyard, Dawit watched Michel lean closer to Jessica, practically nestling her ear. In his old skin, Dawit would have shot Michel six times over already. Berhanu was waiting to allow Dawit to defend his wife. They were under attack.

Dawit focused his mind to a pinpoint.

Where is Fana? Dawit asked Fasilidas.

SHE WILL BE HERE, BUT FANA DOES NOT MOVE QUICKLY.

Dawit's finger ached from being so primed to shoot Michel. He called to Michel privately, not for his hidden troops or acolytes to hear.

Is this where our truce dies, Michel?

Michel backed away from Jessica, as if startled by Dawit's presence. The pressure from the barrier was suddenly gone, and Dawit ran down the steps unobstructed. Berhanu and Fasilidas thundered behind him.

Jessica's face was contorted. Pain?

SHE IS NOT PHYSICALLY HURT, Fasilidas said. I DON'T KNOW THE REST.

"I meant no harm, signore," Michel said as Dawit ran past him. Even with a mask, passing so close to Michel was like having another walk *through* him, a warm jitter. Michel lowered his eyes, posing contritely. "I wanted her to know how much Fana needs her."

Dawit went to Jessica, searching for damage to his wife. Jessica's eyes were dazed, unfocused. Her thoughts were too noisy to read in her excitement. How would he know if she had been altered by Michel? Even Fana might not know.

Berhanu ventured a thought to Dawit: TO THIS COWARD, HER MIND IS A CHILD'S.

Jessica's muddied eyes brought more than rage to Dawit. For the first time since Miami, he imagined his life's abyss if he lost her. When he had given Jessica the Blood, he had foolishly expected to have her with him always. He should never have left her alone.

"Jess, I'm coming with you," Dawit said. "Give me that key. We're leaving now."

If Michel meant to stop him, let him try.

"No!" Jessica held the key to her chest, guarding it. Wild-eyed.

Dawit moved closer to shield her state from Michel and the onlookers. He stroked her shoulder with his free hand. *What did he do to you?* Dawit asked Jessica silently.

"He let me see," Jessica said. "He showed me why."

Gibberish! Dawit's trigger finger throbbed, the aftermath be damned.

"No, David, I'm all right," Jessica said, sounding more like herself. "I needed to see."

The worst conclusion was obvious: Michel had altered Jessica's thoughts and will. And dear Fana might only be like Icarus, flying too close to the sun.

But the mission need not fail here.

Michel was new to civility, and a slow learner. Higher telepaths could trample less-practiced thoughts easily, and Jessica was the weakest among them, except for the singer. Jessica's state had been fragile long before she encountered Michel. Fana would come.

Dawit hoped his reasoning was his own.

"Never have direct communication with Fana's mother," Dawit told Michel, a public rebuke for the witnesses. "Address our party through Teka, or under mutually agreed-upon terms. Never restrain me or anyone in Fana's party again. Am I clear?"

"Whatever you wish, signore," Michel said quietly, sounding as eager to please him as the boy whose face he wore, ruddy with embarrassment. "Please tell Fana I meant no harm."

His anxiousness seemed too staged to be genuine. Or was it too genuine to be staged?

There was commotion on the steps. A lamp came on, illuminating a growing crowd keeping a distance near the building's doors, everyone in bedclothes. Michel's father, Stefan, was the most anxious, standing at the top of the stairs with a hunting rifle.

Dawit knew that Fana had appeared from the change in Michel's face, as if he were shrinking. Being Michel, perhaps he was. As Fana walked down the stairs toward the courtyard, Michel's eyes raced right and left, looking for somewhere to hide.

I'M GRATEFUL FOR YOUR RESTRAINT, SIGNORE, Michel's voice whispered. *YOUR LOVE FOR YOUR WIFE IS A MODEL FOR ME.*

And then Michel was gone. Michel's dog barked once, circling the spot where Michel had stood. An impulse made Dawit look toward the doors across the courtyard, and he found Michel standing at his father's side. Twenty meters in a sheer instant. Only a visage?

The next time Dawit glanced toward the steps, Michel and his father weren't in sight.

Rami and the singer emerged from the palace doors, and Dawit gestured for them to come, so that their entire party would be outside. Dawit tried not to let his rage from Jessica's stupefied eyes cloud him while he watched Fana hug Jessica, who was sobbing as if Fana were her mother.

"I didn't know, baby," Jessica kept saying, almost an incantation. *What has he done to her?* Dawit asked Fana.

HE LET HER TASTE WHAT CALLS US, Fana answered, but her thought sounded noisy, distracted. She'd described a clear abuse of her mother without a ring of judgment! How far would Fana have to drift to meet Michel?

It's inexcusable, Fana.

"It was . . . clumsy," Fana said aloud. Softly. "He didn't mean to hurt her."

"Do his intentions matter?" Dawit asked Fana. "He swayed her. It is the same result."

HIS INTENTIONS ARE EVERYTHING.

Was she speaking of Michel, or herself? She had mesmerized the singer the same way. The singer now looked petrified as she paced the outer ring of their circle, awaiting her future.

"David, I'm fine," Jessica said. Dawit winced, noticing that she was calling him by his Miami name. "Let's go back in with Fana. She needs us to help her get ready."

Dawit cursed himself for not realizing that Jessica was too fragile for the journey to Michel's. Fresh from her dream chamber, she should never have been so close to him. Now the cost of his miscalculation was clear.

Dawit gazed toward Teka: *Well?*

Teka, Fana's deepest believer, had no answer for Dawit now. Teka had confided that he barely recognized Fana's thoughtstreams since they had arrived at Michel's, and Teka knew her mind better than anyone except Khaldun. Fana was racing so quickly that Teka couldn't follow her. Berhanu, of course, thought they should have come to Michel only in war.

Dawit sent Fana a thought: *Will you stay even if your mother is a casualty tonight?*

Fana's silence appalled him. Was she thinking about it, or too shy to say the answer? Dawit's insides collapsed with his keenest grief since Kira had died at his hands. Was another child being destroyed before him?

TRUST ME, DAD. The voice was still too far for his comfort, but he could hear Fana.

Dawit kissed Fana's forehead. He wished he could bundle her into the car with them. But, like Teka, Dawit had followed Fana as far as he could.

"Safe journey, Duchess."

Teka sent him a mental nudge: *JESSICA CAN FORGET HER VISIT FROM MICHEL. FANA COULD DO IT EASILY—MORE EASILY NOW THAN YESTERDAY. SHE IS GROWING, DAWIT.*

Perfect simplicity!

But, however altered she was, Jessica held dominion over her mind. Dawit spoke to her in a hush. "Jessica, we could restore your earlier mindset, before Michel's interference," he said. "Your opinions would be as they were. You would only forget you saw Michel out here—"

Jessica shook her head. "Fana, don't you dare." At last, she sounded like Jessica again.

"You wanted to leave," Dawit said. "You argued passionately."

"Dawit, no! I won't go, and I want you to stay too. She needs us here—all of us. I can't go back to not knowing. You can't learn backwards."

"You see what he's done to you," Dawit said. "Let Fana persuade you instead."

"She already did—she woke me up in Lalibela and asked me to come with her," Jessica said, grabbing Fana's hand. She entwined their fingers and rested their joined hands across her breast. "You've got a tough trip ahead of you, don't you, baby?"

Fana nodded beneath her mother's soothing voice, her head bent as if she'd been released. Jessica stroked the length of Fana's hair down her back, and Fana closed her eyes beneath Jessica's caress. A single tear streamed from Fana's closed eye.

Michel and Fana were allied already. They had both won Jessica.

Was this his wife, or Michel underneath? Dawit wondered. The same question was in all their minds, except Fana's. Her mind was nowhere near them.

The singer was standing near the car, ready to climb in. Her anxious eyes wanted to go.

"We can't leave Fana alone when she's with Michel," Jessica said, her fingers moving lovingly across Fana's locked hair. "This is why we're here. Damn him for the way he showed me, but now I know, and I can't unlearn. I'm worried about my head too, but I have a test: I'm still me as long as I have this in my hand."

Triumphantly, she held up the car key she'd never stopped clutching.

The key clinked gently against its gold key chain: the crest of Sanctus Cruor.

BLOOD PROPHECY

Even bees, the little almsmen of spring bowers,
know there is richest juice in poison-flowers.
—John Keats

Me and my crew's gonna roll.
We're on a Party Patrol.
We're losing control
Out on this Party Patrol.
—Phoenix,
"Party Patrol"

Thirty-one
Montana

Andres Enriquez wasn't what Johnny had expected.
The rancher was about thirty, clean-shaven, with round tortoiseshell eyeglasses and a button-down shirt in striped shades of blue, probably Italian. Five eight, not as tall as Johnny. His build was mild, even small. He had looked bigger in his photograph. Less like a yuppie. While Enriquez saddled his horse, Johnny stared at the blue-felt image of a dragon stitched across the back of his shirt.

When Enriquez had appeared in the stable with sleep-deprived eyes and a USC coffee tumbler, Johnny had assumed he was a ranch guest who had come to live out frontier fantasies and brag to his friends that he'd roped a calf or driven cattle. No rugged bones or hard, weathered lines on his face. No retribution in his eyes. He looked too small in every way.

Enriquez assessed him from the corner of his eye, too, disappointed.

With a short sigh, Enriquez plucked a brown suede cowboy hat from a row of waiting hats mounted on pegs near the stable entrance. He took a moment to be satisfied with the hat's fit in the small square mirror on the wall. Fashion.

"You ride," Enriquez said, a question dressed as statement. A prerequisite.

Johnny had hoped he wouldn't be asked to ride a horse. Tallahassee wasn't a big city, but he was a city boy. He hadn't ridden a horse since junior high school, when the horse behind him had bitten his leg on a hiking trail. Johnny didn't like riding horses. Hated it, in fact.

"Sure," Johnny said. "Let's ride."

After one false start, Johnny mounted his huge sand-colored horse, clinging to the saddle for balance. His horse followed Enriquez's down the wooded trail, nearly matching its pace. The horses were well trained, clopping in no particular hurry. The wide trail took them away from the guest ranch's stables, toward the thickets of pine trees. The air smelled of pine, dead leaves, and, vaguely, manure.

Two horsemen trailed after them, bulky men Johnny had noticed following him to the stable. Bodyguards. Three days ago, the scenario would have made Johnny nervous.

"This was my first horse," Enriquez said. "My father and I trained him together, in the vaquero way, from when I was ten years old. My father was harsh. I would train more softly now. But the barest touch on the reins, this guy knows where to go. We share a mind."

Except for his Spanish words pronounced with flourish, Enriquez spoke flat English, with a careful lack of an accent, either Mexican or western.

"Must be an old horse," Johnny said, reaching for a response.

"Horses live forty years—they're not dogs," Enriquez said. "But sure, I want him to live a long life. He's the only one left now. Papi is gone. Charro, gone. Arturo. It's sobering to wake up one day and your only family is a horse."

Enriquez stared pointedly at Johnny. He had never been talking about the horse. Finally, Johnny saw the hollowed anger in his eyes. Their negotiation had begun.

Johnny's heart raced. "I can—"

"Uno momento," Enriquez hushed him calmly.

Two riders approached from the opposite direction, whipping off their hats to wave in an exaggerated cowboy style. "Howdy!" called the one with the beer belly.

"¡Buenas dias, senores!" Enriquez said, suddenly in character with a cheerful grin. "I truly hope you are enjoying your stay at El Ranchero!" He poured on a thick Mexican accent. The riders told him how much they loved the ranch, how it was a childhood dream come true.

The moment they passed, Enriquez's grin dropped from his face. "This place makes people happy," he said. He sounded baffled by the idea of happiness.

"You'll see why one day," Johnny said. "God willing."

Enriquez gazed at him with stripped eyes.

"I already see it every day," Enriquez said. "Welcome to my daily dose of sanity."

The sky opened in front of Johnny. They had reached a cliff overlooking the basin at the edge of the world, a memory from when everything was new. Fiery fall foliage painted the mountains' slopes, reflected in the basin's lake of orange, gold, and red below. Johnny realized he had never seen a real autumn before. God had sent him a clear map, with space and colors. No evil could touch them here. *We can do this,* he realized, awed.

"My condolences on the loss of your family," Johnny said.

Enriquez didn't answer, staring at his daily meditation.

"I can't bring your father and family back," Johnny went on, "but I can promise you a long, healthy life. And anyone you love. Even your horse." Pet owners had their own internet Glow network.

"I've always been very interested in Glow," Enriquez said. "It once brought a cousin back from the dead, or close enough. He'd been shot four times. That made me a believer."

Johnny and Caitlin had considered approaching Enriquez as a Glow supplier for Canada months before, since his ranch was a perfect cover. Drug runners already had effective networks—but they had decided that the Enriquez family's history of violence didn't represent the ideals of the Underground Railroad. No drug wars in the name of Glow, if they could help it.

What's changed? Johnny asked himself with Fana's voice, always inside him now.

They had lost Fana. Everything had changed.

But what's changed?

"We can get you enough Glow to last fifty people a hundred

years each, maybe longer," Johnny said. "You get to choose who gets it and how much."

"Only a hundred years?" Enriquez said. Definitely a businessman.

"We say a hundred years to be fair," Johnny said. "The truth is, we don't know yet. You'd be one of the first to find out. It's possible a man lived twice that long. Remember: health is the one thing people would trade everything for." He almost said *mortals*.

"You brought a sample?"

Johnny heard the two bodyguards approaching behind them. One of the men's horses whinnied. Despite the open air, Johnny felt claustrophobic. Did Enriquez somehow know that he had Fana's Blood in his veins? He wasn't armed, he hadn't gained super strength to overpower them, and he wouldn't get far running away on his horse. His new earlobes tingled, his only evidence that the Blood would protect him from injury. All he'd lost was his earring. But no blood would keep him from getting captured. Fear of imprisonment was one reason the Lalibela immortals had created a prison of their own.

"The sample will be delivered once we both understand what we want," Johnny said, keeping his voice calm. "If you don't mind, I don't want your men listening, Mr. Enriquez."

Enriquez considered, and gestured for his men to move back. They turned their horses to find another vantage point, out of earshot. Johnny watched them walk down the trail before they turned their horses around to observe nearby a stone outcropping. Something darted through the carpet of dry leaves below Johnny's horse. A rabbit, maybe. He almost jumped.

Enriquez sipped from his coffee tumbler. "Is your father still alive, Mr. Wright?"

Johnny's heart skipped. Was Enriquez threatening him? Now that Fana was gone, he couldn't be sure his parents had enough protection from their immortal minder. Johnny had hired a Cape Town firm himself, but Phoenix's security had failed. There might be a breach in the security, or Michel might be the breach.

"Why'd you ask?" Johnny said.

"To see if you can imagine what it would feel like to find your father nailed to a wall. You walk in to find his skin so pale that you don't need a coroner to tell you he's been drained of every drop of blood."

Exsanguinated. Johnny's stomach turned as he thought about Caitlin's friends, the family who had died harboring them at the safe house in Arizona. They'd lain in bloody pools in their beds, drained, too, with a bloody message left behind on the wall: AND BLOOD TOUCHETH BLOOD. The stench in the doomed house seemed to clot Johnny's nose again.

"No, I can't imagine my father like that," Johnny said. "But I've lost people to him too." His voice almost broke as he thought of Fana. "And as bad as that is, he's worse than you've seen. He has a deadly biological agent, and he wants to own the world the way he owns Nogales. He's already begun spreading a plague."

From where they sat astride the horses, facing the vista, it was easy to imagine the world emptied. Except for birds, there were no living creatures as far as they could see.

"God's watching us, so I won't paint a pretty picture about Charro," Enriquez said. "My brother wasn't always that way— he had bad influences—but he was greedy, and people are dead because of him. Federalistas, mayors, wives, girlfriends. I knew, but I didn't know everything. Women and children? He never told me, but I knew the rules. If it had just been Charro who died, or me, what could I say? God's judgment. I always expected it. But Arturo? My cousin was only sixteen, a good kid in school. And then Papi . . ." Enriquez filled his lungs so he could go on. "Papi was a crippled old man. When I saw him nailed to the wall, the *way* he was nailed, I knew God doesn't live in that church. Whoever did it enjoyed his pain."

"No," Johnny said. "*He* enjoyed your father's pain."

Enriquez was silent as the mountain. His face colored as he slowly crossed himself.

"Others have tried, but he always knows," Enriquez said. "You die where you sleep, with your blood on the wall. His legend's on the radio, The Curse of El Diablo. *Tres Ojos* in the Back of His Head. You'll die if you speak his name in vain. In Sonora, get this, the children *pray* to him in school. Light candles for him. They're turning a demon into a *santo*. Or a god."

At least Enriquez knew what they were up against.

"He has a weakness." Johnny swallowed the knot in his throat. "A woman. He's getting married Thursday morning. A public wedding, in the tower. He'll be exposed."

Enriquez's face came to life, shocked. His lips fell apart. "Where'd you hear that?"

"I know the woman he's marrying."

Enriquez whispered to himself in Spanish. "If that's true, I should be paying you."

"Your payment is for the risk," Johnny said. "It may not be enough."

He wouldn't lie to the man he'd hired. If he couldn't convince Enriquez with the truth, he would find a way to do it himself. He would never lie in Fana's name.

"Ah," Enriquez said, understanding. His face flattened. "That's why my gringo homey called me instead of risking his own *culo*."

"He has influence. He's bought off your government and most of mine. He's made friends internationally. He's gotten away with mass murder, and he's about to unleash something way beyond genocide. There may not be another chance like this."

"No," Enriquez agreed, nodding thoughtfully. It was as good as saying yes.

"This woman, his fiancée, risked her life to get close to him and expose him for us," Johnny said as his throat tried to close. "She can't be hurt. If she's hurt, there's no payment."

Enriquez's nodding stopped. He looked troubled. "That's harder. When bullets fly . . ."

"That's a deal breaker. You won't get your Glow."

Hunger flared in Enriquez's eyes. He would have killed Michel for free, but he wanted the Glow for his trouble. "Then we don't need an army," Enriquez said. "We need a sniper, and I know a good one. Him and a little backup. A smaller circle's better anyway. Fewer leaks."

"Leaks don't worry me," Johnny said. "Make sure your sniper's nowhere near Nogales when you contact him. He shouldn't come within a hundred miles before he has to. I'd suggest farther away. We can give him satellite photos of the area."

"Oh, I know exactly where that damned place is."

"I want to meet your sniper," Johnny said. "But don't mention *his* name to anyone. Or his title. Or the name of the sect. None of us should." He pointed to his eyes. "*Tres Ojos.*"

Enriquez nodded. He crossed himself again. "Yes," he said. His voice was faraway.

Johnny and Enriquez understood each other fine.

"In my family, you expected to die young," Enriquez said. "Even if you had your head in the sand like me. If one of you farts in the wrong direction, the whole family's dead. I grew up scared. But if I have something to die for, maybe I can pay my way into Heaven."

"Amen." Johnny scratched his tingling earlobe. He wished he hadn't lost his earring.

A chill made Johnny long for a heavier jacket. The expanse of the open valley and fifteen hundred miles south to Nogales might not be enough space from Michel. He could be hiding in the colorful treetops. Or inside one of Enriquez's men. Michel could be Enriquez himself.

But it had begun. Enriquez's Glow sample would be delivered as soon as Johnny called the courier from a local company to bring it, unaware. Enriquez would use a Glow strip to test it. Within an hour, a gunman would get the order to shoot Michel on his wedding day.

If Michel was shot, Fana could take over the battle. Or Dawit. All they needed was a chance to overpower him. Tomorrow, Michel could be dead!

But if not . . .

Johnny's heart knocked in his throat.

Fana had been right: the Blood wouldn't protect him from Michel.

It was time to write a goodbye letter to his parents.

Thirty-two

Although the room was cool, Jessica dabbed away beads of hot perspiration from Fana's forehead with a washcloth. Fana's first fever in eighteen years. Fana's eyes were still closed as she sat by the fireplace in the room Michel had made for her parents.

Fana had suffered a lifetime of trances, but this one was far different. Jessica tried to remember her daughter's patience as she waited for Fana's eyes to open—a sign that she was near them, temporarily freed from her Blood fever. She and Dawit had spent hours at Fana's bedside when she was young, watching for the fleeting moments when Fana would open her eyes to the world. Once again, Jessica looked for signs that her baby girl was still there.

Jessica had always known that Fana would go to Michel, to the Shadows, but knowing was different now, so deep and wide that there was nowhere to run. She didn't have enough tears left to fill the hole in her. Just let Fana stay awhile longer, and open her eyes from time to time so Jessica could check in and see her daughter again.

Teferi, Fasilidas, Berhanu, and Teka had encircled the room, trying to erect a mental web to protect their group's thoughts, an attempt at privacy. Michel would know he wasn't welcome. Jessica was a part of the tighter circle around Fana. They had all fallen into place, slowly closing in, plugging the gaps. Dawit beside Jessica, and Rami beside Phoenix, both musicians quietly playing their violins. Fana's teacher sat across from her, close enough for her to hear his breathing. Fana had always known she would need her circle of voices with her.

Somehow, maybe because of what Michel had shown her, Jessica knew it was time.

Fana pulsed Jessica a memory: *Will I look different when I lose my baby teeth, Mommy?* Fana had asked when she was three, before times turned bad. Fana reminded Jessica of the brightness of the afternoon out by the kraal with the goats in Botswana, and her own voice still alive in Fana's memory: *YOU'RE GOING TO LOOK A LOT OF WAYS WHILE YOU GROW UP, FANA,* she had said. *YOU'LL ALWAYS BE BEAUTIFUL.*

Yes yes yes yes, she had tried to tell Fana even then. She would cry later, but now Fana needed her to rejoice in the truth of their shared memory. Fana would always be beautiful.

Fana opened her eyes to stare at Jessica, unguarded.

"I couldn't have been strong enough without you, Mom," Fana said.

Fana spoke out in the air, where words had weight. Where Jessica could always hear them again and again without the help of Dreamsticks. There hadn't been enough tender talk between them, only the battles, and now the time had passed.

"I love you, Fana," Jessica said, choosing her words to Fana carefully, in case they were her last. "You have a gift, sweetheart. Kill him, if you can."

Fana's open face fell into impatience. *HOW CAN YOU SAY THAT NOW?*

"He told me to tell you my thoughts," Jessica said. "He knows it's the best thing. Otherwise, he knows he'll hurt you."

BUT YOU SAW US, Fana said.

What had Jessica seen? She had seen two showers of light crossing, a sky of flaming embers. New pathways gasping to breathe, a horrible aching.

"I don't know how to explain what I saw," she said.

"What he made you *think* you saw," Dawit reminded her gently.

"You and Michel may be two halves of something bigger," Jessica told Fana. "That's why it hurts to stay apart. If you keep fighting, maybe you'll get weaker. It's already started: your visions are hazy. You've been saying it for months, and now I understand why. But Teka says . . ."

Teka cleared his throat, preferring to speak for himself. "I said it's *possible* that the reaction could be eased if Michel's heart stopped," Teka said. "His remaining thoughtstreams should wither. But we don't truly know. Why wouldn't he have killed Fana to quell his pain?"

"Then he would lose her power for the Cleansing," Dawit said. "He wants hers too."

"He doesn't want to hurt me," Fana said. "But he would kill me if he had to. It would be . . . crippling, I think. But better than dying. So I can't hurt Michel without hurting myself. Weakening myself. I might lose gifts."

"It might be worth it, Fana," Jessica said. "Why take a chance on changing his mind?"

"We're stronger as two," Fana said.

"You're strong enough as one," Jessica said.

"Be decisive," Dawit said. "If he's torn, you have the advantage."

"Don't try to shun the Shadows entirely, Fana," Teka said. "Use them for strength. Learn them. But always distinguish between them and you."

Jessica gave her a small mirror. "Have a way to know who you are," Jessica said. The car key still dangled from her hand. Jessica had never let go of it.

"Be vigilant, Fana," Dawit said. "He's declared his plans to overtake you."

The room was like a library, or a museum. The first thing Phoenix had noticed was the original da Vinci painting of a mother and child hanging over the fireplace in a protective glass case. Phoenix had never learned to be moved by the painting's cross or the child's destiny, but the artwork made her miss her son so much that she nearly swooned. What other hardships had Mary borne for her child? What were her stories?

Phoenix was surrounded by others, but she still felt alone, except for the painting.

Phoenix couldn't stop thinking about Michel's eyes from the courtyard, their first meeting. Even while Michel had been introducing her to his followers, his dead eyes had told Phoenix that he would gladly arrange her abduction again, without a rescue this time.

Michel was loathsome, and he stank. Phoenix had brushed up against something hot and tarry when she walked within ten feet of him—the Shadows? She wanted to go somewhere and wash the smell of him off her, but she couldn't leave Fana alone.

Fana might go to him at any time.

Fana might already be gone.

Phoenix heard a beautiful solo, a soprano's song, and realized it was the music from her own arm capering across the violin's strings. Middle Eastern, East African, and something she didn't know. Fana was conducting the fast-paced melody from inside her, the way Scott Joplin's ghost had.

PLEASE PLAY FOR ME, Fana whispered. *Play* and *pray* were so much alike, Phoenix did both. Rami followed Phoenix's lead. Since Rami was a telepath, playing with him was like hearing her own thoughts in harmony. The sensation lifted her higher, floating above the room. She would need to float. Fana expected Phoenix to follow her across the planes between life and death, calling to her with music.

Phoenix's arm improvised on its own from what Fana had taught her, and Rami both led and followed. The music trilled, raced, and played. She and Rami mined the notes between the notes. They veered into rhythms and basslines, plucking motion into the air. They were playing "Party Patrol," a song she had once believed was silly. Beneath her.

"Yes!" Fana cried, elated. She jumped to her feet. "I love this song! I want to dance!"

To remember her body, Fana danced.

Thirty-three

Fana's skin was still sweating as she made her way down the hall, this time without the mortal girl Inez to lead her, or her sweet Fasilidas trailing behind. Shallow panting followed her, bouncing from Michel's stone walls; she had to remind herself that the panting was hers. Her heart was still dancing.

Michel wasn't in his studio. His stoic void met her at the oak door. The door was locked; she rattled the lock open with her thoughts, as effortlessly as a cat burglar, but the canvases stood alone in the darkened room. No one pitched across the painted rain forest and thick wooden beams on the high ceiling. Michel's absence seared her.

Fana pulsed for him, searching for his thoughtstreams, but he didn't answer. He had told her he didn't want to lead her. He was giving her a way to change her mind.

Fana was as desperate to find Michel as she had once been to flee him. Now that she was ready, she didn't want to wait. She would never be stronger, fresh from a circle with her family and the music of their voices. Fresh from dancing! She could have danced until dawn, but Fana had reached the limits of her body. The Blood link to him blotted everything.

"Michel?" she called, knowing how much he liked to hear his name. But he resisted. He was going to make her come to him.

A small shadow moving in short lurches near the floor stopped Fana's steps. Her eyes focused in the dark: Adam was wandering the halls. He jumped to her, climbing to her shoulder. Adam immediately began grooming her, picking at her hair.

Fana swatted at his careless tugging. "Adam, where's Michel?"

"The Most High is nowhere and everywhere," the chatter monkey said, sounding more lucid than usual, more human. Already thoroughly indoctrinated.

"Have you seen *Michel*?" Fana said.

Adam shrieked laughter, leaping from her shoulder to a shelf. "There's nobody named Michel!" he said. "Michel doesn't live here!" Adam rounded the corner, amused by his lie.

Chatter monkeys weren't guides, Fana remembered.

Fana followed a hidden memory, tracing the winding, private stairway one flight up at the far west of the building, past the collection of silent paintings on the wall, impassive eyes watching her climb. Michel's bedchamber might be the only room on the floor, nestled in a corner away from the soaring cathedral; far from the sealed chamber that echoed its sorrows even now, the one that housed his Cleansing Pool.

The walls seemed to tremble. He was close. The smell of the Shadows wafted gently from the floor, and Fana inhaled. Her mind sharpened.

Michel was in his room, waiting for her, she realized. He had known that she would come.

The wing was dark, and his door was nearly closed, open a crack to let out a sliver of light. Music floated from the room. Had he plucked the music from her recollections? It was Cuban music the way her father had taught her to love it, at its roots. La Reina, Celia Cruz, singing an old love song in her earthly, impassioned warble. *Tuya y Más Que Tuya*, she sang. Yours and More than Yours. She sang of dreams of her beloved lulling her to sleep.

Michel had given her music on her first visit, she remembered, a song called "Black Tears," as sad as their meeting; as inevitable as their parting. The sound of grief, about a connection so deep that it could cause you to die.

Michel knew the right language for her.

Michel's room was large, of polished medieval brick, barely furnished except for a bed elevated ten feet from the ground, jutting from the wall, and a sofa and bookshelves on the floor for reading. Except for rugs, his room looked more like a tomb.

Michel's three Sanctus Cruor robes hung in a glass case across the room, suspended in a shrine to his duty. The case had rows of light bulbs, but the lights had been turned off. Fana hoped the Most High was gone for the night.

Michel was near his tall picture window, staring outside at the waking sky as he hovered a foot above the ground. He bobbed slightly, floating in a gentle sea. Michel's crimson silk pajamas shone in the moonlight. Without trying to, Fana noticed his open pajama shirt.

As soon as she stepped across his threshold, one headache died, replaced by another. Her mind was falling into sections that didn't remember how to knit together, clamoring for him.

Michel didn't look at her. "I hope I didn't scare your mother," he said.

"Of course you scared her. But I'm glad she saw." Fana hadn't come to chide him. She was glad her mother had stayed, that she could hear the muffled burr of her mother's thoughts.

"Are you here to wake me, Fana?" Michel said. "Or to put me to sleep?"

He had been listening to them, of course. He always listened.

"I don't know," Fana said. "Is this all another lie, Michel? Your way of bringing me here? If you're forcing me here, I can never trust you. I will kill you. Don't doubt it."

"You'll try," he corrected her. "Just as others will try."

He knew why she was in his room, so he could afford to be blunt.

"I'm not others," Fana said.

"Your mother's voice . . ." Michel murmured.

"This is *my* voice."

Michel floated, skating across the opposite wall as quickly as a shadow. "The truth, Fana?" he said. Her heart jumped at the endless possibilities for his lies.

"Always."

"My pain is real. But did I share it with you to bring you here tonight? *Non lo so.* I can't say. My abilities hide from me, yours hide from you. Teka, our teacher, recognizes our union, the call of our Blood. So does the Prophecy. I've taken every precaution, far too many, so I know I haven't tried to pull you. But *si*, I have wondered too."

Michel's intentions mattered. That was what she had told her father.

"Teka is *our* teacher?" she said, surprised.

Finally, Michel smiled at her, a hint of warmth beyond their transaction. "Of course. I will teach you the Shadows, and he will teach me the Rising. Did you think I don't want to learn your ways? Why should you know things I don't?" His grin was a promise.

Michel's smile, such a rare sight, trapped her again, his essence shining in his eyes. They were poised at the edge of themselves. The air swelled with his presence near her, along the side wall. The ache in Fana's head made her grind her teeth together, hard.

"Promise you won't try to take me tonight," she said.

"Promise you won't try to kill me tonight."

Neither of them promised, but neither of them mentioned the Cleansing.

Could this be the only place and time for them?

An image in the corner of Fana's vision took her eyes to the massive mural on the wall. She had to turn to see it behind her: a perfect rendering of her engagement dinner to Michel a year ago. Hers was the only face visible. Fana had forgotten how Caitlin had dressed her dreadlocks with countless white bows, and the white dress she had worn for Michel, which made her look festive somehow. Or the bright red lipstick her mother had painted on her lips, remembering her lesson from Gramma Bea. Her grandmother was in the portrait, too.

Now Michel was behind her. She hadn't heard him fly to her, or his feet lighting on the floor, but her shoulder brushed against his chest. He stood only close enough to let her know he was there, so she would feel how much he wanted her. Fire roared over her as her body and mind conspired, feeding each other.

"This is beautiful, Michel," she said.

"Only the woman is beautiful," he said. "You are beautiful, Fana."

He slid his arm gently around her waist, but he didn't whisper thoughts to her. Even as he touched her, his hot skin pressing to her, he kept his distance. He gave her one last chance.

Then . . .

Michel swayed with her to the music, gently changing it for her ears, his mental touch nearly soft enough not to notice. Suddenly, Celia was singing in a chorus with Benny Moré and Vicente Fernandez, while Mario Bauzá's orchestra built a wall of sound to embrace them, an army of brass. She heard Michel's tender words buried in the music: *COME TO ME, FANA.*

A pathway opened, a sun's worth of light. He ruptured himself for her, showing more than he'd planned, surrendering to his need to fuse with her.

Be decisive, her father had said.

Fana decided.

Fana's jump felt more like flying. First she rose only a few feet, cool air caressing her face. *Yes, I've always wanted to fly.* Far away, maybe a solar system away, his lips kissed the side of her neck, kneading her flesh into a ball of sensation. Fana smelled the paint from his mural, saw colors blending. Then Fana raced beyond sights, smells, and skin, tumbling and twirling, tossed in the midst of their storm.

Then . . .

She chose you tonight, but she will not choose your way.

If you cannot prevent her suffering, honor her by enjoying it.

Feed from her. Let it begin.

His father's voice chased Michel because his father's voice, by now, was his own.

Forgive me, Fana.

Michel held Fana as if she were a moth, by a delicate wing. Fana was tumbling, senseless, trying to gather pieces of herself inside him. She liked the feeling of flying, so he disguised the chaos as flight to help her join with him.

Fana was magnificent; a warm, vibrating bath. She was so clear, so crisp! Her beauty made him ache to fill himself with her, to follow her currents. Just to peek . . .

But no time. *Now.*

Fana had offered her gift to his door, her brave sacrifice, and so he would be kind. She would wake without remembering fear or struggle. He would preserve everything about her except her Blood mission. She was gaining strength from him, less confused with every heartbeat, so he couldn't wait. It would never be easier.

But . . .

Fana called to Michel from the places he had not seen, so many dots of unexplored light, an undulating massage. How could he preserve what he had never known? He heard her childhood laughter, her untold mysteries.

LET GO OF ME, MICHEL, she said. Her own voice, still preserved.

Fana would fight, but he could hold her.

For a rare instant, Michel didn't know what he would do.

Then he let her go. The moth flew free.

He followed her wondrous blaze.

Michel rocked through Fana, his own hurricane. Seeing the shape of him taught her to see new shapes in herself, pulling and expanding her awareness. How had he learned so much without a good teacher, only riding the Shadows? Michel was a miracle. His father had fed him the only way he had known how, but Michel might be as strong as Khaldun. Was she?

Fana sailed through Michel's strength, wrapping herself in it, wondering how much of it she had given him and how much he had given her, already confused about where she ended and he began. Each new space in him brought a new delight, so much to learn. He reminded her of everything she'd forgotten about how to make rain.

Fana raced past a corner she couldn't see, a piece of him tucked away in secrecy, but she didn't linger. She would have time to learn him. He probed at the spaces she'd held from him, too, but he respected her barriers when he found them. The barriers tripped up their speed, but why reveal weaknesses?

One part of them was not free to play; one part of them always had to remember.

Still, they dived into each other, hurtling through each other's memories, tasting every thought they could find. They were hungry for each other, so they gorged.

Their bodies, somewhere far from them, found each other, too.

Neither Fana nor Michel heard the tolling bells that woke the mountainside.

Thirty-four

The man who opened the door to room 306 of the Motel 6 off Interstate 45 southeast of Houston looked like he was sixty or sixty-five, easy; like somebody's grandfather who complained about bad eyes and sore joints. His records said he was fifty-six, but life had ridden him hard. He had hollowed bags under his eyes, and his breathing gurgled slightly in his chest, probably from smoking.

But a shot of Glow would get him into shape. He had to be ready tomorrow.

Enriquez had said he was the best.

The stranger recognized Johnny from the vidphone, so he let him in, closing the door efficiently. The room was dim, barely lighted by a weak fluorescent bulb near the bathroom and a weaker lamp between the two twin beds. The curtains were as thick as blankets, blocking even the Texas sun. No suitcase was in sight. The sniper hadn't turned on the TV. The walls carried the smell of deep-fried dough from white food wrappers in tight balls in the trash.

"I hate Houston," the sniper said. "I should've said Fort Worth. Better food."

The notion of food, stopping to eat, was beyond Johnny. Houston was more than a thousand miles from Nogales, but it might be too close. That was all Johnny was thinking.

"Just kidding." The sniper outstretched his hand, and arm muscles flexed. "I'm Raul."

Johnny shook Raul's hand. "John Jamal Wright." He used his name from the news.

The cross hanging from Raul's neck reassured him; a small, sterling silver testament to faith, not fashion. He wore a plain wedding band, tightened by time on his ring finger. *He knows both God and love,* Johnny thought. Raul's features might be Maya: dark brown skin and a broad forehead. His snow-white hair was tied into a long ponytail.

When Enriquez had mentioned his hitter's military experience, Johnny had assumed he was recommending someone who'd retired from the Mexican military. Wrong.

Raul Puerta was a retired U.S. Marines sniper. He and Raul would be their own army.

"An honor, Wright," Raul said. His eyes were full of things he wanted to say. "The war on Glow is a sin. A medic brought some out in the field—it's liquid gold. I've never seen anything like it. And, man, I heard ops we're doing that turned my hair gray—civilians getting snatched, misinformation, cover-ups. That singer . . . what's-her-name. The loonies are running the asylum. You guys are heroes doing God's work. Get it to the damn people."

Hiring a sniper didn't feel like God's work, but Johnny thanked him.

"Let's nail this crazy son of a bitch," Raul whispered.

Raul turned on his cheap bedside clock radio to hide their voices from neighbors. A woman was singing a Spanish ballad so loudly that the tinny speakers rattled. Johnny almost asked Raul to turn off the music right away. He rarely ignored his hunches. Anything could be hiding an omen or a message, but Johnny let the radio play.

Johnny sat on the bed opposite Raul's. "Here's what we know . . ." he began.

His intelligence said that the wedding would be on Thursday morning, a window anywhere between five a.m. and noon. Raul should be in place by five a.m. at the latest, since an earlier public event seemed unlikely. In past public appearances, followers had two hours' notice if they wanted to see him in person. News of his appearances sent Nogales into a frenzy. Raul would be alerted as soon as a time was announced.

Johnny talked about their target as *he,* and Raul followed his lead: Where would he be standing? How long would he be exposed?

Johnny had to admit how little he knew, offering satellite images of the surrounding area that weren't enough. Michel's unholy home always looked blurry in photos, hidden in shadows. Johnny was guessing even about the wedding's location; he was convinced that it would be in the tower because of a stubborn memory from the time when Michel had tormented him with visions of his future with Fana. He had seen a domed tower.

The singer on the radio captured the agony of wondering what Fana was doing at that moment. Johnny tried not to think about Michel's face, to forget his name. The plan to kill him felt like a wish. Even with a good sniper, what were their chances?

"You've left me a lot of question marks, kid," Raul said.

"Then we need luck," Johnny said. "Maybe more than luck."

Raul shrugged. "Here's our luck," he said, and opened his duffel bag.

The gun was in pieces. As a collection of thin parts painted in camo green, the gadget didn't look like luck, or even a good omen. It looked scratched up and secondhand. It wasn't any more impressive than Enriquez or Raul. Or Johnny.

Raul sat on the floor like a child at playtime and began assembling it between the beds, where it would be hidden from the door. Twisting, snapping, patting, metal clicking against metal. It took him only a few breaths, about thirty seconds. Assembled, the gun was four feet long. Its oversized scope looked like it could see footprints on the moon.

"This is the Intervention," Raul said. "No bull—that's the name. Handheld ballistic computer. Laser range finder. This is the reason the U.S. Marine Corps has the best snipers in the world." The room brightened in the gun's aura.

Johnny ran his fingers across the gun's tiny scratches; its past life. A former marine was almost as good as an active unit, Johnny realized. They might as well have the cavalry.

"What's the range?" Johnny said.

"How far you need?"

"To be safe . . . half a mile?" It sounded feeble. Michel would hear Raul breathing. Their reports on Michel said he had military patrols within half a mile of the church for crowd control. "But farther's always better."

"I can give you a mile, if I can get past any obstructions," Raul said.

A mile! Raul grinned at Johnny's surprise, his teeth so tobacco stained they were brown. "In '04, my guys shot a barrel three times from 1.3 miles with this baby. World record."

"Don't count on a world record," Johnny said, nervous. Raul's psych report had looked fine after twenty-one years in the corps, but maybe he was delusional. Maybe they all were.

"Course not," Raul said. "I just need a mile."

One mile's cushion. A mile's protection. Johnny didn't know if he should feel assured by the adjustment, but he did. Raul knew his capacities from practice. Johnny wondered how many men he had killed, or if Enriquez had hired him before. He was disappointed in himself when he realized that he wouldn't ask.

"What else do you need?" Johnny said.

"I have a few guys, but I only need my spotter. We figger all we'll get is the cold shot."

"What's that?"

"The first one," Raul said. "Might take the bullet three seconds to get home, but it'll travel faster than the sound. He'll never hear it coming."

Having the plan mapped out with the familiar assurance of physics made Johnny's heart celebrate. He envied the spotter who would go to the mountain with Raul and the Intervention. He wanted to hear the *crack* of the gunfire with his own ears.

Someone knocked on the door, two polite raps. Raul caught Johnny's eyes, wondering.

"That must be the Glow," Johnny said.

Johnny could have brought Raul's sample himself, but protocol said always to hire a courier. Raul covered the Intervention with one of the brown bedspreads before he got up to answer the door, not rushing an ounce. He moved in a calculated, economical way. He wasn't the kind of man who tripped or made missteps. His finger would be steady on the trigger.

Raul signed for the package, a standard padded envelope.

Once the door was closed, Raul raised the package to Johnny: *May I?* Johnny nodded.

The hypodermic was inside, already filled with a dose of Glow. More like fifty doses, but it was hard to dilute Glow enough for a single dose. Most people used more than they needed. The solution was barely pink, more saline than blood. Raul held it up to the lamp's anemic light, shaking it.

"You can't tell by looking," Johnny said.

"True that," Raul said.

A slight wheeze from Raul's lungs gave away his eagerness as he breathed faster. Raul pulled a black rubber strap out of his back pocket. With the hypodermic between his teeth, Raul deftly snapped the strap around his upper arm. He flicked at his skin to pop a vein.

"Been a while since my last dose," Raul said, poising the needle. "When it's the real stuff, man . . . There's this feeling you get right when it hits your bloodstream . . ."

When Raul plunged the hypo, Johnny looked away. He had seen shots administered at clinics, but no one had ever shot up in front of him. Raul was a joyrider. If Raul knew that the Glow was from Johnny's blood, he would never let Johnny leave the room. Johnny would become his personal bank account and fountain of youth; his morning cup of coffee and his nightly whiskey shot. Johnny shivered. Eventually, people would notice that he didn't age. If he lived long enough.

"There it is," Raul said, his eyes closed. He exhaled hard through his nostrils, in bliss.

"Makes you feel like you can do anything," Johnny said. He thought about the mountain, the *crack* of the gunshot that might echo for miles.

Raul nodded. "La Reina," he said absently.

"What?"

Raul nodded toward the radio. "Celia Cruz—La Reina. My mother loved her."

The radio came into crisp focus. The song sounded sad to Johnny despite the dance tempo, as if the singer had Fana's voice. Johnny remembered what *La Reina* meant from high school Spanish: The Queen.

"If the bride gets shot, no more Glow," Johnny said. "Scrap the mission if she's at risk."

No one could claim that they had misunderstood. Johnny wouldn't have known about the wedding if Mahmoud hadn't told him; and Jessica has sent him to Mahmoud. Johnny had promised Jessica not to hurt Fana. And if Fana was hurt, Michel might have a chance to destroy what mattered about her. Whatever Michel had done to Fana might be undone after he was shot.

Raul raised his eyebrows. "Scrap it?" he repeated thoughtfully, head cocked to the side, as if he were already seeing Michel in his laser-guided sight, another everyday target.

"If she survives, maybe we all will," Johnny said. "Only shoot *him.*"

"If you say so," Raul said. He didn't sound convinced.

"Sorry to be a jerk, but I need your word," Johnny said. "Swear it on your wife."

Raul's eyes narrowed to slits. He didn't want his wife brought into the room. He looked like he wanted to remind Johnny about the bigger stakes, like the outbreak in Puerto Rico. But he nodded, resigned. "You have my word. I swear it on Martha." He said her name like a prayer.

Johnny shook his hand, clasping tightly. They didn't let go right away. Raul's word might mean something, or it might not. Plans went wrong.

"I like the way you walk, kid," Raul said. "Straight and sharp. Hope your dad's proud."

"My parents are too scared to be proud." The letter he'd sent his parents would only scare them more, but they deserved a warning. Johnny didn't dare dwell on his parents. "But maybe one day."

Johnny shut off the radio, not sure why. He didn't ignore any signals, anything that felt too right or too wrong. Something about the music bothered him, even if it was beautiful. The music might bring him closer to Fana somehow. To Michel.

With the radio off, Johnny listened in the silence, waiting for a hint that he'd been found. The silence was worse than the sad song.

Johnny wished he had an appetite, or that Raul didn't mind the food in Houston.

He would have liked a last good meal before the wedding.

Thirty-five

Violet waters lapped against a pink and lilac sky, blending at the distant horizon.

Fana was drifting in her ocean of colors, wrapped in a warm blanket of water. Part floating, part flying, massaged by the ocean's fingers. Serenity. Spanish singing flew past her ear, and a stray thought—*Johnny?*—before both were gone. The wind carried violin strains to help her remember her way back, but she didn't follow the music. Not yet.

Fana had never traveled so far, even when she was three. Fana dived beneath the water, knifing through the rainbow of glowing shapes and tendrils, water massaging her lungs.

She saw a shape approaching from the murkiness below, the deeper waters.

Hair, shoulders, his face. His image appeared as a strobe: here and gone. A hint of his mental marker. Fana flipped, speeding back toward the surface. She swam faster, and he gained on her. He grabbed her foot and tugged, forcing her to stop swimming.

In Michel's first grip, Fana hadn't been able to remember her own name. His presence had been poised above her like a giant, ready to reduce her to a wisp of smoke. The scope of him had taught her how strong she could expect to be, if she learned.

Then Michel let her go. Again.

Michel popped above the water, damp hair hugging his forehead and neck. He was smiling, although his face flickered in and out of sight. In the mental landscape, physical appearance was an afterthought. Her mind flashed Michel's image because she perceived his mental marker, but they didn't need eyes to see here. She could feel his smile.

"There!" Michel said. "Found you again."

"I was barely hiding that time," Fana said. "It's taking you longer."

Playing with him taught her fastest. Fana had found Michel when he was hiding once, but she couldn't hold him through pure strength, yet; she darted and dashed in his thoughts, confusing him. He lost himself when he chased her, the hunter in him fully engaged. Challenging Michel was the best way to hold him.

Michel was studying her, too, of course. He had discovered how much she enjoyed trusting him; how much she liked feeling his strength, and his letting go.

Michel swam through Fana, their flickering images melding. His passage wasn't entirely clear—their thorny places snagged—but he was still a bath. Each time they came together, their minds washed new passageways clear. Fana luxuriated in the spaces where she and Michel fit. They practiced holding each other like wriggling fish, feeling the tug, letting go. Catch and release. They were magnificent.

Warm raindrops kissed their faces as they floated on their backs. Fana had brought Michel to her childhood resting place, back to the scents of salt water and sugar, where warm water licked her ears and the soles of her feet. But she didn't show him everything that had driven her here as a child. Secrets slowed their fusing, but they each kept a few.

A lone bright purple rum bottle floated in the water, bobbing between them. A message! Which of them was it for? Fana hoped Michel wasn't sending himself a grim message from the Most High to wake them from their peace.

Fana unfurled the parchment rolled inside the bottle.

Teach, the single word said in Ge'ez, the language of the Letter of the Witness.

Fana and Michel both scanned the water for the bottle's sender. A flat ocean's horizon embraced them in every direction. Except . . . .

"There!" Fana said, pointing.

A small dot of a boat, maybe a canoe, lay barely within sight. A figure waved from the boat. Was it a man? A woman? Fana raced toward the boat, until she realized she wasn't moving no matter how fast she swam. The boat always receded from her.

Was it Khaldun? Had he been waiting in her shared thought-streams with Michel?

"Is that the Witness?" Michel said.

"I think so," she said.

"Then he's come for our union, to see his Prophecy live."

They weren't willing to tell each other their private questions, but they both shouted after Khaldun, whose name, Fana remembered, meant "eternal." Their combined voices thundered in the skies. Fana lost track of how much time they called for him, but he never came.

Don't forget to teach, Mom had said. Mom was his messenger, too.

"The Letter never mentions killing anyone," Fana told Michel. "The Witness never wrote that killing is a part of the Cleansing. How did the revelation come to you, Michel?"

Even now, when he had never been more open to her, she asked carefully.

The water surged, carrying them like a mother's arms as Michel considered his answer.

"The Witness asks us to interpret his words," Michel said. "Words are only a path."

"Was it . . . your father's doctrine?" Fana said. "Was the Cleansing the reason he broke your mother's mind and stole you? Was she afraid of what her son would grow up to be?"

It was hard to know whose questions she was asking, or whose mother had been more petrified of raising a monster. So much was a sea of mirrors.

Looking for Michel once, Fana had stumbled across a space filled with tall file cabinets, as dusty as fifty-year-old artifacts in an office basement. Most of the rusting drawers had been labeled "Teru," except a few labeled "Mama," written in crayon instead. Drawer after drawer had been locked. All Michel had given Fana was a glimpse of a red ball rolling back and forth across a braided Turkish rug, and a woman's cooing laughter.

"Come, Fana," Michel said.

He took her away from her ocean, plunging her to his depths. His speed dizzied her as he pulled her. Anxious thoughts chased after her, small popping bubbles, but she ignored them and enjoyed their speed. Michel would release her again.

And if he didn't, she would face it.

The cold murkiness below them formed sudden shapes. They raced through a forest of faces: men, women, and children, captured in their moments of greatest agony. Their screams raked through Fana, clawing at the door to the appetite she had locked away.

Fana's heart screamed for them. She couldn't catch her breath.

"I can feed on suffering, but it's too much," Michel said. "This is *now*, Fana. This very instant. Children. The starving. The pawns of conflict. The sick. The Shadows live near me, so this is what I hear. I always have. You'll hear it now too."

"We can heal the sick."

"And then what, Fana?" Michel said. "What about the ones after them? Should they live forever too? We can't save them all." Was it Michel's voice, or her own?

A rum bottle sped beside her, diving with them, so Fana unfurled the parchment inside:

Learn, it said.

A stench grew, the water more viscous and harder to wade through. Missiles sailed toward Fana, a glittering wall of dead fish with clouded eyes. Bigger creatures tumbled past in the maelstrom, frozen in death. Otters. Seals. Porpoises. The ocean screamed around her, boiling red.

"'And the very planet shall die,'" Michel said, quoting the Letter. "This is what happens without the Cleansing, Fana. This is what happens if we are childish."

Overwhelmed by the screaming, Fana pulled away from Michel's nightmare vision, and she was relieved when he let her go back to her tranquil ocean. The figure in the boat was still visible, silhouetted against a fuchsia sky. She liked keeping him in sight.

The water foamed beside her, and Michel broke through in a fountain. His image shimmered in the water's spray.

"We can't hide here, Fana."

He could be her father talking to her mother in her dream chamber, she thought.

"Why not?" Fana said.

"Our wedding! I have to tell the people. There are preparations. I can't find your dreams of a perfect wedding—didn't you ever imagine one?"

Michel was more practiced at passing between mental and physical realms, like changing his clothes. He sounded like a flustered bureaucrat, and Fana had forgotten about the wedding! Fana realized that she had never imagined her wedding, except a child's fairy-tale portrait of a prince and princess. A physical ceremony seemed silly when they were learning so much swimming inside each other. But the symbol was meaningful to Michel.

And she might have trouble finding her way back to her body if she stayed too long. She wouldn't rely on Michel to lead her. Violin music reminded Fana which way to go, and she followed her muse.

Somewhere nearby, she also heard muffled singing: Celia Cruz. La Reina.

"Look what I found!" Michel said.

Michel's image flashed to her. He was holding a waterlogged wooden chest over his head with both hands. The chest was closed, although it had no lock, engraved *Johnny* in her script. The singing was trapped in the dripping chest. Johnny was thinking about her.

Johnny's memory chest seemed too small; it had felt so much bigger before. How had Michel pried open the lock? Or had the music done it?

When Fana tried to take the chest, Michel swung it out of her reach. And he complained about childishness!

"Don't look in there," Fana said.

"We'll be married in hours, and you keep him from me?"

"I haven't seen plenty of yours," Fana said. There was one woman, Gypsy, he had sent to his Cleansing Pool; he kept the rest of her locked away. "I won't think about him when I'm with you. Just like I promised. You said you wouldn't either."

They both knew Michel liked to keep his word to her. He sighed.

Michel heaved the chest away, where it splashed and floated before it began to sink. Bubbles rose as it disappeared from sight. Fana longed to dive after Johnny, to soothe his furious pain and fear. It was hard to remember why she shouldn't.

"Your mortal who dreamed he was a god," Michel said, almost sadly. "You had every right to choose him for the Blood, Fana. You'll choose each one who's saved."

"We have to read the Letter carefully, Michel," Fana said. "Together."

"Of course. A joint reading will be our first public act as husband and wife."

Everything was a ceremony to him.

"Friday is too soon to begin the Cleansing," she said.

"Yes," Michel said. "Friday is too soon. Saturday, perhaps."

They were learning how to meet each other! Their journey would be painstaking, a slow-growing plant, but she would challenge his interpretations one at a time, and he would challenge hers. They would ask questions in each other's voices. With time, they would become something new. They would have their own Way.

The physical world called to Fana in the frenzied, exhausted music of Phoenix and Rami. Hours had passed.

A third floating bottle bumped against Fana, so she unrolled the the parchment inside. Once again, the word was written in Ge'ez.

Grow, it said.

"He tells us what we already know," Michel said, his voice fading to the physical world.

Fana had been about to say the same thing.

As if they already shared one mind.

Thirty-six

Wednesday

At noon, there was a knock on Fana's parents' door, where the group had congregated. Phoenix had her own room with a collection of pianos, she'd been told, but she wouldn't have left Fana even if she'd wanted to. After the strange episode between Jessica and Michel in the courtyard, Phoenix didn't want to be alone at Michel's.

Fana was meditating by the fireplace, where she'd been since the late-night dancing, speaking only occasionally. Phoenix was beside her, always keeping her in sight. Fana seemed not to hear the knocking, and no one else answered the knock. None of them wanted anything on the other side of that door.

"*Perdóname!*" an apologetic woman's voice called from the hall. "Fana is here with us, and she is ready to return to you."

But Fana was here! Fana was four feet from her, close enough to see the stray hairs across her brow. Close enough to touch. Now Fana's closed eyes looked suspicious, too quiet. Twenty minutes before, Phoenix had asked Fana if there was anything special she should play, and Fana had gently shaken her head. But . . .

"Fana?" Phoenix whispered.

The girl by the fireplace didn't move. The longer Phoenix stared at her, the paler she seemed. Her face blended into the color of the flames.

Phoenix jumped to her feet, her heart rattling. She'd talked herself out of being scared after the dancing, because everything had fallen still and seemed all right.

"Stay away from the door," Dawit told Phoenix and Jessica,

hushed. Jessica stared at the girl by the fireplace as she rose from her chair.

When the door opened, Fana was standing in the doorway, wide awake. There were two Fanas, impossible and identical. The Fana sitting by the fireplace was wearing jeans, her eyes still calmly closed, but the Fana at the door wore a Victorian-style nightgown of bulky cotton. Phoenix might have worn a gown just like it, somewhere in the past.

"What the . . . ?" Jessica whispered.

The Fana at the door wasn't exactly awake, Phoenix realized. She stood with a slight sway, as if she'd been drinking, her eyes staring at nothing. Her face was so calm it was empty.

Maybe Michel had that effect on everyone. *Maybe my turn is coming.*

"Which one is really Fana?" Jessica said, alarmed.

And at that moment, the Fana by the fireplace faded into the shadows to nothing, an illusion. Gone. Phoenix might have screamed, if she could have moved.

"We've got you, Duchess," her father said, and he and Fasilidas carefully led the newly appeared Fana into the room. "We're here."

"He has some nerve, sending her here in a damn nightgown," Jessica said.

He. Phoenix was standing on the outside of the others, watching them move as if she were in a tank filled with water. The disappearance of the Fana by the fire hadn't made an impression on anyone else, except for an irritated scowl Jessica cast in the empty space's direction. Phoenix was the only one who was paralyzed where she stood.

"Don't be overly alarmed," Teka said, although the others weren't alarmed the way they should have been. "Fana seems fine, only deep in trance. She is with Michel, but she does not seem frightened or in distress."

"That we know of," Jessica muttered.

Phoenix pulled herself out of her shock as she watched Dawit and Jessica lay Fana down in the low, elegantly carved bed from Asia. Jessica had told her that she and her husband once had a bed like it; it had originally been an opium bed. Fana sank down, her eyes closing. To Phoenix, Fana looked like her mother in her ruffled coffin.

"What just happened?" Phoenix said. "What's going on?"

As Teka explained it to her, Phoenix learned how much she still didn't know about Fana's people. She couldn't wait to tell Carlos about it. And Marcus, one day.

One of Fana's gifts was the ability to create a three-dimensional aura, a visage. Teka could do it, too, and a few more of their kind who had high telepathy skills. Usually a visage needed tending to interact with others, but Fana was powerful enough to leave a visage as a decoy. None of them had guessed that Fana had gone to Michel, even her parents and teacher.

When had Fana left them? Had the real Fana been dancing?

"Keep playing for her," Teka said. "Keep her close."

Phoenix forgot her questions while she and Rami played. She had once followed a ghost across planes, so she knew where Fana was, how difficult it might be for Fana to find them.

Phoenix hadn't touched a violin in years before arriving in Mexico, and she'd already been asked to play for hours. The pads of her fingers were tender from the strings, her arm sore from her wild bow. And Rami was tireless. Sometimes Phoenix wanted his melodies out of her head so she could rest. She was also hungry, but she had gotten used to hunger in detention, and none of the others touched the bread, wine and pasta the attendants brought.

WHERE I LIVE, OUR MUSIC NEVER STOPS, Rami said, speaking to her head like Fana. And he offered more than his voice. When Phoenix's arm felt like it was a lead weight, or on fire, Rami lifted her arm with his strength.

"Yes, but faster, faster," said Teka, their conductor. "She's closer now."

Harried attendants knocked on the door incessantly, bringing dresses, flower samples, and menus for Jessica to approve. Michel was making his wedding plans. Or was it Fana?

Jessica's worn face and reddened eyes made her look like she was arranging Fana's funeral instead, but she met with the attendants dutifully, sitting with the women at the tea table near the fireplace. The women were so frantic to make Jessica smile that Phoenix wondered if their lives depended on it.

"Yes, *esta bien*," Jessica kept saying, barely looking at the fabrics. "Anything is fine. You choose." Her lack of interest brought the women to tears as they gave each other worried looks: *They* should choose? They were terrified of displeasing Michel.

Phoenix remembered her barefoot wedding to Carlos on a beach in San Juan before a handful of family and friends, an easy day that had planned itself. Still, Phoenix pitied the attendants. She called over her shoulder: "That one! Fana will love that one," when one dress's white gauzy lace caught the corner of her eye. The women showered Phoenix with teary thanks, and Jessica blew her a grateful kiss, glad to be done with it.

Would Fana wake up in time for her wedding?

By six o'clock, nearly dusk, Phoenix needed bandages for her blistered fingertips. When she couldn't play, she sang while Rami's violin sang with her.

"*My soul gets cold from standing still . . . if I can't test my wings, I'll die . . .*" Phoenix sang to Fana's sleeping face. "*Don't wanna die for a while . . . I think I'll fly for a while . . .*"

Fana's eyes popped opened. Phoenix was so startled, she thought she'd imagined it.

"I've always loved that song," Fana said. Her voice was sleepy, but her eyes were bright.

Fana smiled as if she'd never been gone.

Jessica's day-long prayers had been lost somewhere in Michel's palace. Throughout the long hours, watching Fana's placid sleep, Jessica had hoped to hear the wails and shrieks of Michel's faithful through the halls, the sign that he was dead.

Not only hadn't Fana killed Michel, she still planned to marry him. Jessica hadn't realized how much she had hoped for a different outcome until Fana opened her eyes, her plan unchanged. Jessica's disappointment blistered against the walls of her stomach.

But at least Fana was back. She hadn't died helpless in her sleep in a nightgown soaked with blood. But how much had Michel changed her?

Fana looked giddy enough to float in the day's last light as Jessica and Dawit stood on either side of her on the balcony overlooking Michel's woods and courtyard, watching the bustle of wedding preparations. A caravan of trucks was making deliveries, a chorus of loud beeping when they backed up, supervised by a swarm of Sanctus Cruor officials in crimson vests and skullcaps. Twelve white horses trotted in a disciplined line as costumed horsemen rehearsed formations. A royal wedding. To Jessica, it looked like preparations for a circus.

The stone domed tower above them speared the sky. Two silent bells hung from the belfry, the highest point. Below the bells was a gaping open-air platform where Michel planned to exchange his vows with Fana. The tower's belfry was supported by thin columns of polished stone, but Jessica could see straight through the tower to the purple sky over Sonora. The Most High had made several addresses there, his attendants had told her.

To Jessica, Michel's tower looked like a castle keep. Fana's dungeon.

"He's agreed to delay the Cleansing," Fana said. "At least by a day."

"That isn't nearly enough," Dawit said. "Not for what you're trading!"

Jessica noticed again the way Fana seemed to be standing on her tiptoes, how she kept clinging to the balcony's carved stone railing as if her weight were pulling away from her. Sometimes Fana's feet seemed not quite to touch the ground. Was she levitating?

Jessica might never understand everything Teka had tried to explain about Fana's mental union with Michel, but she knew what sex looked like. Now Fana was shining with a different kind of fever. Fana wouldn't be the first woman to confuse sex with a man with having power over him.

"You're marrying him, Fana," Jessica said, speaking slowly to wade through Fana's busy mind and floating feet. "That's all he'll give you? A day? That's ridiculous."

"Today I have one day," Fana said. "Tomorrow, another day. Or a week. Or a year. I'll help him interpret the Cleansing a different way. We just need time."

"If you haven't changed him by fusing, what makes you think you ever can?" Jessica said. "He's seen everything you want from him."

"I don't expect to change him," Fana said. "We'll change each other. We already are."

Jessica didn't have the gifts to burrow into Fana's head, but she could see the difference in her already. Fana's eyes never met hers or Dawit's when she spoke to them now; she was halfway with them, halfway somewhere else. With Michel, probably.

"Will he wear his Sanctus Cruor robe to the wedding?" Dawit said. "If so, you can't predict what he'll do. His beliefs may prove too deep for him, with so many followers here. To him, this wedding represents the union in the Prophecy, the signal for the Cleansing. He's waited his whole life for this day, Fana."

Fana nodded, considering. "I'll ask him not to wear his robe," she said.

"Be prepared if he does not agree," Dawit said. "You may lose ground."

Fana smiled to herself; a secret.

"What's funny?" Jessica said.

Fana shook her head. "It's not funny. I just wish I could show you what I gained."

"Don't trade away the world population for good sex and flying lessons," Jessica said, and Fana's smile vanished.

"I wouldn't do that, Mom." Fana looked embarrassed, a hint of her former self. Jessica noticed Fana holding more firmly to the railing. Was she worried about literally drifting away?

"Just checking to make sure you're still there, sweetheart." Jessica dangled her car key for Fana, to show her what commitment looked like. "We can still go."

"You can go," Fana said. "You gave me everything I needed. He won't stop you."

Fana's terseness stung, but maybe she would go. She could meet Alex and Lucas in Nigeria to help brace for what might come after the wedding.

"Would you prefer us to go, Fana?" Dawit said. There was a trace of hurt in his voice.

Fana still didn't look at them, gazing down at the courtyard.

"I'm getting married," Fana said. "Every bride wants her parents there."

Please don't wear your Sanctus Cruor vestments when we're married.

When Fana pulsed the thought to Michel, the sounds and sights from the physical world dimmed, and her mind brightened. Her parents' voices faded, and the busy thoughts of the workers frantic to make Michel happy. Fana's awareness narrowed to Michel, riding the new streams that tied them. She dived into him with ease.

Her timing was bad: Michel was in a meeting with his father in his chapel. His father was trying to persuade Michel to let him administer the vows. She and Michel had agreed on Teka instead, and Stefan, as always, was angry; accusing blasphemy, predicting disaster.

Fana's message so surprised Michel that he didn't answer at first. But silence was better than the instant outrage that would have come before their fusing.

Don't trade away the world population for good sex and flying lessons. Her mother's voice, faraway. Fading to nothing . . .

HOW CAN YOU ASK THAT OF ME? Michel finally said. *THIS IS THE WEDDING OF THE MOST HIGH TO HIS PROPHESIED MATE.*

Your robes are a symbol of your station, Michel. I want to marry the man—not a symbol.

Michel whisked her to the chapel with him, so that she could see the gold writing from the Letter of the Witness that filled the wall. His father's voice was a muffled burr. She could smell the tequila in Stefan's glass.

THE PEOPLE HAVE NEVER SEEN ME WITHOUT MY ROBE, Michel said.

Our real union was last night, Michel. You weren't wearing your robe then.

She reminded him of her ocean retreat, and how they had played in the warm water. She tickled him in one of the new mental passageways they had built.

YOU ASK TOO MUCH, FANA.

Please consider it. You don't have to answer now.

I'M SORRY, Michel said, *BUT YOU HAVE MY ANSWER.*

She would marry the Most High after all. Fana marveled at how unafraid she was. No answer from Michel would have been good or bad; it simply was. She had known that fusing with Michel wouldn't give her control over him unless she was ready to risk fighting him. She wished they could go back to learning each other instead of the constant arguing that the physical world's concerns thrust on them. Her mental streams hummed from his voice, tugging to follow him, just as hers tugged at his.

But she couldn't play with Michel tonight. How would she find her way back in time for their wedding? Phoenix and Rami needed to rest.

Brightness coaxed Fana back to the balcony with her parents, where the sun was setting. It was almost as pretty as her mind's ocean, except that the physical world's colors were so much duller. Had the colors here been brighter yesterday?

Fana was dizzy from her balcony's height, startled to brush against the railing as her feet found the tiled floor again. She'd been floating! She had never levitated on her own, and now she could barely remember how to walk.

What else was waiting? What else could she be?

Fana nestled between the auras of her parents, enjoying the feeling of them on either side, her ocean in the physical world. Colors might grow duller, but her parents' auras were a different kind of bath: pure love.

"I'm getting married," Fana told them. "Every bride wants her parents there."

Thirty-seven

Thursday
Wedding Day
6:30 a.m.

They came from everywhere, following the ringing of the bells that had started at five a.m. They braved the road, glutted with traffic. They took shortcuts through the woods, where they were questioned and searched by soldiers. They rode cramped in cars and trucks, or weaved dangerously on motorcycles and minibikes. They trudged on foot with their children trailing behind them, or riding on their shoulders.

As far as Raul's binoculars could see, Nogales's faithful were streaming to the church.

The women wore white dresses, and the men in jeans had white T-shirts or dress shirts. When it had still been dark and Raul had been scouting through the infrared, the pilgrims had looked like ribbons of milk spilling across the rocky woods and mountain.

The church's courtyard was filled. The overflow already ran the length of the church's driveway, down the road, and into the surrounding woods. Thousands of people would never be close enough to see or hear the ceremony when it started, but they might all hear the gunshot.

Eight o'clock. Ninety minutes to go.

"How many, you think?" Martha asked him.

"Twenty-five, thirty thousand," Raul said. "Might be more, if they'd had any notice."

Martha's voice beside Raul was as constant as his heartbeat. She lay five yards left of him, eye always trained through her spotting scope. Like him, she was draped in heavy, grassy camouflage. They had found a spot in the high grass and shrubs near a cluster of knotted tescalama-tree roots, like a web of aged fingers clamping the soil in place behind them. The roots would give them footing when it was time to run.

He and Martha had met at the range when both of them were long past the age of expecting to meet someone new. They had almost the same story, word for word; one afternoon had taught them their experiences and grievances in common. Martha had been raised in Texas, too, a *gringa* with a wide face, cherry cheeks, and beer-blond hair who'd left her parents the day she turned eighteen in 1979 and enlisted in the army. Then her true life had begun—until things changed. It wasn't every day you met a perfect soulmate *and* a world-class spotter just as pissed off as you were. And no one had ever looked as good as Martha in a ghillie suit.

There hadn't been a sliver of sunlight when they'd chosen their spot at four-thirty. Before the night's clouds had burned off, rain had dripped on them for twenty minutes, long enough to turn the ground slick.

When the bells had started ringing at five, Raul had thought it was an alarm.

But the church had only been calling to its supplicants, the sole wedding invitation. The first had started coming right away, as if they'd been camped out down the road. Within a half hour, the traffic had been steady. Within an hour, the road to the church had been jammed.

"Know what, baby?" Martha said.

"*¿Qué pedo, rubia?*" She loved it when he spoke Spanish, but his English was better.

"This isn't just talk anymore."

"Nope. We're way past talking."

How many nights had they stayed up late talking about how the fanatics and narcos were destroying Mexico, and how the feds back Stateside were burning the Constitution to try to shut down Glow? The key, they'd realized, was to understand the *connection*.

They weren't the only ones who could see that Washington was on its knees to S—

Raul stopped himself before he thought the sect's name. He wasn't superstitious like his cousin Andres, but he knew how to dodge a jinx on mission day.

Andres had called him for jobs twice before, but never this big. He and Andres had to stay away from each other. Raul was glad he'd enlisted back in 1995 after a long stint as a Dallas cop, before the DEA had heard of the Enriquez cartel in Sonora. He'd liked bragging about his cousin's gangster family when he was growing up in El Paso, but the connection had stopped being cute a long time ago. Andres was a second cousin, but still.

Five years ago, Raul had done some work for him in Mexico, getting rid of some people the world wouldn't miss. Andres had paid him so well that he hadn't done it again. But they'd talked for the first time after Tio Tito and their little cousin Arturo were murdered. Butchered—that was the word for the old man's death. They traded tragedies.

Raul had told him he'd left the corps because of kidnappings and cover-ups that made him wonder which flag he was fighting for, the one with the stars and stripes or the one with the teardrop of blood. He and his cousin had felt like family for the first time since they were twelve. Hell, Raul had thought Andres was going to ask him the favor right then and there. Or maybe Andres had been waiting for a good soldier to make the offer first.

So it had never been said. Not then.

But John Jamal Wright had brought them back together. With their share of the Glow, Raul and Martha had decided to open a small clinic, maybe in Canada. Maybe in Mexico, where anyone who ran Glow ended up dead. Until now, maybe.

Raul's radio beeped in his ear. "Eyes front," O'Reilly said.

O'Reilly's brother had run Glow in Boston, until he'd been tortured in detention for six months by feds. O'Reilly's fight to free his brother had given him a whole new attitude.

"I got 'em," said Martha, her binoculars raised. "Security guards."

Raul tracked the rocky terrain. A patrol of six soldiers was climbing, looking for a vantage point to watch the crowd. Through the binoculars, the soldiers looked like they were on top of them, but they were three hundred yards downhill.

One of them might see the muzzle flash. Or flashes, God forbid.

"We'll have to haul it," Raul said to Martha. "After."

"You think?" Martha said.

Getting away had looked free and clear when they first camped, since they were on a hillside opposite the church, just under a mile away. They'd figured on scrambling on foot behind the treeline for half a mile and jumping into the truck at the rendezvous point. After that, the road waited.

But the patrol could finger them, and there was no time to reposition.

He had his own army, and it would rise like a dragon after the gunshot.

Raul licked his dry lips. Every other part of him was drenched with sweat.

He and Martha had told their neighbor they were hitting Vegas for a few days, leaving their dog, Wolfie, and a spare key behind. They had cleared the sink of dishes and taken out the garbage so they wouldn't leave a smell. They hadn't talked about not coming home.

For the hundredth time, Raul wished he and Martha weren't too old to have kids. But thank God they didn't have kids.

Raul treated himself to the view through Ole Susie's scope, a beautiful sight: an empty platform under the belfry, so clear he could see bows on the white ribbons wrapped around the columns. The pulpit was in the middle of his sight, between two columns. A picture postcard.

He hoped the wedding would start on time.

Thirty-eight

7:50 a.m.

A bracing pipe organ played Mozart's "Ave Verum Corpus," trembling the walls. The choir in the balconies joined the song. At least a hundred elementary-age schoolchildren dressed in white lined the palace's main hall, gently tossing gardenia petals to the floor as Fana passed. The church's main hall was a wonderland of gardenia and hibiscus flowers.

I'm getting married, Fana realized. Just like Michel had told her, her imagination had never treated her to a wedding day. What kind of mate could have fit her? She had expected to be alone the way she'd been alone in her ocean. *Life is something you touch,* Gramma Bea had told her right before she died. Fana brushed against Gramma Bea's spirit when she called out the memory; a hug from her grandmother.

Why had the idea of this day filled her with so much fear?

Michel was a challenge, but his hand was everywhere in the beauty around her: he had chosen the musical pieces, the choir, the children, as gifts to her. The ceremony itself was a gift to the crowds, who were giddy with their hope for lasting life, lasting love. At least for a day, joy smothered the misery of the distant hall that housed the Cleansing Pool. Even Mom, trailing behind her with her wedding party, could feel the beauty in the music.

And something else! Peace. Fana realized she could hear the music only because she wasn't caught in the heads of the hundreds of faithful inside Michel's church, or the thousands more waiting outside. Noise, her lifelong struggle, was solved. Since her fusion with Michel, she could control the noise like a volume wheel, up and down, nearer or farther, this person or that person. The novelty distracted her. She warmed herself in the love of a schoolboy who blushed when she smiled at him, skated past her father's trepidation, enjoyed Phoenix's wonder. Fana surfed across the chaotic noise outside, let it lift her like her inner ocean's wave. Her soul sang with her new abilities.

But you're getting married, she reminded herself. *Don't wander too far.*

Fana searched for Michel in the flock of crimson robes and skullcaps proceeding toward her from the opposite direction in the hall, the Sanctus Cruor initiates carrying their sect's flag on medieval-style poles. Michel's essence was everywhere, as solid as mass, but she couldn't find his physical body.

Fana stopped walking to wait for him at the designated place, where the corridor met the narrow walkway to the tower. There, they would hold hands and walk to the tower together.

Why couldn't she see him?

Suddenly, his scent was under her nose. Fana was toe to toe with Michel before she recognized him, confused by his appearance. He had cut his dark hair short, preserving only the curls across his forehead, the way he'd looked when she'd first met him as Charlie on the Underground Railroad.

And he wasn't wearing his Sanctus Cruor robe!

Michel was dressed in a military-officer-style white suit with a waist-length jacket and sash, his chest pinned with two rows of Sanctus Cruor medals. A thin golden ceremonial sword with garnet stones on the hilt hung from his belt, just below his navel.

Michel had transformed himself into her prince.

Fana felt her father's relief, her mother's surprise. Teru's pride. Stefan's outrage. The initiates' wonderment circled the hall, as if Michel were nude. Fana saw herself through Michel's eyes: her favorite white scarf from Lalibela, bare shoulders, and layers of shiny white taffeta. To him, she was beauty itself.

A BRIDE SHOULD BE HAPPY ON HER WEDDING DAY, NO? Michel said.

He held out a white-gloved hand to her.

• • •

Dawit blinked. Michel, who usually hid himself behind his robes, wielding his vestments as a weapon and shield, wasn't dressed as the spiritual leader of Sanctus Cruor? Fana's mission was succeeding already!

AND SHE HAS ONLY BEEN HERE TWO DAYS! Teka said, excited. He shrouded his private thoughts with a powerful mask. IMAGINE WHEN THEY DEBATE THE LETTER, THE MEANING OF THE CLEANSING. SHE IS GAINING INFLUENCE, JUST AS YOU SAID.

But Michel was gaining influence over Fana just as quickly. Where would they meet?

Fana's bridal dress brought tears to Dawit's eyes, but not because of its beauty. The small victory, to Dawit, was bittersweet. He had counseled other leaders to marry for the sake of peace, but his own daughter? His faith in Fana's plan seemed like a betrayal to her, no different from Mahmoud wresting him from his life with Jessica in Miami.

His daughter looked serene, even happy; Michel's fairy-tale clothing had delighted her.

But for how long?

Jessica squeezed Dawit's hand hard. He knew her thoughts, and she knew his. "Dear God," Jessica whispered. "Please protect her. Give her power, Lord, but give her wisdom too."

Teka nudged Dawit. HAVE YOU HEARD FROM MAHMOUD?

No, Dawit said. Should I have?

I HAVE FELT HIM MASKING STRONGLY SINCE I SENT WORD OF THE WEDDING. AND HE HAS SUDDENLY COME TO MIND.

Dawit almost missed a step. Teka's abilities far surpassed Mahmoud's. How could Mahmoud create a barrier strong enough for Teka to feel from so far—especially since Teka's time with Fana had improved his gifts so much? And if the mask wasn't Mahmoud's alone, who was helping him? And why?

You should not have told him, Dawit said.

THE COUNCIL ELECTED HIM LIAISON, Teka said.

If Lalibela were to rise against Michel, could this be the day they would choose? Of course! Would Mahmoud be bold enough? And who else would join him?

Some of their own party might. Berhanu might.

Any attack on Michel would pose a risk to them all, so Dawit sent private pulses to Berhanu, Teferi, Fasilidas, and Teka to be sensitive to any Brothers who might be nearby. *Lalibela might be about to move against Sanctus Cruor,* he said. Berhanu's surge of excitement was so well contained that Dawit barely noticed it.

Do you serve Lalibela, or do you serve Fana? Dawit asked Berhanu.

Berhanu did not answer him.

"What's wrong?" Jessica whispered to Dawit.

Dawit only shook his head to hush her. Michel was the best telepath in Sanctus Cruor's ranks, but Stefan could intercept thoughts, too. He didn't want his unease to spread.

Trumpets sounded from the traditionally dressed mariachi players on the balcony.

Hand in hand, Fana and Michel began their walk to the tower.

Michel, then Fana, climbed the narrow, winding tower steps, while the rest followed. Fana picked up her dress to keep from tripping over it as she climbed. It was a long climb, with little elegance in the rougher stone to reflect the rest of the morning. Their retinues followed them at a careful distance.

Michel and Fana emerged in the tower, holding each other's hands.

The tower's marble platform was oversized, with enough room for the twelve who followed Michel and Fana to fan out behind the waiting pulpit, facing the crowd below. Dawit glanced up at the massive bell, hanging in stoic silence above them.

Fana and Michel strode to the front of the tower, facing the courtyard, and waved. As if they had already rehearsed. An open target.

As Dawit scanned the breadth of the crowd below, he noted innumerable hiding places in the trees, outcroppings, and hillsides. Only a few hundred soldiers were spread within a crowd of more than twenty thousand: decoration, not security. The tower wasn't even equipped with bulletproof shields. Michel thought he was truly immortal.

As Michel and Fana waved, cheers and chants rang through the courtyard, up and down the driveway and into the woods, rumbling like an earthquake. If he and his Brothers couldn't detect Mahmoud in the endless crowd, only Fana or Michel could. Michel believed he could rely on his speed and perceptions, but he might miss something.

Was warning Fana the same as warning Michel?

Feel for Mahmoud and our Lalibela Brothers, Dawit told Fana. *Be careful.*

NONE OF YOUR BROTHERS ARE IN NOGALES, Michel said curtly. *NO WEAPONS BORN IN YOUR HOUSE OF SCIENCE ARE HERE—EXCEPT YOURS.*

Dawit didn't know if Michel had intercepted the thought or if Fana had shared it, since Fana didn't send him a response. Had Michel blocked Fana from hearing him? Dawit wished he hadn't brought up Mahmoud's name without evidence against him. Dawit pulsed an explanation to Michel, but Michel sharply barred the communication; a twinge behind Dawit's eyes.

LEAVE US IN PEACE, SIGNORE, Michel said. *THIS IS OUR WEDDING DAY.*

Berhanu and Fasilidas gave Dawit knowing looks; they had heard Michel's rebuke, too. Berhanu grinned to himself, amused by the irony; Dawit hadn't seen Berhanu smile in ten years.

The crowd fell into a reverential hush as soon as Michel and Fana stopped waving. Only the hawks and sparrows thrashing in the trees dared to break the silence.

When Teka took his place at the pulpit, Dawit brushed away Stefan's loathing and envy. He had no room for thoughts of Michel's father.

Teka spoke, his voice amplified by large speakers echoing across the mountainside.

"Bless the Blood," Teka said, in Spanish. The crowd repeated the blessing, instantly hushed again. "The Letter of the Witness writes of 'mates immortal born . . .'"

Distantly, a woman shrieked with ecstasy, overcome.

"But what unfolds before us this morning is far simpler and grander than Prophecy," Teka said. "We are witnessing the union between Michel Tamirat Gallo and Fana Beatrice Wolde: They have chosen each other today."

Over Texas
8:05 a.m.

Johnny Wright kept his TV on CNN, which was showing footage of a political event somewhere in the flat Midwest. Hats and balloons paraded while candidates told lies. Johnny wasn't wearing headphones to hear the TV; he was too anxious to stand any noise beyond the racket of the engine at his first-class window seat. *Breaking News*, he tried to will his TV screen to announce. *Assassination in Nogales.* He could almost see it.

Johnny hadn't expected to board a commercial airliner again, but the inspiration had hit him when the colony plane landed in Dallas. He wasn't afraid anymore. He would be safer if he flew commercial rather than the Lalibela Colony jet. At the airport, faced with the massive panel of worldwide flight destinations, Johnny had tried to make himself buy a ticket for Nigeria to be with Caitlin and the others, his new family.

But Johnny had never been able to make peace with hiring somebody else to do it. Unlike his new Lalibela Brothers, he couldn't live with hiding. Mark Christian, his alias, had boarded nonstop North American Airlines flight 999 for Nogales.

Johnny stared at the time stamp in the corner of the CNN screen and its slowly shifting numbers. The wedding had started five minutes ago.

Johnny rested his head on the flimsy pillow he'd been handed as an early-morning passenger, but leaning against the window only made the engine noise more unbearable. If pacing the aisle wouldn't bring attention to him, Johnny would have been on his feet. Had it always been this hard to sit still, or was it because of the Blood?

On a plane bound for Nogales, any of his neighbors might be

agents. Johnny had cut off the crown of minidreads people knew from his photos, so his only costume was short hair, a thin mustache, and nerdy black-frame glasses. Malcolm X glasses.

A flight attendant, a middle-aged black woman with broad hips, leaned over to offer Johnny a mimosa from a silver tray. Johnny stared at her swinging necklace, a garnet teardrop that looked like blood. Johnny only shook his head and waited for her to move on.

He wished he could risk calling his parents. He could barely remember their voices.

Johnny wasn't supposed to be using a cell phone, his usual ruse, so he tried to speak softly enough that his neighbor, a heavy man in a too-tight sports jacket, wouldn't hear him.

"What's up?" Johnny said under his breath to his radio, toward his pillow. He couldn't pull off a casual tone, biting the words. Talking to Caitlin was all he had.

"Nothing yet," Caitlin said, always on standby. "But it's jammed solid, so it's still on. Maybe it hasn't started." Johnny had his own access to the Nogales sat photos on his wristphone, but he didn't want his eyes on that structure even through a satellite. Until the gunshot, Johnny didn't want his name to be whispered anywhere near him.

Maybe they weren't getting married in the tower. Maybe that was it.

"Any visual?" Johnny said.

"I've tried every angle," Caitlin said. "Same problem."

Too many shadows. Johnny tried to take a deep breath, but his lungs were locked up.

"How you doing?" Caitlin said.

"Not real good."

Caitlin sighed. "Why are you on that plane again?"

So I can do it myself if I have to, he thought. But Caitlin already knew why he would be landing in Nogales in an hour. He'd timed his flight so that if something had happened to Fana, he would be there for her.

"You'll know when I know," Caitlin said. "Good luck, Johnny."

"Thanks," Johnny said, but luck was only the beginning of what he needed.

Once the lighted sign above him freed him to unfasten his seat belt, Johnny got up to go to the bathroom, mostly because he needed to walk. Johnny hadn't seen any initiates in regalia on the plane, but he could tell from their faces that most of the passengers were pilgrims. Johnny remembered chatter from commercial flights, people talking to one another, or at least reading, but the passengers bound for Nogales sat with straight backs and flushed, thoughtful faces, as if the plane were taking them to the shores of the New World. They were old women, young men, parents, teenagers, black, white, Latino, all of them ready to have someone they could believe in.

He isn't the one, Johnny thought. *But if you keep looking, you'll find the way.*

The curtain between the cabins hung near the bathroom, and Johnny's glimpse to the coach cabin made him freeze and look again. Did he know that beard?

In the rear of the plane, the passenger staring at Johnny looked like Mahmoud.

"Dammit."

Raul hadn't spoken a word to Martha in an hour, as silent as their radios. He had sunk into the details around them, floating on adrenaline. His ear caught every pebble rolling down the hill, every breeze in the leaves, every distant car horn. That was the thing he and Martha never needed to say: they felt alive only when they were disappearing into a mission. There was no other feeling like it, except Glow.

"Goddammit," Raul said, his second word in an hour. His finger was getting itchy.

"Easy," Martha said.

When the groom had first stepped out on the tower platform, he'd stood in Raul's sight like he was posing for a photo. But Raul had forgotten he was so young, or he'd thought the pictures he'd seen were older. The kid was only eighteen or nineteen. Most soldiers were kids, but his surprise at the groom's youth cost half a second. Raul had lost his perfect shot when the kid shifted left to start waving to the crowd.

Raul and the kid were dancing now.

Whenever Martha helped Raul lock on, the kid bobbed or artfully blended against someone else's profile. The SOB planted himself behind a column and lingered out of range forever, taunting Raul with the white fabric of his jacket on his gilded shoulder.

For the first two minutes, maybe three, Raul thought the kid was lucky. *Really* lucky.

But after six minutes, Raul was remembering his cousin Andres's mumbo jumbo about *Tres Ojos*, Three Eyes. How the kid claimed to be an immortal, and you should never think his name. A worm of fear ate away at Raul's reasons for being in Nogales sweating in a ghillie suit. He imagined being forced to watch Martha nailed between trees, hanging like a scarecrow, an image so vivid it was like a memory. His mind was as itchy as his finger.

Time to turn on his jukebox.

An old Lynyrd Skynyrd tune revved itself in Raul's mind, "Gimme Three Steps," a dose of southern-fried inspiration. Raul needed the kid to walk three steps away from the column. He and Martha needed only three steps to stay out of the dragon's mouth. *Gimme Three Steps, God.*

The bride and groom lined up at the altar, and the kid offered Raul the back of his head.

Raul's beautiful postcard was in focus again.

"Ready?" Martha said. "Send it."

Raul never heard her. He had already pulled the trigger.

Thirty-nine

We *are witnessing the union between Michel Tamirat Gallo and Fana Beatrice Wolde: they have chosen each other today.* Teka's voice guided Fana and Michel back to the tower when their thoughts tried to run away with them.

FROM THE FIRST TIME I FELT YOUR AURA, Michel said, *I KNEW YOU WERE A QUEEN, FANA. EVERYTHING MY MOTHER SHOULD HAVE BEEN.*

We'll heal your mother, Michel. Together, Fana said.

Bands of light wound between them, wrapping them more tightly. What a sensation, to be held and to hold another!

Fana, do you choose this man to be your husband? Teka said.

I do, Fana whispered, somewhere far below. But the rest of her was launching through the rapids of their newly conjoined river. She couldn't stand her ignorance.

I need to learn, she said.

I want to teach you.

I have to teach too.

You already do, Michel said.

Michel, do you choose this woman to be your wife? said Teka.

I do.

Fana rounded a new corner of herself, and was swept up in the Rising, high above the tower, pulling Michel away from her ear. Michel chased her, pouncing to follow her with a cat's playfulness, but he didn't have her speed in the Rising. Bright light emptied Fana's mind except for the hum of the jet's engine, somewhere over Texas.

A realization sparked in her thoughts: Johnny was coming to Nogales.

Why? Fana's knowledge raced, yanking her ahead of what she knew, raising the barricades she'd tried to protect her loved ones with. And then Fana knew.

Was her sudden maw of fright a kind of love?

Fana's mouth, her limbs, even her thoughtstreams couldn't keep up with the knowledge. She stood frozen in an endless moment, watching from above, unable to race to the places where Michel could hear her.

The Shadows whispered to Fana in the growling voice she remembered from when she was three: *YOU SEE? YOU DESTROY EVERYTHING YOU TOUCH.*

One side of Michel's face dissolved into a red spray. Gone.

Fana's eyes couldn't stop staring at her white dress, soiled with her husband's blood.

By the time Jessica heard the gunshot echo across the mountainside, Michel was already slumped at Fana's feet, as if to curl around her legs. His blood had streaked her dress in a single line, like paint from a roller. Had he tried to embrace Fana as he'd fallen?

Michel's mother, Teru, was the first to scream. Her wail pierced Jessica so deeply that it dug out tears. No mother deserved to see her child shot down, even one with the Blood.

What have I done? Jessica thought, and, *Thank you, Lord.* Two sides of her roiled at war.

Gunfire began from several directions below, and the ground shook with stampeding feet as people tried to run. Screams spread through the crowd, and Jessica's heart withered. Her legs wobbled, and she nearly sank to her knees.

How could she have thanked God for gunshots? What had she become?

There were children in the crowd. A catastrophe was being born.

And Fana! As Fana stared at the perverse blood on her bridal gown, Jessica had never seen such raw bewilderment on her child's face.

What have I done? That might have been the only question remaining in Jessica's mind.

Jessica ran toward Fana, but a barrier she couldn't see knocked her away. Berhanu's breath huffed behind her, and Jessica realized he'd pushed her aside with a mental stream. The impact was so unexpected that Jessica stumbled to the floor.

Berhanu snatched Michel up as if he were weightless, hoisting his limp body over his back. Michel looked so much smaller now, unrecognizable. Jessica looked away from Michel's horrid veil of blood. The bullet's wound had ripped away the top side of his face, leaving a horror. He would not wake right away.

Jessica wondered why Berhanu was trying so valiantly to help Michel.

Then she realized he wasn't.

Stefan roared out in Italian, his gun raised at Berhanu. Stefan was red-faced and livid, and Jessica heard her own rage in his voice. A parent's rage.

Until the shooting started, Jessica hadn't realized there were so many guns in the tower.

Dawit fell on Jessica to shield her with his body, but she never blinked, so she saw a blur as Dawit's knife left his hand. The blade flew into Stefan's neck, embedding there. Stefan's gun flew over the edge of the tower. He tried to yell in pain, but he couldn't make a sound.

Well-orchestrated chaos played around Jessica: stone columns chipping from bullets that ricocheted against the bell above them, bodies diving and falling. Through wisps of smoke, Jessica saw lovely Fasilidas slumped in a heap, bloodied.

Only Fana hadn't moved, except to raise her head to show her eyes.

Jessica didn't like what was in Fana's eyes. The bewilderment was gone. Her eyes were on Michel, who still rested in Berhanu's thick arms.

"PUT HIM DOWN!" Fana screamed, racked with pain.

Dust flew into Jessica's face as Dawit's gun vaporized in his hand. All the guns in the tower floated away in tiny clouds.

Fasilidas, Teferi, and Stefan all lay sleeping, gone for at least six hours, probably eight. The survivors squared off against one another, wary. Berhanu, closest to Fana, hoisted Michel over his shoulder, looking for a way out of the tower. Berhanu's leg was splotched red from a gunshot, but he was still on his feet, lurching under Michel's weight.

As Berhanu turned around to face Fana, his face was pained. The Life Brother's nose was bleeding, a sight Jessica hadn't seen since Fana was three.

"I'm going to burn him," Berhanu said, staring defiantly at Fana. "To ash. And then you, and all of us, are free of him. I do it in *your* name, Fana. And for the Lalibela Colony!"

Jessica had never heard Berhanu make such a long speech. Blood peeked from Berhanu's other nostril, and his jaw trembled. Berhanu was a powerful telepath; he was engaging with Fana, wrestling.

But he was losing, and badly. Jessica saw it in the burly man's eyes.

Berhanu staggered to address the crowd, thrusting Michel's prone body over his head.

"Any of you who find this corpse, burn it to cinders!" he yelled in Spanish. His voice roared across the mountainside, woven inside the gunshots. *"Scatter it in the wind!"*

Berhanu heaved as if to toss Michel over the tower, but he staggered backward again, dropping Michel to the platform. Berhanu's last look was to Dawit, his final words silent.

With a cry, Berhanu took three running steps and launched his large frame over the side of the tower. More frantic screams rained below, but Jessica heard only hers.

"Fana, no!" Jessica said to Fana's eyes, trying to find her in the holes torn by the gunshot.

Dawit went to Michel and reached for his neck. Jessica thought he might try to break it—but instead, he felt for a pulse.

"Fana, it's not as bad as it seems," Dawit said. "His heart is still beating."

But Jessica wasn't sure she had heard him. Fana didn't look like she could hear anything.

• • •

"Johnny? Did you hear me?" Caitlin's voice said, excited. "He's hit. I dunno how bad yet. All hell's breaking loose down there. Tell me you heard me."

But Johnny Wright heard only the knocking of his heart. Caitlin was drowned out by every ounce of the blood throbbing through his veins.

Johnny felt his palms press against the armrests, flexed arm muscles launching him to his feet. His body was taking flight without him. Right leg, left leg; sure, swift motion. Johnny's body left his seat and walked to the aisle of the plane.

He tried to tell Caitlin something was wrong, but he had lost control of his mouth. Crushing dread wrapped around Johnny, sodden and final.

Just two minutes earlier, when Mahmoud had winked at him from the rear of the plane, Johnny had believed again. Aside from Fana's concert with Phoenix, or waking up after Fana gave him the Blood, seeing Mahmoud might have been the finest moment of his life.

It's too late! He knows! Johnny tried to shout his thoughts to Mahmoud, with no idea how. Could Mahmoud see him past the curtain? Did Michel have Mahmoud, too?

Johnny's leg bumped hard against an armrest as he rushed past, a jolt of pain to let him know what was coming. Could he talk to Michel by thinking his name? Would it do any good?

What did you expect me to do, Michel? What would you have done?

Johnny stopped at row 6, leaning over to the sunburned man sitting on the aisle in 6A.

"I'm John Jamal Wright," Johnny heard himself say.

The man's face lit up with recognition. Johnny tried to scream at him, Kill me!

Don't make me hurt anyone, Johnny begged Michel. *Just let it be me.*

Johnny watched his own limbs move in a horrifying blur: an elbow to the man's jaw, a deft snatch into his jacket for his Glock, and a dizzying *crack* against the man's skull with his forehead, all in a blink. Then the explosion as he shot the air marshal in the temple.

Please, Michel. Not like this. Only punish me.

Johnny heard his own voice yell in a roar as he stood in the aisle. "Ladies and gentlemen," he said, "welcome to my Hell!"

The screams washed over him like a waterfall. The pleasure horrified Johnny, stroking his mind. Was *this* how suffering felt to Michel?

"I'm John Jamal Wright!" his voice said. "Turn on your phones and call everybody you know. Tell them it was me. When the plane goes down, we'll all be in pieces."

Real death—not just for him and Mahmoud, but for two hundred people he didn't know.

Is this how you treat your own followers, Michel?

Johnny's arm jutted straight out. He hadn't had a chance to turn his head before the gun fired again, and more screams pierced him somewhere new. From the corner of his eye, he could see only the white hair of the old woman he'd shot, and his spirit sobbed.

Michel, please just take me.

"Anybody else ready to die?" Johnny heard himself say.

Caitlin's shocked voice whispered in his ear, "Oh my God. It's okay, baby. I'm here."

Johnny wept with joy, in the place Michel couldn't touch. He tried to slow his heartbeat so that he could hear every nuance in Caitlin's voice from the radio in his ear.

"You came so close," Caitlin said, as if that was consolation. "He was hit."

Where was Fana? Had she been hit, too? Couldn't she tell that Michel was killing him?

"Fight him, Johnny," Caitlin said. "You've done it before. You can fight him."

Johnny couldn't find muscles to fight with. There was nowhere to flex or pull; he was only riding. Johnny turned, lurching toward the pilot's cabin.

He watched his arm rise again as he fired his gun at the lock, and the mangled lock fell open. Was this what life was like for Michel? Everything parted for him?

The gunshot made Caitlin squeal in horror, but she didn't leave him. "Fight, baby. *Fight,*" Caitlin said. "I know you're in there. I know you hear me, Johnny. Put the gun down."

He shot the pilot seated to the right of the door without looking over his shoulder, so he never saw his face. He listened to the copilot reason for a while, and then beg, and Johnny was forced to luxuriate in the repulsive allure of his fear. Johnny was relieved for both of them when the copilot was dead, too. Caitlin strangled her cries with every shot.

The world moved beneath his feet as the plane veered. The screams were sweet torture.

"Johnny? If you're still there, pick your moment, *one* moment, and give it everything," Caitlin said, impossibly calm. "Mahmoud's heard the shots by now. You're not alone."

Mahmoud was behind Johnny in the cockpit as soon as Caitlin said his name. Johnny knew before he turned around, because *he* knew. Johnny's body spun, fast. Mahmoud had a shiny black knife ready, fashioned from material he'd slipped past the airport's metal detectors.

"Bad luck for you, isn't it, Mahmoud?" Johnny heard himself say, the words humming in his throat. "To die in a plane crash?"

Other passengers had gathered behind Mahmoud, men and women ready to storm the cockpit. "He can't shoot all of us!" a hoarse man shouted. A rallying cry traveled through the cabins, replacing terror with wild hope.

"Drop the gun, Hannibal," Mahmoud told Johnny gently. "Try to move your fingers, one by one. Leave the rest to me."

"Help him, Johnny," Caitlin whispered. Caitlin's voice slowed his heartbeat.

How had he done it? How had he ever shot Michel's men in Mexico?

"*Fight,* Johnny," Caitlin said. She'd stopped hiding the tears in her voice.

Johnny's index finger wouldn't obey, tightening on the trigger. Mahmoud was ducking, but he wouldn't be quick enough.

Bless me, Lord, the way you bless Fana in the dragon's den.

Time slowed a fraction. If Johnny hadn't been waiting for the
moment, he might have missed it. The bullet tore into Mahmoud's
left bicep, missing his heart by a mile.

Mahmoud didn't show pain at his injury. He gave Johnny an
impressed grin.

WELL FOUGHT, MY SON, Mahmoud said as he threw his knife.

I love you, Fana—

When the blade pierced him, Johnny was the only one on the
flight who heard his cry.

Forty

The world ended and began with a gunshot. One world gone, another world born.

Phoenix had ducked gunfire more than once, so she knew how to dive away from death. Teferi had caught a bullet meant for her, fired from Romero's gun. She had seen Romero glare at her with a lunatic's loathing before he'd taken aim at her, petrified by the power in her music.

But the gunshots weren't as bad as the smell.

Phoenix hadn't noticed the stench until Berhanu threw himself off the tower, a sight that would have been harrowing enough. Phoenix had smelled a bare hint of the odor on Michel when she met him, maybe on the soles of his feet—but now the stench was stewing like thick crude oil floating to the surface of things. Chaos nourishing itself.

A gunshot had ripped the seams open, freeing blind fury.

"Fana, it's not as bad as it seems," Dawit said, although things were far worse than they seemed. Phoenix jumped at the *chug-chug-chug* of an automatic weapon spewing random death.

"His heart is still beating."

The guns in the tower had turned to dust. That was the first thing Phoenix had to write about. Phoenix tried to remember everything, because someone would have to tell the story. Someone would have to sing the songs.

Phoenix wasn't surprised when Dawit went flying backward away from Michel, as if he'd been blown in a gale, falling against a column. Michel still lay unconscious, but some part of him was awake. Hadn't Dawit just said that Michel's heart was beating? Dawit better step off.

Clouds were covering the sun, faster than clouds should move.

Phoenix kept her eyes open, trying to see it all.

Someone had to remember.

Someone had to bear witness.

Michel, where are you?

The colorful, glittering radiance was gone, replaced by remarkable pain. The call to fuse with Michel had startled her—the severing of Michel, so suddenly, so cruelly—added new dimensions to pain. Fana was blind as she looked for him, limping, unable to fly even in her thoughts. Shadows choked her, leaving Fana to wade through a dripping, formless muck. Fana was up to her knees in Shadows.

She *felt* him. She knew his breathing. Heard his heart's weak beating.

But the bullet had torn down the lights between them. As long as Michel was unconscious, his thoughtstreams were roaming mindlessly, disordered. The Shadows were cradling Michel while he slept, harnessing his rage. Michel was nothing but Shadows now.

Michel, wake up! It's still our wedding day.

A flicker brightened a passageway in the distance, but he was out of her reach when she tried to follow, just around the next bend, diving deeper into the dark. And oh, the smell! There was a symphony of suffering steeping in that smell, a stewpot cooking. Fana couldn't wade too deeply into the smell, or she would forget she hadn't come to feast.

Fana had experienced the first pull of the Shadows with Berhanu, watching his nose bleed like the Life Brother she had killed when she was three. No fumbling or struggling to find his heart; the Shadows were better at killing. Brushing against the Shadows was sticky, so it had been hard to pull free. Berhanu had been bleeding from both nostrils—*she* had made it happen—even as Fana tried to let him go.

Berhanu, a guardian she loved, would die like an offering to the Cleansing Pool?

If not for her games with Michel before the wedding, she would have been overpowered then. But she braced, pushed back, wriggled, washed away the smell.

And she'd torn herself away from the Shadows' surge in time to send Berhanu leaping out of the tower, an escape from the Shadows' exsanguination. At least Berhanu would wake after his fall, if Michel's followers didn't butcher his corpse to mincemeat.

But Berhanu had betrayed her.

IT WILL BE A TEST, FANA, BUT KEEP CONTROL.

She wished it were Michel's voice, but Teka's voice followed her instead. At least she had a guide! Fana was glad her teacher had always known what he was preparing her for.

The Shadows whispered secrets to her in colliding voices. A flash of too-bright light, and Fana saw the charred bones of two people lying side by side with a sniper rifle between them. They had combusted in an instant, tracked by Michel's angry Shadows. Somewhere far from her, the Shadows gaining speed, riding a horse. A rider in a cowboy hat was racing at a gallop, leaping from a cliff, an endless, petrifying fall. The conspirators were dying.

Who else?

A sudden cry of pain filled Fana's core, one she knew. Johnny! The Shadows had found Johnny high above the world. She had murdered Johnny by giving him her heart long before she'd damned him by giving him her Blood.

Fana hadn't thought she could absorb new pain, but Johnny's last cry ripped at her.

Michel, stop it!

No one but Michel could stop the power the Shadows drew from him for their blindly rampaging rage. The Shadows believed they were doing his bidding.

Light flickered, gone before she could track it. Had he heard her? Where was Michel now that the bullet had set him adrift?

Heal, Michel. Call the Shadows back.

How long would it take? Other Life Brothers might need six or eight hours to wake, maybe longer for a head injury, but Blood-born healed faster. Could Michel wake in two hours? One? Could she protect his body that long? Could she fight his Shadows that long?

If she couldn't, she would have to kill him today.

Fana's grief unearthed her anger, and the Shadows tried to carry her away again. Every part of her ached from her shorn bridges with Michel, body and mind. Her solitude felt foreign now. Fana was raw to her core. If she killed Michel, would she always feel this battered and incomplete? Wouldn't she rather kill them both?

THE SHADOWS WILL TELL YOU LIES IN YOUR OWN VOICE, Teka reminded her.

When Fana was still, new knowledge came to her: sixty-seven men, women, and children lay dead below the tower because they had come to see her wedding day. Sixty-eight. Sixty-nine. Concerns from the physical world squalled, calling to Fana. The Shadows were exciting Michel's guards to grief-stricken murder. The Shadows were sweeping the courtyard, siphoning fear in their mindless protection of their host. A storm.

But Fana had lived through a storm before.

USE THEM WHEN YOU MUST, Teka said. A SWIMMER MUST SWIM WITH THE RIPTIDE'S CURRENTS, NOT AGAINST THEM, OR SHE DROWNS.

Teka had never spoken of her drowning before. But she hadn't learned the Shadows yet. Michel had just begun to teach her. When he'd tried, she had run. She had lost a lesson.

Her mind's darkness gave way to the gray morning light and the dreary colors of the physical plane, hardly better than the muck of her mutilated thoughtstreams. Michel's absence stabbed her, but Fana fought her grief because grief would only make her angry. The Shadows smelled sweet when she was angry. They smelled sweet already.

When Fana felt her feet on the ground, her ears awash in screams and gunfire, her mother's shattered eyes were waiting for her. Fana forgot the gunfire.

"I'm so sorry, Fana," Mom said in a ghost's voice.

Fana hoped her mother would beg her to soothe her mind's raucous pain, because she would refuse her. Fana remembered what she couldn't help knowing, what Mom had hidden so feebly: Mom had encouraged Johnny to kill Michel. She had sent Johnny to Mahmoud. And Mahmoud had told Johnny about their wedding. Mom could have snuffed this day before it was born.

"You only had to trust me," Fana said to her mother's pain-crazed eyes.

Fana clamped her mother's thoughts away, turned away from Jessica's wretched face. Fana was so angry, so undone, that she was afraid she might see her mother's nose bleed.

Her mother had betrayed them.

The Shadows would hunt for Jessica, too.

The back of Dawit's head rang from impact against the solid stone. Red spots danced.

His vision doubled and snapped back to focus as he watched Teru kneel at Michel's side, cradling her son's bleeding head. Caesar appeared in the tower, barking wildly as he circled Michel and Teru. Caesar's teeth gnashed like a row of swords.

DON'T TOUCH HIM AGAIN, Fana told Dawit. Soaked with sorrow, and worse. Her mental stream had flung him away.

We must get him inside, Fana. All of us. There's a sniper, he said.

NOT ANYMORE, Fana said.

Fana sounded altered enough to remind Dawit that his daughter wasn't the same girl who had left Lalibela—she was a product of her fusing with Michel. Worse, a fusing gone awry. Dawit did not know the new Fana entirely, but he hoped he knew her enough.

Was the dead sniper Mahmoud? Dawit's heart shook. Was his dearest Brother gone?

Jessica went to Fana, trying to hold her hands. "I'm so sorry, Fana," Jessica said. "But people are dying—listen! You have to make it stop."

Jessica seemed oblivious to the stranger in Fana's eyes. Dawit went to Jessica's side and gently took her arm, prying her away. Would Fana hurt her mother?

Your mother didn't cause this, Dawit told Fana.

YOU HAVE NO IDEA WHAT SHE'S CAUSED, Fana said.

Michel triggered this attack, Fana. None of us asked for war. "Call down his men, Fana!" Dawit roared aloud, hoping his voice could reach her faster, jarring her from her stupor.

The volleys of gunfire across the mountainside suddenly fell silent, an afterthought. Perhaps all the guns had disintegrated to dust.

But the look Fana gave him dried Dawit's throat. Was she Fana or Michel? Had Michel taken her while he was unconscious? He should have destroyed Michel himself!

Teka's voice whispered gently, *DON'T ANGER HER, DAWIT. SHE IS CAUGHT WITH MICHEL WHILE HE SLEEPS, DEEP IN HIS SHADOWS. SHE NEEDS TIME TO GET FREE.*

Time is more precious than oxygen, Teka.

The tower platform was suddenly crowded with Sanctus Cruor: troops, clerks, and scribes. Dawit had eliminated his most feared power vacuum when he put Stefan to sleep, but Romero was telling his men that Dawit and his party were involved in Michel's shooting, that Dawit had attacked the Holy Father. Romero might be as bad as Stefan, or worse.

The guns were gone, but the tower gleamed with swords' blades.

Dawit was unarmed, and his best fighters lay sleeping. Or worse—dead. Michel's followers would incinerate Berhanu, Teferi, and Fasilidas if Fana didn't intervene.

She has me, Dawit, had been Berhanu's last words to him.

Fana knelt beside Teru over Michel and joined his mother in stroking his hair. Dawit was certain that Fana was restraining Romero, who would have tried to lock him in a furnace by now, but Fana didn't glance back at him.

Teka helped Dawit flank Jessica and Phoenix in a corner, near the tower railing. Phoenix was the most fragile, afforded a single death. Only four remained? Where was Rami? His gentle Brother had been in the hall outside the tower when the shooting started.

I'LL PROBE FOR HIM, Teka said. *I DON'T FEEL HIM YET.*

The loss of Berhanu hobbled them, but the grief was worse. Berhanu was the finest warrior Dawit knew.

Berhanu loves you like a daughter, Fana, Dawit said.

Fana barred his thought, a slap behind his eyes.

Romero bowed to Fana. *"Mia regina,"* he said, awaiting orders from his queen.

"Take my party to my parents' quarters," Fana told Romero. "Bring Michel to mine."

At least Fana would not hold them in a cell.

Caesar was subdued with a rigid restraining leash to wrest him away from Michel. The animal thrashed and howled as if he had been shot, too. Michel's attendants brought a gurney and draped themselves over Michel, lifting him, their faces streaked with tears.

The bodies of Teferi and Fasilidas were gathered roughly, bound with ropes. "They sleep in service to you!" Dawit called after Fana as she followed Michel's gurney. "Let Berhanu wake for a trial, Fana. Teferi's children see you as an aunt. Protect our wounded!"

"The way your filthy jackal protected the Most High?" Romero hissed at him. "He will hang from the lampposts, a piece on every corner. I'll chop him myself."

Dawit tried to lunge at Romero, but four men held him and shoved him away, urging him back with jabs from their swords. Fana never looked back, following her new retinue into the palace. Berhanu was lost. What of the others?

SHE CANNOT HEAR YOU, Teka said sadly. *SHE IS BARELY WITH US, DAWIT.*

Dawit suddenly looked for Jessica, who stood at the tower railing, and for a moment he thought she meant to jump. But Jessica only stared down at the aftermath of the attack.

"Don't look, Jessica," he said, but it was too late, so he joined her at her side.

Berhanu's body was gone, removed. A thin man had died splayed in the fountain, turning its waters dark with his blood. Dozens of others were scattered across the emptying courtyard, most of them encircled by grievers, some left alone. Their blood was vivid against their white clothing. A woman screamed as she held her young daughter's riddled corpse.

"Oh no," Phoenix said, joining them at the railing.

"Johnny came to me, Dawit," Jessica whispered to Dawit. "He wanted to . . ."

She didn't need to say the rest.

We think it was Mahmoud, Dawit told her quietly, but comforting Jessica brought pain. Was Mahmoud the dead sniper? Dawit's stomach dropped.

Jessica's face shook. "Dawit, I told Johnny to go to Mahmoud. *I told him.*"

Dawit's heart trembled. Jessica hated Michel enough to have enlisted Mahmoud? Dawit had underestimated Jessica's power to keep her own secrets. If only she'd confided in him!

The day was suddenly heavier.

Dawit took Jessica's shoulders, guiding her eyes away from the slain bystanders below. "You are not responsible, Jessica," he said, wishing it didn't sound so much like a lie. "You thought you were protecting our child."

Jessica sobbed into his chest, joining the chorus of mothers' wails.

Without the constant crackle of gunfire, Dawit realized he heard loud buzzing above him. He gazed skyward at the quickly gathering clouds draining light from the sun.

"Sing for her, Phoenix," Teka told the singer suddenly, urgently. "We have lost Rami—"

"*No,*" Phoenix said with a gasp.

Dawit turned to Teka, startled. *RAMI TRIED TO GO TO BER-HANU,* Teka explained.

"So you must sing, Phoenix," Teka finished calmly. "Don't stop until they're gone."

"Until who's gone?" Phoenix said in a frightened whisper.

Teferi pointed up at the sight that had fooled Dawit's eyes. They had never been clouds.

"Have mercy on us, Lord," Jessica said. "We didn't know."

WE MUST PREPARE OURSELVES, DAWIT, Teka said. *IF FANA FAILS.*

The sky was bloated with bees.

Forty-one

He stands at the altar beside his prophesied bride, who is as beautiful as her promise. She has chosen him, and he has chosen her. The call of the masses swells to the heavens. He is repeating his vows. And then there is pain, and whiteness, and . . .

Michel blinks. His vision is washed in crystalline brightness, but he studies the moment before he lets it drift away. Stefan is posted at the pulpit before him in his vestments, beaming with rare approval. Michel expected to see Teka, Fana's teacher.

"Why do you wait, Michel?" Stefan says. "They are ready to be Cleansed."

Michel gazes at himself and realizes he is wearing his Cleansing Day vestments that he and Stefan argued about; the crimson robe he had left hanging in its glass case because . . .

Why?

His highest echelon is here, encircling him: Stefan, Romero, Bocelli, the Four Horsemen. The leaders, the judges, the propagandists, the thieves. All have come to bear witness. The scribes' pens scribble his every gesture on their parchments. His gold-plated copy of the Letter of the Witness lies open on a stand before him.

His book is turned to the page titled "The Cleansing."

Michel's spirits surge. He should have known the Day had come from the sweet smell in the air. When had the Shadows ever been so pure? When had he ever heard such a song?

And his bride is here! Michel blinks, as if he has been dreaming.

Fana waits beside him beneath her Ethiopian scarf, her burnished shoulders bare, and her smile, oh her smile! Has she been here all along? Why are they waiting?

Michel scans the tower once more: Where is his mother? Why won't Teru come to watch her son fulfill his destiny?

MICHEL, WAKE UP, Fana's voice says, distant and desperate.

"I'm ready, Michel," smiling Fana says, moving her bridal scarf aside. Her brown skin shines at him. Fana's thoughts don't match her face. Which Fana is lying?

"For the Cleansing?" he says, to be certain. Hadn't she said she needed another day to be convinced? He can teach her the necessity. In turn, she is teaching him patience.

"Yes, Michel," Fana says. "You've shown me what needs to be done. I'm ready to stand at your side for the New Days."

Thousands of faithful outside of the church scream with joy. The morning wakes the sky.

I DON'T WANT TO FIGHT YOU, MICHEL. WAKE UP.

Fana smells like gardenias. He wants to bury himself in her. She lifts her face toward his, offering the parting petals of her lips. *In the name of the Letter,* he thinks somberly, and leans down to taste his kiss. . . .

But her eyes! Just as her eyes enchant him in his bedroom mural, Fana's eyes intrigue him with their defiance, their lack of joy. Fana's essence is in her eyes.

MICHEL, LET ME GO.

Too late, Michel realizes that Fana's happy face, not her voice, is lying to him.

What's happened?

He is standing at the altar . . .

YOU PROMISED NOT TO TAKE ME TODAY. WAKE UP, MICHEL.

Michel tries to hurl himself out of his dream, but he has forgotten motion, sensation. He is watching the groom with the masses, from a distant perch. He is watching from the knoll a mile away, near the knotted stand of tescalama trees.

Michel has never been taken. There were times he wished he

hadn't ridden the Shadows so far, believed he'd gorged for impure reasons, like in Kano. In Puerto Rico. But he has never been paralyzed. Voiceless.

In more than fifty years of life, how has he never contemplated the simple horror of it?

He watches his twin groom cup his palm behind Fana's neck, holding her. His pleasure sickens him.

Forgive me, Fana.

Michel weeps as he watches himself take Fana's long, sweet kiss.

"*Stop it*, Michel," Fana whispered fiercely to her sleeping husband's bloodstained ear. She could barely make herself look at the mess the sniper's bullet had made of Michel, but Michel's face was a gentler mess than his thoughtstreams. The anger of the excited Shadows tugged at her from the tatters that had joined them. The Shadows were spinning a dream to trap them both, strengthened by their fusing.

"Don't make me kill you," she said.

What was that twinge? The pain of Michel's resistance?

As soon as his attendants had lain him on her bed and she'd touched his forehead, whispering for him to wake, a jolt like a fishing lure pulled her under, *deeply* under, before she popped back up for a breath. His touch, but none of his mental markers. Michel was sleeping, but his power was awake. The Shadows had found another way to her.

"Michel, wake up—or I'll have no choice. I'll have to stop your heart."

Would that be enough? Michel was already beyond the dimensions of his damaged brain. What if his thoughtstreams could live without his body?

She might have to drain his Blood. There might not be another way, if she could remember how. She hadn't done it since she was three, and she'd had help from the Shadows.

Either way, her mind would be savaged without Michel.

The second tug came, sustained pulling. And the smell.

Deafening buzzing sat over Michel's palace, bees pelting the glass windows like hail.

Michel, you're asleep. Let me go!

Fana had lost her protection from the blizzard of distractions. She'd programmed Romero with orders to prevent further bloodshed, but she worried for Berhanu. For all of them. If she couldn't find Michel, or wake him . . .

The scope of the consequences humbled Fana, her first deep taste of fear.

Had it been a mistake to come to him? To bring her family to him? Should she have tried to kill him right away, the way poor Mom had begged her to?

Fana breathed. She tried to reach Michel's body through the Rising—to skirt the call of the Shadows. She hoarded a moment of peace the way Teka had taught her, but peace had never been harder to hold. Fana's thoughts roamed through Michel's brain matter, searching for the bullet's damage, trying to remember the lessons she'd learned from Johnny.

And she *had* learned.

She *did* heal Michel faster than he would have healed alone. But that knowledge was closely followed by her certainty that it was somehow too late, that Michel's sleep would be shorter, but still far too long. The next tug from Michel was so strong that Fana was woozy, holding her bedside table for balance.

I'm sorry, Michel, she said. *I tried to wake you up.*

Fana found Michel's heart, wishing she had tried to stop it as soon as he was shot. She should have let Berhanu take him to the furnace. Fana had learned from Johnny; she didn't fumble. His heart's slickness squirmed against her. She wrapped herself around it, smothering it, locking herself tight. She tried to still Michel's heart with all her strength.

Frantic barking boomed outside her locked door, and nails scrabbled against the polished wood. Caesar knew.

Michel let out such a long gasp that Fana thought his eyes had opened, he was awake.

But Michel had a dead man's face. An inhuman screeching

behind her ears almost made Fana forget herself. Michel's heart slipped from her, thrusting her aside with its wild beating. Pain erupted in her head, worse than her torn thoughtstreams with Michel. As Fana fought to blink her eyes—the smallest actions at a time—her nose bled right away.

Fana wished she had brought her mother to her room. Mom had been her first guide past the Shadows. The Shadows had pushed Mom away from her.

SWIM WITH THE CURRENT, FANA, Teka said. DO NOT FIGHT AGAINST IT. YOU'LL FIND YOUR WAY AGAIN.

Reminded by her teacher's voice, Fana inhaled and reached for the peace of the Rising.

To her shock, her body fell from Michel's bedside to the floor, her limbs jutting in awkward directions, a rag doll. Fana couldn't blink her own eyes.

His strength with the Shadows was a wonder. He had her already.

We tried so hard, Michel, Fana thought, but she couldn't move her mouth.

She had lost her voice, and so had he. They were caught together, married after all.

Fana rose.

She is up to her nose in the Shadows' muck, breathing the stench in hot bursts. She seals her lips tightly, but she can taste the sweetness teasing her tongue. Her tongue flames for more, but she pinches her lips, a wall.

The murky warm sludge has risen, covering her nose. Her eyes will be next.

A brief flicker. Is Michel telling her he's sorry? Yes, she is certain he is. She can feel the pulses of his helplessness, trapped in his healing sleep.

When the Shadows rise above her head, tugging her hair down, too, Fana holds her breath and seals her eyes. She listens for Phoenix's singing, her parents' voices, but ooze plugs her ears. Fana's lungs burn to breathe. Hot tears gather behind her eyelids, with nowhere to go.

She has read about how painful it is to drown.

Shadows leak into her mouth, her lungs. Finally, Fana opens her mouth wide to the muddy waters, refusing to gasp and choke. She drinks as much as she can hold.

WELCOME HOME, FANA, says the gravelly voice she has not heard since she was three.

Forty-two

Bees pasted across the windows sealed out the day's sun in Jessica's chamber with Dawit. Jessica pressed her palm to the warm windowpane, absorbing its vibrations, stronger all the time. Were the bees swarming all of Nogales, or just Michel's prison?

Phoenix had never stopped singing. She sat on the floor, rocking in the doorway of the empty closet, where she was wrapped in a blanket, ready to cover herself and slam the door if bees escaped into the room.

"Why bees?" Phoenix said, half spoken, half song. "Bees nurture us from flower to flower, tree to tree. They bring us so much sweetness. Bees spread *life* on their wings." She improvised a sorrowful scat at the end, the sound of the courtyard's massacre.

"Bees aren't the Shadows," Teka said. "They're only attracted to the scent."

Jessica remembered being wrapped in a blanket of their venom's sting when she had rescued Fana from her hurricane trance. Like any of God's creatures, bees had many faces.

"The soldiers, they shot their own people," Phoenix sang, heartbroken, shaking her head. "Killing their fruit, their own seeds—men, women, and children. Why? Why? Why?"

"Think of the Shadows as an entity of living rage," Teka said. "The fusion between Fana and Michel attracted the Shadows in a way I have never known. They have great potential within both the Shadows and the Rising. Perhaps this was Khaldun's prophecy of the Bloodborn. But . . . this unnatural rupture has freed the Shadows. While Michel sleeps, Fana faces their potential for destruction alone. Casualties may . . ."

He didn't finish. Jessica winced, remembering the sniper's bullet. Teka had already explained that they might see the start of the Cleansing.

"The Shadows siphon rage from their hosts," Teka said. "Their worst impulses. I believe that's why the soldiers were shooting. The Shadows are too thick here today."

As thick as bees, Jessica thought, her palm facing the busy mass on the window. She might have persuaded Johnny to trust Fana if she had trusted Fana first.

"How is her fight, Teka?" Dawit said quietly. Jessica had asked Dawit and Teferi to speak aloud instead of lapsing into telepathy. They couldn't afford the price of secrets today.

Dawit was sharpening a ceremonial Ethiopian sword that had been hanging over their bed as decor, his only remaining weapon. The guns in his travel case had turned to dust. His steady lashing across the blade with the stone, back and forth, made her anxious. Jessica was afraid she knew Dawit's plans for the sword, although she couldn't bring the thought to light.

"Her heart beats, she walks," Teka said, solemn. "But I cannot find her."

Teka and his understatements! "What does that mean?" Jessica said.

Teka sighed. "She is lost in the Shadows, Jessica. For a time, at least."

Had any parent ever been told so gently, *Your daughter is dead*?

Dawit's sword sang against the sharpening stone, joining Phoenix's song against the steady hum of the bees. Dawit's rigid, grieving face could have sharpened the steel.

Jessica would always remember the sight of the casualties in Michel's courtyard, but she prayed she could one day forget Fana's glare. Would it be the last thing between them? The loss of her daughter's love was far more frightful a prospect than the Shadows.

Please, Lord, guide us through this day. Give me my daughter back, or give me the strength to carry out her mission.

"We'll try to reach Fana as long as we can," Dawit said. "Jessica has reached her in the Shadows before."

"And Michel likes to hear his name," Jessica said. "So call him."

With her voice hoarse from her songs, Phoenix sang about love overcoming pain.

"Then we'll finish the mission for Fana," Jessica said. She sounded confident, reasoned, steady. "We'll prevent the Cleansing in her name." She heard herself speaking the words, but would not contemplate their meaning. She forced away the memory of Dawit's hands around Kira's neck as he strangled the life from her.

Dawit's blade went quiet. His eyes closed for several seconds before he began sharpening again, his head low.

"Yes," Teka said. "That's what she would want from us."

Phoenix sang of climbing mountains past the clouds, and how much they would see.

Above them, the tower's bell tolled.

"If the Shadows want the Cleansing," Dawit said, "we know where to find Fana."

Berhanu's course, and quick timing, had been best. It would have been far easier. At least Dawit had chosen Fana's guardians well.

"What if we stop his heart?" Dawit said. "Destroy his corpse?"

"Two Bloodborn have never fused, as far as I know," Teka said. "You're asking me to predict the future. I am not Khaldun."

"Your best guess, Teka."

Teka was dressing himself in the crimson robe he had liberated from the guard they had lured into the room, straightening his collar in a mirror. The unfortunate young man lay with a snapped neck in their bathroom, and a small pile would soon join him. Jessica had asked Dawit to kill as few people as necessary, but they didn't have the luxury of prisoners. They would need three more robes and weapons to reach the Cleansing Pool.

Teka paused. "In truth, the damage to Michel's brain is so severe that he should be as good as dead, until he heals," Teka said. "Our Blood lives as long as the heart beats, so he could be more vulnerable during his sleep. But stopping his heart may not be enough. If the Shadows have found a host in Fana . . . Michel might take refuge outside of his body too. He had fused to her. He might have the ability."

"He might live when he has no physical body?" Dawit said. *Was Michel a god?*

"They are energy as much as flesh, Dawit," Teka said. "He might live through her. Or, one will absorb the other. We know Michel has proven stronger, in the Shadows. He has taken her literally in his sleep."

Could Michel walk forever wearing his daughter's face? Dawit wondered.

Teka swallowed painfully, and Dawit shared the bitter burn in his throat. "I think we must assume . . . that she had not advanced far enough in the Rising."

Just as Jessica had warned!

"And . . ." Dawit had promised an end to their constant telepathy, but he couldn't bring his next question within Jessica's ears: *What if both bodies are destroyed?*

Teka made certain that Dawit saw his wretched eyes when he answered, *IT IS THE SAFEST COURSE . . . IF WE CAN.* Teka walked quickly away, overcome.

Dawit held the edge of the sink, suddenly unsteady. He dared not look up to see his face in the mirror. The man in the mirror had vowed never again to hurt one of his children.

He felt someone watching him, and saw Jessica in the bathroom doorway.

Jessica ignored the dead man on the floor without questions. She walked directly to Dawit to hug him to her with surprising strength.

He wouldn't have to tell her. She had seen Fana's eyes in the tower.

"We have to be sure," Jessica whispered.

Dawit nodded, pulling Jessica's face to his chest, wrapping his arms around her ears. He tried to speak and couldn't.

If they survived the day, they would have the rest of their lives to mourn.

Invisibility. They walked Michel's hallways like ghosts.

One man walking almost pace for pace with Phoenix in the crowded hall glanced at her curiously, looking for a good angle to see her face, then his eyes moved on. Phoenix couldn't remember the last time she'd walked invisible in a crowd. Fana's teacher had concealed their small circle in the bowels of Hell. They heard the occasional *perdóname*, but Teka said their faces would seem blurred, indistinct, as long as they walked close to each other and the safety he had built. They joined the sea of crimson robes flowing like blood through the building's hall.

Michel's home was so grand in its stately reverence, bigger than life. The candlelight alone was enough to feel God peeking down. God wasn't afraid to visit anywhere. No wonder Michel's followers thought they'd found God's living room.

The ringing bells sounded happy. Apology, invitation, promise.

Most of the people were harried, robes askew and hair windswept with the stories they had to tell. They'd been there since the wedding, and ninety minutes felt like a lifetime ago. Sanctus Cruor was trying to keep its head on straight. Chatter was quiet in the processional, but everyone had plenty to say in hushed snippets.

"He said he was immortal," a woman whispered behind Phoenix, before she was hushed.

Romero was waiting at the crowded archway to the Cleansing Pool, shouting for organization, directing people right or left. Phoenix stiffened when she saw him, remembering the rage on his face when he had tried to shoot her in the tower.

REMAIN CALM, Teka said. *HE IS A VERY POOR TELEPATH.*

Romero seemed to stare straight through her.

Alem waited squarely around the corner when they entered the Cleansing Hall. Their Brother who had given Michel the virus stood in their path.

Dawit readied his hand on his sword's hilt. Were they thwarted so quickly? Alem was as close as Fana had been to her groom in the tower, staring with his copper-colored eyes. Alem looked straight past Teka's group mask. Perhaps his ties to his Brothers were too strong to be fooled.

Alem did not smile, but he grasped Teka's shoulders. *BROTH-*

ERS, he said, his face contorted as if he'd been holding his breath. *BERHANU IS GONE.*

Was Alem still a Brother who loved them? Did that mean that Fana could be wrested from the Shadows' spell, too? Alem touched Teka's face fondly, and then Dawit's. His eyes shone like pennies in a bright stream, past madness.

HE BEWITCHED ME, Alem said. *HISTORY FORGIVE ME.*

We mean to stop it, Dawit said.

YOU CANNOT, Alem said, full of certainty. *IT IS AS GOOD AS DONE.*

Alem's eyes shifted to the center of the Cleansing Hall, toward the pool . . . but higher. Thirty feet above the floor, a shadow moved against the ceiling, gliding like an eel.

When Dawit glanced toward Alem again, their Brother was gone, his head bobbing as he excused himself past the followers crowding the door, on his way out. Alem would not help them, but he would not hinder them, at least. He was running from damnation.

Safe journey, Brother, Dawit thought.

Michel was propped on his throne overseeing the Cleansing Pool, his condition unchanged since Dawit had seen him at the altar in the tower. He had barely been wiped clean—not that much could have been done for his appearance. His prince's suit had been replaced by his crimson Cleansing robe with the Sanctus Cruor crest prominent on his chest. His blood didn't show against the matching fabric. He listed to one side, his damaged face hidden against his shoulder.

Wake, Michel, or sleep always, Dawit said. Even if he roused Michel from sleep with anger, Michel would be kinder to Fana than the Shadows. She was gifted at reasoning with him. She had come so close!

Michel did not stir. He made no answer.

Movement across the ceiling sent a cold, wet tendril across the nape of Dawit's neck, as if Fana had reached down to touch him. Dawit looked up in time to see Fana zip to a darkened corner in the rafters, gliding between oversized banners, her Sanctus Cruor robe flapping behind her. She was still a bride, dressed in white.

She was fast. He would have preferred a crossbow to the knives he'd stolen.

Beside him, Jessica clamped her hand over her mouth. She had seen Fana, too.

Phoenix's hoarse singing was ever-present, but Dawit heard her raise her weary voice. *"My soul gets cold from standing still . . . If I can't spread my wings, I'll die . . ."*

They needed Teka's protection, so their group moved slowly through the masses. There was no seating except in the crowded balconies. Dawit recognized some of the world leaders who had come for Michel's wedding, now present for a different event entirely. Dawit was too far to probe them. Did they understand? What had Michel promised them?

MICHEL MIGHT WAKE SOON, Teka said, excited. *THE SHADOWS HAVE MASKED HIM, SO I CANNOT HELP HIM HEAL. BUT I FEEL HIS HEALING—HE IS GLOWING.*

Dawit whispered the news to Jessica, and her face brightened with hope. Could any of them have imagined a day when Jessica would rejoice to see Michel?

While they stood within the huddle of the faithful, Phoenix sang to Fana and Michel, asking them to bring their union back to solid ground. Dawit felt a sharp pang, missing Rami. He'd wanted to ask Alem for word on the fate of their other Brothers' corpses, but his concerns of the world had narrowed to the Cleansing.

Dawit stared at Michel, the sleeping puppet king.

Could I get to him? Dawit asked Teka.

Teka shook his head, emphatic, as he sent his hurried message. *IMAGINE HE IS IN A SEALED CASE. NO GUNSHOT OR KNIFE WOULD DISTURB MICHEL NOW. WE SHOULD NOT MOVE AGAINST THEM UNTIL IT BEGINS, WHEN THE SHADOWS TRAVEL SUCH A DISTANCE WITH HIS VIRUS. BUT BY THEN, IT MAY BE TOO LATE.*

His words were so deeply hidden that Dawit could barely hear him.

The Cleansing Hall went silent, all eyes skyward.

Fana hovered directly above the Cleansing Pool in her now-spotless white vestments. Her dreadlocks gently framed her cherub's face. Fana looked so much like his child that he hoped she had found her way back.

Fana's voice crackled above them from end to end.

"Thus is it written in the Letter of the Witness," Fana's voice said, and Dawit's hopes melted. " 'And so a man and woman, mates immortal born, will create an eternal union at the advent of the New Days. And all of mankind shall know them as the bringers of the Blood.' "

There was no healing in Fana's recitation—only hunger. Only Shadows.

I'm going to slit your throat, Michel, Dawit taunted him. *Just as I slit your father's. And then I'll shovel your pieces in the furnace. Millions may die, but so will you. So will Fana.*

Yes! Teka encouraged him. *I MIGHT HAVE FELT HIM STIR.*

The bees beat the rooftop like a hurricane.

Fana's voice went on. "All peoples of the world shall face a time of Cleansing," she said. "The Cleansing will bring weeping, but it will bring feasts and rejoicing. The Cleansing will bring sorrow, and it will bring new life. During the Cleansing, husbands will cling to their wives, and mothers will sit vigil over their children. Without Cleansing, wars shall flourish. The air will be choked with smoke. The sun will scorch the earth like fire. The oceans will turn to poison. The very world itself will die."

What about Fana? Dawit asked Teka.

SHE APPEARS RIGHT BEFORE ME, DAWIT, YET HER MIND IS QUIET.

Fana would not fight her way back in time. Fana might have been erased from herself.

If only he had a gun! Even a mortal's gun would be faster than his blades. To reach Michel and Fana, he would need to be virtually two places at once. He could envision a dozen swift strategies with Berhanu and Fasilidas by his side, even if Fana flew like a peregrine falcon across the ceiling. Teka was a mighty telepath, Khaldun's most loyal student and Fana's finest teacher, but he was an untested warrior.

I WILL DO WHAT I CAN, DAWIT, Teka said. *I WILL GO TO MICHEL.*

They both knew that Teka couldn't bear to destroy Fana, even if he could reach her first.

"Today," Fana's voice boomed, "you will be both witnesses and participants . . ."

Dawit received an excited pulse from Teka, a nudge to look to his left. All he saw, at first, was a sea of robes. Then an olive-skinned young man wearing a beard leaped to his vision.

Mahmoud was within ten yards of Michel, then gone. Dawit knew Mahmoud's stealthy approach well. He planned to strike.

Tell him to wait! Dawit told Teka. Mahmoud was too far out of his range for a pulse.

Mahmoud straightened, suddenly still, and turned over his shoulder to meet Dawit's eyes. Teka had already sent his message, and helped Mahmoud find them.

Dawit's oldest friend inclined his head in a joyless, respectful bow.

Mahmoud would wait. For now.

Jessica nearly drowned in conflicting emotions when she saw Mahmoud bow to Dawit. She'd almost forgotten how much she despised him.

Her terrible burden with Dawit felt heavier, more inevitable, with Mahmoud so close to Fana. Mahmoud did not love Fana. He would celebrate to see her die.

"*Where are you, Michel?*" Jessica suddenly heard herself scream out in the open when she'd only been trying to send him a thought. "*Are you too weak to protect your new wife?*" Yes, Lord, let him come, Jessica prayed. *Let him come in a rage and strike us all down, but let him save Fana. Give Fana time to bring him to her Light.*

Appalled followers grumbled and shouted at Jessica. She saw a commotion in the crowd as Sanctus Cruor guards made their way toward her to remove her.

Phoenix looked at Jessica with wide, startled eyes. Her song faded on her lips.

"Keep singing to her," Jessica told Phoenix. "Stay close to Teka's mask."

Dawit's eyes on her were as childlike as Phoenix's. *JESSICA, NO—*

Jessica pushed through the crowd in front of her, struggling to make it as close as she could to Fana, to stand beneath her daughter's shadow. Jessica moved only ten feet. Rough hands clawed at her arms, her robe, her hair, nearly staggering her from her feet. A man's elbow knocked Jessica's jaw so hard that her vision went white, and she would have fallen if not for the bodies smothering her.

"Do not touch her," Fana's voice said, somehow gentle despite trembling the floors.

As quickly as she'd been surrounded, Jessica was alone, penned into a wide, empty circle. Jessica's heart pounded. Which Fana was floating above her? The gentleness in Fana's voice brought hopeful tears to Jessica's eyes.

"Fana?" she whispered. "Sweet baby?"

IT IS NOT FANA, DEAR JESSICA, Teka's voice said sadly in her ear.

Jessica glanced at Dawit, who seemed ready to spring to her. She shook her head *no,* and his face withered . . . but he stayed back, his eyes expecting the worst.

No one could say Jessica hadn't known love.

The room swayed, and Jessica let out an involuntary gasp, her fingers trying to grab something to hold; fistfuls of air. She waved her arms for balance and found none.

Her feet weren't on the floor!

The room grew bigger beneath Jessica as she floated higher. She braced for a wild swing, but she hovered until she was ten feet above where she had stood. Jessica hadn't realized she had such a deep, primal fear of heights until her limbs flailed in panic.

Jessica looked up, hoping to see Fana's face, but Fana was too far behind her. She whipped her head around to search for her. Instead, she felt a wave of dizziness as she saw the crowd staring at her, moony faces upturned.

I CAN EASE YOUR FEAR, Teka said.

"*I'm not afraid of you!*" Jessica shouted, her answer to Teka. Almost the truth.

I LOVE YOU, JESS, Dawit said, faint but unmistakable. Jessica didn't have to touch the warm dribbling from her nose and ears. She knew her blood from the smell.

I have faith in you, Fana, Jessica said, a whisper from her mind. *I know it isn't you.*

Fana's voice flowed like wind through the Cleansing Hall.

"I love humankind so much," the Fana-thing said, "that I sacrifice my mother."

Forty-three

The world was all tumbling and mud, until she heard the Words.

"*I have faith in you, Fana.*"

She stuck out her hand, or where she imagined a hand should be, and caught something. It was rough, and would have scraped her if she'd had skin, but she held on tightly. A tree root in the mud! Freed from the mud's tumbling, she hung on to work on the puzzle of the Words.

I have faith in you, Fana. She remembered the precise order.

Who was the "I"? What was faith? Who was Fana?

Asking the questions exhilarated her. Shaped her.

Who was the "I"?

She was the "I."

What was faith? (Knowing?)

Who was Fana?

The last question niggled at her. She was certain she had known, once.

Who was Fana?

She was Fana.

She had a name.

Her name meant Light.

When Light remembered her name, the Shadows parted.

Michel, where are you? Please wake up.

Years seemed to have passed, but it might have been only minutes.

Fana swam to the surface of the mud, gasping at the thin sheen of air. She spit the syrupy sweetness from her mouth, looking for flickers of Michel in the dark hallways.

Heal, Michel. My mother is dying!

She heard something rolling slowly back and forth below her, the length of a room. Every sound was a clue. She was too far above the surface of him, looking for him in his reflections. She had to dive back down.

Fana took her mother's Words to guide her, so that she could remember herself again.

I have faith in you, Fana.

Fana dived again, this time without pausing or fighting. The Shadows washed away some of her remembering, but she knew she was looking for Michel.

The muddy waters were rushing now, gaining speed, moving toward something larger, a place too deep to swim. The waters tried to carry her, so she swam the way her teacher had told her, riding the current for a while instead of swimming against it. When the water felt no resistance from her, the current let her go.

Fana swam the way she chose again. When she got lost, she followed the singing.

The waters brought her to a dreary office building, flooded nearly to the ceiling in mud. Ruined light fixtures above her dripped in Shadows. She saw an open door, the first open door she'd found, so she floated inside with the tide of clouded water. The office was flooded, too. Rows of submerged file cabinets stood in regimented lines, only the top drawers dry.

But the drawers were locked. TERU, the typed labels read.

She had been in this office before! Had she found Michel's thoughtstreams?

He had opened one drawer for her.

Fana heard a young child's laughter. She swam in the mud, following the laughter, until she found a file cabinet in a corner against the far wall. The top drawer was cracked open exactly the way Michel had left it for her. MAMA, the label said in crayon.

The child's voice was a very young boy's. His laughter giggled from the rusted drawer.

Fana pulled open the drawer and found a soccer ball. Michel's mortal friend. (*Nino's ball?*) When she touched it, the waters lurched, rising to Fana's chin. Fana tossed the soccer ball behind her and reached deeper into the drawer before it could flood with the mud.

This time, she found a bright, shiny red ball. A younger child's.

Fana held the ball between her hands, remembering how a ball felt when you were three. She closed her eyes, savoring the joy of it.

When Fana opened her eyes, she was on her feet, on solid ground, in a large gray living room. Piano, sofas, display tables with statues. Tall windows stood in rows across the walls, but the windows were covered in thick curtains, as if the house had something to hide.

Not a house—a *castle*, in Tuscany. A grand, fading Turkish rug spread from one side of the room to the other; a soft ocean for play in a house of cold, uncomfortable floors.

A *bounce-bounce-bounce* sound issued from the stairwell behind her, and the shiny red ball she'd dropped fell impossibly slowly behind her, until the last bounce rolled it to her feet.

A young boy near her squealed with laughter.

"*Dammi la palla!*" the boy called. Give me the ball.

The child was sitting alone across the rug, on patiently folded knees. He was such a well-behaved child. All the staff marveled at it, especially his nanny.

A nest of black curls spilled across his brow. In the winter, his skin was the color of honey. In the summer, he turned nearly as brown as his mother.

"*Dammi la palla, Mama!*" Michel said, his baby teeth shining at her.

He laughed when she picked up the ball. She sat on folded knees across from him. She tested her fingers on the ball's firmness, and pushed.

The ball rolled the length of the floor, until Michel caught it on the other side. As the ball rolled toward him, the room began to lose its light. He squealed, rolling on the floor with delight. *Life rolls in cycles of good and bad*, Gramma Bea said in her ear.

"Mama's turn now," Fana said. "Roll it back, Michel."

Michel pushed, firm and sure, and the ball came back to Fana.

She held it tightly. Sunlight peeked above the curtains, brightening the room, and Fana saw her face in the standing mirror beside her. She was wearing her favorite white scarf, and she looked like Teru's twin.

But she was Fana.

In her reflection, Fana noticed two shapes on her lap: toys! One was a handmade rag doll with three heads, a gift from children who loved her and relied on her. The other was a small plastic container of jumping beans. The worms inside the beans jumped when they were too warm, because they liked to sleep. They were freed of their beans only when they became moths, and then they could fly! But they flew only for a few days before they died.

When Fana saw her face in the mirror again, she was round and fat, too. Chipmunk cheeks! She grinned at herself, glad to have her baby teeth back.

"I want to play with you," Fana said, "but we have to go somewhere, Michel."

Michel beckoned to her, impatience sagging his chubby cheeks. *"Per favore, Fana! Dammi la palla!"*

"Only one more time," she said, and rolled the ball back to him.

They played for an instant; a day, a night, a day, a night.

She had found Michel's hiding place from the Shadows.

Forty-four

Dawit's world fell away when the Cleansing began, everything wrong in a breath.

The terrible stream of Jessica's life dripping to the floor ravaged his eyes. And Fana floated above her, impassive, willing her mother's Blood to flow.

Was it all the Shadows, or was Fana angry about the wedding? Dawit didn't know.

How could he kill any creature dressed so convincingly as his daughter? Unless Michel intervened, both he and Fana had to be destroyed, neutralized beyond simple sleep. How could he? How could he carry her to the incinerator while he trembled with sobs?

For the first time, Dawit knew that he could not trade his daughter for his wife, weighing the tragedies. Even saving Jessica could not compel him to destroy Fana before she drained her mother's Blood. Dawit's limbs shook with helpless frustration and horror.

But for her mission? Yes. He could.

Dawit's knife was ready in his hand as soon as he saw the blood throughout the room, enough nosebleeds to fuel a plague. None were spared. Phoenix, Teka, and all the rest of Michel's believers who had been so happy to envision a world made just for them shared the same fate. The Shadows were feeding from them for the Cleansing.

The virus was loose. Jessica would not be the only loss, nor a room in a single hall.

MICHEL IS AWAKE, Teka said, just as his knife went flying toward Fana.

• • •

When Michel woke, at first pain made him senseless. His body was nearly dead, and Michel had never experienced the stripping of his body. He touched his face, repulsed. He wanted to flee from his skin. All of him roiled with confusion: where was he?

Then he saw his dear angel floating above him in the white Sanctus Cruor queen's robe he'd made for her. Michel looked at his own clothing. He was dressed for Cleansing Day.

The Shadows were feeding in a howl.

From his throne—yes, he was in his chair for the Most High—Michel saw a room crowded with nosebleeds. The Shadows tried to smother him with the irresistible surprise, betrayal and suffering of hundreds of supplicants. His pleasure was so great, it was pain.

But Michel brushed the Shadows away with the lessons he had learned from Fana. He could not feast until he understood how he had left his wedding tower.

Had Stefan administered the vows? Had Teka? Such confusion!

Teru's shrill scream suddenly echoed across the Council Hall from Stefan's balcony, where she stood alone.

"*No!*" she screamed, pointing at the rafters. "*Stop this, Michel!*"

A woman hovered below Fana, her wide-eyed face streaked with blood. Blood crawled like tears from the corners of her eyes. Was it Fana's mother? Michel looked up at Fana again, horrified. Fana's face and mind were wiped clean. Where were her thought-streams?

What has happened? Who is doing this?

Michel tried to reach out to Jessica to stop her bleeding and bring her back to solid ground, but he could not find a way to touch her; it was like fighting endless billowing curtains. His mind felt as weak as his healing body. Jessica was wrapped in Shadows.

She was dying, draining of her Blood.

Fana, what are you doing? Your mother won't wake if you take her Blood.

Fana's father suddenly came to Michel's sight. He was staring up at Fana with an expression Michel memorized so that he could paint it, the embodiment of Pain itself.

Dawit cocked his arm back to throw his knife. Michel's mind was sharpening, but it was still moving so slowly that the knife surprised him. Dawit was so fast that the blade was flying before Michel could send a mental stream to swipe it from his hand.

Michel almost turned the soaring blade to dust. Almost.

Set me free, Michel, Fana said. The sound of a flea in his ear, begging. Fana was so lost in the Shadows, Michel felt barely a trace of her. But the soft words helped him understand what he had seen on Dawit's face, and Dawit's pain was contagious.

Michel was too weak to free Fana from the Shadows.

He allowed Dawit's knife to fly.

Dawit's blade was sure, pinning Fana's heart still. Her gasp filled the hall.

Fana's mother fell first, in a rag doll's heap. Then Fana plunged down from high above, spinning, her gown flying behind her, trying to catch the air. Below, the supplicants scattered.

When Fana's thoughts died, Michel screamed.

Until the last instant, Dawit was certain that Michel would turn his own knife back on him.

But it was worse: instead, Dawit watched the blade plunge into Fana's heart to the hilt. He heard his daughter gasp in pain, and saw his wife and child tangle on the floor.

Even if the world died, at least Fana might live, or some version of her. He might have lost his wife, but he had been spared the worst, even if the world had suffered.

Supplicants crushed one another as they squeezed back through the doors, or lined themselves against the wall, trying to clear the Council Hall.

When Michel lurched to his feet, Dawit didn't move or flinch. Michel's face was healing, half of it sewing itself into blistered scars.

Dawit tried to look at his fallen daughter, but he could not. Perhaps when she woke.

Scurrying footsteps brought Phoenix and Teka to Dawit to huddle over Jessica. Was she lost to him? Waking grief tightened his muscles, caught his breath. Dawit knelt beside Jessica, pressing his palm to her warm forehead.

THEY ARE SLEEPING, Teka said, and Dawit was lightheaded with relief. BUT THE CLEANSING GOES ON, DAWIT, Teka finished.

Michel took pained, halting steps, dragging himself toward his bride, who was crumpled a few feet from Jessica. Michel was oblivious to any other concerns.

"Michel!" Dawit shouted, his voice rising above the room's chaos.

Michel stopped, raised his eyes to him. Dawit had never seen eyes filled with such a void. The man behind those eyes might as easily collapse to the ground or strike him dead.

"You gave her your word!" Dawit said. "The Cleansing should not be today."

Michel made a wild motion, as if to wave Dawit silent. Then he continued his lurching steps toward Fana. He could barely stay on his feet, but he knelt to scoop Fana into his arms, and he willed himself to stand again. Fana lay limply, her hair swinging as he walked.

A strangled sob tore from Michel's throat.

THE CLEANSING HAS STOPPED, DAWIT! Teka said.

For the first moment since the tower—in truth, the first moment since Fana had first run away from home and found herself in Michel's web—Dawit believed disaster had been averted.

Dawit felt Mahmoud before he saw him.

Mahmoud was in the balcony beside Teru, raising his gun. Dawit's second knife was in his hand, ready to throw even as he realized that Mahmoud was out of his range. Dawit never had the chance to throw his knife. He had already run out of time.

Teru gasped, or Dawit might have thought he'd dreamed it.

In one instant, Mahmoud had been biting his lip with rare emotion, his body leaning forward in his readiness to take his target, and then . . .

Mahmoud's gun clattered to the marble floor.

Mahmoud vanished in a puff of pale dust that floated across the floor. The unimaginable sight stole Dawit's breath. He could not make a sound, but his eyes screamed with the horror of it. Watching beside him, both Teka and Phoenix gasped.

Dawit stared at the empty balcony, unable to look away from the space where his most beloved Brother had just stood, ready to join him in battle. If he stared long enough, hard enough, would Mahmoud reappear and grin at him at his joke?

The emptiness was beyond conception.

The air shimmered, hot, as Michel walked past, carrying Fana.

YOUR FRIEND CAME TO OUR HOME TO HARM US ON OUR WEDDING DAY, Michel said. *I'M SORRY FOR YOUR LOSS.*

An apology, however polite, was not nearly enough. Dawit shook with empty rage.

"What will you do with Fana?" Dawit said.

"Fana is safe, signore," Michel said, not looking back. "We are together. She will rest with me until she wakes."

"Michel!" Dawit called sharply.

Michel staggered to a stop, and gazed back at Dawit with the unruined side of his face.

"She is the most precious being ever created," Dawit said. If he had thought it would make a difference, he would have begged Michel to preserve her. Not to enslave her.

Michel's eyes shimmered with tears. "I know Fana in ways you never can," he said. "You need not tell me who she is."

Trust us, Dad.

Fana's voice? Or a memory in his ear? But how—if her thought-streams were dead?

I TOLD YOU, DAWIT, Michel said. *FANA IS WITH ME.*

Michel let Dawit hear a peal of his daughter's laughter, the exact moment he'd first made her laugh when she was three. Dawit wasn't ashamed of the father's tear that stung his eye.

But he could not forget the mission Fana had risked her life for.

"How many were infected?" Dawit said. He had lost track of time, but fewer than five minutes had passed between the time of Jessica's first nosebleed and the time he'd been forced to bring Fana down. Maybe only one or two.

Michel sighed, and looked at Fana's sleeping face. He hated for her to hear.

NINETY THOUSAND, Michel said. *AN ACCIDENT. BUT NOW*

IT IS CONTAINED. PERHAPS WE CAN HEAL THEM WHEN SHE WAKES.

"When is the Cleansing, Michel?"

Michel turned away from him with an unsteady step, carrying away his bride.

"I do not know the future, signore," Michel said.

THE NEW DAYS

Live as if you were to die tomorrow.
Learn as if you were to live forever.
—Mahatma Gandhi

It is very beautiful over there.
—The last words of Thomas Edison (1847–1931),
upon waking from a coma

Epilogue

New York
Two Years Later

It was overcast in Manhattan, but the crowd in Central Park sounded like sunshine. The cheers were the sound of joy. GLOW FOR LIFE, the banners on the trees read, reminding everyone why they were celebrating: Glow was finally legal in the United States. The law had finally caught up with the people.

Phoenix sang "The Bees" from the stage overlooking the North Meadow, crammed with vibrant human life snaking through every visible corner. Thousands more spilled into nearby meadows even if they couldn't see her. The police had told her there might be a million people at the concert. More would have come if she had given more notice.

Her last note hung over the crowd in the trial-roughened voice she had brought back with her from Nogales. A new voice; not as smooth, but so much stronger.

In a flash, she saw Fana's laughing face. Music was the only place where Phoenix and Fana still met. Phoenix felt Fana coursing through her as strongly as she had at the first Glow concert, an electrical shower. Fana sent gold dust floating over the listening crowd, into stray windows, and into the cars that honked as they passed. Spreading healing.

Most of them hadn't known they were sick, or why. Doctors caught so little.

That was what bees did—they spread life. Most people preferred to heal at concerts, if they had the chance, but now they could have

Glow in the privacy of their homes. Legal Glow would make it easier to get it to everyone who needed it. Clarion had bought and leased hundreds of buildings for Glow clinics across the country, taking control of hospitals in poor neighborhoods. The U.S. revolution was about to begin.

"Thank you!" Phoenix said to her old-school mic, the one she asked for especially because it reminded her of concerts she'd seen as a child. "That's a song I wrote in Mexico."

The crowd roared gratitude and love. People chanted her name, but Phoenix knew they were chanting to the music, the healing, not to her. She hadn't asked for any of it. Until the music came with its sad beauty, Fana's wedding day had been hard to live with.

"Heal!" she told New York. The country. The world. "Safe journey, everyone!"

They were still calling her name, but Phoenix left the stage. She'd already done three encores. Everyone was giddy backstage, even roadies, who weren't used to giddiness at concerts. Glow made everyone giddy.

"Mom, you're a rock god!" Marcus said, giving her a bear hug. Not even ten years old, and he was nearly as big as a roadie in his Phoenix Glow Tour T-shirt. Marcus looked more like her father every day. Like his grandfather and namesake, Marcus was her biggest fan.

"I'm not a god," Phoenix said. "I'm just making music."

Phoenix never used the term *god* lightly. Her best friend, her sister, might as well be a goddess, but she'd never used the word. Maybe the word for Fana hadn't been invented yet.

Carlos was in his usual spot backstage, by the curtain stage right. Trying to be invisible. Phoenix would never have thought Carlos would come with her on a Glow tour. Time truly healed everything.

Carlos rested his forehead against Phoenix's. "Beautiful, Phee," he said. "So beautiful. I wish Mami had been here."

She nodded. She'd seen a woman near the stage with braids like Carlos's mother, and another who'd looked just like Mom. Reminders that they were always nearby.

Police swarmed everywhere. Phoenix would never look at police the same way, but at least they were trying to protect her these days. *For now,* Sarge's voice reminded her.

"Are they here?" Phoenix asked Carlos, and he nodded, taking her hand to walk with her down the metal steps on the other side of the stage. They were led and trailed by an army.

The women's glowing faces were waiting for her in a roped area. Two hundred women waited for her in folding chairs beneath a hanging tarp, barely covered from the drizzle. It looked too much like a pen for Phoenix's comfort, but the women's shining eyes didn't mind. Most of their faces were wet with tears, not rain. When they saw her, they rose to their feet, rocking upright, many of them holding their chairs for support.

"Nobody touches Phoenix!" Gloria, Phoenix's cousin, barked. "Please stay where you are and let her come to you one by one."

Phoenix walked through the lines of women, one after the other, the faces of the world. Africa, Asia, Europe. Phoenix had always loved New York for its faces. Pregnant women always sought her out, some from great distances.

One by one, Phoenix rubbed her hand across the rounded bellies.

"Bless this child," Phoenix said, touching each woman's stomach, gazing into her hopeful eyes. *Bless this child, Fana. And bless this child. And bless this child.*

New York had been hit hard.

Birth rates were dropping. In New York City, just like in regions of China, researchers estimated that two out of ten men and women might be infertile. The percentage of live births was higher internationally, so the babies were born healthier, but fewer and fewer people could conceive. Scientists didn't know why. There were already reports of stolen newborns.

Outside this Central Park sanctuary of music and joy, the world was panicking. Fana had explained it to Phoenix in her typical blunt way: *WE THINK THERE ARE TOO MANY.*

Fana's compromise with Michel; their shared vision.

"Bless this child," Phoenix said, pressing her hand to a warm, living belly.

Fana, bless this child.

Phoenix shied away from the thirsty, longing eyes of the woman she was touching. The woman trembled so much that Phoenix thought she was cold. "You're . . . an angel," the woman said, barely able to speak the words.

"I'm just a singer," Phoenix said.

Lalibela

The young man called himself Mark, although it was not the name his parents had given him. He had forgotten his birth name, and his age, but so had many of his Brothers.

He should not be alive. His teacher had told him he should be dead because of what he had done. There were stories that he had faced down a demon. He had challenged a king. All the stories were fantastic, and none of them sounded true.

The truth was a lost memory.

He hoped his punishment was just, but it was hard to imagine that he had done anything bad enough to warrant being robbed of his memories. He would never want to hurt anyone. He wanted to dedicate himself to healing the sick.

His Brothers took the Blood for granted, but Mark knew he was newly immortal, so the Blood fascinated him. He eagerly followed news about Glow from upworld, and had donated Blood for use by the new clinics in the United States and Mexico. Mark agreed with Yacob, his teacher, that their Blood was a gift to everyone. He agreed with Fana and her Blood mission.

But that was all he could do for Fana's mission. For fifty years, Mark would be confined to the Lalibela Colony. He had forty-eight years left to serve—that, and his memory wipe, had been the sentence for his crime. His spirit was restless, but how could he consider an apprenticeship in the House of Science a sentence? It was a privilege. In some wings of the House of Science, the laws of physics had their own mind.

Yacob waited in the garden, as he always did, to show Mark his way. Yacob wrapped his arm around him like a father. "Mark, our walls are empty but for us," Yacob said. "For the first time in centuries. We're the only two who aren't in the delegation."

The Lalibela Brothers were on their way to meet with the Bloodborn in South Africa, where the new colony was being built. Mark had tried not to think about it, but now he would think about nothing else. He had never felt more like a prisoner.

"I wanted to meet Blessed Fana," Mark said, choosing the Fananites' title for her. Seeing her would be blessing enough. To be in the room with her.

Yacob sighed. "You think of her too much. Your head is filled with free space doing nothing. You need to meditate more, youngster."

Yacob had warned him not to overlook his studies in the House of Meditation. If he studied his meditation diligently, Yacob had said, one day he would learn to hear thoughts and send visages. He must follow the path of the Rising, not the busy sounds in his head.

But today, Mark would think only of Fana. He had been enchanted by her since he first heard the stories about how she had started the Underground Railroad to share her Blood when she was only a child. She'd had so much vision so young!

Fana's parents visited Mark from time to time. They had known him in his former life, where he had first met Fana as a child. Her parents shared stories about Fana's days living like a mortal, or the time her father chased him from a window in the woods. Sometimes, her mother brought him photographs of Fana as a child—to look at, not to keep—and he could almost remember himself. He might not deserve their kindness, but he was grateful.

"How can I see her?" Mark asked Yacob. "What if I petition?"

NOT NOW, Yacob said. Yacob was sad for him when he mentioned Fana. *NOT YET.*

Mark wondered again what he had done to deserve his punishment. His banishment.

But there would be other delegations, and he wouldn't always have such strict prohibitions. Yacob had promised him that he would be free one day. Until then, he only needed the Blood in his veins to help heal the world—even if it was a world he couldn't see.

And Mark didn't need to go to South Africa to be closer to Fana. She was with him always. She came to him if he only thought her name.

In his dreams, she called him Johnny.

The New Colony
KwaZulu-Natal
South Africa

Their lovemaking stirred the still morning.

She had dozed off in the woven rope hammock swinging in the balcony overlooking the mountains and valleys in every direction. At dawn, he slipped in to entwine himself with her. His touch was as fresh as his first caresses, when she had known him by another name. A new promise. So much better than a dream.

When their bodies squirmed, she wasn't shy with her calls. Two eagles answered her, breaking into flight. The moment brought wonder to her waking mind. Her mate in her arms, so close to the basin that had given birth to human life. The earth seemed to rumble with its history, shaking the treetops with footsteps across the vast valley, past open bushveld and acacia forests.

She could see and feel so much more now that she was meditating properly.

Thank you, Lord, for blessing me. Please help me bring your blessings to others.

Her daily prayer.

Jessica closed her eyes to feel the sun on her face. God spoke to her in the sunlight, and in the evergreen valley that spilled below them in an endless tangle toward the lush mountains that ringed the reserve. The reserve was in the heart of Elephant Country. A large herd moved slowly through the thin morning haze, at least a dozen adults and six smaller elephants in an unbroken snake toward their water hole. Once, these had been hunting grounds for Shaka Zulu and his storied warriors. Hunters were banished now.

"Good morning, *mi vida*," Dawit said to her ear.

"Morning, baby."

They knew each other's bodies and movements so well that they nestled with ease on the hammock, slipping hips and elbows free. Would it be such a bad thing to stay in a hammock all day? Maybe there were virtues to uninterrupted communion.

An hour passed before she noticed.

"Jess," Dawit said, hushed. "Look."

His eyes were trained to the woodland. His grin could mean only one thing.

Where?

THERE. BY THE SCRUB TREE.

They were sending thoughts to each other. She was learning telepathy! She couldn't send thoughts to just anyone, but she could reach Dawit. Teka said that neither of them should be strong enough to carry the other—not without more training—but they were doing it more and more.

Jessica saw forest canaries circling the trees.

The birds? Jessica said.

NO—LOWER. NOT QUITE TOUCHING THE GROUND.

She blinked, and there they were, almost too far to see without binoculars, speeding through the scrub brush. They undulated like they were swimming, coasting on their backs, relying on their inner eyes to see for them.

But so, so fast! Like watching lions hunt. Here and then gone, hidden in the low trees.

Fana took Jessica's breath away; a rare sighting of a creature nearly more myth than real. At least she had recognized Fana that time, with her hair flying behind her. Fana hadn't been hidden in feathers or fur. Or in the empty air itself.

"I miss her," Jessica said.

It was strange to miss someone who shared the grounds, whose door was only ten minutes' walk away. Fana had come to the breakfast table with her and Dawit yesterday—Fana's body, anyway. Fana had smiled, asked about Alex and her cousin, and smiled some more. But only a part of Fana came for breakfast every Sunday; the rest was too far to touch.

Dawit rested his chin on Jessica's shoulder and sighed. He might miss Fana more. He had been more of her friend, less a devil's advocate. More accepting of her path.

"I wish . . ." Jessica began, but she stopped herself. Out of respect for Fana and Michel, she left her lost wish for the past unspoken. Maybe her deepest wish was that Fana had been born without the Blood, with the chance to live a different life.

She isn't ours anymore, Dawit.

SHE NEVER WAS, JESS.

Khaldun had told her from the beginning that they would only be Fana's shepherds. He had charged them with giving her enough love to be ready for her destiny. Had they succeeded more than they failed, or failed more than they succeeded? Some days, she still didn't know.

"I'm a childless mother," Jessica said. "That's how it feels. And I can't tolerate what they're doing. Infertility is cruel—taking that dream away from so many parents."

Dawit paused. He avoided the subject when he could, but she knew he approved of the new version of the Cleansing. Like many of his Brothers, he thought overpopulation had been ignored too long. Immortals had long memories, and they remembered different times. Most of them favored creating a smaller, healthier human population; the immortals were a unified front at last. The entire Lalibela Colony was on its way to toast the planet's new future.

But what gave them the right?

"They see it as the gentlest way to regain balance," Dawit said finally.

"Well, I won't stop fighting her. I know she's sick of hearing me, if she's listening."

SHE'S LISTENING, Dawit said.

He waited, and said aloud, "We can have children."

He said it in a matter-of-fact way, as if they had ever discussed having more children in twenty-five years. Her pregnancy with Fana had been a surprise; they'd conceived her the night he first told her about his Blood, the end of the world as she'd known it. Now Jessica's mind vibrated with surprise and possibilities; but mostly pain. She hoped he hadn't expected a smile.

"The world has enough Bloodborns," she said.

"Raymond isn't."

Alex's baby had been born a year ago Friday, and he didn't even have the Blood to heal his scrapes and cuts, much less Fana's enhanced gifts. But he'd come with his own kind of magic; he was the spitting image of their father as a boy, down to his curly hair.

"Maybe they got lucky with Raymond," Jessica said.

Dawit chuckled. "I'd hardly call inheriting mortal blood lucky."

"You know what I mean."

Alex had accepted the Blood Ceremony from Fana only six months before she learned that she was pregnant with Raymond, and her pregnancy had been uneventful. But Jessica and Teru had died and received the Blood *during* their pregnancies, creating Fana and Michel. What if other circumstances could produce children like them? Or a percentage of all children of the Blood would be born with Fana's gifts?

Two Bloodborns were altering the world population like their own private game board. What would others do? Khaldun had warned of an ungovernable race.

"If Fana gets pregnant, that baby might as well be ours," Jessica said. "No one can raise a child while they're staring into space."

It was hard to imagine Fana and Michel pulling free of each other long enough for a child, disturbing their private cocoon. Whatever Fana had given up, Michel had given up no less. They had crossed to somewhere else together, away from everyone. Michel's father was as heartbroken over his lost son as she was for her daughter.

"Who knows if she'll even have a child?" Dawit shrugged. "They are the first—so much is unknown. Why should we wait for Fana?"

He was persisting. She checked Dawit's brown eyes, and they were earnest and unblinking. After all they had suffered as parents, did he really want to begin that journey again? Jessica would give up her Blood to undo her mistakes with her children.

"It seems wrong that we have the choice and others won't," Jessica said.

"A few others won't," Dawit said. "Most will. There will always be more children. You know Fana would see to that. We're talking about us now."

I can ease your fear, Teka had said. The minute Jessica had first held her new nephew, she'd realized she could be a mother again. She should have known that Dawit had noticed. Pain flared deep in Jessica's stomach.

"I still hear them, Dawit," she said. "My two babies screaming for their lives with those tiny voices. I don't want to do that to a child again."

"We won't." His voice was a gentle breath. "Never again."

"How do we know that?"

Faith, Dawit said. He gestured toward the South African morning. About twenty zebras had appeared near a ridge a hundred yards away, a family. For three days, they had come at the same time every morning to look for one of their missing. They looked a long time before they moved on, and they would probably be back tomorrow.

Dawit kissed her lips lightly. "Since humans first walked here, fear has chased behind us," he said. "And yet . . ."

"We survive," Jessica said. The longer she lived, the more she understood the concept.

A deeply buried tremor woke in Jessica's bones, a reminder of how close they had come, so close. She saw the blood and marble in her last dying place. Jessica could never sanction the plague of infertility, but the new Cleansing was not the horror that Michel's would have been.

Fana had sacrificed herself to change it. Her child had done that. *Their* child.

What mother since Mary had been so proud?

Jessica searched for Fana in the landscape again, hungry for any pieces she could find.

"There!" She sat up, supporting herself on her elbows, and Dawit looked.

In a flicker between the far-off shrubs, Fana sped through the dancing shadows like a sunbird, striving for the speed of light.

ACKNOWLEDGMENTS

When *My Soul to Keep* was published in 1997, I never could have imagined how the story of Dawit, Jessica, and Fana would continue to live and find new readers so many years later. First, I want to acknowledge the readers, booksellers, and editors who have brought my childhood writing dream to life.

At Atria Books, thanks to longtime editor Malaika Adero for her feedback and sisterhood; publisher Judith Curr; assistant editor Todd Hunter; and publicity manager Yona Deshommes. Thanks to my longtime agent, John Hawkins of John Hawkins & Associates. On the film side, thanks to my manager, Michael Prevett of The Gotham Group, and to the warriors who have fought to bring *My Soul to Keep* to the screen over the years: Blair Underwood; Frank Underwood, Jr.; Nia Hill and D'Angela Steed of Strange Fruit Films; Rick Famuyiwa; Tim Reid; and Zola Mashariki at Fox Searchlight. We all wear our battle scars.

Many thanks to the busy writers and readers who provided valuable feedback during the writing of this novel: Steven Barnes, Darryl Miller, Terence Taylor, Ernessa T. Carter, Anika Noni Rose, Ivan Roman, Nnedi Okorafor, Monica A. Coleman, Steve Perry, Dawit Worku, and Dr. Lee Pachter. I wasn't always able to use your advice, but thank you so much for your time, comments, and care.

Many thanks and best wishes to Mitchell Kaplan at Books & Books in Miami; Blanche Richardson at Marcus Books in Oakland; and James Fugate and Tom Hamilton of EsoWon Books in Los Angeles. Your stores always feel like home.

Thanks to my oldest friends, who keep me sane and help me

remember: Andres Enriquez, Luchina Fisher, Olympia Duhart, Sharmila Roy, Craig Shemin, and Kathryn Larrabee.

And last, thanks to my family, my world: Mom, Dad, Johnita, Lydia, Muncko and Carol, Uncle Walter, Aunt Rita, and Aunt Priscilla. Special thanks to Muncko's son Brian Tabada, killed in combat in Afghanistan on February 27, 2011, for his sacrifice and his seeking heart.

To my husband, Steven Barnes, whose voice is loudest of all in my head when I am writing, the true prince I was searching for. To my stepdaughter, Nicki Barnes, who has followed her acting dreams and made me more proud than I can say.

And to my son, Jason Due-Barnes, who makes me laugh, dances with me, and is already one of the world's great young men.

Friend me on Facebook: www.facebook.com/tananarivedue
Follow me on Twitter: www.twitter.com/tananarivedue
Tananarive Due Writes (writing blog): www.tananarivedue.wordpress.com
Tananarive Due's Reading Circle (main blog): www.tananarivedue.blogspot.com
Website: www.tananarivedue.com